THE
KASHMIR
TRAP

MARIO BOLDUC

THE

KASHMIR TRAP

A MAX O'BRIEN

MYSTERY

TRANSLATED BY NIGEL SPENCER

DUNDURN
TORONTO

Editor: Shannon Whibbs
Design: Jennifer Gallinger
Cover design: Laura Boyle
Cover design (French edition): Chantal Boyer
Printer: Webcom

Library and Archives Canada Cataloguing in Publication

Bolduc, Mario, 1953-
[Cachemire. English]
        The Kashmir trap / Mario Bolduc ; translated by Nigel Spencer.

(A Max O'Brien mystery)
Translation of: Cachemire.
Issued in print and electronic formats.
ISBN 978-1-4597-3348-0 (paperback).--ISBN 978-1-4597-3349-7 (pdf).--
ISBN 978-1-4597-3350-3 (epub)

        I. Spencer, Nigel, 1945-, translator II. Title. III. Title: Cachemire. English.

PS8553.O475C3213 2016   C843'.54   C2015-907804-0
                                                     C2015-907805-9

1 2 3 4 5   20 19 18 17 16

  Canada

We acknowledge the support of the **Canada Council for the Arts** and the **Ontario Arts
Council** for our publishing program. We also acknowledge the financial support of the
Government of Canada through the **Canada Book Fund** and **Livres Canada Books**, and the
Government of Ontario through the **Ontario Book Publishing Tax Credit** and the **Ontario
Media Development Corporation**.

We acknowledge the financial support of the Government of Canada through the National
Translation Program for Book Publishing, an initiative of the *Roadmap for Canada's Official
Languages 2013-2018: Education, Immigration, Communities,* for our translation activities.

VISIT US AT
Dundurn.com | @dundurnpress | Facebook.com/dundurnpress | Pinterest.com/dundurnpress

Dundurn
3 Church Street, Suite 500
Toronto, Ontario, Canada
M5E 1M2

AUTHOR'S NOTE

This novel, based on real political events, is nevertheless a work of complete fiction, and, except for public personalities and incidents already known through the media, neither the characters nor the events are real. Some historical chronology has been altered for narrative purposes.

The whole universe is borne along by violence.
No living being can refuse to admit responsibility for war.
Who could sleep while others are dying?

— Translated from *The Mahabharata*,
adapted by Jean-Claude Carrière

PART ONE

GENGHIS KHAN

1

An architect enraptured with Louisiana had designed this palace, three storeys of it overlooking a cornice, typical of old Creole homes in the Deep South. Massive columns gave it a Greco-Victorian look, a definite aura of wealth that was confirmed by its four garages, each one wide as an avenue. Max O'Brien had learned from reading *Car and Driver* that one of them contained a veritable Ferrari room, decorated in red and black, in the middle of which sat a marvel of an Enzo, a Modena 360. The owner rarely took it for a spin, and then only on special days: summer, for instance, cruising down Fifth Avenue in order to get stuck in East Village traffic, then back again to its special shrine for the rest of the year, surrounded by furniture and mementos emblazoned with the Scuderia logo.

In this upscale New York suburb, each crossroad ended in a circle of houses just as spectacular as this one.

The neighbourhood was a magnet for the rich, who used such dead-end loops to insulate themselves from the rest of the world on huge fenced lots with fortressed homes.

Each one, of course including the one where the Ferrari lived, was equipped with a sophisticated Securex L2245 security system, the very latest in personal protection — "Fort Knox has nothing on you!" said the ads for Bells & Whistles, a surveillance company based in Queens. In the pages of the *New York Times* they showed a tough, imposing baseball umpire, whistle in hand. On the menu were break-and-entry sensors, motion detectors, sirens, cameras, and other dissuasive measures, all relayed to headquarters, which looked more like Cape Canaveral than the dingy closets of any ordinary security companies.

Naturally, this included all the old-school features. About a hundred well-selected, well-trained agents with spotless records and in exceptional physical condition, some with expertise in martial arts, patrolling the neighbourhood day and night, on foot and in cars. Dogs, too, trained to attack and intimidate. Huge monsters just drooling for the chance to lunge at any intruders and chew them to bits, or so the yellow-and-black notices posted on fences and at the entrances proclaimed.

At the annual Burglars' Convention and in the exclusive catalogue of places to consider knocking over, if such amenities existed, houses protected by Bells & Whistles would probably be marked off-limits with a big red star. Okay, hands off. Would the amateur weekend hiker try Mount Everest? What about Jacuzzi-waders plying the English Channel? Thinking of doing a Bells & Whistles place? Un-unh. Suicide, baby, suicide.

So, of course, this morning, that is exactly what Max was planning to do, and in broad daylight as well. The haul would be 14.2 million. He could have his pick of these places, but he chose Chez Ferrari for three specific reasons. First, the house had been sold several times in recent years, and the previous owner, creator of the start-up Chronodesk, the San Diego computer giant, had passed it along to one of the heirs to the Toolbox stores — a chain selling office furniture kits out of Tampa — the present owner of the house in question.

The second reason was that Gerry Monaghan, the heir, had taken an extended vacation in Ireland on the recommendation of his accountant, so he was spending the better part of a year at his cottage in Dún Laoghaire (eighteen rooms and a view of Dalkey Island), reaping the tax benefits offered to artists by the Irish government. He was, in fact, author of the book for the musical comedy hit *Dip-Dip-Do-Yay!* launched in 1989 on Broadway and reproduced from time to time by regional troupes all over the U.S.

The third reason was the Ferrari.

Normally, to pull off something like this, Max would need a formidable team to neutralize the horde of security agents, the dogs, and the surveillance system. He'd also need a mole inside Bells & Whistles to cover him so he could work in peace. Max was no ordinary thief, and for backup he had just one man, Jiri Schiller, a crook of his own ilk. Max had chosen him for his diploma from the Boston University School of Law. Specializing in real estate, Jiri had inherited from his old man — a trucker — a big physique, an equally big mouth, and a ravishing smile that swept both bankers and women off their feet.

Max had chosen his victim with the same care as the Monaghan residence. Bill Lockwood had just been named head of the mortgage department at the Chase Manhattan Bank on Madison Avenue. Newly arrived from Cincinnati, he was full of the usual clichés — if you can make it in New York, you can make it anywhere, et cetera — and considered the promotion an opportunity from heaven, a springboard to who-knows-where. Today, whiz kid in mortgages: tomorrow, financial adviser to the President of the United States, why not? Max had hung out at the Manhattan Plaza Health Club tennis courts enough to know he was a blowhard, vain, pretentious, sure of himself, and, of course, ambitious. He also knew Lockwood had played hardball to get where he was, to the detriment of colleagues who lacked his "killer instinct." He laughed about it under the shower after beating Max to a pulp.

Divorced, with no children, Bill found Max (no ... uh ... better make that Max's alter ego Robert Cheskin) the ideal confidant, whose ear he could fill with dream-bubbles and still not fear ridicule. Max had let on he was divorced, too, and in a custody battle with his ex over the house and Ferrari, *his* Ferrari. Imagine, he'd waited over three years for delivery! The house? Easy. There was always some excuse for not inviting Lockwood over, and anyway, the banker was too busy for a social life. His morning tennis games were the only exception to a long day at the office, his career coming before all else.

In fishing, the wait is the hardest part, but the most important. Patience is a crook's best friend, Max liked to say. To steal, you need to weave a web, and that means not being in a hurry. With Bill Lockwood, he took his sweet time, and only went into action after the web had become a masterwork of lace. Max could have waited longer, but that would have been a mistake. The amateur thief gets wrapped up in his own prowess and mesmerized by his own lies. His new identity is precious to him. It is reassuring and comfortable, so he puts off the time for action as long as he can. To move on feels a bit like death. A part of you disappears.

That morning, Max called Lockwood to announce that he and his ex had finally agreed to settle on the house. It would be put on the market, and they'd each get half the proceeds. Max could sense Lockwood getting jumpy on the other end of the line. He was flapping his tail in circles around the bait. So much for Step One: the sucker was on the hook. Now for Step Two. It seemed the German buyer needed a mortgage, so naturally Max had recommended Lockwood: "Wait till you meet him. He's great guy." This was far better than working with a bank in Stuttgart, which had no U.S. subsidiary anyway.

"Mmmm," hummed Lockwood, smelling blood in the water.

Becoming a member of the club was a wise choice … a multimillionaire client had fallen into his lap, just like that. Not an ounce of effort required. They'd done right giving him the job in New York.

"Just one small problem," sighed Max. "The buyer won't touch the Ferrari."

Lockwood was amazed: "What kinda moron is he?" he yelled. "A German? So what, Schumacher's German, isn't he?" Max couldn't believe it either, but it was their problem now, and they were stuck with it …

"Look, I owe you a big thank-you for handling this so fast and smoothly. You know what Nancy's like, always changing her mind," Max said. "I'll let you have the Ferrari as a gift for, say, fifty grand."

In the preceding months, Max had made a point of mentioning the Ferrari often and emphatically, watching Lockwood salivate each time it came up. He'd even gone so far as to doctor pictures of the car in *U.S. Weekly* and print up a fake edition of the magazine complete with an article on the painful divorce of Robert Cheskin, no actual pictures, of course, but plenty of interior and exterior shots of the Monaghan place (not really). That took brass. So, Lockwood, without ever setting foot there, felt he knew the place inside and out … its "owner," too. Nothing could possibly make him doubt his friend's sincerity. The whole thing, their "friendship" included, was an elaborate fiction from the get-go, and now the intimacy of that private relationship was about to get propelled into the public sphere. This was the keystone of the con man's art.

So Step Two could be checked off, and now all Max had to do was let out some line so the fish believed it was free, and it wasn't too late to change his mind if Lockwood wanted. He could call a halt and back up all the way if he so wished. Actually, no, it was too late for that. This was an offer he couldn't refuse. Blinded by the Ferrari that would soon be his for a pittance, he personally walked Jiri

Schiller's mortgage application through the system, after Max brought him to Lockwood's office. He even offered the services of his own notary, an important client of Chase Manhattan. Max, of course, graciously accepted. This Lockwood was an open book: he was going to hand-deliver his chance multimillionaire acquaintance to the bank and pile up some more brownie points for the future. Max could tell that Lockwood knew he was making out like a bandit on this one. Certain that he was, in fact, the *real* con man, Lockwood would obligingly jump like a fish straight into the frying pan.

The last step, the actual "frying," was the transaction itself, and it took place early one morning in the Park Avenue office of Notary Warren, who had Schiller fill out all the necessary documents — after duly verifying all the fake property titles Max had manufactured — and handed a cheque to the "Vendor" for the amount of the mortgage obtained from the banker the day before (minus fees, of course). Lockwood's $50,000 for the Ferrari would be directly payable to Max at noon tomorrow, when Lockwood would take possession in a shopping-centre parking lot not far from Monaghan's house.

Max then deposited the cheque in an account he'd opened a few months prior at a branch on Third Avenue. Half of it he promptly transferred to an account he held under yet another name in Geneva, the other half going to Jiri Schiller in Frankfurt. What did he spend it on? Well, the first $11.95 went on a miniature Ferrari he saw in the window at F.A.O. Schwartz. He'd have it sent specially wrapped to the Mortgage Department at Chase Manhattan, care of Bill Lockwood.

As the saleslady was copying the address, Max suddenly felt a wave of fatigue creep over him, as though the weight of six months of lies suddenly fell on his shoulders right there at the counter. He was completely indifferent to the fate of Bill Lockwood. He was just a pigeon, a tool to get a few million out of Chase Manhattan. A drop in the bucket of their affairs. If, once in a while, Max felt himself about to go soft on anyone, he thought about what had happened to his father. There weren't enough Bill Lockwoods in the entire world to make up for what had been done to him, his life ruined and plunged into deepest despair.

Max hailed a taxi and headed for Brooklyn Heights, his real home from the start of this affair. His bags were already packed, so all he had to do was grab them and head for the airport.

Hawaii, Jamaica, the Azores … the choice was his.

2

Juliette awoke with a start. The room was completely dark, and David was absent. She leaned toward the alarm clock: it read 11:30 p.m. The emergency meeting had gone on forever, as always. She had no trouble picturing them all around the oval table in the conference room on Shantipath, listening to High Commissioner Raymond Bernatchez unloading on the people in Ottawa once again.

"They don't grasp the first thing about the situation here in India!" As if to say, he, Bernatchez, the former pro football player, knew anything more than the newspaper clippings provided by the Press Service — this according to David. The first secretary, William Sandmill, was probably chewing his nails without letup and casting a look of dread at Bernatchez, obviously terrified to say anything lest he rile him further. The young Indian employee, Vandana Dasgoswami, was sparing no effort to calm everyone down so they could "get some perspective." Claude Langevin from public relations had arrived late, as usual, despite the fact he and his small family lived right there in the compound. Sunil Mukherjee, Bernatchez's personal secretary, ever the "liberated" Brahmin, as he called himself, was the one to whom the high commissioner turned whenever he wanted a reading on this particularly bewildering country. It was Henry Caldwell, commercial affairs adviser, who would normally be running this meeting if the presence of Bernatchez were not called for. Two years away from his retirement, "Old Caldwell" was disappointed to be finishing his career so far from the family farm his brother had just willed him, and he dreamed of returning to his native Saskatchewan. He spent his lunch hour immersed in the Massey-Ferguson catalogue or else the seed book a colleague at Agriculture Canada sent him every month.

That afternoon, thirty-five Hindus had been massacred by Islamic extremists near Jammu, the winter capital of the state of Jammu and Kashmir, a reprisal for the murder of a thousand Muslims in Gujarat last March. In turn, fifty-nine Hindus had been burned alive in a railway car in the northern state. Such was the analysis of experts.

"You know what the worst part is?" David exclaimed when he told Juliette about it over the phone earlier that evening, "Just comfortably watching this storm and doing nothing."

"But what else can you do? Remember what Vandana said: 'We are nothing in the great horror of life'?"

"Yeah, well, she's wrong."

The hecatomb, or rather this series of them, only worsened an already-tense situation between Hindus and Muslims. It was one that had turned poisonous in December 2001. A suicide squad had attacked Lok Sabha, the Indian Parliament, in the heart of New Delhi, not far from Maharani Bagh, where David and Juliette lived. Responsibility for the assault had been claimed by Lashkar-e-Taiba, an extremist Islamic group, possibly the most deadly, based in Pakistan and fighting for either the independence of Indian Kashmir or its annexation to "the land of the pure." Their specialty was terror strikes like this: a fire fight that had killed a dozen, including the commandos themselves.

Since then, and despite the shockwave and the breaking of diplomatic ties between India and Pakistan — whom New Delhi accused of supporting the jihadists — it was business as usual. "The illusion of normality," David said. Now the Jammu massacre had undone all that, just as Canadian investors had recommenced their involvement in India, or so said High Commissioner Bernatchez. How to convince Canadian businessmen that things were now normal and would stay that way, despite the occasional "isolated incident" that shouldn't affect long-term relations between the two countries? Now, repeat after me, nervous investors: one billion inhabitants ...

The Montreal conference next month was aimed at calming everyone down, and now it might be postponed yet again, hence the emergency meeting of the relevant High Commission employees.

"You think this will take all night?" Juliette had asked, already knowing the answer.

"There's nothing I can do." *As usual*, she thought. Emergency or not, ever since the conference had loomed on the horizon, her husband had been keeping insane hours. He'd come in late when she was already in bed, ignore the cold plate Daya, the cook, had left in the fridge, and get right back to work early in the morning. Juliette suspected that Sandmill and Mukherjee, who were supposed to help, had left him to do it all alone. Okay, fine, so Bernatchez had unshakeable confidence in his young diplomat, but that wasn't a good enough reason for David to risk burning himself out. However important Indo-Canadian trade relations were, they did not merit ruining his life.

He was taking on too much, as usual, Juliette recriminated, and his colleagues had noticed it, here and in Ottawa. He could always be reached at any time, day or night, not to mention the businessmen — oops, sorry, business*people* — who'd bombarded him for weeks with questions about the political situation in the region, as though he, David O'Brien, an obscure diplomat in New Delhi, had any control over the great international cauldron. So he'd answer them in predictable diplomatic doubletalk. "Canada's third official language," he liked to say.

This evening, her husband's absence had upset Juliette more than usual. She'd been waiting for the perfect moment to announce her pregnancy ever since Dr. Rangarajan at the Apollo Hospital had confirmed it; this was to be an event they'd remember forever, but the right time just never seemed to come along. Last week, David had gone to Kathmandu and left her alone, this time with his mother, Béatrice, who'd briefly stepped ashore between cruises on her way back from Thailand: "How bored you must be. I know. I've been there."

Béatrice was likeable enough, not a burden, generous and well-meaning, but a bit too much for Juliette. Elegant and distinguished at fifty-three, she could still turn heads. She had boundless energy and stormed through other people's lives with a vitality that was more than Juliette could stand. Besides, she just loved giving advice and instructions, which was all well and good, because, after all, she'd "been there." Lately, though, Juliette just wanted to be alone with David.

Béatrice had finally gone back to Montreal the day before, but not before saying hello to Bernatchez, "poor Philippe's friend." Finally, Juliette would have David all to herself. So she had the big table with the white cloth set in the dining room, asked Iqbal the gardener to choose some flowers specially, and had Daya put a bottle of champagne on ice. Next, she slipped into her finest dress, but the phone rang, and David told her the meeting would be dragging on.

Juliette's favourite time of day? Early in the morning, her "India moment," as she called it. The rest of the day was spent with diplomats' kids at the British School, which didn't seem like India to her at all. It was an artificial oasis wholly apart from the sounds and smells of the country they were in. Here, in this neighbourhood, it was a different matter. The backfiring rickshaws zigzagging between overloaded buses; the shouts of merchants pushing *tongas* and carts to market; the *"namastes"* of the *chai-wallahs* — tea sellers — meandering through the new city looking for customers; the kids running after her the minute she stepped into the street and begging for candies, shouting, "*ladu, ladu, ladu*," then getting back to their games as though nothing had interrupted them.

Ever since they'd arrived in India, Juliette had taken to lounging in bed in the mornings, since she taught only in the afternoons. David didn't dare wake her. He ate alone the breakfast Daya left him, then got behind the wheel of the Volvo he'd picked up from his predecessor last June (along with the house and the guard, Adoor). In Ottawa, the couple had shared a small apartment in the Glebe before finding themselves in charge of a Spanish inn that made them feel like unwelcome guests. Still, Juliette was convinced she'd done the right thing following David to the ends of the earth.

Her friends, though, not so much. Juliette had cut short her studies of ancient languages to serve canapés and pastries to other diplomacy-widowed wives in a country where it was way too hot. Her future had been thrown away — "What about the master's degree you wanted so badly?" — so she could act as a stand-in at embassy cocktail parties, a *memsahib*, a super house-slave, surrounded by inferior house-slaves. The young Juliette just smiled.

Upon arriving, she'd enrolled in Hindi and Urdu classes at Jawaharlal Nehru University: Hindi so she could tell Daya he could really lay on the spices, and Urdu to beg Iqbal not to plant marigolds, which she hated. Okay, they were very popular in India, but there was no need to turn her garden into a flower market, was there?

Then, in August, she'd found a job at the British School, or rather the oh-so-British Mrs. Fothergill had rounded her up to become part of her shock troops: "We mustn't let the Yanks educate our children, must we?" she said over her cup of Darjeeling. She had an aversion to all things American, especially teachers. Juliette and David found the weekends far too short for Agra and the Taj Mahal, Jaipur and the Palace of Winds, the ancient city of Fatehpur Sikri. And Delhi, of course, old Delhi, where they had fun getting lost in the bustling, dirty, fascinating life of its little streets.

But international politics soon caught up with them, and September 11 elbowed their contentment aside. By October, the invasion of Afghanistan brought war far too close for comfort; then in December, and much closer to home, came the suicide attack on India's Parliament. March delivered the Gujarat massacres next, and yesterday the events in Jammu. In a matter of weeks, Juliette and David had bid farewell to the carefree and innocent life of their arrival in Asia the summer before.

Juliette awoke to the sound of the shower … *David, at last.* She hadn't heard him come in. She slipped on her robe and joined him in the kitchen. He was already on his way out again, briefcase in hand. "I slept on the sofa so I wouldn't wake you. Meeting at eight. Gotta go."

"So the conference is off?" she inquired.

"Nope. Not so far. Still on."

"Promise me you'll be home early tonight."

David took her face in his hands. They were icy. She realized for the first time how tense he really was. She'd noticed his increased stress in recent days, but she'd put that down to Béatrice or maybe Bernatchez. Now, though, she had the impression it was something else. What was going on?

"I can't help thinking about my father," he said. "I've become just like him, and I feel just what he felt."

Normally David never mentioned Philippe. It was almost as though the immense and monumental figure of his father was no longer his. So why now?

"What's with you? You're acting strange."

David merely took cover behind his diplomat's facade, and Juliette was baffled: she sensed that she'd lost him. *Well, here goes nothing*, she thought.

"Look, David."

"I'll try, till nine o'clock, tops. I promise."

"David, I need to say …"

"Nine o'clock."

She knew what this meant. He was going to spend all evening in a meeting or on the phone … and part of the night. The big news would have to wait. The champagne, too.

She noticed Luiz in the courtyard, standing by the Volvo. He was the High Commission's clerk and a specialist in urgent photocopies, endless faxes, and updates on local restaurants with a modicum of cleanliness and where you could go without fear of bumping into other Canadians passing through. The young man was from Goa and lived close by — his mother worked as a cleaning lady for a Dutch manufacturer. Luiz had taken to David and had been begging for lifts ever since David made the mistake of picking him up after work. Rushing out of the house, David tossed Luiz the keys and turned to Juliette as she held her bathrobe tight around her.

"Nine o'clock," he said, and she smiled. He smiled back, looking like a kid who was late for school, lingering among the bougainvilleas. She had never loved him more than that morning and she regretted she hadn't told him just now, hadn't held him tight and led him back to the bedroom with its bed still warm from their bodies, and made love to him once more.

Luiz was already behind the wheel and sliding the key into the ignition when David opened the door and got in, and they immediately sped away — of course, a day like any other. She'd relive this moment over and over in the coming months, this gentle parting as though on tiptoe. Then their love and their future, all of it, suddenly vanished in the humdrum glare of sunlight. What was it again that happened next? Raymond Bernatchez's evening phone call? She couldn't remember.

"Juliette …" The high commissioner never disturbed them at home. She instantly expected the worst and steadied herself against the wall. "You'll need to be brave," he said.

She thought of David and the announcement she'd wanted to make. Wonderful news. What a fool she'd been for thinking their lives could be one long, unending holiday along a flower-strewn path marked at intervals with unforgettable moments: "the illusion of normality," as David described it. It was Vandana who had it right: "We count for nothing at all in the great horror that is life."

3

There was the nasal call for Delta flight 148 to Rome, and the passengers shuffled to the counter. Max O'Brien was one of them, ticket in one hand and Italian passport in the other. The crowd ground him to a halt directly beneath one of the three TV monitors. He looked up as someone turned up the volume. CNN showed the usual pictures of desolation: this time the carbonized carcass of a car blown up by terrorists in New Delhi, with one dead, Luiz Rodrigues, and one seriously injured, David O'Brien, both employees of the Canadian High Commission of India. Max stood immobile, paralyzed for a long time, his eyes fixed on the screen, his world pulverized yet again, and left so fragile that soon nothing of it would remain.

"Your ticket, please, sir?"

Max roused himself as the nasal voice reached him from behind the outstretched hand. Passengers around him were complaining. He left the lineup.

Juliette was sorry she'd made fun of Béatrice when she got off at Maharani Bagh, her suitcases filled with gifts. "Oh, I know the feeling. I've been there before." And for once she was right: "Déjà vu all over again." As soon as the Gulfstream landed at Dorval, David's mother had taken charge. She'd managed to get security to keep the journalists, those blood-sucking, carnivorous parasites, as she called them, away from the hangar where the ambulance awaited. She barked in the face of the muscle men from the Royal Canadian Mounted Police: "This just isn't the time, got it?"

Shrugs all around, sunglasses removed and replaced, wristwatches requiring nonstop attention, fingers pointed and threatening, hands outstretched, but Béatrice wasn't giving an inch. "I don't give a good goddamn about your investigation."

Juliette was still caught up in the whirlwind of the day before, when she'd headed for the Apollo Hospital after Bernatchez's phone call. The bombing had happened in the northern part of Delhi along the banks of the Yamuna, he told her. Their car had been booby-trapped. Pity that was all they knew for the time being. "David's dead, David's dead," she kept repeating as she ran through the hospital corridors, as though the mantra could somehow bring him back. Then she saw a familiar face, Dr. Rangarajan. She knew his smell, the timbre of his voice, gravelly as though he were always on the verge of coughing or clearing his throat. He held her tight for comfort with the words one always says at times like that, but she heard none of it. Then a *thanedar* in a uniform and moustache with an officer — also moustached — showed up and Rangarajan cleared off. The officer was in charge of the preliminary investigation and had Juliette tell them absolutely everything, even if, at first glance, it seemed utterly banal.

She felt like answering, "It doesn't matter. Nothing does anymore. He's dead."

"Madame, he is still alive."

Juliette could have kissed them, both of the moustachioed cops. She wanted to see David, yes, absolutely, but she couldn't. Just as she started screaming, Bernatchez ran toward her with Vandana and Mukherjee and took her hand, vowing to catch the cowards and to make sure the Canadian government would never let these monsters get away with it. She couldn't have cared less about them or any other government, of course. All she wanted was to be with David, alone.

"You're both heading straight back to Canada," Bernatchez told her.

There were a doctor and a nurse aboard the Gulfstream supplied by Worldwide Air Ambulance Service and Dr. Mitchell from the High Commission, whom Juliette had never met. Neither one was very chatty, which suited her, since she was in no mood for conversation. She was numb from the sedatives and sealed inside a flying clinic. Through the porthole, she watched India drift away, perhaps forever: first little pinpoints of light, then nothing … total blackness.

What was it the *Mahabharata* said: "All the creatures of the night crowded round me, deformed and terrifying …"?

For the first time on board the plane, a longing for cocoa, an irresistible urge to bite into a piece of chocolate — *maybe because I'm pregnant*, she thought. Maybe it was just the sedatives she'd taken. Why now, all of a sudden? It was as though her brain had decided to come to her defence and keep her from thinking about what had happened to David. This yearning had nagged at her all night.

Now at the end of the corridor of the intensive care unit at the Montreal General, she was sitting in a little room rigged up on the ninth floor, munching a Toblerone as though her life depended on it.

"He's still fighting, fighting hard."

Juliette turned her head toward a shadow engulfed in the blinding light from the downtown buildings that shone through the open windows.

Dennis Patterson.

Without a thought, she threw herself into his arms. She wanted to seem brave and stop crying, but it was too much for her. With every new visitor, the pain rose in her face, a torrent she couldn't control. Patterson waited it out, then took her aside. He was bigger than she or David, and he held her by the shoulders like a fragile, delicate rose. As old as Bernatchez, but having aged better than the former pro football player, he was visibly proud of his white hair, and his bushy eyebrows made him look like a retired Santa.

"I know he'll get through this. Dr. Dohmann's an exceptional neurosurgeon." He sounded like a get-well card: sweet, sonorous, pious wishes, when what she really wanted was the truth and some explanation, here and now.

"Why? Why him?"

Patterson just shrugged. "A ton of reasons, I suppose, and nothing to do with who he is or what he represents."

"What are these RCMP types saying?"

"Not much for now, but they have a man there."

Juliette knew who it was: a heavyset guy with very short hair whom David had introduced at one of their soirées. He seemed nice enough, certainly discreet, but she couldn't recall his name. Patterson said he'd be helping the Central Bureau of Investigation (CBI), India's FBI.

"Helping? Wait a minute, I don't understand!" Juliette yelled. "Two employees of the High Commission in a bombed car, and the RCMP is just looking on?"

"Imagine if it was the other way round and an Indian diplomat in Ottawa got bombed on Elgin Street. What would people say if the Indian police took charge?"

Juliette couldn't care less what people thought. She remembered incidents with American or British diplomats and the squads of FBI or Scotland Yard that showed up. The Mounties, however, were just leaving one officer on site to get eaten alive by the CBI.

"That's the way things are done, Juliette," said Patterson.

"The way things are done?"

Bernatchez had promised: "The Canadian government would not let these monsters get away with it."

Words, words, words. "You know people in the department. You could do something. I'm sure a call to the right person in Ottawa would get them more involved."

"Look, Juliette. It's frustrating, I know, and I agree, but there are bilateral agreements …"

"Do something."

"I've talked to the minister, and he's not against the idea of offering, say, additional logistical help to the Indian police."

"Additional logistical help? How about a pen-and-pencil set with John A. Macdonald on it?"

Patterson sighed and made Juliette look at him. "Look, the important thing is for David to get better, stay alive. He's going to need both of us for that. You especially."

Hallmark, Hallmark, Hallmark.

She felt abandoned, coddled and silenced, cut off from reality.

It was night again, and Juliette had hardly slept since her arrival in Montreal: just short periods of agitated sleep, awaking in sweat, stunned and disoriented. She wanted to be set up next to David, in the same room, at all times, but for both medical and security reasons, Patterson had explained, they couldn't let her. She no longer felt like fighting and obediently followed Béatrice home.

On her way out of the hospital, she chatted briefly with two Mounties from the airport who asked her the same questions as the Indian police before they left. What were they doing here anyway? Shouldn't they be in New Delhi helping out their fellow officers?

"Look at them pretending to be useful," she yelled as she climbed into the taxi. "Good for what … raking in their pay?"

"Do you remember those old films?" Béatrice replied, "The Indians. Not your kind, the others with feathers: Apache, Comanche, Cheyenne, who knows? When they attacked the pioneer wagon trains headed west, rows of them appeared on the mountaintops, menacing in their war paint, and fell on the poor settlers for no reason. We were never told why. No need. It just happened, like rain. No one justifies rain, do they?"

What was she getting at? Juliette thought.

"Well, terrorism is just the same, like Indians in the movies or rain in summertime. No need for a motive or a rationale. The goal of terrorists is to terrorize. That's all there is. In other words, why even bother to investigate? What is there to find out? In any event, tomorrow or any moment now, three or four groups will claim responsibility for the attack, most likely Lashkar-e-Taiba. David was just one more statistic, and mere statistics don't get investigated, they just pile up, nothing to get upset about. Then they get shuffled to the bottom of the pile. Vague, impersonal statistics. Open it," said Béatrice, pointing to the glovebox.

She did, and inside was a firearm, very small, a .25 calibre of the kind you might slip into a handbag. Juliette was surprised to see Béatrice had one.

"In El Salvador I was constantly afraid, so I took shooting lessons without saying anything to Philippe. Go ahead. Pick it up."

"I've never used a gun."

"Easier than a tube of lipstick. You'll see."

Juliette closed the glovebox. *Enough violence. Why make more?*

Along Route 87, Max, now travelling as Peter Flanagan in a rented Ford Taurus from Kennedy Airport, heard on the radio that his nephew hadn't regained consciousness after the attack but the surgeons were hopeful they could bring him back: "His heart is solid, and he's strong, so he'll pull through." Max also learned that David hadn't travelled alone from Delhi; Juliette was with him, bent over the stretcher, in tears, naturally. Max knew his nephew was married but hadn't met the young bride yet. After the death of Philippe, his son David had cut Max off, or rather he had fallen into oblivion.

He crossed the border at Rouses Point using one of his American passports. The customs officer, already blasé about the security measures introduced after 9/11, barely glanced at it, cellphone in hand, more interested in lecturing his eldest daughter about letting everything lie about the house than hunting potential terrorists. Max then went directly on to Montreal. He thought about stopping at Mimi's first, but the pain, like the curiosity, was unbearable. He just had to know, to understand.

David's mother lived in a building, the Rockhill, in Côte-des-Neiges, where she'd moved after Philippe died. Béatrice could have gone back to Ottawa to be near her son when he was recruited by Foreign Affairs, but Montreal was more her style.

"Do you know how many years I've spent in boring capitals, practically going to bed at curfew? Ottawa's pretty and calm, but no thanks!"

Juliette fell asleep fully dressed, and it was the doorbell that cut into her dreamless sleep. It was daylight, and she heard voices. *This is it. They've come to tell me it's all over*, she thought. In the kitchen she came face to face with a bulky, grey-haired, uniformed policeman who respectfully stood aside, surprised to see this little thing appear from behind him. A second man sat at the table, a smaller, younger plainclothes officer. He got up when he saw her and offered a cold, hairy hand, very official.

"Detective Sergeant Luc Roberge, Quebec Police Force. I'm very sorry to bother you. This is Officer Morel." The officer nodded. Juliette turned to Béatrice, who was leaning on the counter and paying no attention to her.

Why did she let these two in?

"What's happened is absolutely horrible," Roberge continued. "Since 9/11, it's as though everything's upside down. Totally."

Juliette said nothing, so he went on.

"I hope he makes it through. Sincerely."

Hallmark Plus.

He coughed. "I realize this is a delicate moment, but you may be getting a visitor …"

"Visitor?"

Roberge turned to Béatrice, looking for encouragement and getting none. "We have good reason to believe that Max O'Brien will soon be back in Montreal," he went on. "He's sure to know his nephew's in a coma from the media. We think he's bound to show up."

Roberge was stickhandling, so Béatrice came to his rescue: "Sergeant Roberge is from the Economic Crimes Squad."

"I thought I'd already mentioned that."

"They want to arrest Max. End of story."

"We've been after him for fourteen years." He seemed strangely proud of this sorry record, adding, "My team is convinced he'll get in touch with one of you."

"Why me?" asked Juliette. "I've never even met him." This was true. David had only mentioned the name a few times in passing. She knew David's uncle had been wanted by the police for several years: a crook who was not involved in her life, or David's, for that matter.

"All I'm asking is for your cooperation. He is brilliant, but sneaky and manipulative. You mustn't believe a thing he says, ever."

Béatrice waved his business card. "Message received, Sergeant. If he ever does show up, one of us will call you, right, Juliette?"

She nodded.

4

As he parked the Taurus on the third floor of the Montreal General parking garage, Max suddenly realized he'd come without even making a plan. He'd driven back to Canada on a whim, abandoning the most elementary caution. Why had he come anyway? David was in a coma and couldn't speak, and even if, by some miracle, his nephew recognized him and allowed him to stay, what could they possibly talk about?

Your father asked me to keep an eye out for you, but while you were getting blown up on the other side of the world, I was in Manhattan swindling a banker — again! I'm so sorry. Max sighed. His presence seemed increasingly pointless, wrong, in fact. Never mind. He wanted to be with him, and he ought to be with him.

Max slammed the car door, cast a quick look around, and made his way to the hospital. No cops anywhere. Not surprising, really — terrorists never finish off their victims. They leave them to suffer right to the end. Why not do as much damage as you can? No journalists, either. He learned later that they'd been corralled in a smoking room on the ground floor, and there weren't that many anyway. The operation was over, and the radio was saying that David had survived … just barely. Now he was stable.

Max did spot a security detail, though, but not the usual hospital agency, which struck him as odd. At the entrance, the regular guards' uniforms were burgundy. These ones wore navy-blue jackets. They were also armed and looked all ready to play commando.

"Can I help you?" An agent had appeared behind him with two more hanging back, and before Max could answer, the man added, "Journalists aren't allowed here."

"I'm family."

The guard looked him up and down. Max realized right away that something was off. Two more agents ambled up in case they were needed as backup. There was no time to lose, and Max tore off down the corridor, looking for stairs to get him out of there fast. Already, he was cursing his carelessness.

He bumped into a nurse, who dropped her tray of meds with a howl of fright. First he tried the door to the stairway, which he opened without looking, but other agents had been called in and were swarming up from below, cutting him off. Max jumped over the handrail, delivering a few punches as he went, but it wasn't enough. He was being held firmly, his head hurting, against the bars of the railing. He'd stumbled upon some real pros.

"What are you doing here?"

"I came to visit my nephew."

The men looked at one another. One pulled out his cellphone and stepped away to make the call while they took Max back to the corridor. The nurse was crying, and a well-intentioned guard was helping her pick up the things she'd dropped.

Max was taken to a windowless room that must have been where the on-duty doctors came for a rest because it had lockers, a washbasin, and a toilet with the door half open. Someone offered him a coffee, which he refused with a grunt. Then they left him alone with one guard. What was this setup for? Why didn't they hand him over to the cops? Maybe that was next. A few moments later, he imagined Luc Roberge showing up with an evil grin. *After all these years, I finally get my hands on Public Enemy Number One!* Luc Roberge. Max had practically forgotten him till now. Of course, it was his turf he'd stepped onto, straight into the cop's waiting hands. What a screw-up!

When the door opened, it wasn't Roberge he saw but Béatrice, and the guard had disappeared. Béatrice stood apart from other women her age, thanks to her long years in the diplomatic corps, her manners, and her attitude: lofty, very erect, and impeccably elegant. She was radiant, even in this naked, cold, and impersonal room. Max hadn't seen her for years, ever since the death of Philippe in 1990, when he'd shown up incognito — thanks to all the "wanted" notices — to be with his brother's remains. He'd taken a big risk then, too, but he'd trusted Béatrice, who, during the night, had smuggled him into the funeral home on O'Connor Street in Ottawa. While she stood lookout at the back of the hall, he'd gently made his way through the floral arrangements, as though he had the place to himself. Philippe with the discreet and modest red maple leaf pin on his lapel, for which he'd given his life in El Salvador. Max didn't know how long he'd spent beside the coffin, looking but not crying — he'd already done that. When they were outside in the parking lot, Béatrice announced majestically, "From here on, I never want to hear from you again. Don't write or speak to me or David. Nothing at all. You no longer exist."

Then Max had shown her the *International Herald Tribune*, the paper Philippe had used to communicate with him once upon a time. Béatrice tossed it in the street. "Never, you hear me? Never."

So this was to be a double mourning. Her husband was dead, and Max was shoved into the shadows. The idea was to protect David now that Philippe was no longer around. What galled him the most was not this decision; that was hardly unexpected. It was her intransigence … and all with that bedroom voice of hers. Max knew seduction; it was the basis of his craft, and he could only admire the finesse and subtlety of hers. The outcome was the same, but oh, how she said it. Max had gone from being a necessary evil to just plain evil.

A century later, here she was again, standing before him, attractive as ever. She looked disappointed in him, as though his appearance only meant more bad news, just another rock in the avalanche of the past twenty-four hours.

"How is he?" Max asked.

"The doctors are confident; in fact, downright encouraging."

After long pause, Béatrice said, "I knew you'd come."

Max smiled sadly. He couldn't tell if she meant it or if it was just her way of saying it was too late again, that it was time to lay a wreath and choose a picture for the card.

"I want to see him."

"He's in a coma. He doesn't recognize anyone."

"I want to see him," Max insisted.

"What's the point?"

Before she could stop him, Max stepped around her and continued down the corridor. The teary-eyed nurse was gone, and the mercenaries were clogging the coffee machine, leaving only one guard at the door on the other side. He rushed Max to keep him from going in, while others moved in to back him up. Then behind him, Max heard Béatrice: "Okay, it's okay."

The man hesitated, then stepped aside. Max glanced across the hall at Béatrice and opened the door. The room was in shadow, but his eyes easily spotted the bed in the corner behind a curtain. He approached and pulled aside the curtain. The bed was empty.

David was actually on the next floor up. Dennis Patterson's idea, Béatrice said. "It's for his security," though someone seemed to have forgotten to give his change of address to the doctors, who were conspicuous by their absence, until Max noticed shadows behind glass at the opposite end of the room. The patient was intubated and plugged into various respirators, monitors, intravenous drips, and luminous dials. David's eyes were closed, of course, his hands by his side as though at attention.

Max spent a long time staring at his nephew, his face thickened with bruises, probably with medication too. The boy had aged since the last photos Max had seen in *CanadExport*, the Foreign Affairs newsletter. Max was confronted with a young adult; in fact, an adult, period.

"Are you Max?" a voice came from behind him. A young woman holding a piece of chocolate was sitting in a straight-back chair by the door. She had blond hair and blue — very blue — eyes, practically an ad for Lufthansa. This model was tired, though, worn out by long hours in front of the cameras. He went over to Juliette and held out his hand. She smiled weakly, but her hand was burning hot. He could easily see David falling for this one's charms.

So, the family was all here: the dignified but grief-stricken mother, the devastated wife, and the unconscious son-and-martyr. And, oh yes, the American uncle. The mysterious uncle who always shows up unannounced, the one they only talk about in hints and whispers.

"I suppose the armed guards were Patterson's idea?"

Béatrice nodded. "No point in taking chances." She glanced in the direction of Juliette, who had her back to them and was contemplating Montreal's buildings massed against the river, which looked like a distant grey sliver blending with the sky.

"If you had an ounce of decency, you'd go straight back where you came from. You've seen him. Now go."

"I want to know what happened, the whole story. I want to find those bastards and make them pay!"

‡

Juliette turned to look at the newcomer. This man was the first thing to make any sense since it all happened. When he'd come in, he looked like a loser in that worn raincoat. Worn out like him. Still good-looking, but old-ish and running on memories and bygone days. Some globe-trotting con man hunted by the police for the last fourteen years! Somebody had it all wrong.

The conversation was starting to interest her, and she drew closer. Finally, something was happening. Strangely, though, Béatrice said, "What's the use? Do you think that will bring him back?"

"Look, Béatrice, I'm sick of getting here too late." He headed for the door without even a glance at Juliette, who was still intrigued and shocked by what Béatrice had said. Angry. Before she had time to catch him, he was gone. Juliette turned to Béatrice.

"Why did you —?" but Béatrice was already on the phone "— what are you doing?"

"My duty ... hello, Detective Roberge? This is Béatrice O'Brien ..."

5

Here Greek Avenue turned into Little India, and flags with the crescent moon or the spinning wheel replaced the blue-and-white. On Hutchison Street, a right-turn at the Al-Sunnah Al-Nabawiah Mosque, and Max was stuck in traffic taking in the scenery: a veiled woman at the bus stop, mustachioed men in conference in front of the Ratha Driving School, other men farther off buying lottery tickets. *Hmmm ... I thought the Qur'an forbade that.* Next, a left turn onto Ogilvy. On either side, there were Sri Lankan grocery shops selling products "direct" from Colombo. The beginnings of turbans, saris, and traditional *shalwar kameez*, in front of a video store specializing in Bollywood films. Posters in strident colours featuring Hrithik Roshan, the latest heartthrob, and his star-struck leading lady Kareena Kapoor, had replaced the purple curtains announcing the Cretans' Association

— long gone, along with the pastry window displays — piles of baklava engorged with dripping honey.

Max parked the Taurus near Athena Park on Jean Talon. Soulless blocks of grey concrete with fake windows just for decoration, called the Labyrinth to please its former Greek tenants, now served an Asian diaspora. Here were the offices of immigration lawyers, temp agencies, schools that taught languages, a tae kwon do academy, and Thai restaurants, and, naturally, import-export agents. Among them was the workplace of Dennis Patterson. Max had tried calling him, but he was at lunch, his secretary said. Max would not take no for an answer and was told Patterson always ate at noon in the ground-floor cafeteria.

"I'm sure he'll call you as soon as he gets back."

Those who worked in the Labyrinth could eat their way around the world every lunch hour. The kitchen had a fast-food version of just about everywhere, with steaming vats standing out in the open for those in a hurry. You could go from China to North Africa to Mexico to Italy without jet lag, just some heartburn. Behind the counters, caterers in colourful costumes bustled constantly. A long lineup could cost them faithful customers who might not come back to New Orleans once they'd been to Polynesia and its sauces. You had to shake a leg, get excited, and convince the customer he was getting some serious effort.

Max scanned the room: the white spots of tae kwon do outfits everywhere — the students ate there, too — and in front of the Mughal Palace, advertising vegetarian food, a young Indian woman was barely managing the daily specials. Dishes of *masala vada* and *roti* orbited her under the menacing eye of the turbaned boss, who was stationed behind, making the lemonade. Two other employees, both male, did hardly any better. Sooner or later, all three of them would probably be shown the door by the lemonade-maker.

But Max wasn't here with the hungry throng to feel sorry for the immigrant proletariat. He'd just spotted Dennis Patterson sliding his tray along in front of the Indian girl. The former diplomat had aged, and his breath probably smelled of Scotch, as usual. They'd first met when Philippe brought his classmate from the University of British Columbia home with him. Patterson had drunk all night long, even then, and Max recalled Philippe mentioning it. He even overheard a conversation between them years later. Philippe was warning Patterson about his habit, saying it could hurt his career.

His brother had predicted correctly. Philippe had charged up through the ranks in fourth gear, whereas Patterson, after a distinguished beginning, had marked time. Parked in Ottawa behind a desk on Sussex Drive while his friends were posted around the world, he had left Foreign Affairs mid-career and wandered from one law firm to another — he'd trained as a legal adviser — before opening a consultancy in international relations in the basement of his bungalow in Repentigny.

That was the best decision of his life. There was a real, concrete need for Canadian companies just waking up to the opportunities of "emerging markets," as the jargon had it. There couldn't be any gaffes or approaches to the wrong people. In this blind uncertainty, Patterson was their seeing-eye dog. It wasn't his job to tell them which country to go to, but simply how to get there with as few problems as possible.

Though a poor bureaucrat, Patterson turned out to be a dynamic entrepreneur; he hired other defrocked functionaries from the department and unceasingly developed his manic attention to significant details: *You're invited to visit a Japanese colleague. Do you wear a tie or not? Jacket?* By virtue of his effort and eighteen-hour days, he became indispensable in his domain, and now he employed twenty people on the eighth floor of the Labyrinth, drove two Mercedes — one sport, one not — and owned a summer home in Sutton. All this did not stop him from enjoying the chicken curry special at $5.99, soft drink included.

"Luc Roberge is after you. He's already met Béatrice."

Max already knew where the emergency exits were and that a second elevator was located on the south side of the building. He also knew there was an alley behind some stands beyond the storage room. From where he stood, he could also see the saloon door to the kitchen in the Mughal Palace, which was in constant activity with employees going back to the storage to fill up on beef bhuna or shrimp biryani. Even if Roberge found his way here, Max was sure he'd be able to sneak out. He might be Public Enemy Number One, but only to the cop. They'd have given Roberge a partner, two at most, but ones better suited to working on a computer than tailing anyone in a car. Photocopying would be more their style than high-speed chases through the city streets, so nothing much to worry about in that department, at least for now.

In Max's absence and after Philippe's death, Patterson had been David's surrogate father. This way, Béatrice was sure he had everything he needed and his inheritance handled properly. Money management wasn't Béatrice's thing. Spending it was. From the U.S., Max had discreetly kept an eye on things via some contacts in brokerage houses, and amazingly, he found absolutely no misdoing on Patterson's part. He administered Philippe's pension with complete honesty, leaving no room for reproach on investment matters. So, despite his alcoholism, Patterson was a much better guardian than Max, though Béatrice had never given Max a chance to prove himself.

Patterson seemed to read his thoughts: "Love abhors a vacuum," he said. "I simply stepped into the space that was available."

Béatrice had David in Rabat, Morocco, but Max first saw him at age three. He'd been living in New York and only came back to Canada incognito, always at great risk, but never encountered any serious problems. He and Philippe had arranged a code to be printed in the *International Herald Tribune* want ads. Their get-togethers seemed more like secret meetings, always furtive, always in a crowd: in the middle of a park, on the Metro. Two big kids having fun unknown to anyone close to them, but Max had to be more and more careful. Roberge had realized how close they were and was sure to use this "weakness" to grab Max one of these days. Family reunions became more dangerous. That didn't stop Max from sending birthday presents to David via Philippe, but this, too, had its risks. Young David had been fascinated by this American uncle who rarely showed up, and when he did it was unannounced, quickly and on the sly. What else could they say to the boy? That Max was on the run from police in three U.S. states and two Canadian provinces? Of course, this couldn't go on forever.

In December 1987, when David was nine and the little family was back in Ottawa for the holidays, Max and his brother set up a meeting at the Plaza in New York. But Béatrice showed up instead, the *International Herald Tribune* in her hand … quite a surprise for Max. Over smoked salmon and under the loudspeakers moaning a disco version of "Jingle Bells," she asked Max not to try to see his brother again. Béatrice wasn't going to let her husband risk his career on these escapades.

"So why didn't he come and tell me himself?" Max was annoyed.

In fact, Philippe didn't know about his wife's manoeuvring. He thought she was in Montreal to finish up her Christmas shopping, and she was not about to clue him in either. She wanted Max alone to make this decision and bear the brunt of the blame for the estrangement.

"And if I refuse to go along?" he said unconvincingly.

"You won't." She smiled sadly, placing her hand on his. "You love Philippe too much to make him risk his future."

She was right, and he knew it. The sacrifice was his to make, and he only wished he'd been the one to take the initiative. In a way, it was humiliating that it came from Béatrice, but being cut off from Philippe meant being cut off from David, too. She pushed away the untouched salmon and reached into her purse, pulling out a gift-wrapped box with a red ribbon that Max recognized.

The Walkman he had sent his nephew. Every year he sent a present. She held it out to him and he slipped it into his pocket. This, too, he understood, and he nodded.

"This will be our little secret."

He nodded again.

"Thanks, Max, for Philippe."

Central Park was covered in snow. The hack drivers took him for a tourist. The sky was grey, so more snow was coming. Max and Béatrice had parted inside the hotel: she was booked on the four o'clock flight to Montreal and Ottawa, where David and Philippe waited. Max walked aimlessly across the park with his hands in his pockets, ignoring the cold wind that scorched his face. Emptiness, a bottomless pit from which he'd never escape. He emerged at Fifth Avenue across from the Metropolitan Museum. At a distance, a homeless man lay asleep on the sidewalk, his whole life contained in the torn and scattered plastic bags around him. Max got out the Walkman and slipped it into one of the bags, unnoticed, then continued on his way to nowhere.

6

"What identity did you come under?" Patterson asked.

Max wasn't in the mood to regale him with stories from his travels. Maybe some other time, so he got straight to the point.

"What happened in New Delhi? Who's responsible?"

Patterson wiped his mouth, then took another swig of beer. The former diplomat was worn out. His eyes were red, glassy, as if he hadn't slept in days. "No idea here, either," he replied after a while.

"Did you talk to David just before it happened?"

Max shook his head, disappointed. "No. I knew he was busy."

Patterson sighed loudly. "Ha, we thought globalization was a one-way street. For trade, maybe. Not violence. Take that crapfest in Singapore, for instance, which unleashed a horror show in Caracas, then a catastrophe in St. Petersburg."

Max wasn't there to hear the day's headlines from an international-relations consultant.

Patterson turned to him. "David was in the wrong country at the wrong time."

"Look, Patterson, I'm not one of your clients, okay? Explain."

"It could be any one of five groups, from what I could get out of my CSIS contacts." Patterson considered the Canadian Security and Information Service diligent in its handling of the incident. "First, there's the Hizb-ul-Mujahideen. They're the biggest. A thousand Muslim fanatics, very highly trained, probably in Pakistan. Great planning ..."

"Like the Indian Parliament attack?"

"No, that's another Islamic group, Lashkar-e-Taiba, at least according to the Indians and CSIS. Their trademark is suicide missions, preferably spectacular. They're based in Pakistan, but India, especially the disputed state of Kashmir, is their playground."

"And the other three?"

"Similar style. This is a contest in violence of the most raw kind. Jaish-e-Mohammed, Harakat-ul-Ansar, and Al-Badr, all of them active in Kashmir, naturally. One of those is responsible, I'm certain. Remember the Hindu victims the other day in Jammu?"

Max couldn't see the connection with David. Why attack Canada? Why a diplomat ... and not even the most important one, a rookie? An isolated, desperate move. It made no sense.

Patterson shrugged. He had no idea either. No one had come forward, and even if they did, it might not mean anything. Often two or three groups claimed the same action so as to cover their tracks.

"India's a powder keg these days, because of Kashmir," Patterson went on. "Poisonous Kashmir: a conflict left over from the dismantling of the British Empire in 1947. Since Partition, the Indians and Pakistanis haven't let a chance go by to get at each other. Three wars already. Three times India has won, once in 1947 and 1948, once in 1965 — both wars over Kashmir — then again in 1971. Nothing changed for the locals. They were still cut in half by the demarcation line with the two armies facing off at the foothills of the Himalayas: a million soldiers and sixty-five thousand dead in over fifty-five years.

"In the wake of September 11, and with Al-Qaeda, the conflict took on more resonance. A new scope, too. Before then, the only victims were in Kashmir. The rest of what went on up there stayed there: jihadist and Kashmiri rebels versus the Indian Army — home-made carnage. But now India is accusing the Pakistani Inter-Services Intelligence, the most formidable secret service in all of Asia, of covering for Islamic terrorists and helping them deploy all over the country. So, you might say things are tense." Patterson paused, then added, "Especially now they both have the bomb. Sure, our minister of foreign affairs tried to cool things down, without taking sides, of course. As far as Kashmir's concerned — like any other conflict of this type — Canada has to keep on good terms with both countries."

"So David was just an unlucky victim? No Italian or Japanese diplomats out on the street that day — oh, hey, wait, a Canadian!"

"I can't think of any other reason."

"What do we hire security people for, then?"

"When in doubt, it's good to be prepared for the worst. You never know … a Hizb-ul-Mujahideen hit man shows up at the General Hospital with an AK-47 slung on his shoulder —" Patterson looked up "— I know it's crazy, but I wanted to reassure Juliette."

"The Mounties questioned her?"

Patterson looked at Max a long while. "Béatrice is right," he said ironically, "you're going to stick your nose into this, aren't you?"

Max glanced at the half-open door to the Mughal Palace storage area, just as some Indian employees opened another one onto the street. Just for a moment, with both doors ajar, Max saw through to the other side of the building: parked in the alley was a police car with removable flashing light on the roof. No one was at the wheel. Could this be Roberge already? Again Max's eyes roamed over the cafeteria. It was less busy now. Employees had finished lunch and were headed back to their offices. He looked around for Roberge's profile, but didn't see him. This time, Patterson picked up on his nervousness. No point in pretending.

"You called them, didn't you?" Max asked, but Patterson just smiled.

"I have absolutely no interest in making life easier for Roberge. You know that."

That left Béatrice. Why had she turned him in?

A man in a uniform shirt appeared at the north exit and another one at the south. They seemed to be looking for someone: it had to be him. So they hadn't spotted him yet.

"Look, I need an intro to the high commissioner, Bernatchez."

"Don't get involved in this, Max. Stay away from it."

A third agent emerged from among the stands, a flabby guy pretending to be engrossed in the Mexican menu. And another among the tables. Then a bustle of activity behind the display of *chalupas* and *enchiladas*. There were shouts and the sound of a plate shattering, then a struggle on the ground. When the agents got up, they were firmly grasping a young Latino. Screeching of walkie-talkies followed — a successful raid right there in the Labyrinth.

Another illegal on his way back to Chihuahua, courtesy of Her Majesty, thought Max. *One more broken dream.*

The cops ignored Max and Patterson as they went off with their prize, looking proud, shoulders straight.

Patterson resumed the conversation. "The situation there's explosive. Way beyond our abilities, and yours, anyway."

"I don't give a damn."

"You're going to take off after Islamist terrorists all by yourself?"

"Sure, why not?"

Patterson shook his head hopelessly. "These guys are even worse than the Salvadoran army, Max, harder to get hold of."

Max closed his eyes. He could see Philippe's office on Avenida Las Palmas, the chalk outline on the floor, the Policia Nacional officer by the door, pretending to be somewhere else, not wanting to disturb Max's reunion with ghosts. *I'll see it through to the end*, he told himself. *I'll keep my promise to Philippe.*

7

The last of the trees had been cut down, or would be soon. The dirt roads had been cleared and marked out. Cranes, tractors, a giant Meccano set. From his window, the young Max could see the first construction sites, the first wounds. Houses going up as far as the eye could see; all identical, lining up like fresh scars. Against the advice of Max's mother, Solange, his father, Gilbert, had quit the poorly heated apartment on Lajeunesse in the summer of 1962 to seek out something new at the opposite end of the island. His new fortune and his family's.

He'd convinced Stéphane Kavanagh, his banker and friend, to take a chance on him, and in the following weeks, while everyone else was getting worked up about the Cuban Missile Crisis, the two Irishmen were at the kitchen table, totally wrapped up in something else. It was a contest of dreams and hopes. Solange pretended to be won over by her husband's arguments — the future king of Roxboro, as he said with a smile as broad as you please, shaving cream still on his face. Max remembered that Sunday when the four of them (Philippe was there for the day this time) went to scout out the plot for the ultimate sacrifice. Solange, not wanting to be a wet blanket, though she was wary of her husband's impulses, faked her enthusiasm for the clearing of the street, the beauty of the lot, and the size of the river.

Gilbert O'Brien was a veritable home-handyman visionary. All these houses were going up at high speed, and one day they'd need improvement, renovation, or at least a change of colour. All these tenants becoming home owners would sooner or later get bitten by the toolkit/electric-sander bug. Their mortgages were all sewn up thanks to Kavanagh, who in return financed Gilbert's business on Gouin Street. Yep, a tidy little arrangement. Solange went along without a word, Philippe and Max, too, despite the sacrifices: new neighbourhood, new school, new friends. Then, when Philippe left home to avoid the exhausting daily trek to college, Gilbert had to resign himself to the boy getting a room in town. He'd be a long-distance partner in the dream.

Max was inconsolable. He idolized Philippe, his teacher and protector. Philippe had six years on his brother and brought a whiff of the outside world to Lajeunesse Street. With him around, dressing, eating, and talking were all different: everything was "modern," a modernity learned at college side by side with the daddy's boys of Greater Montreal. Gilbert had spared no expense. The Jesuits cost him an arm and a leg, but he paid without blinking. It was an investment in his son's future, his own, too. Did he already have Philippe in mind to pick up the reins after him, or was he thinking of Max as the "handier" of the two? Whichever it was, the "empire" was still in the planning stages. It kept Gilbert awake at night. He spent sleepless nights adding details here and there. By dawn he'd be ready to pass the torch to both of them, as they went out to conquer the world in their turn. His office became a time machine to the future.

Solange was the one left waiting in the present. Then one day she'd had enough. She was seeing another man on the side, one who "understood" and who did not live in a fantasyland. Her confrontation came as a complete surprise to the "king of Roxboro," who felt she'd betrayed him. Gilbert hadn't seen this coming. She wanted a new life that wasn't Gyprocked, screwed, and asphalt-shingled into place. She wanted out with her kids, but Philippe refused to leave. So did Max. They both clung hard to Gilbert, shutting out their mother's arguments. She insisted, she lamented, then she slammed the door in a fury.

Gilbert, supported by his friend Kavanagh, was heartbroken for months. Then life started up again, and the king of Roxboro got right back to work. On Saturdays, Max filled in for Philippe, who was absorbed in his studies, and helped his father in the store. Early on Sunday evenings, Philippe would disappear to his small room on Amherst. When he was gone, Max paced the floor, not knowing what to do. He had trouble fighting the sadness brought on by big brother's absence. Fortunately, there was Kavanagh, a constant guest at their table after

Solange walked out. Likeable, open, and "modern" in his own way, he gradually replaced Philippe, who showed up less and less.

A love lost turned into new prosperity for Gilbert. He had been right, and Kavanagh the banker was delighted. Business at the hardware store doubled every trimester, and it was time to expand right away. The housing boom surpassed all expectations, and the king of Roxboro reigned supreme. Gilbert invested more and more, and Kavanagh backed him up. The bank made bigger loans on the strength of even greater projected income. Gilbert spent more than ever and didn't mind sinking everything he had into the project. Success became almost a monotonous routine: no bumps or sharp turns in a road as wide as tarmac leading straight up into the clouds.

The fateful day was one Max could never forget. The radio said it was the coldest day of the year. They came to get him while he was in math class late one afternoon. *Way to go*, he said to himself. He hated differential and integral calculus. Philippe was in the principal's office, fresh from Vancouver, where he'd been studying political science since September. Then Philippe took him out to a waiting taxi. The driver already knew where to go. He headed straight for downtown, but road construction led him back to Gouin and the hardware store.

By the time Philippe realized what was happening, it was already too late. The store was closed … on a Friday. Max looked for his father, but the place was deserted.

"We're going to a hotel for a few days," Philippe said when Max turned to him. "The house has been seized, too. It's the bank's now."

"What about Papa?"

"He'll be here soon."

Kavanagh had six stitches in his face where Gilbert had hit him with a nail-puller. From the police station, he'd called Philippe in Vancouver instead of a lawyer, and Kavanagh declined to file charges, so Gilbert was able to join his sons at the hotel by evening — motel, actually. A pretty grubby one, too, in a slummy neighbourhood. The windows hadn't been opened in weeks, due to the cold, and the room hadn't been cleaned ever, except maybe a superficial once-over. All three slept in the same big bed, three world-weary musketeers chewed up and spat out by fate. Gilbert turned on the light in the middle of the night. He had to talk, confess, get it off his chest. He was washed up. Kavanagh hadn't kept his word and had let his superiors take a piece out of the king of Roxboro. The vultures had swooped down on his business and torn it to pieces. It was the saddest night in Max's short life: a filthy little bulb overhead, worn-out furniture, and the hum of traffic in the distance.

"Why us? Why?" Gilbert couldn't get over it. He never did. After the nervous breakdown, he wound up in the woodworking section at Castor Bricoleur, where he coasted along. He'd come home with his hands full of splinters and never even bother to pull them out. All desire to make an honest living or even "make an effort" deserted Max, too, which resulted in petty crimes to round out the month's expenses, a borrowed car to impress a girl his age in the neighbourhood, some vandalism, a few misdemeanours here and there: nothing original, just run-of-the-mill impulses. Then one day, he took off after Kavanagh to give him a taste of their calamity. Another dose of the old nail-puller. But the banker had pulled up stakes. *Aw, the hell with him*. Max had to get on with his life, and he wasn't about to let anyone get in his way, not like his dad. Little crimes led to bigger ones, bolder, riskier. Max was bound to end up in jail sooner or later.

Then along came Mimi.

Before her, Montreal had always spelled misery and hard times for Max.

The first time he got out of the Bordeaux prison in 1972 — it seemed like only yesterday — there was no one but the bus driver. Gilbert hadn't passed the news along, so Philippe didn't know Max was out. No sign of his father in the little apartment on Bagg Street, either. That's what Max thought at first, because of the drawn curtains and locked door. A neighbour came and let him in. There was Gilbert, sitting in the shadows with a cat on his lap. He'd never liked animals before.

"I don't want you here, Max. I put all your stuff in that box. Take it and go."

It was only a shoebox of souvenirs he didn't want anyway, and he tossed it in the first garbage bin he came across on his way to Mimi's place — an ex-cellmate had given him the address.

Mimi was the eldest of the three and stood in as mother for the other two: Antoine, who was Max's age, with his nose buried in *Popular Mechanics*, was the intellectual in the family; Pascale was secretive and melancholic, looking at him that day through wide teenage eyes, more curious than frightened. The tenants were the collateral damage of the justice system, and Mimi had seen plenty already, so what was one more or one less? And what did these bewildered black sheep live on? Max had an idea, but he wasn't about to ask. To each his own. They barely said "hi," then one day they disappeared. A halfway house to crime is what it was. That's the way Max was headed, too, inevitably. Mimi, though, liked nothing better than to exercise her maternal instinct.

She was taken with Max, and she stood behind him unobtrusively. A slight glance or a word or two once in a while, nothing more. She was cautious as if she were afraid he'd panic.

One morning, she found out what he was up to — a gas-station holdup, just one more dumb move — and she took him out to a restaurant to explain a few hard realities, as she called them. Not just any restaurant … the Château Champlain, swarming with waiters decked out in formalwear. Max had never eaten in a place like this before. He had trouble believing Mimi could manage such luxury. Okay, she had money, but not *that much*.

"What's the matter, Max? I've never been here before either."

She'd chosen a table at the far end near two businessmen in suits and ties whose discussion involved airy sweeps of their pens. Mimi at once struck up a conversation with them. They were only too glad of a pretext for getting off business matters, and she was especially charming: a smile here, a burst of laughter there, and her timing was perfect. Max twiddled his thumbs until they ordered … the same thing as the two business types, who were now back in the thick of their number-columns. After dessert, and feeling stuffed, Max was still wondering what this life lesson was that she wanted to teach him. Till now, they'd just talked about trivial stuff, as though intimidated by their surroundings, nothing heart-to-heart. Max was confused. Mimi had brought him here to talk him out of a burglary, but they were surrounded by things only money could buy — lots of money. Max figured after the burglary he'd invite her out for a life lesson, too.

When they'd finished eating, Mimi caught the attention of the businessmen once more. On the ground was a leather wallet one of them had probably dropped.

"Is that yours?"

Intrigued, one of the men scooped it toward him with his foot, but it wasn't his or his colleague's. Mimi took it from him and said, "I'll give it to the waiter. He'll want to know which table it was under. If he looks this way, signal him, would you?"

Baffled, Max followed her to the counter where the overworked waiter was trying to juggle three different orders.

"Our boss is getting the bill, so just give it to him."

"Your boss, where?"

Mimi pointed to the two businessmen, and one of them, as expected, waved to them. The waiter nodded and went on about his task.

Once out on the sidewalk, Mimi walked Max away, but not too quickly. Bewildered by what he'd just seen, Max didn't dare ask any questions, though he was dying to.

Then she said, "There's more than one way into a life of crime, Max. Some ways are smarter than others."

Over the following months, there was a change in the program — a new career, new things to learn under a new teacher. Mimi taught him the ABCs of the con game with great patience. Gradually, he gained confidence, inventing his own swindles and updating the old ones. He threw himself into the pigeon hunt with the energy and enthusiasm of a neophyte. Soon, the world of grifters kept no secrets from him. He joined a network of fraud artists and plunged himself into all kinds of schemes, playing more and more key parts as his experience grew and his talents gained recognition. He stole smart, without violence or intimidation. Mostly from businesses or those they profited, and that set his conscience at rest. Max didn't lead just one life, but ten, twenty, fifty … lives that overlapped constantly, so he had to look in the mirror to remember who he was.

Now he was coming home to Mimi for the first time in years. She'd started renting rooms to students from the Université du Québec nearby, the area a little more respectable than the hoods of the old days. Noisier too, though. As soon as they hugged and took a good look at one another, and told one another they hadn't aged a day — actually, she had, but he didn't mention it — students came running down the stairs. Mimi rolled her eyes in exasperation, then smiled, a dimple in her right cheek. Despite the wrinkles, really nothing had changed. Some women can retain that "little girl" look forever, and she was living proof.

"I can't tell you how good it is to see you! They told me you were in New York."

"New York and other places."

She smiled. Again the dimple. He stroked her cheek. He was happy to see her as happy and steady on her feet as always. Antoine, too. A little stooped maybe, and wearing slippers, but still with his head full of projects that worried Mimi. She'd moved on, but not Antoine. He'd turned the basement into a print shop. He still worked at Dorval Airport, but on weekends he made fake documents: passports, social insurance cards, travellers' cheques, the way other people had fun with stamp collections or building the Eiffel Tower out of toothpicks. Who for? Illegal immigrants "fresh off the boat," sort of, who needed that kind of thing. The middle of the room was occupied by a Xerox 3275, HoloText 283 that even embedded holograms right in the photo, and a TypoFlair 2220 — the very latest in plastic lamination — plus other machines whose purpose Max didn't know.

"See, this is where I come to unwind," Antoine said with all the pride of a weekend artist. He and Max had been partners a long time. Under contract for Air France in the 1970s, Antoine had developed European contacts in Montreal and all over Canada. Some worked for French companies, and he let them in on unbelievable investment opportunities, blue-chip stocks in corporations that didn't exist — especially in Asia — or bold and inventive ways to keep the French tax authorities from getting their hands on hard-won travel allowances. Max and Antoine's victims weren't really victims, strictly speaking, since their losses were handed on to their employers, who probably profited from similar schemes in the peace and quiet of their Paris offices. Later on,

Pascale had joined in with her own special roles to play: the Monaco socialite who would do anything to protect her husband, Count Whatever, from financial ruin; the elegant Brazilian with a fortune from South African diamond mines; or the young charity-fund manager hounded by the Austrian government and ready to entrust her holdings to someone reliable but enterprising who, naturally, had the welfare of the tropical rainforest at heart, especially at a return of 28 percent.

Pascale, Pascale, Pascale.

Mimi's brother raised his head from the HoloText machine, his face bathed in pale blue light. "Is David going to make it?"

Max had no way of knowing. All he could do was repeat what it said in the papers.

Antoine placed a consoling hand on his shoulder. That was his way, and it was worth all the condolences on earth. In a voice close to a whisper, he asked, "Do you still think about her?"

Max pretended not to hear so he could keep up a front. But he couldn't pull it off with Antoine. "Pascale? Sure, all the time. You?"

"Always."

The love of Max's life, Pascale and he had married in 1974 on a whim. Or was it love at first sight? They adored each other and couldn't imagine living apart. They couldn't even go twenty-four hours without seeing, touching each other and leaping into bed. Then suddenly she was gone, just like that. Then dead in India. Max never got over it. Ever.

8

Doctor Dohmann was a frail man, an ex-smoker, and it showed. His hand was forever sliding into his right jacket pocket searching for that phantom pack. *Highly respected, but a victim like all of us*, thought Juliette, *with his little tics left over from the past*. With his pen, he pointed to a detail on the MRI on the computer screen: dark, amorphous stains that Juliette refused to connect with David's brain.

"See here? A subdural hematoma from violent trauma. The explosion probably blew him against the door. There are other lesions from the shockwave, but the first is more serious. That accounts for his present condition."

She wondered if the Indian police would receive this information. The RCMP would insist on seeing it first, of course. Still, what did it change? David was in a coma just the same.

"Will he survive?"

The doctor's hand returned to the jacket pocket, then to his face. He removed his glasses, gently, but it cost him great effort.

"I don't wish to give you any false hope. He's stable for now, and he's recovered from the operation nicely, and fortunately, despite the cerebral edema, the intra-cranial pressure is diminished. Still, there's no guarantee he'll come through it. Not yet, anyway."

"And if he does, he will be … I mean, will he be …?"

Dohmann understood perfectly well. "The David you know and love? I hope so, of course, but it isn't very likely."

"Diminished, then?"

"Yes. We'll just have to see how much. Memory loss, unbearable migraine, personality changes, apathy, indifference, mood swings. This would be the optimum result. Or …"

"A vegetable?"

"It's too soon to say. First he has to get through this, and it's not yet certain."

Juliette looked away. Being in the room had sud-denly become unbearable. She was mentally preparing to leave when Dohmann added, "There's something else."

"Yes?"

Dohmann seemed ill at ease. "I don't know if the police have mentioned this."

"Mentioned what?"

"Not all the marks on his body were from the explosion."

"What do you mean?"

"Lesions on his neck and chest ... and the joints of his fingers, too ..." He cleared his throat: "They're from before the car bomb went off, and completely different in nature."

Juliette was speechless.

"In other words," Dohmann went on, "when the car blew up, your husband was already in bad shape."

"Beaten?"

"Possibly."

"And Luiz, the driver?"

"I don't know. I haven't seen the autopsy report. In any event, the body was blown to bits."

David beaten? Tortured? What on earth for? For what purpose? Revolted, Juliette left the office. She so wanted to share her distress and horror with someone, Béatrice, for example, even Patterson. But she was alone at the hospital. She also desperately needed to sleep, but knew she wouldn't. From now on, she couldn't afford to feel tired. She had to be alert, for both of them. In the common room at the end of the corridor, the vending machine spat out the over-sweetened American chocolates that gave her heartburn. Even Toblerone, the one exception, was getting to be too much for her. Dr. Rangarajan said something about sweets, didn't he? What was it? She couldn't remember. She slipped the money into the slot and got mint chocolate for a change, the only type she hadn't yet tasted. She was distracted, and it was no surprise she didn't notice the man sitting in a high-backed armchair facing away from the door. When she realized it was Max O'Brien, she gave a start.

He got up and smiled: "Sorry, I didn't mean to scare you." It was a sad smile that showed the fatigue in his face. She noticed the bags under his eyes. He gestured to the chocolate. "I was sure I'd find you here." She was about to mumble some banality when he added, "I'm sorry I left in a hurry yesterday."

"Is it true what you said about getting to the bottom of this?"

"What do you know about me?"

"Practically nothing. The black sheep of the family, a repeat criminal. The man of many faces. Béatrice mentioned some horrible things about you. If you've done even half the things she says …"

"What about David? What does he say?"

Nothing. Max didn't exist. In the lead-up to the wedding, his name hadn't come up once. Worse than dead. At least the dead get mentioned, remembered, but Max? Nothing at all.

"I sent him several emails at the High Commission, but he never answered."

This was news to her: "What about?"

"Oh, nothing special. I wrote to Béatrice, too. I'm not sure why. It wasn't to get back into the family; I just wanted to connect. Tell them I was still around. I thought maybe time would win out over the past." He seemed pained by this. "Just before Philippe went to El Salvador, he made me promise to look out for David. It was stupid. There was no way I could do it, and even if I could, David would never allow it." He looked away. "When I heard about the bombing, it came back to me. I felt I'd let Philippe down; not taken him seriously. I was wrong. David was all that was most precious to Philippe, even more than Béatrice. Entrusting him to me was Philippe's way of helping me redeem myself. Do you see what I mean?"

She didn't really, but let him go on.

"It was an emergency exit. He was showing me a hidden passage, a way back in, unnoticed in the wall and papered over, and all I had to do was open it. I didn't."

Juliette was still in a fog, so he went on.

"The explosion is another door, a way out, one more chance, and this time I'm not going to miss it."

Juliette listened to him soliloquize, his head slightly tilted, till finally he looked up at her. "I'm leaving for New Delhi tonight."

He expected her to give a start and wade in against him, like Béatrice, for instance (if he dared tell her), but Juliette seemed to go along with it. He realized she was at a loss, that she didn't trust either Béatrice or Patterson, much less the RCMP or the CBI.

"I want to catch them, too," she said, finally.

"I'll help you."

"Tell me."

With the police, everything had been dragged out of her painfully and oh-so-slowly, but with Max, it just poured out naturally: first the High Commission and the past frantic days before the Montreal conference at the end of the month, involving government officials and some private companies. The prime goal was to stimulate economic activity between the two countries. Forget about the poor, the lepers, overpopulation, and the caste system. Think economic development, the middle class, and skilled labour.

"Who's taking part?"

"Every Canadian business already working in India, or those who want to be: information technology, recycling, pharma … then there was Béatrice's lightning descent."

"To do what?"

"See her son and empty all the shops in Connaught Place. We took her to the airport two days before the attack. What else? Mrs. Fothergill dropped in uninvited just as we were about to have supper. That persistent Japanese diplomat looking for a squash partner. Didier, the librarian at l'Alliance Française was in a panic …"

"And before Béatrice got there?"

Juliette clammed up. *Should she tell him? Was it even relevant?*

"Dr. Rangarajan confirmed I was pregnant."

Max was the last person she ever expected to share that secret with. No one had even breathed his name at her wedding, and now he was her confidant, and Béatrice was still in the dark. The fact was she didn't even want her mother-in-law to know, though she really ought to tell her. When the time was right. Max had to know that it was because of Béatrice's invasion that she didn't have time to tell David; well, that and her stupid decision to wait for "just the right moment." Besides, he was about to head off to Kathmandu.

Max was intrigued by this. In Nepal, the Canadian Co-operation Office provided support for various development projects. David travelled to Kathmandu from time to time for meetings, get-togethers, and rundowns on the political situation, of course. Things were tense there these days, and Nepal was in a state of civil war, with Maoist guerillas seeking to overthrow the monarchy.

Juliette sighed. She recalled asking David to find a replacement. She hardly saw him as it was: first preparations for the conference, and then he'd be returning to Canada.

"You weren't coming with him?"

"I'm a teacher. I couldn't get the time off."

"And he wouldn't drop Kathmandu?"

"I couldn't very well force him."

"Did you fight about it?"

"No, we never fought."

Well, sometimes, about having a baby, for instance. It was his idea. Juliette hadn't wanted one at first. There had been shouting, doors slammed, periods of seemingly endless silence. He absolutely had to have one. She tried to reason with him, but her arguments didn't stand up: *Look, we hardly see each other as it is. And a baby on your first posting … in India …?* In her heart of hearts, she felt he was getting round her again. First, she'd followed him to Delhi, then this baby thing. Surely it was his turn to give a little. It had to do with principles or something she didn't believe in, when in reality, she wanted a child as much as he did.

"So he went to Nepal," Max underlined.

"With Vandana, a colleague."

"You know her well?"

"Great girl, a good friend."

"And the political climate in India?" Max went on, "Islamist terrorists, for example, might he have done something to rub them the wrong way?"

"No idea."

"He told you everything?"

"Uh-huh, we had no secrets."

She immediately wished she hadn't said it that way. This wasn't Béatrice she was talking to, for once, and he didn't need to be convinced.

"The past few days?"

"Same as always, except the political situation, the deaths in Jammu a few hours before."

"Any connection?"

"In India there always is," said Juliette. "Everything's connected to everything else. You can't separate anything."

In David's tight little circle, there was the prep for the Montreal conference, Béatrice's impromptu visit, and the official trip to Kathmandu — all in the week leading up to the car bombing. In the background, the deteriorating political climate, the suicide assault on Parliament, the Gujarat massacre, and the killings in Jammu. Whatever meaning there was to the incident involving David was to be found in one of these events, maybe even all of them.

"You're right: everything seems to be connected, but how?"

She looked at him and understood then and there that she could trust him, no matter what Béatrice, Patterson, and that Roberge character said out of annoying, fake politeness.

"He told me something that morning just before he left: 'I keep thinking about my father. I've become like him. I feel just what he felt.'"

Max stared at her intently, as though that one little expression had snapped him back to something in the past she couldn't have known about, something that just might have led David to his fate.

"And another thing. Dr. Dohmann thinks David was injured *before* the bomb went off." She summed up what the doctor had told her, as Max listened in rapt attention.

"What time did David leave the High Commission that day?"

"I don't know, just that he promised to be home by nine."

"It happened on the banks of the Yamuna. Is that his usual route home?"

"Not at all."

"So a kidnapping, then, just as he was leaving the office perhaps? David and the chauffeur were then held for several hours by the kidnappers, who got rid of them later in the evening. No message, no demands, just executed after a short episode of brutality. Very strange."

Juliette shook her head: "But why?"

"That's what I'm planning to find out."

9

India? Tropical? Sure it is! Eleven years before, in 1991, Max had the surprise of his life when he got off the plane in the early morning to find the airport freezing. The touts paced up and down the deserted concourse wrapped in wool blankets or huddled together sharing *bidis* — small hand-rolled cigarettes rolled with eucalyptus leaves. *Taxi-wallahs* clapped their hands to keep warm, and someone ordered someone else in English to "close that bloody door." Travellers awaiting the first flights of the day noisily slurped their scalding hot *chais* as they sat on cardboard suitcases. Even the *bhikari* had their seasonal rags on. Delhi was a northerly city. Back at home, Max had expected to sweat in a soaking shirt caked in dust from the roads. Instead, he rubbed his hands in time with Antoine in their first-class compartment on the Poorva Express, which runs from Delhi to

Varanasi. Indians stared at the two in amazement, a bit the way Montrealers would gawk at a couple of tourists wandering along Saint Denis in February: "Hey, *Sahibji*, you should've read a guidebook. You don't visit northern India in winter."

Visit ... *uh-huh*, like the lovers at the Akbar Road Hotel who also chose the wrong season and, shivering, stumbled into the former British residence converted to a European-style inn, whose name they could never dredge up. Max and Antoine were just back from Varanasi and waiting for a flight to New York via Geneva. Antoine, who never spoke anyway, suffered his marathon of pain in silence. They'd had three days to kill. Originally they figured they'd spend more time in India for a change of scene, but everything reminded them of Pascale. Every tourist in a *kurta* pyjama, every *baba* in a *dhoti*, any young woman in a *salwar* or *ghagra* somehow seemed to be her appearing in the middle of a crowd. After the cremation in Varanasi, Max had tried to change their booking for a quick return to the States, but the flights were filled, all except this one via Switzerland.

The inn was a lugubrious place, chilly too, like the rest of the city. The sight of these two young tourists, happy and in love, with whom they shared the Victorian mansion, cut him to the heart. His room was unbearable as well. Its only window opened onto a billboard: INDIA IS FOR LOVERS. He had avoided the hotel whenever he could. He couldn't stand the sight of couples cuddling at breakfast. Unable to bear the silence of his travelling companion or the spectacle of that billboard any longer, Max spent his time at

Connaught Place and always ate alone at The Most Welcome Restaurant, an American fast-food place near the Middle Circle.

This time, though, Max's arrival at Indira Gandhi in the middle of the night was in a much more dramatic and public setting. At the Heathrow stopover, the Indian papers were full of news about the deteriorating political climate. The day before, in Srinagar, Kashmir's summer capital, masked men in police uniforms had assassinated Abdul Ghani Lone, a moderate leader (said the experts) of the Hurriyat Alliance, the political front of the Kashmiri separatist movement. Ghani Lone had often opposed the Islamists, who, he said, were trying to seize control of the entire movement. Max recognized the name of Hizb-ul-Mujahideen, one of the organizations Patterson had mentioned. The Thousand Fanatics. The Indian government claimed these "madmen" had decided to neutralize the seventy-year-old leader once and for all.

What followed was a chain reaction. India accused Pakistan once again of supporting Hizb-ul-Mujahideen and the others via the ISI (Inter-Services Intelligence), who used them to interfere with the Indian Army in an attempt to destabilize the region. After the attack on Parliament, then Jammu, and finally blowing up a Canadian diplomat in his car, the murder of the Muslim leader was the straw that broke the camel's back. Prime Minister Atal Vajpayee decided to react.

War was about to be declared.

That meant even more problems for Max. Both Canada and the U.S. had announced the "imminent" departure of their diplomatic personnel, and that would result in empty offices and furniture under dust-covers. New Delhi under siege: the airport shut down, armed men everywhere, sandbags, camouflage nets, and tanks on the tarmac. Actually, none of that was happening. Nothing dramatic at all. Except the heat. For real, this time. The sort of stinking heat that brings on nausea. Sure, in the arrivals hall there were a few soldiers done up in spotless uniforms, too spotless, as if they were getting ready for Independence Day. Pants nicely pressed, shoes shined, they circulated inconspicuously among the crowd of passengers, *taxi-wallahs*, and ever-present touts.

It was two in the morning, but the heat was so leaden you would have sworn it was noon. It seemed like forever since he'd left Montreal. During an interminable stopover in London, he'd bought a *Lonely Planet* guide. Apart from military vehicles, the road from the airport was deserted. He couldn't actually see the *jhopadpattis* — slums — that lined it, but he smelled them in every unbearable trickle of water the car waded through. Once in town, they were constantly overtaken at high speed on the red-dirt avenues by khaki Jeeps and police cars. More than once, a kamikaze in uniform almost drove the taxi off the road. At times, the traffic was stopped by *thanedars* — police — who inspected the interior of every vehicle by flashlight.

"*Aray saala* … beat it," the driver muttered as soon as they were out of earshot.

"You think it'll be war?" Max asked, but the driver just shrugged his shoulders.

"Threats, threats, but they never do anything."

"People must be afraid. There's no one in the streets."

"We're in the embassy district."

Around the Oberoi Hotel, as if to vindicate the driver, the military was even more discreet.

A young woman in a flowered sari, with a wreath of marigolds round her neck and a red dot on her forehead — the *bindi*, as Pascale had once explained to him — greeted Max in the lobby as if he were a distinguished guest. A persistent bellhop, with a Texas accent from his apprenticeship days in Houston, showed him to his room. Max had the impression he was expected to comment on it, as all tourists did, but he wouldn't be one of them. He talked about the threat of war, but again all he got was a shrug.

The immense room opened onto the pool, though it was deserted by now, a huge blue stain glistening against the darkness. Max pulled the curtain to block the glare and tumbled onto the bed without unpacking. He didn't know whether to sleep, rest, or send for a bottle of Scotch. One thing was certain: he had to think. How much was he sure of? The Indian papers he'd devoured since London kept up the same refrain. No terrorist group had claimed responsibility for the bombing that had gravely injured the Canadian diplomat and his driver, but no one was distancing themselves, either. The police were exploring all possible trails: a polite way of saying they hadn't a clue what to do next. One thing nagged at Max, though. There was no mention of a kidnapping. The Indian authorities had not given that piece of information to the papers. Was it to keep the diplomatic community from panicking?

What else did he have to go on? Well, there was Kathmandu, the business trip that landed David in the middle of a civil war right before the kidnapping. At Heathrow, Max had done some research into the Maoist rebellion Juliette mentioned, as well as the massacre of the royal family by the crown prince the year before — regicide and patricide against the world's most breathtaking backdrop.

This was turning out to be a trip marked by death, but how could it not be? Max never let go of David's remark: "I keep thinking about my father. I've become like him. I feel just what he felt."

Was striving for excellence how Philippe had erased Gilbert's failure? Max, on the other hand, had strived for a life of crime, not honours and distinction. Big brother had impressed everyone in Vancouver. They fell all over themselves offering him grants as if the money were burning a hole in their pockets. When he graduated, one of his professors had encouraged him to apply to the Department of Foreign Affairs. He won the job and distinguished himself at it. But Ottawa was just a stepping stone for the ambitious Philippe, a place to garnish his already impressive list of contacts. Like Gilbert, he had a head full of dreams. Max, however, had tossed out his illusions with that shoebox. Yet the two were so much alike. What drew them so close together? Sadness, maybe. Or memories.

Stretched out on a bed that was far too large, Max again rummaged through his disjointed past. Philippe visiting him in Bordeaux Prison, not dishing out the expected sermon or words of caution or advice, just there to help. "If you need me …" But Max the delinquent youth didn't expect anything from anyone. Big brother was on his way to Tokyo for three years — his first posting.

"I've become just like him," David had said. What did he mean by that?

Since Philippe's tragic death in Central America, the memory of his face had started to fade, but the attempt on his nephew's life had brought it all back. The two became interchangeable, like photocopies.

Until now, the two had belonged in different space-time compartments. This trip to India had dissolved that barrier. Now he felt Philippe's presence more than ever.

Like Pascale.

At the orphanage in Varanasi, when Sister Irène mentioned cremation, Max had imagined some discreet, antiseptic ceremony or other: a virtual cremation, in fact; out of his and Antoine's sight. He saw himself flying back to New York with the urn in his suitcase, like some oversized souvenir snagged at the last minute in the duty-free shop. Instead, Pascale, his love, lay on the crisscrossed sandalwood logs and branches the attendants would rearrange countless times. They conducted the cremations on the *ghats*, the steps leading to the Ganges, while family and friends watched from a safe distance. He and Antoine had stood beside Sister Irène, rosary in hand. Upon arriving there, they'd been assailed by a swarm of the infirm — and not so infirm, in all likelihood — crouched at various levels, begging. Now, though, they were left in peace, the three of them alone in their sadness.

The nun had paid for the cremation and wanted to make sure the orphanage was getting its money's worth, stoically watching the scene that had been pushed out of Max's mind by events of the past few days. The phone call in the middle of the night from Varanasi, a stranger phoning to give him news, bad as well as good, of Pascale, who wanted to see him. She wanted to "explain it all," but she was dying. The cancer had left her barely weeks to live — he'd searched ten years for her, everywhere, first with Antoine, then alone, until Mimi and Antoine persuaded him to move on: "You can't live on memories forever."

Who says?

Max could have gone on looking forever if that's what it took. He would have crisscrossed Europe in all directions, located friends of hers, contacts, and business connections. He had no idea whom she'd left with, but there was someone; he was sure of that. They'd fled to Germany for a while, then disappeared again. Still Max wouldn't let go. He'd find her; he knew it. He'd persuade her to return. All these years, she'd been living in India, and he was just now finding out with Antoine. She was in a convent and orphanage run by French nuns, and had just been welcomed there in the previous weeks. This Sister Irène said in her Toulouse accent and with a smug smile: "I grant you that Hinduism and Buddhism can bring some comfort, but in sickness, there's nothing like the sympathy and compassion of the Christian faith."

Max and Antoine hadn't gone to Varanasi for a study in comparative religion. They just wanted to see Pascale and take her back to North America to get medical help. Sister Irène had turned to them and said: "I'm afraid it's too late …"

Pascale had passed away the previous day. She'd left some things for Max and her brother: letters, jewellery. The two of them followed the nun down the corridor; there were *bachas* — children — everywhere, but girls only. Max had read up on this: in India, the birth of a girl is considered a financial burden. Later, when she was old enough to marry, her future husband's family would demand a huge dowry. One girl could perhaps be managed, but two would be prohibitive, and a third was better gotten rid of so as not to ruin the entire family. This is where Sister Irène came in. The orphans — abandoned children really — were left on temple steps or under the carts of *chai-wallahs*. Sister Irène gave the poor things a second chance.

The nun opened the door to a pure-white cell, bed linen washed and changed. There was jewellery Max didn't recognize; Antoine either. Pascale must have got it after she left. Max gave it to Sister Irène, who nodded her thanks. There were three letters: for Mimi, Max, and Antoine. Max's seemed jumbled, but he recognized Pascale's chicken-scratches, a bit clumsier, it's true, but they bore the same expressions, phrases, and spelling mistakes. It must have been difficult for her to have even put these few words together in her weakened state. She asked Max's forgiveness for wrecking his life and regretted leaving without a word. What explanation would she have given? No way of knowing. Pascale was as reserved in her final letter as she was in life. A photo fell out of the envelope as he placed the letter back inside. He picked it up and saw Pascale in what must have been her last months, looking old and tired. Her smile was bitter and resigned. She was dressed in a sari with a bindi on her forehead, an Indian costume that was far from comic to Max.

Standing in the doorway with hands folded, Sister Irène seemed as much at a loss as they were. She came over to Max and held him in her arms. He didn't know nuns were allowed to go that far. Of course, this was India, "pagan territory," and Sister Irène was a model, forever setting the standard. Sympathy and compassion were always her guiding principles, and she said so freely.

Hours later, she accompanied them along the Ganges to the *ghat* in Manikarnika, where the cremation would take place. Max didn't know Westerners had this right. By way of response, Sister Irène smiled in Indian fashion and shook her head. She knew very little of the road Pascale had taken. Pascale had simply shown up about ten years ago and joined a Buddhist community, as young foreigners do at the outset. Then, after a few months, most go back home, where they can take a shower, eat with utensils, and move on with their own lives, not one belonging to a group, religion, and culture of which they can never really be a part. Their intense and inevitable spirituality takes on the more comfortable form of a photo album.

Against all probability, though, unlike those other foreigners, Pascale had taken root in India, wavering between open, welcoming Buddhism and closed, hierarchical Hinduism.

"You know you can't convert to it. It's sealed off from everything else."

"There are enough of them already," Max shot back. "They don't have to worry about recruiting."

Sister Irène smiled. Their rickshaw, like Antoine's, was stuck in a monstrous traffic-jam: rickshaws as far as the eye could see, utterly paralyzed, as well. It was like Friday evening at the entrance to New York's Lincoln Tunnel.

Max had no idea whether Pascale's body had been carried across the city on a bamboo stretcher, as was the custom, but now she rested on a pile of logs placed one by one to keep track of the price of this ceremony. The priest was about to set fire to the pyre when he suddenly turned to Sister Irène and pointed to something on the body. They conferred in Hindi for a moment, then Sister Irène asked Max and Antoine, "Do you wish to keep her ring?"

The officiant hadn't waited, however, and was already taking it off to hand to Irène, who gave it to Max. He recognized the "jewel." He'd made it himself in the prison workshop at Temagami, using recycled metal from tin cans, then given it to her when she visited the following weekend. She had cried and cried, so much that the guards, who were used to bursts of tears, came over to see if she was in hysterics. So this was all that remained, this ring of twisted scrap metal. Max was on the verge of tears now, too, and slipped it into his pocket as they lit the fire.

The smoke danced over Pascale's remains, then flames lapped out from the centre. Max heard the crackling of wood and saw sparks tracing a path in the sky. Hypnotized, he watched without understanding, still in shock from the chintzy ring, the poor photo, and the letter saying nothing. Antoine stared rapt at the fire, walled in silence as always.

Pascale was burning well. Licked by flames, her body was now black. An odour of burning skin and hair invaded the *ghat* and blew toward them. Smoke was coming from every direction as Max closed his eyes. When he reopened them, he saw the fire had dwindled after the men stopped piling on wood. Max turned to Sister Irène as she apologized: "The orphanage has little enough money for the living, let alone the dead, and wood is expensive."

"What will they do with the ... what isn't burnt?"

"It will go in the Ganges. The river's full of human remains ..."

Animals too. Climbing out of the rickshaw, he had seen a cow drifting with the current. He spoke to the man in charge and pulled a pile of rupees from his pocket. The man understood. He weighed out some more logs and threw them on. The flames grew again, stronger and higher. Antoine turned away, and Max saw he was sobbing off to one side, alone. His eyes met Sister Irène's, and he felt like crying, too. He did.

Once Pascale's body was completely consumed, Max and Antoine went down to the level that bordered the Ganges, their hands clutching ashes: some of wood, some of Pascale, who knows? Still, a ritual is a ritual, and Max felt both solemn and ridiculous at the same time. Antoine released them first, and the ashes vanished in the wind over the water. Then Max did the same, turning to Antoine, perhaps to hug him. What do you do at a time like this? Anyway, Antoine was gone. Max spotted his friend climbing up the ghats at full speed, as though chasing after someone. Max followed. What was this about? He caught up with Antoine, out of breath on the last level.

"He was here. I saw him," he said looking around nervously. "He was watching us."

"What are you talking about, who?"

"Some Westerner," Antoine said. He'd already noticed him in the station at Varanasi, but thought he was dreaming … and now today, here.

"What, a tourist?"

Antoine turned to Max: "The guy at her place that night …"

Max recoiled. Her "kidnapper" — her lover — had come here to see her off, too.

10

The voices of sunbathers in the pool snapped him awake. Max O'Brien opened his eyes and snatched his watch off the dresser: 4:00 p.m. He'd slept almost twelve hours — his first rest free of nightmares in a week. He opened the curtains. The pool was swarming with the usual tourists, beached on deck chairs. Young Indians in livery went among them handing out drinks. The heat seemed crushing and the war just a bad dream.

Max spotted his friend Jayesh in his Speedo trunks with an American newspaper on his knee, a Kingfisher beer nearby.

When Max strode up a few minutes later, Jayesh exclaimed, "Why don't they pay José Théodore a *decent* salary? He should just take off for Colorado like Patrick Roy. Sometimes you'd think they don't want to win the Stanley Cup at all."

Max sighed. If there was one thing that absolutely did not interest him, it was hockey. Jayesh Srinivasan, though, born on Birnam Street in Montreal, was the greatest (the only?) Indian fan of the Montreal Canadiens and goalie José Théodore. Today, around the pool at least, it was no contest. Jayesh had the air of a geek on vacation, a computer whiz weaned off his technology. Slicked-back hair, dark shades, discreet tattoo on the shoulder — a change of style, he called it — Jayesh had the look of a playboy. At the age of twenty-nine, he had decided to try his luck in India, after a stretch of work with Max: three years of cons in the big U.S. cities, playing a Saudi investor in search of greedy pigeons longing for a quick score. Tired of such easy pickings, Max imagined him at the High Commission of India in Ottawa explaining to some bureaucrat why he wanted to "go home" to Tamil Nadu where his family had lived. Then followed four years in Mumbai, a choice he stuck to wholeheartedly … except for the lack of hockey. Even so, he followed all the gossip in *USA Today*, and from his parents in Montreal, as well. They'd never understood the decision of their only son. Siddhartha Srinivasan, now a retired star salesman from Cummings Chevrolet Oldsmobile on Décarie, felt cheated by his "ungrateful son," who had rejected America, the costly and much-sought-after gift they had bestowed on him.

"The case has been handed to Chief Inspector Dhaliwal," he said, draining his Kingfisher, "a hard-ass from the Indian Army trying to make his mark in the CBI. I have to admit, he's had some success, too."

"And the RCMP guy, what about him?"

"Josh Walkins, till now a gofer, paper-pusher, and maker of paper-clip chains — he's in charge of the internal investigation."

"Which means …?"

"No way they're letting the Indian Police inside the High Commission. Same with David's place. Walkins passes along whatever they get to Dhaliwal … who in turn sends a cc. to Lal Krishna Advani, minister of home affairs."

Despite the collaboration, the Canadian cop was a mere over-the-shoulder spectator to the real players in this card game.

"What have they got?"

"No idea, *yaar*. All very hush-hush, but I have a contact, and we'll soon know."

"How about the High Commission?"

"All packed up and ready for the airport shuttle, same as the Brits and the Yanks."

A young woman dived into the pool. Jayesh followed her closely with his eyes, then returned his attention to Max. "Besides, things are worse since yesterday. You know what Prime Minister Vajpayee did? He just went on up there, to Kashmir and the Pakistan border, and told his soldiers: 'The hour for decisive combat has come, and we will win this war,' or something like that. Same stuff from the Pakistanis. President Musharraf had his National Security Council meet in Islamabad and banged his fist on the table. These two nutbars are sharpening their knives on Kashmiri backbones. Then they spread the cloth and set the table."

Jayesh could describe the generals' "hors d'oeuvres": the Indian bombardment of the Azad Kashmir, or Free Kashmir, controlled by Pakistan since Partition. Hajira had seen twenty dead in a week, nine of them the day before in Abbaspur, then the Pakistani response in Manyari near Kathua, where sixty houses were destroyed. All these fireworks against a backdrop of national mourning in Srinagar. Abdul Ghani Lone, the moderate Kashmiri leader just killed by Muslim extremists and buried amid much grief and anger …

In short, it was a complete train wreck.

But Max wasn't seeing it. The country on the verge of war? That was hard to believe for any of those sitting around the pool at the Oberoi. He knew nothing of India, and even less of war. Perhaps this was how all wars started, with no one believing it, then, all of a sudden, fighter planes screaming overhead, refugees travelling in convoys, foreigners stranded in the airports. At least one thing was certain: with war on their doorstep and the embassies virtually closed, it would be much harder to catch the perpetrators.

"Do you think he'll make it?" Jayesh was referring to the still-comatose David.

"I don't know."

The Most Welcome Restaurant still existed: Formica furniture, electric signs, colourful uniforms, but a different clientele. Max had previously seen only tourists here, those who were fed up with filthy dives (while the Most Welcome Restaurant would have flunked a health inspection in any major European city, it was still a notch above the local grease-encrusted spoons). But now there were Indians here in place of the foreigners, many of whom had probably already fled the country. They were well-dressed, even hip-looking young people who wouldn't have been out of place in Soho or Greenwich Village. Most striking was the air of prosperity about them, social climbers eager to show off their nouveaux riches.

Jayesh had ducked into the restaurant briefly to make a phone call. "Some transactions don't belong on the cellphone, *yaar!*"

After he climbed back into the Maruti, they drove for quite a while. It seemed as though they'd never run out of city. One slum hot on the heels of the next, growing back in like fungus after Indira Gandhi's disastrous attempt to root them out in the seventies — that was how Jayesh summed it up. By all means, get rid of the symptoms of poverty, just not the cause. *Nussbandhi* (vasectomies) had been forced on the poor, civil liberties suspended, and a state of emergency declared for months on end. That was modern India's darkest chapter. Then in 1991 came a sudden change. The country opened up to private capital and foreign investment and the results had been positive. This time, Max saw numerous changes: the young upstarts at the Most Welcome and the Maruti that Jayesh was driving instead of an old Ambassador, for instance.

There was no mistaking the general air of economic recovery, but the religious misery of India still showed through: the deformed and crippled beggars and the *sadhus* covered in ashes and barely clothed stole the spotlight from this new India, as though refusing to be pushed aside. At a red light on the way out of town, a leper approached the car, asking for change and waving his stump in Max's face; next were the slums, the *jhopadpattis*, with kids in rags jamming the sides of the roads, so resigned to their situation that they didn't even reach out for charity. Through all this wash of human catastrophe, Jayesh showed little or no emotion, just waving aside one beggar in exasperation, the way you'd listlessly shoo away a fly, knowing it would soon be back. *Odd, this Jayesh*, Max mused, wondering if the Srinivasans felt that their family monkey god Hanuman was playing a joke when they bore this playboy, homesick for the old Indian motherland.

Jayesh felt Max's gaze on him. "Okay, we're almost there. Next village."

He braked for two starved-looking cows feeding on a pile of garbage by the side of the road, then honked his intentions of passing the cart in front of him. But the Maruti was still stuck behind a Mercedes — not the first Max had seen this time, though there had been none on his previous trip in 1991.

"Hey, it's one of mine," yelped Jayesh.

"The Mercedes?"

"I sold that one and some others."

"Seriously, back in your father's dealership?"

Jayesh roared in wholehearted laughter. He pointed to the slow-moving car in front, way too precious for these roads. "You know what the import tax is on a car like that? Three hundred percent. Big shots from Malabar Hill in Mumbai have to pay not just the price of the car plus transport, but bribe the Vajpayee government 'legally' three times the purchase price."

Max hadn't yet cottoned on, but he knew his young friend had made out on this somehow.

"It isn't just the poor who are unhappy here, the rich are, too. Actors in Mumbai, computer whizzes in Hyderabad, crooked lawyers and lobbyists from Delhi — who do you think they turn to?"

"Mother Teresa?"

"Naaah. Jayesh. If they want a Cadillac or a Jaguar or a Merc, I get it for them."

Honk … this time for a herd of pigs, something only the *dalits* are allowed to eat, so now they were in Untouchable country. This slum was their castle.

"The law is clear about this," Jayesh continued. "Indians who buy toys overseas can bring them back free of duties and taxes."

It began to dawn on Max.

"All those Indians working in Kuwait or the Emirates as cleaning staff, floor washers, and street sweepers spend, what, maybe a year or two there? Then they come home with the money, plus a little something for their better half," said Jayesh.

"And with your help, a Mercedes they've never seen and never will," said Max.

"Paid for by my client along with a small return for my contact and a commission for *bibi*."

"The police look the other way?"

The same good-natured roar of laughter.

The Maruti now went down a dusty road flanked by small, modest houses, luxurious compared to the slums on the main street. Jayesh stopped in front of one, and two kids in filthy pants appeared in the doorway, but an adult male hand forced them back inside.

Max followed Jayesh into the house. A woman in a cotton sari bade them *namaste*, then immediately retreated into a back room with the children. Buckets beside the table told Max the neighbourhood had no running water, at least for now. The place was clean, with minimal furnishings. A policeman's uniform hung behind the door.

"Ashok Jaikumar works at CBI headquarters," Jayesh explained, as the man nodded left to right as Indians do to show agreement. "He's in on all Chief Inspector Dhaliwal's meetings."

Jaikumar ran his hand through his oily hair and invited the two men to sit at the table. He had on a *kurta* pyjama, as always when he was inside, was about thirty years old, his head held high, even lofty, as shorter men often do. He seemed proud at being questioned, rather like the finalist in a quiz show. He offered them tea and *barfi*, boiled-milk sweets, but the two visitors declined.

"Exactly what do you want to know?"

First, how far the investigation had got and Dhaliwal's thoughts on it. Apparently, Dhaliwal was at his wit's end. It resembled nothing he'd ever seen before.

"Any connection to the group that attacked Parliament?" Max asked.

"That's what Dhaliwal's team thought at first: Harakat-ul-Ansar — they'd intercepted some of their activists a few days before; or maybe Jaish-e-Mohammed — they're also very active in New Delhi. The police had their inside informants, moles, in fact, and at least a general notion of the jihadis' comings and goings, but embassies and consulates weren't on their hit list."

"A change of strategy, maybe?" Max asked. "I mean, who'd have thought that Lashkar-e-Taiba would one day launch an attack on Parliament?"

"Sure, especially with ammonium nitrate–based explosives. They're a favourite with terrorists," said Jaikumar.

"Not to mention kidnapping," Max added.

The policeman was surprised to find Max so up-to-date on what, until now, had been kept from the media, and equally surprised to discover he knew about David's wounds from before the bomb attack, something the investigators found intriguing, needless to say.

"What, in fact, happened between the time David and his driver left the High Commission —"

"Witnesses put it at about 4:30 p.m.," cut in Jaikumar.

"— and the car bomb six hours later by the banks of the Yamuna on the other side of town?"

Baffled, Jaikumar shrugged. "The police are leaving no stone unturned, and Lal Krishna Advani, the minister of home affairs, is following the investigation closely. You know Inspector Dhaliwal is from Gandhinagar, in Gujarat, the same state Advani represents in Parliament, and he keeps him constantly up to date, verbally, of course, as one does with politically dangerous files like this."

Jaikumar was biding his time, holding something back till he got the price he wanted. Out of the corner of his eye, Max saw Jayesh pull out a huge roll of rupees, and he dropped some bills on the table. The policeman looked at them for a long while without touching them, then said, "The RCMP fellow searched the diplomat's house from top to bottom, went off with his computer at the High Commission, and then scanned his appointment book, address list, and agenda."

Jaikumar slid the rupees into a drawer under the table. Now it was time for the grand revelation. "The day before the kidnapping, do you know who the young man saw? Majid Khankashi, imam at the Kasgari Mosque, better known as Genghis Khan to the Hindi press."

Jaikumar was proud of his scoop and happy with the money, so he added, "An opinion-maker with considerable influence in Jammu and Kashmir State, where he comes from, and Delhi, too, of course. He's suspected of being the *éminence grise* of Hizb-ul-Mujahideen, perhaps even an agent of Inter-Services Intelligence."

The policeman paused for a moment before continuing, "Did you know the Volvo exploded near Yamuna Pushta, a Muslim slum?"

Max persisted. "What was David meeting him about?"

That Jaikumar could not say. There was no way to interrogate Khankashi, because the imam had disappeared the day after his meeting with David, the day of the explosion itself. He was suspected of hiding out in Kashmir or elsewhere on the Pakistani side.

"Why?"

Jaikumar shook his head. The massacre of Hindus in Jammu, maybe, plus the killing of Ghani Lone. Khankashi was suspected of contracting it out or at least being involved in some way. Every time there'd been a flare-up of violence in recent months, fingers had been pointed at Indian Muslims. Being a Muslim in India was not good, not good at all. The slightest skirmish or lawlessness rained public hatred down on them. They were the whipping boys, the scapegoats. They'd always been suspect in this country. Were they even "real Indians"? They probably had some secret agenda in collusion with worldwide Islam, for instance. If they had to choose between India and Al-Qaeda, which would it be? The events of these past weeks spoke for themselves, didn't they? Then again, maybe Genghis Khan was wary of meeting the same fate as the Kashmiri leader. What if he wasn't responsible for the killing? What if he'd just taken off? That was the hypothesis of the investigators.

Genghis Khan, thought Max, *our first real lead.*

11

The citizens of Delhi might not be taking the threat of war seriously, but the authorities had both thumbs on the panic button. In order to protect the Canadian High Commission, the minister of home affairs had pulled out all the stops. Heavy-set and heavily armed troopers in khaki lent support to the regular security agents, casting the same wary eye over visitors at the entry point. So, this was it. Canada was now officially a member of the victims-of-terrorism club. As Max got out, the taxi made a U-turn on Shantipath and headed for the "normalcy" of downtown. Here the scope of the upheaval struck him. More of the same frenzy in the waiting room, though with less noise and fewer raised voices. Under the Canadian flag, Indians in ties and wearing perfume, with slicked-back hair, were waiting for visas or work permits. Obviously, recent events had put them in even more of a hurry to get out of here ASAP. Max went up to the counter where a young bilingual woman ("in the two official languages" according to the small blue panel on her left) accepted Mr. Brokowich's passport — provided by Antoine — as he asked to see Raymond Bernatchez.

"Unfortunately, the high commissioner is —"

"— I have an appointment," Max cut in. "He's expecting me."

Patterson had done things right: a couple of *hmm*s and *yeah*s on the phone and an electronic click came from the door on the right. Under the envious gaze of the mere mortals in the waiting room, Max disappeared into the office complex.

"My name's Sunil Mukherjee, secretary to Mr. Bernatchez." He held out his hand. He was young with grey hair, probably in his forties. His large glasses gave him a serious, professorial look. Max followed him down a corridor of photos showing winterscapes, no doubt to help visitors cool off, then up some stairs. Mukherjee walked fast, never looking around. On the second floor was a half-open door and a desk covered with papers and a bouquet of flowers — no doubt David's office. Max felt like going in and sitting down as he had in Philippe's embassy office in San Salvador under similar circumstances. Mukherjee was waiting up ahead before another half-open door. That was Bernatchez's office.

When Max went in, the high commissioner was on the phone with his broad back to the visitor. This man,

Juliette had primed him, used to be a pro football player, though flabby now from lack of training. The chair swivelled round and Bernatchez waved Max to a seat, then went back to his previous position. Faced with a wall of back once more, Max discreetly surveyed the usual run of family photos: three offspring in graduation robes, smiling and full of the joy of life ("Thanks, Dad.") and a more recent one taken in India, probably his wife, with Indian children in her arms.

"Sorry for the mess, Mr. Brokowich," Bernatchez got up with his hand outstretched for Max to shake. "Dennis tells me you felt it was essential for us to meet."

Now Max's cover had to be flawless. After supposedly talking to David in Kathmandu on the phone, Brokowich had decided, after weeks of hesitation, to go over the heads of his board ("such nervous Nellies … you have no idea") and take part in the Montreal conference anyway. Patterson was terrific and a great help, but he was worried after what happened to his contact, David ("How horrible … awfully sad"), and now this impending war as well. So, on his way from Singapore to Montreal, he had decided to stop over in Delhi to check on things.

After meeting with Juliette, then Patterson, Max realized that several businessmen had threatened to pull out in light of recent events. Though Patterson was the guest speaker, he'd advised his clients to put their investment plans on hold: "just till things settled down." If this had been happening across the board, Bernatchez's phone must have been ringing off the hook for a week.

Bernatchez replied accordingly, "There's really nothing to be worried about, I assure you."

"You are pulling out, though."

"Absolutely not. Just the families and non-essential employees. I'm staying, and so are my principal collaborators."

Max couldn't prevent a hint of a smile. "Easy when one's well protected."

"Look, Mr. Brokowich, things aren't nearly as bad as you seem to think."

"Oh, it's not just me, it's also *The Times*, *France-Soir*, the *Washington Post* …"

"The Indians and Pakistanis have been having these squabbles for fifty-five years now."

"I feel a bit better."

"Believe me, there won't be a war."

"Still, a Canadian and his chauffeur were killed."

"Oh, David didn't die, and there's no proof it was linked to Kashmir, either. We mustn't confuse two separate issues." Bernatchez was getting impatient, no doubt wishing he hadn't agreed so readily to Patterson's request that he meet this jumpy businessman. Normally, he'd leave this to some underling or Indian secretary, but it was too late now, and a mistake he wouldn't make again. "Since 9/11, the rules have changed, and our old standbys don't work anymore, but despite appearances, including what happened to David, I don't believe Canada's presence in India is …" he groped for words "… let's say *exacerbated*, for either party. On the contrary, you'd be ill-advised to reconsider your intentions."

Max sighed and pretended to be won over. Bernatchez smiled, sensing victory already, and was in a hurry to get rid of this guy.

"There are a few details to settle, of course, and David will no longer be in charge, only for the time being, I hope." The high commissioner heaved himself out of his chair and looked to the right of the doorway to a smaller office. "Vandana. Where is she? Oh, dammit, that's right. William, come in here."

Moments later, a nervous, frail man appeared in a well-cut suit, quite unlike the one Bernatchez was wearing.

"Vandana's taken over David's files," the commissioner explained, "She'll be in charge of communications with Montreal and all that, but she's out at the moment. Allow me to introduce William Sandmill, our first secretary. He'll be organizing Montreal too."

As soon as the underling arrived, Bernatchez made his getaway, leaving Sandmill to politely throw this bum out, his "old friend" Patterson notwithstanding.

"The Spanish Embassy," Sandmill explained, "has decided to organize a reception in solidarity with us to defy the terrorists, as they put it, to show that we diplomats are not to be intimidated. Vandana's there now, getting things ready." He glanced at his Bulova. "Come and wait in my office. We'll be more comfortable there."

He guided Max down the hall and the stairway, bypassing the photocopy and vending machines with a smoothness his boss would probably envy, explaining on the way that the whole subcontinent was in upheaval — that was undeniable — but there was also a good side to all this. A large coming together of ideas, cultures, and religions was underway, the mixture bubbling and overflowing from the pot sometimes, but progress, finally, after centuries of stagnation. The West had a role to play in this renaissance.

Max barely listened to his spiel, as Sandmill led him into the huge, sun-filled office he shared with an Indian colleague.

"This is Mahesh Tevari."

They shook hands. The young man was timid and self-effacing.

"Mahesh is in charge of our relations with the Indian Ministry of Commerce and Industry and of our local delegation. In Calcutta, the consulate deals with it. The same thing in Bombay."

"Mumbai," corrected Tevari.

"Bombay, Mumbai, I never can keep them straight. They've changed all the names, and it's so confusing." Sandmill turned to Max: "Would you like something to drink, Mr. ... uh ..."

"Brokowich."

The first secretary was well informed and knew India like the back of his hand, insofar as such a thing could ever be. He was selling Bernatchez's soap with conviction, reinforced occasionally by Tevari, who grunted or nodded his agreement. Max wanted nothing more than to believe them both. Then an older man showed up in the doorway, looking for Vandana as well, the veteran Caldwell. Mukherjee appeared once more with a glass of tea for each of them.

"Have we answered all your questions, Mr. Brokowich? Are you more at ease now?"

Max nodded. Just then, the sound of voices came from the corridor, and Langevin, head of public relations, came in, his jacket slung over one shoulder. He was talking on the phone in Spanish with his colleague at their embassy, talking about the reception and solidarity cocktails. He turned down the tea that Bernatchez's secretary offered him.

Watching this, Max tried to imagine David functioning in such a universe and couldn't manage it. Maybe he didn't know his nephew well enough, or possibly he'd known him mostly through others: Béatrice, Patterson, and now Juliette. A huge sadness suddenly crept over him.

David's name kept coming up in conversation. Max looked up and asked the 100,000 rupee question: "Who do you suppose carried it out? Who did it? Why?"

Sandmill and Tevari exchanged glances. They couldn't open up to just any stranger without consequences. The whole commission was walking on eggshells.

"I don't know," said Tevari, "but nothing's the same since …" Perturbed, he looked away.

"David isn't just a colleague," said Sandmill, "he's a friend to all of us."

"I can guarantee you one thing, Mr. Brokowich," ventured Tevari, "Indians are as sad for this as you are."

Touched, Max acquiesced.

"Vandana, everyone's been looking for you!"

It was Caldwell from the other end of the corridor. When the young woman approached Sandmill and Tevari's office, the former signalled her in. Vandana was pretty, with very long hair held by a golden comb, and magnificent, very determined eyes. "A great girl," Juliette had said.

12

Within the four office walls, however, Vandana Dasgoswami didn't seem so sure of herself, more like a startled young girl as she cast a nervous eye on Max. No point putting up a front with her. No need for a cover like with Bernatchez. Her friend Juliette had communicated directly with her from Montreal and explained who Max was, that he'd soon be in Delhi under an assumed name ("It's complicated. Don't ask."), and would need her help. Vandana was clearly afraid and needed reassuring, warming up in a sense, as soon as possible. She was indispensable to him.

"The flowers were from you?"

"Excuse me?"

"On David's desk."

She seemed even more ill at ease, sad and stressed too. Max mentioned David's visit to Genghis Khan the day before the bombing, which she didn't know about, but his relationship with Imam Khankashi was public knowledge. They met regularly after his stay in Tihar.

"Tihar?"

"The biggest penitentiary in India," she explained. "Ten thousand prisoners. The imam was held for a year without trial and in dreadful conditions, as you can well imagine. He was suspected of every crime you can think of, naturally. Technically, David didn't work in the consular service, but he managed to find a lawyer and get him a fair trial."

It finally clicked for Max. The imam had Canadian citizenship. "Eight years in Downsview, Ontario, before coming back after the Ayodhya Massacre."

She was going too fast for him, so Max asked her to begin again, slowly, beginner-style. Vandana explained that India was a layering of civilizations, one on top of the other, with mixed results, but in Ayodhya in Uttar Pradesh, the stratification had solidified. In the fifteenth century, a mosque had been built at the legendary birthplace of the god Rama. Sure, it was wrong, but history was history. It was either move on or be constantly at war. The Hindus, however, were not about to let things go, and Ayodhya became the symbol of a cause and a rallying-cry.

"Then, in December 1992, all hell broke loose. A bunch of Hindu crazies took apart the Babri Mosque stone by stone. But that wasn't enough for them. Next, they emerged from the dust cloud that remained and headed into town, pillaging and massacring to their hearts' delight. Sectarian violence then spread all across the country.

"The Islamic Hizb-ul-Mujahideen was bent on vengeance," Vandana continued, "and attacks occurred all over, especially in Kashmir. Back in Canada, Genghis Khan didn't miss an opportunity to spew his hatred of Hindu nationalists. He was the perfect target, the ideal bad guy, and easy to scoop up.

"He was in prison on and off. The last time was in the fall of 2001. Alone, isolated, and helpless, he had no illusions about Indian justice, least of all the hope for a trial. He was bound to lose anyway, and he was already paying through the nose to the RSS guards."

"RSS?"

"Rashtriya Swayamsevak Sangh, an association of national Hindi volunteers, extremists — fascists, in fact. They are paramilitary and have existed since 1925 — one of them killed Mahatma Gandhi. They're fanatics who get off on trashing Muslims whenever they can, and aren't ashamed to look up to the way Hitler tried to solve 'the Jewish question' in Europe.

"With thirty million militants, they've supported the Bharatiya Janata Party of Prime Minister Vajpayee, were in on the founding of it, in fact, and the government appreciates their support big-time," Vandana said. "Benign neglect and willful blindness, complicity, as a matter of fact, and all it wants from the BJP it gets. The RSS spreads terror with impunity wherever it goes. The Ayodhya Massacre couldn't have happened without the connivance of local authorities.

"Once Genghis Khan was free, the RSS pressure never let up. The one in charge of neutralizing him was Sri Bhargava. He's the most violent member of the RSS, and he has no political ambitions," she said. "His sole objective is simply to kill all Indian Muslims, or at least throw them out of the country, starting with Genghis Khan.

"In Hindu mythology, Durga is a merciless goddess on the warpath against ignorance; hence Bhargava's name for his outfit, Durgas, even more radical then RSS. And this *gougat* won people over. Hindus saw him as the answer to Islamic terrorists, a kind of James Bond of 'Hinduness.'

"As a result, all over the country, Bhargava and his Durgas took control of the terrorism. They used Islamist methods — bombs, martyrdom, et cetera, without ignoring the old methods, such as boycotts of Muslim shops, demolition of mosques, or pogroms in Muslim neighbourhoods. They even opened dozens of specialized schools — *shakhas* — focused on anti-Islamic doctrine, which followed the lead of *madrassas*, Qur'anic schools that sowed the seeds of radical Islam across Pakistan and elsewhere: similar methods, indoctrination, even misinformation."

"Genghis Khan versus Agent 007; extremists in a struggle to the finish ... would this Bhargava go so far as to kill a foreign diplomat?" Max had gradually been building toward a theory. "If David was buddy-buddy with Imam Khankashi," he continued, "James Bond might have found out and wanted to teach him a lesson. See what I mean? Maybe not just him, but also the other Western diplomats who might be tempted to side with the bearded boys."

Vandana recoiled slightly. She was sick about this whole thing, and it showed. Despite a very professional effort at masking it, she felt terrorized, too. Her position at the High Commission and her Western clothes made one forget she was Indian, that she lived here. She had a husband, family, perhaps children, all perfect prey for extremists. Max had read somewhere the story of a Hindu grandmother disfigured by acid simply for offering a glass of water to a Muslim labourer. Acid in the face was also the reward bestowed by an enraged Islamist on a young girl for wearing jeans on a bus in Srinagar.

"What files was David working on the last few days, apart from visiting the imam?"

Vandana sighed. She'd already been asked this a dozen times by Josh Walkins of the RCMP and his Indian colleagues. "Active and current files, I forget which," she responded wearily. "He was preparing to leave for Montreal … the conference."

"Lots of meetings with colleagues, I suppose."

"Yes."

"Did he make any phone calls, receive any visits?"

"Phone calls, but no appointments that I remember. I took care of it at Mr. Caldwell's request. The few days in Delhi before his departure weren't enough to finish up the Kathmandu files along with the run-up to Montreal."

Kathmandu again.

This trip had been playing on Max's mind. He put himself in David's place — having to go home in the middle of the night after preparing the Montreal conference. Endless meetings with Bernatchez, Caldwell, and company. There were a thousand details to attend to and time was running short. The investors had to be reassured, fussed over, and given tender loving care; a huge job. Still, David had to go to Kathmandu in the shadow of the mountains ... with Vandana along, too. Two fewer pairs of hands to do Bernatchez's bidding.

That didn't take into account Béatrice's impromptu visit. David hadn't seen his mother for months, and yet he chose that very moment to leave town.

Odd.

"Kathmandu — what exactly happened there? What did you do?"

"Meetings and get-togethers."

"What about?"

"A literacy project we've been on for months with CIDA, the Canadian International Development Agency."

"Even during a civil war?"

"The situation's calmed down a bit," she replied unconvincingly.

Max sensed she was hiding something, but what was it? He'd felt it from the beginning. A professional liar himself, he knew how to spot an amateur who'd never make it to his level of the game. The ones with no talent for it, like Vandana, didn't have the skills for his kind of work.

"You're right," she said, changing the subject, "I left the flowers."

13

David lay hidden beneath layers of therapeutic materials, and Béatrice hovered over him with a facecloth, which she used very tenderly to bathe his face, afraid of hurting him further. *I feel like Virgin Mary at the foot of the cross in a half-tone Renaissance painting*, thought Juliette. Outside the door, security agents kept watch. She was a member of their group now. She knew their habits, their tics, and their first names. They shared the same routine. The fountain at the end of the corridor, for example, was their turf. When they came into the room, however, it was always on tiptoe, but it was more for her and Béatrice than for David. He'd become part of the furniture, a thing, a pall.

At first, the two women had taken turns at his bedside, but now they left together in the evenings. Once in the apartment at the Rockhill, Juliette found Béatrice crying alone in the dark. Then they hugged each other tight. Juliette had just decided to tell Béatrice about her pregnancy, but she was no longer brave enough.

There was a long, plaintive ring of the phone in the night, and Juliette ran to pick it up before Béatrice had time to ask "Who could that be at such an hour?" Juliette knew somehow it was Max on the line.

"How's David?"

His voice was surprisingly clear, though it came from the other side of the world.

There was so much to tell him, but she couldn't get a thing out. Like a bashful young girl, she got all tangled up in polite phrases. *I must sound like an idiot.*

Max, genuinely polite, pretended not to notice.

Since yesterday, David had become feverish and developed pneumonia. She told him about her last discussion with Dr. Dohmann, the EEGs he'd shown her. Barring a miracle, there was no hope, he had said. She spared him the details of her fainting, her legs folding just like that in front of everyone, then the crying in Béatrice's arms, both of them in tears.

"What will you do?" Max inquired.

She closed her eyes: "I don't know. I believe in miracles."

Max did, as well, but what was that worth compared to the belief of Dr. Migneault? Dohmann's replacement was a thorough young doctor with a shaved head, a bit tough-looking. Béatrice suspected this was to pre-empt the appearance of baldness. Juliette and Dr. Migneault shared a love of chocolate. She pretended to hope, but knew she could not. She found herself in an office with

Béatrice and a corpulent social worker. Patterson stood in the hall, discreetly out of the way.

"The decision is yours and yours alone," Migneault said with the appropriate flutter in his voice. "We can wait for weeks, if you wish, but his condition will not alter." He glanced from the social worker to the pair of them. Juliette knew what was next.

"David is clinically dead," Migneault said.

Whatever he said afterward didn't register with Juliette. All her thoughts were for David. She pictured the timid young man who'd approached her in the cafeteria at McGill University, relived those evenings discussing international politics, those long walks in Westmount parks when he passionately but patiently explained the inevitable nature of things in general and the world order in particular. There was the coffee spilled in that Sherbrooke Street Restaurant and the young waitress's irritability. What about that absurd shirt he absolutely had to hang on to, the stolen bike he never got back, his hopeless attempt at wearing contacts, or his illegible signature, and that mix-up at the post office — "Just why, tell me, do you have to write as though you're retarded?" His last birthday was at Montebello. Never another. Never growing old. Dying young. Dying, period.

Moments later, out in the corridor, Patterson was all solicitude. Words of encouragement were the very last thing she wanted to hear, neither his nor Béatrice's. They'd abandoned David, and now it was her turn to do so. Dohmann and Migneault, too. *What cowards we all are.*

Chocolate, once more, chocolate.

David was not allowed to die, not until she decided. The terrorists had done their worst by leaving his fate in her hands.

"Mukherjee remembered saying goodbye to David late in the afternoon," Max continued, "about four-thirty. Luiz was with him on his way back, then nothing, the car just disappeared. No witnesses, just an explosion by the Yamuna in the evening. Near a Muslim slum ... on top of it."

"I don't suppose anyone's talking."

"Majid Khankashi — Genghis Khan, they call him," Max said. "Vandana told me he and David met often. Did he ever tell you what about?"

"No."

Juliette regretted not having been more curious. David returned home from the High Commission worn out. Why bother him with questions?

"He never came to see him in Maharani Bagh?"

"Just evening phone calls ... David never brought his work home with him."

"Except for the conference."

"That's right."

"They met the day before the explosion."

Juliette hadn't known that. Anyway, she never asked him about his movements. Why not ask Khankashi himself?

Disappeared ...

She remembered once having met him by accident with David in Old Delhi near the Kasgari Mosque. The impeccably trimmed beard allowed a glimpse of what Juliette considered an enigmatic smile, one given to showing joy as well as sadness. He offered them tea in a nearby café. She'd felt no apprehension at the time. In the crowded streets, passersby eyed them with respect, and yet the papers portrayed Genghis Khan as a bloodthirsty Islamist, despite his being a Sufi mystic. How could there be a monster behind such a harmless facade? Why was David committing the blunder of being seen with him in public? She'd brought it up that evening, and his answer was, "If Sri Bhargava invites me to tea, I go. Both of them monsters, perhaps, but my job doesn't exempt me from horror or allow me to pretend such people don't exist."

"Sri Bhargava, founder of the Durgas," said Max.

"Ah, Vandana told you about them?" replied Juliette.

"Yes."

"Do you think he sponsored the attack"?

"I don't know. Did David meet him or make contact?"

"Not at all."

"What about members of the RSS or other Hindu groups?"

"David never mentioned it."

"Any complaints to the High Commission about, say, 'connections' with the imam Khankashi?"

"Nope."

"Any comments, accusations, or even threats from Hindu personnel? Or anyone, for that matter?"

"Never."

"What about helping the imam ... any insinuations or hints?"

"No, I'm telling you, no! David knew his job to a T, as well as his mandate. He was in New Delhi to represent Canada and its citizens, not to mix in India's internal controversies."

She recounted for him a discussion they'd had.

"Having tea with a Muslim extremist, isn't that taking sides?"

"Khankashi's no extremist."

"That's definitely not what the Indian papers are saying about it, David."

"Only the ones that support the BJP, not all of them."

Max was puzzled: "You're sure he said it that way?"

"What do you mean?"

"Khankashi's no extremist."

Police and security officers were rushing down the corridor and out of the stairwells, out of breath, sweaty and excited. Orders were bellowed. Juliette got into the middle of it all as Béatrice exited the elevator, where a uniformed man stopped her from going any farther.

"What's happened?"

"They arrested someone in the kitchen."

They sent the two women home with an escort and a policeman to keep watch overnight. What was all this?

The Rockhill turned into a fortress with the comforting presence of a patrol car in the parking lot. Another officer with a hat too big for him said good night to them in the corridor and touched the butt of his handgun as if to say *Don't worry. I'll be right here.*

Béatrice closed the curtains with a dramatic sweep. There might be snipers hidden in the building facing them. No point taking chances. Juliette could not sleep and felt guilty for not staying with David.

The phone rang. It was Patterson back from his information hunt.

"The unidentified man was walking in a suspicious way through the hospital basement. An employee thought he looked strange, so he alerted security."

The rest of it followed the usual pattern: The supposed cook didn't have his ID with him, nothing. He tried to ditch the security agents before the arrival of the police; then there was a foot-race through Orthopedics, a fight in Obstetrics among a crowd of panic-stricken mothers, and finally the takedown in Rheumatology.

"Was he there for David?" asked Juliette.

The police didn't know. They hadn't finished questioning him. Patterson promised to keep them posted.

The next day, Dr. Migneault found Juliette at the vending machines. "I'm sorry I didn't put things too well yesterday."

"No, you were right. Why insist on overdoing it?"

"In the face of life's horrors, we don't count for much, nothing at all."

14

Max and Jayesh went through the Palika Bazaar followed closely by *bhikharis*, a whole family of them in rags with hands outstretched. When the two men reached the limits of their territory, they turned back. They emerged at Connaught Place, and more beggars followed in their wake. Jayesh ignored them, the same as the others.

The two men stopped under the arcade of the Regal Cinema. Nearby, next to a column, a shoeshine boy called out for customers in a tired voice. Most people paid no attention to him, but one man stopped, rolled up his pant leg, and put his foot on the small wooden box. The shine began without a word. When it was done, the customer tossed some coins on the ground, but the shoeshine boy didn't seem at all insulted. He fell upon the coins scattered on the pavement amongst the passersby, before returning to his spot by the column.

"*Dalit*," murmured Jayesh, "untouchable."

Max turned to him and Jayesh explained: "If the shoeshine boys touch the leather shoes, which are made from cowhide, they're impure. That's why that guy threw down the money instead of putting it into his hand."

Jayesh was a *Vaishya* — merchant class, third rung on the Hindu social ladder — and this explained his father's occupation. Even in America, Siddhartha Srinivasan respected, in his own way, his place within the caste system.

While Max was speaking to Juliette on the phone the day before, Jayesh was at the Kasgari Mosque impersonating a CBI investigator: "Just a few more questions about some things we need to clear up." He'd met the "second-in-command" of the imam Khankashi. He was told the imam had kept in touch with David because both of them were on the same wavelength, especially about Kashmir. The imam would never openly acknowledge such a thing. Genghis Khan had supported the separatist movement from the beginning, while still keeping his distance from Pakistan. It wasn't easy. The brutality of the Indian forces, especially in Srinagar, played right into the hands of Pakistan. Pervez Musharraf's government would have welcomed this son of Islam safely home from Hindu territory with open arms. Khankashi was an idealist, though. He professed to believe in a multi-ethnic India, as Gandhi and Nehru had imagined it. An India where Hindus, Parsis, Christians, and Muslims could live in harmony with respect for one another.

"So, you're thinking bluff?"

"Of course. The usual sitar song to put people to sleep while the Islamist killers of Hizb-ul-Mujahideen build up their arsenal, courtesy of the Pakistani secret service."

"Sufis and jihadists fighting side by side ... pretty weird, no?"

"I'm telling you, showbiz. Whatever. The imam shouting from the rooftops that Muslims are second-class citizens, worse than untouchables. From time to time, some *Dalits* get roughed up, but Muslims get exterminated ... with the government's blessing. No problem with putting Hindus first in everything in this country: schoolbooks get 'revised' to showcase Brahmin heritage.

"In a situation like this," Jayesh went on, "Genghis Khan has no choice but to walk the straight and narrow, and for years the Vajpayee government has been longing for him to step out of line so they can put him away. So what does our holy man do? He cites proverbs from the Mahatma and yet he still rips into the BJP and the Islamists every chance he gets — James Bond included. I wouldn't be at all surprised if one day we found Khankashi stuck away in the country eating bread and water while he weaves the cotton threads of his *charkha*, like Mahatma. It would be just like that asshole to slide back into the old passive resistance number!

"David's association with the holy man had tongues wagging among Bhargava Hindus, without a doubt; not that he made a point of publicizing it, but it was no secret either. I mean, tea out in public in Old Delhi. He had to be doing favours for the imam on the q.t., in the guise of diplomacy."

Max came back to Vandana's theory that James Bond had probably used David as an example to other diplomats that they had better play in their own sandbox. "Maybe, but if so, why didn't they claim the attack? Terrorism has a marketing scheme all its own, but it's been a whole week and nothing. Old news. There's been Afghanistan, then Kashmir and the worsening situation between India and Pakistan took centre stage and stepped back into the general melee."

"But getting back to Genghis Khan," said Jayesh. "Whatever his Islamist reputation, especially among the papers loyal to the BJP, he denounced the World Trade Center and Pentagon attacks of September 11 — against the spirit of the Qur'an, he said."

"I bet that put a chill on his Islamist buddies in Pakistan," guessed Max.

"Precisely."

"Yet the Indian cops are sure he's hiding out in Karachi."

"They have no idea where he is, so they dream up any old thing, as usual. I think he's still in Delhi and laughing his ass off."

"So, a fake 'moderate,' is that it?"

"That's what the Durgas are saying. They'd do anything to get their hands on him. Bhargava would love to finish him off personally."

"And where exactly is he? How do we get in touch, talk to him?"

"No one knows but his closest cronies."

This was just getting better and better with both suspects disappearing into thin air: Genghis Khan to his lair and James Bond into clandestine retirement. One thing was certain, though. Dhaliwal and his team were going to have to treat this one with kid gloves. If they did tie the attack on David to his contacts with Khankashi, it would make waves that might drown them all, even Bernatchez and the High Commission. For instance, if Dhaliwal could prove that David had "privileged" connections with Muslim officials — already suspected of financing or protecting Kashmiri terrorists — Canada would be in hot water, just when its businessmen were about to break into this new market and important contracts were to be signed at the Montreal conference.

Was Bhargava the culprit? It was a sexy hypothesis, but it couldn't withstand serious scrutiny. Hindu extremists didn't give a damn about world opinion. Their country's "Hinduization," as they put it, was domestic business, a religio-nationalist delirium that knew no diplomatic scruples. What was it Vandana said? As recently as March, Prime Minister Vajpayee had crossed his arms while fascist groups in Gujarat staged pogroms against Muslims for two months without denouncing or forbidding them or even sending in the police. A government like that was not going to bother about a diplomat — Third Secretary to boot — being friends with the imam of a mosque.

Nope. The answer had to be somewhere else.

Summer 1984. Max was living in the U.S. under three different names and passports, still a Canadian citizen according to two other passports he hardly used anymore. Now he was in Hy's Steak House in Toronto, specializing in T-bone, filet mignon, and surf 'n' turf, sitting on a leather seat worn in by an army of clients every day at noon in the thrall of red meat. Philippe sat facing him; he was soon leaving for Bangkok with his small family. David was six and mischievous-looking in the photo his father had thumbed a million times. Philippe looked up with that winning smile he often showed. Max smiled back, but for different reasons.

"I found Stéphane Kavanagh," Max said. This was the man who'd ruined their father. Philippe's smile vanished, which surprised Max, who had also never heard his brother raise his voice. He was normally so calm and collected.

"Stay away from that guy!"

"He put us out on the street."

"Ancient history, all of it. Forget it!"

"Forget it? He's living a totally normal life as though nothing happened."

"DON'T YOU LAY A FINGER ON HIM!"

Max didn't get it. Since finding the piece of garbage, he was determined to clean his clock, and his own brother, who'd suffered as much as all of them, was telling him to sit on his hands. Max's thirst for revenge had grown over the years and kept him awake at night, even in his cell, and now Philippe was telling him to forget it. He didn't realize that vengeance was Max's food and his fuel.

Deathly silence followed. A pall fell over their farewell dinner. Philippe was perturbed and only pretended to wrestle with his steak. Finally, he pushed his plate forward forcefully, the noise of clanging cutlery turning heads.

"Look, one wrecked family is enough. We don't need two."

"Who says he has a family?"

"You found him already. You knew where he was and didn't tell me ..."

Philippe had made his own inquiries at the same time as Max. Stéphane Kavanagh had a teenage daughter.

"I don't give a damn about his family!" Max yelled.

Philippe looked around nervously as though searching for help. It was a reflex, an indication of deep discomfort left over from childhood.

"What is it, Philippe? What's going on?"

"You don't know?"

"Know what?"

"Who do you think he had his family with?"

Philippe didn't need to say any more.

Solange.

Max had been content just to find the guy. Philippe had gone deeper into his life and stumbled on a marriage certificate with Solange's signature. She'd started a new family with Gilbert's banker. The rest was easy to figure out. She'd used Kavanagh to push the king of Roxboro over the edge to ruin. On purpose.

"She did it to punish the three of us."

Now it was Max's turn to push away his plate.

Solange.

No wonder Kavanagh had shown such interest in Gilbert after Solange left and urged him to "expand" the business and stretch his investments beyond his means. He'd done it simply to please his mistress. Now, though, it seemed she and Kavanagh were scraping the bottom of the barrel. In fact, the whole family was, Philippe told him.

"I don't give a damn if they're having problems!"

"I didn't say you should, Max."

"Then don't start in on me tonight, okay?"

"Look, promise me you won't do anything to them. Don't be like *her*."

Promises. Here we go again. Max had had enough of them. He got up and rushed out of the restaurant. He didn't want to give his brother the opportunity to make him soft, to turn him into a man without convictions, or memory. Philippe was too down to try to stop him. He probably despised himself, cursing his magnanimous spirit. Max felt as if he'd lost his one and only friend.

Philippe was right. Kavanagh wasn't doing so well. He was working as a cashier at a plant nursery, earning barely enough to support Solange and their daughter.

Max sat in his car for hours watching Kavanagh through the store window, surrounded by climbing plants in clay pots. What should he do: listen to Philippe or his own tortured conscience? One day, Solange came to pick Kavanagh up from work. Max hadn't seen her for centuries, and it was like staring at an old photo. Missing her? Maybe. Love? Definitely not. Philippe was right, though. *You couldn't hurt all three of them. No point lowering yourself that far.* Then Solange started laughing, the same laugh as that night when she'd tried to order them to follow her and they had clung to Gilbert instead. A defiant laugh that still carried a chill. He started the car. He'd made up his mind.

Tricky business, ruining a rich guy. A poor one like Kavanagh would be child's play, a no brainer. Max could do it with his eyes closed. In the end, Max didn't have the stomach for it. A touch of shame at the last minute? No, more like doing as his brother had asked him. Ruining Kavanagh and tossing Solange out on the street wouldn't be worth losing Philippe's respect. Still, he had to justify what he was doing — or rather, not doing — to the one who had been most affected.

The Melchior Residence on Viau Boulevard. The small pension afforded by Castor Bricoleur wasn't enough to cover Gilbert's costs — uniformed nurses, meals in his room, a huge garden — but Philippe (and Max, too, though discreetly) sent the necessary amounts.

Gilbert was sitting in a wheelchair looking out the window, as always, as Max knelt down and told him what he'd found out about Kavanagh, Solange's cruelty and vengeance. Gilbert listened religiously without reacting. He no longer had the slightest idea who Stéphane Kavanagh was or what he'd done. He didn't even recall owning a hardware store or dreaming of dominion over the northern suburb. Even having loved a woman named Solange and wanting to give her the moon escaped him. No, Max's retelling of their misfortunes was for Max's ears alone, to put an end to it all, to close the book on it. For good.

Why was this painful episode coming back to him here and now, a bare few metres from David's home in India? Perhaps it was the bougainvilleas at the entrance that brought the greenhouse to mind again, and with it his mother's laugh, followed by his determination to put an end to it once and for all. Jayesh's Maruti was parked diagonally by the wall that encircled the only unlit house in the street. Max would love to get his hands on the things that Walkins had taken from the High Commission and then handed over to the Indian police, but even Jayesh with his roll of rupees couldn't buy him that. But David's residence, now that was another story. This was an open book.

The two of them climbed out of the car, and though the sentry box and the entrance gave the impression of constant surveillance, Jayesh had found out the guard had been sick for a week with malaria. The police had emptied the house, and it was no longer of interest, so Max and Jayesh would have free run of the place.

The kitchen door was locked, but Juliette had given Max the key before he left Montreal. They couldn't turn on the lights for fear of alerting the neighbours, but Jayesh swept the place with his flashlight beam unnecessarily, as the immense moon cast a glare over the room, enough for them to make out the contents of the house. They could tell the police had been through every nook and cranny, leaving no drawer, closet, or cupboard untouched.

Max had never been invited here, or to Philippe's home. And it felt strange being here tonight, as though he were an intruder, a stranger, yet one who recognized certain objects, like a trinket that once belonged to Philippe. Here was David's privacy spread out before him, and his presence felt almost indecent. Especially now that he knew certain intimate things about the couple, like Juliette's pregnancy.

On the wall behind the sofa was a collection of photos, again both familiar and foreign: David and Juliette in one another's arms, so obviously in love. Then there were older ones of David as a teenager standing in between Béatrice and Patterson. Some, even older, were of Philippe and Béatrice at the award ceremony for the French high school in Bangkok, or of David shivering by the pool at their house in Ottawa. Then, there they were, all three of them, on a ride at a fair in some country or other. He couldn't tell. Max felt himself being overtaken by an immense sadness. His nephew's life, like his brother's, had unfolded without him. Béatrice's orders at the funeral home on O'Connor had been respected by her son. Max had no longer existed, had just disappeared, completely obliterated and shut out of the lives of both his nephew and brother.

Yet Philippe had always been there, discreet but faithful, despite the Kavanagh episode, often showing up when Max least expected. You thought he was on the other side of the world, and then suddenly he'd be there at the penitentiary with the right words of encouragement, as usual. Max asked for nothing, but Philippe gave him everything. Why was that? Out of love, but also out of guilt, Max figured. Philippe mistakenly felt responsible for what had happened to their father. Perhaps he'd promised himself never again to make the same mistake. Two brothers united forever like the folded blades of a pocket knife.

One day, when he was in Ottawa for a meeting of the Asian bureaus — he was posted to Ankara at the time — Philippe received a message from a Turkish businessman who absolutely insisted on meeting him at the Château Laurier. Max waited with Pascale in Room 506. He was proud to introduce his wife and apologized for not having informed his brother of the wedding: "It all happened so fast!"

Philippe had hugged Pascale and welcomed her into the family. And into a normal life. Almost.

"Hey, look at that, *yaar!*" Jayesh exclaimed as he crouched next to the stairs, facing the wide-open safe beneath the lowest step, its door wedged under the bottom of the banister. Max knelt down for a look while Jayesh swept the inside with his flashlight. Documents such as insurance policies had been removed from their plastic sleeves, so had a copy of the lease on the house, various expired passports belonging to David and Juliette, a marriage certificate, and an airline ticket.

Max took a closer look. The latter was for David via Paris on Air France to Montreal. That would have been for the conference. The dates matched. He took a closer look, especially at the cover it was in — a sort of wax-paper envelope — where David or someone else had scribbled some notes. But the ink had run because of the paper, and the words were illegible. Maybe they had been jotted down quickly while on the phone and copied somewhere else later on. Using Jayesh's flashlight, he could make out one word, *Tourigny*, and some digits, perhaps a phone number.

There was something else inside the envelope: a coin that rolled out onto the floor. Jayesh trapped it with his foot.

"Rupee?" asked Max, coming closer.

"Yes, but Nepalese."

Kathmandu again.

Next morning, the bellboy with the Texas accent brought breakfast to Max's room sporting the smile of one who expects a huge tip. On the tray were a teapot, toast, porridge, and the daily edition of the *Times of India.* Page one had an account of the previous night's clashes in Kashmir, as well as the latest Bollywood gossip and releases from the international press.

There was a photo of David: DIPLOMAT DIES.

PART TWO

LOUNGE LIZARD

15

"Come on, don't be afraid, I'm telling you!"

On the ramparts of Fatehpur Sikri, David held out his hand and flashed that killer smile of his. "You won't fall, I promise. Come on up!"

Juliette slipped her hand into his and felt his fingers closing over hers: "Okay, nothing can happen now." She felt swept up and David's arms held her fast and high. His deep, good-hearted laugh was like a child's as he carried her. She didn't dare open her eyes. That would mean losing her balance and smashing her skull on the flagstones in the courtyard. *How stupid I am!* she thought, *He's here holding on to me. I can't fall.* This man, this man of her life, seemed to be made especially for her protection, she the free-speaking young university student. She opened her eyes. "I love you, David."

Now, that same hand felt soft, weak, damp, and meaningless. *Who'll protect me from vertigo now that he's gone?*

After they unplugged his life support, David didn't die right away as she had expected. There was a moment of suspension, unbearable, as she and Béatrice hugged each other, two wounded souls, already emptied of tears and pain. Then he was gone, just like that, with no further ceremony. The machines confirmed it.

Juliette wanted to be alone now. She didn't throw herself on David's body as she'd done so many times these past few days, but she surprised Béatrice and the personnel by running out into the corridor.

With no one left to protect, the security detail was gone. She rushed into the little room at the end where they'd taken their meals and closed the door behind her. She went over to the window and watched the wind blowing through the trees on Mount Royal, the out-of-breath joggers and a cyclist pumping his peddles.

"You won't fall, I promise. Come on up!"

He was the one they'd pushed into the void, and she felt dragged along with him — a long fall into the night that might never end. *David, David, David.* She ought to be remembering the important things, but what came back to her were the little ones: His way of pinching the crease in his pants when he crossed his legs. His inability to make coffee that wasn't a disgusting mess — *"But really it's so easy!"* — The way he slept tangled up in the covers. The scruffy hair he vainly struggled with in front of the bathroom mirror.... Meaningless little memories like that came flooding back.

There was the wind again and a mother, her baby in a carriage, waiting to cross the street. Juliette's hand went to her belly. "His" child. Suddenly, she just wanted to disappear along with him. Sure, just jump out of the window then and there. Get done with it once and for all. Be with him. What was it the Mahabharata said?

"... the body of the king is laid out with the living body of his spouse. The fire is lit and Madri, without lament, quits her life in the heart of the flames."

She heard the door open behind her as Dennis Patterson stepped gently into the room holding his cell-phone. She didn't want to see a soul.

"The prime minister wants to speak to you."

She looked up at Patterson as he held out the phone to her, more sensitive to manners than sadness, she felt.

"Later ..."

He didn't move, but just stood there holding it.

Oh, all right, let's get it over with, she thought. She took the phone from him.

"Mr. Prime Minister ..."

The sympathy, pain, and sadness resonated in his voice as it did on TV, sincere. Sincerity was his job, though, wasn't it? Well, for thirty seconds at a time, anyway.

Juliette handed the phone back to Patterson, still standing at attention. He wanted to discuss practical details, how things were going to be done. She waved him off: "Not right now."

"Sorry, Juliette."

She turned toward him and fell into his arms as she had the first time, and began crying once more, uncontrollably, into his shoulder. Then she raised her head, her voice quavering. "Has he been identified?"

For a moment, Patterson didn't seem to know what she meant. Then he said, "False alarm. It was a burglar."

Everywhere in the hospital, she'd seen the signs warning patients and visitors to keep their belongings close at hand.

"Creep probably just chose the wrong hospital at the wrong time."

Call Juliette, but to tell her what exactly? Max hadn't a clue. He wanted to talk to her, hear her voice, period. It could wait. Jayesh had left town, knowing that for the time being, Max needed to be alone. From his window, he had a view of the pool, where tourists frolicked without a care in the world. The past caught up with him again. So David's death was one more in the string of deaths that marked out his life. This one was the most unbearable of them all, but who could he turn to for comfort? Pascale would have talked about the predetermined transition from one life to the next, a constant and harmonious cycle of rebirths. The easy pictures of fatalistic Hinduism, like every other religion, he believed, especially for the uneducated and unlettered, deprived of the acquired wisdom of the ages. Small comfort for such an abysmal tragedy. Religion invented to defeat death actually created it, as now in India.

Max felt somehow responsible for what had happened to David: a vague sort of guilt that was hard to pin down, and it was eating him up. Could things have turned out differently?

Alone, Juliette stood before the desk belonging to Patterson's secretary, but the young woman was not there. Patterson himself was in a meeting next door. Should she wait for the secretary to announce her or just walk in? Juliette had been relieved to let Patterson deal with the "arrangements," as he called them. He kept her informed more than she wanted him to. Who cared what happened now? Nothing mattered anymore. Still, she had to sign all these papers. That was why she'd stepped into this maze. But now the secretary had vanished ... *for good?* Wasn't that her raincoat there in the wardrobe with the others? Juliette thought back to the hospital. Here, as well, it would be easy for someone to slip into any of the offices and make off with the coats. That man had been caught in the act. How could she forget? David's death had wiped out everything else. She went on looking at the wardrobe. What had he been doing in a hospital? He'd gone to the trouble of disguising himself as a cook ... good cover. But what if Patterson and the cops had it wrong and he really was there to kill David?

Voices were raised in Patterson's office. Juliette could hear the consultant, grave and soothing, then suddenly Béatrice, her voice high-pitched and exasperated, a voice Juliette had learned to recognize among thousands when she called for news of David. There was a third voice, too, a woman's, that she couldn't identify.

She moved closer to the door.

"At a moment like this," Patterson cut in, "the least you could do would be put aside your differences."

"Are you out of your mind?"

"Béatrice!"

"I refuse, that's all. I, too, have a reputation to think about."

"No one knows anything about it," replied the unknown woman.

"Exactly. I don't want this business suddenly coming out in public."

"Look, I'm sure there's a way to work this out," said Patterson, ever the diplomat.

Juliette gently pushed open the door: "Excuse me ..."

All three stared at her, astonished. They'd stopped talking, so to relieve the tension, Juliette said, "If you're discussing the funeral arrangements, I'd like to ..."

"We weren't expecting you this early, Juliette," exclaimed Patterson, walking toward her. "But you did the right thing coming here."

He turned to the unidentified woman. "Let me introduce Deborah Cournoyer."

The woman, in a grey suit and with a red scarf knotted at her neck, approached, smiling, to shake Juliette's hand.

"Are you with the funeral home?"

Patterson shook his head. "Deborah's an old friend of Philippe and Béatrice."

Béatrice stood to one side, watching and frowning. There was no reading her thoughts, but one might hazard a guess. Of the three, she was the only one still in a bad mood.

"If I'm in the way, I can come back later."

"Your husband was an exceptional man," said Deborah Cournoyer, "and his death is a great loss for us all." She stared Juliette straight in the eye insistently in a way that made her uncomfortable.

Béatrice suddenly switched on again. "We'll leave you two alone." She took the unknown woman by the arm and guided her out.

On her way out, Cournoyer said again, "I'm delighted to meet you. It's a shame it had to be under such sad circumstances."

As the two women left, Juliette turned to Patterson, who was standing before her with a sheaf of telegrams in his hand: "Condolence messages from all over, especially embassies and High Commissions in New Delhi. Foreign Affairs, too."

"What business?"

"Excuse me?"

"Béatrice said, 'I don't want this business suddenly coming out in public.'"

Patterson hesitated a moment, then said, "Nothing for you to worry about, Juliette, I promise."

She looked at him, but said nothing. She'd talk to Béatrice about it tonight.

Patterson changed the subject. "The minister's coming to the funeral."

Killed in the line of duty, so the Canadian flag would be draped over the coffin. Gawkers would clap as they exited Notre Dame Basilica facing Place d'Armes where the *calèche* drivers hustled tourists. Juliette would have to stand erect, proud, looking elegant in a black suit, and next to Béatrice, of course. "I know what to do. I've been there before."

Her head was spinning all at once … must be the heat.

"Then Mount Royal Cemetery for another very short ceremony."

"Private, I hope."

"The media and the public are allowed at the church — we can hardly refuse them — but at the cemetery …"

"And I'll need to say something, I suppose."

"At the basilica? Sure, if you want to. Normally, it would be …"

"Mr. Bernatchez?"

Patterson nodded. "Raymond gets here this afternoon. He'll be at the funeral home and at the funeral itself: the usual tribute, and of course some mention of Philippe. The son joining the father … that sort of thing."

Juliette was incredulous. Patterson gave her a comforting smile. "Don't worry. I'll write it." He waited a moment, then added, "I can modify the program if you want to speak, too."

"No, no, I have nothing to say, not to tourists visiting Place d'Armes, anyway."

As she was getting out of the elevator a few minutes later, Max called. It was their first conversation since David's death. She regretted not having told him about her decision to cut short her husband's suffering. She was afraid that in apologizing she'd break down completely, and she was never going to cry again, ever.

"You going to get through this?"

"Oh yes, I've got an unlimited supply of chocolate," she reassured him.

Max's troubled laugh came over the line. He cleared his throat. He wanted to change the subject. Juliette was expecting some sort of revelation, but he had more questions than answers. He was clearly working hard at piecing together bits of the investigation that first seemed unrelated. He struck her as a labourer lumbering painfully through an overgrown field, moving ahead, but at a very slow pace.

"You knew about the strongbox under the stairs?"

She'd forgotten about it. "Oh yeah, that. David had it put in when we got there."

"What for?"

"It was a gift from Béatrice."

"What?"

"She started doing it in Rabat — a 'secret' vault was essential, she said, so when he was posted to Delhi, she gave it to him."

"What exactly was in it?"

"Nothing all that important. A bit of money."

"Yes?"

"Two thousand to three thousand U.S. dollars, just a precaution. But it would have been better in a bank."

"Any Nepalese rupees?"

"Must've been some. He dipped into them for one trip or another. Why?"

"It was empty. The dollars and rupees were gone."

Juliette was puzzled, but Max didn't think the theft had any connection with the attack.

"I'm sure of only one thing: someone was in that house after you and the police had left."

"Maybe the cops emptied it."

"It's hidden under the stairs. They'd have to know that. I think someone else was there."

"A few thousand dollars ..."

"Who else knew about it besides you two? Household staff?"

"No, of course not."

"Vandana?"

"David may have mentioned it to her."

Max cleared his throat. "Does the name Tourigny mean anything to you?"

"Who's that?"

"It was scribbled on the envelope of David's airline ticket in the vault."

On his way back to the hotel, Max had tried that number in Delhi, then Montreal, then Toronto, even Paris. Nothing.

"You ought to ask Vandana."

16

Luc Roberge had asked Juliette and Patterson to come to his office on Parthenais, but then called later asking them to meet him at the courthouse, where he was testifying in an embezzlement case. He was waiting for them at the entrance, minus Morel, his usual sidekick. He shook hands with Patterson and made the appropriate condolences to Juliette. Then his usual joviality came right back — second nature. *Life goes on.*

"How about a bite to eat?" he asked, taking them in tow. "There's a good little restaurant around the corner."

Patterson tried to duck out, but finally went along when Roberge insisted. The two men talked as though they'd known each other for ages, which surprised Juliette.

"What is it you want?" she asked.

"Just to ask you a few questions, that's all."

The policeman would have grabbed her arm if she'd let him. He whispered a lame joke in her ear to put her at ease. Roberge was the type who couldn't help imposing his good-naturedness on everyone, even at a time like this.

"Very interesting case. A model employee beyond reproach; always knew what he was doing. Well, he put three, maybe three-and-a-half million, dollars in his pocket over eleven years, a little at a time. Seems like nothing, just a discreet fiddling of the company books."

When they came to a red light, Roberge paid no attention and dragged his companions across anyway, ignoring the car horns. A show-off in the spotlight. *This is a setup*, thought Juliette, *but what for*?

"You know what did him in? The flu. Yeah, yeah, a week in bed, says the doctor. Well, it gets worse: two weeks, three, and he had to be replaced in accounting. Some whiz kid with a calculator suddenly smells a rat. At first, no one would believe it, and then …"

Fortunately, the restaurant was nothing like Roberge. It was simple, discreet, settled at the bottom of a quiet street; a romantic sort of place for couples in the evening. The owner had done his best to attract a local lunchtime clientele, even adding a "Judge's Special," but the message hadn't got across, as the place was empty.

"Anyway, the moral of the story is 'beware of conscientious people.' You know, the ones who never take vacations or call in sick. The ones who never give up."

"You mean like you?" ventured Patterson.

Roberge smiled as he slid into a booth. "People think thieves are lazy. Not true. Stealing is a full-time job. You're always on. No let-up. Take Max O'Brien, for instance, he's our regular man-in-the-wind."

Juliette looked up, but Roberge was staring at Patterson. "So, one day he shows up in Montreal and the next he's in New York. He spends his entire life on the road, in hiding."

"Is this going somewhere?" Patterson asked.

Roberge turned to Juliette, then Patterson again. He wasn't so jolly anymore. He was through with the song and dance. "Why have you two been lying to me? Why are you protecting that crook?"

Patterson was about to protest his innocence when Roberge held up his hand for silence: "You had lunch together like old buddies."

He stared at Juliette. "And he came to see you at the hospital. You talked to him. Why didn't you say anything?"

Juliette was mute, and Roberge lost patience. "A nurse identified him. He saw the two of you together."

"That doesn't prove anything."

"We're not in court here, Mrs. O'Brien. I'm not out to 'prove' anything. All I'm saying is, I know you three have been in contact."

"Hey, leave her out of this."

"Look, Dennis, it's nice of you to play the tough guy, but ..."

"You shut up!" yelled Juliette.

She was startled by her own anger. She'd spoken too loudly, and the owner behind the counter was staring at them. She wished she hadn't accepted this stupid invitation. She stood up. "I won't have anything to do with your garbage. My husband's just died."

"I'm sorry. Please sit down." He took her by the arm.

"Leave … her … alone," emphasized Patterson firmly, but Roberge wasn't budging. He fixed his gaze on Juliette.

He said, "I don't wish you any harm, Dennis, either. All I want is your co-operation."

"I don't have to answer to you."

"I know, and normally I wouldn't bother you, but I need your help."

"You're not getting anything from me, ever."

"Please sit down."

She pulled her arm out of his grasp but sat down. Patterson, to her right, was staying silent, almost as though he knew what was coming next.

"Max O'Brien's in India," Roberge continued as he thumbed through the menu. "How do I know? As a matter of fact, I don't know that yet, though David's mother is convinced that's where he is. I could ask Josh Walkins, the RCMP man over there, to get a list of newly arrived Canadians and Americans in New Delhi, say, in the last forty-eight hours. There won't be a ton of them, given the political situation."

He'd made his choice and closed his menu. "But it would be pointless," he said to Patterson. "I can get that information here myself and quite easily, can't I, Dennis?"

Juliette turned to Patterson as he played nervously with his knife. His anger had given way to resignation, though Juliette didn't know why. She looked to Roberge, but the policeman was no longer interested in her. He added, "I'm sure Mrs. O'Brien would be thrilled to hear what you have to say about him."

"Shut up. This is none of your business."

Roberge couldn't help smiling once again. Juliette felt bad for the former diplomat. She now understood the cop's tactic. He'd included her just as bait and pressure for Patterson's confession. She didn't know Patterson well, but she was aware that David's confidence in him was unshakeable. By attacking Patterson, Roberge was also attacking David.

"So what'll it be, Dennis? Shall I tell all to David O'Brien's wife, or will you work with us?"

"Why are you being such a creep?" Juliette said in disgust.

Now she had his attention once more.

"You should be glad. You're this piece of crap's latest victim. I'm only trying to protect you."

"Yeah, well, your methods stink."

"Max O'Brien's are even worse. Ask Béatrice about it. I'm sure she'd be glad to tell what she knows."

Turning back to Patterson, he said, "The minute I learned he was headed for India, I alerted Josh Walkins. I even sent him photos on the Internet — Photoshopped. Amazing piece of software, isn't it? Do you know it? Yup, I knew Max O'Brien was a master of the disappearing act, and figured he was sure to see his old 'friend' Patterson for some specific purpose, like, say, getting himself into the High Commission. A letter from a former diplomat, or better yet, a personal call to Raymond Bernatchez would do the job. That meant revealing the assumed name he was travelling under, and you're going to tell me what that is right now without a fuss."

Patterson went on playing with his fork, while Juliette begged him not to give in to this blackmail, but he wasn't listening. "Peter Brokowich."

Roberge then turned to Juliette with a smile. "Terrific, and now, how about we order?"

Juliette was already up and heading for the exit. Patterson caught up with her in the street. "Look, let me explain."

She was in no mood to listen to him humiliate himself any further. She hailed a taxi and got in. She felt like throwing up, and leaned her head against the window.

Most diplomats die in their beds, surrounded, at best, by their grieving families, and at worst by their souvenirs from another world — exotic trinkets dried out by electric heating and cracked into a thousand veins, not really something worthy of a state funeral. On the website for retired Foreign Affairs people, there would be the inevitable short blurb on the great loss resulting from this death, not just for the family, but for all of society, due to the "selfless devotion to duty and his beloved country." Juliette recalled seeing David turn to the death notices looking for colleagues of his father, who, unlike him, hadn't been "fortunate" enough to die tragically.

Death in the line of duty, however — violent death especially — received the fullest recognition. This was a first-class send-off with all the pomp of Foreign Affairs behind it. Ministers got the wrinkles out of their best suits and shined their shoes. The grieving widow was obviously the heroine of the day, a role Juliette had absolutely no desire to play. She'd have much preferred a more discreet burial, but since David's death she'd let herself be swept along by events. She had some vague perception of everything being arranged around her, as though she had no connection to the whirlwind of energy that strangers were expending on her husband's remains. Patterson had coaxed her to the funeral home on Laurier, shown her the coffin, which she had approved, along with the text of the card. Unquestioning, she said yes to everything. She kept thinking, *I'm not going to cry. I'm going to be dignified*, like those widows of politicians, whose strength of character the media praised to the skies: "She remained erect, not shedding a tear, despite the unbearable grief."

David, in a suit he'd had made to measure by a tailor in the Santushti Shopping Complex, lay in his coffin at the far end of the room. Béatrice fussed over the floral arrangements for the hundredth time. Juliette charged up to her.

"What's wrong? What do you want?" Béatrice cried out.

"The truth." Juliette had had her fill of things left in the shadows, little mysteries, and things implied but left unsaid. The previous evening, she'd asked Béatrice about Deborah Cournoyer and the story that should not be brought out into the light of day, but Béatrice had brushed her off. This time Juliette was looking for answers about Max and why Béatrice always bad-mouthed him. Why was that? She'd turned Max in to Roberge without a moment's hesitation. She stayed as far away from him as possible, as though he were a leper who might infect her. What was the reason?

Béatrice had adopted the pose that David called "her statue pose." "She makes me laugh," he'd said. "She's like a rabbit in the forest when it hears a noise — it freezes completely." Pose or no pose, Juliette was not letting her off the hook till she explained.

Juliette quoted Roberge: "Max O'Brien's methods are even worse. Ask Béatrice about it."

Béatrice didn't budge. This rabbit was unmoved by Juliette's torrent of words.

She moved in again. "What did Max ever do to make you hate him so much?"

Béatrice sighed. "He could have prevented Philippe's death, and he refused. It's as simple as that."

17

The small diplomatic world of India stuck together in their mourning and wanted to prove to the Indians that the terrorist threat wasn't going to intimidate them. On the contrary, this was an act of will, of bravery, and even of heroism. Obviously, the military Jeeps and police cars that Max saw in front of the Spanish ambassador's residence lent courage to the guests. Yet, despite the precautions, Max had no trouble getting past these obstacles. In the immense salon, he faced an Osborne bull in a tapestry hung on the wall above a Gaudiesque bureau. Photos of Toledo and a reproduction of seventeenth-century Madrid were also on show. The Spanish did nothing by halves. The grated door, which separated the servants' quarters from the ambassador's family could be locked in the event of an uprising and was typically decorated with Castilian flourishes.

The ambassador, Don Miguel Ferrer, seemed built to match. His long, emaciated El Greco face was topped by a tangle of wayward grey hair that was borne every which way by the draft from a fan that seemed to pursue him wherever he went, even by the bar near the kitchen door where a group of Sikhs in evening wear stood.

Max stopped a young Indian serving girl, snagged a glass of champagne from her tray, and then went out into the garden. Some of the hardiest were out there defying any possible sniper and seemingly the more excited for it. Guests, fuelled by alcohol, were talking loudly, punctuated by the occasional belly laugh. He'd expected more restraint from David's colleagues, but the vocal display was part of their bluff: "Terrorism won't stop us from enjoying ourselves and indulging in curried shrimp."

There were representatives of other embassies there, as well as Indians, all of them fully decked out for the occasion, downing Scotch and Rioja with typical Western self-assurance and good humour, as if they were saying, "We were present at the end of the world." Around the bar were small groups of entrepreneurs who had shown up, as Max had done, without invitations in order to escape the solitude of the Intercontinental Hotel or an intimate dinner with themselves at the Parikrama. Under other circumstances, Max would have had no trouble at all choosing "pigeons" among these rootless ones and latching on to them for his own profit. For now, he had other things on his mind: finding someone, and that someone was Vandana. But she was nowhere to be seen.

He took another spin around the garden, where groups of Japanese were handing out stacks of business cards, before going back inside. The Sikhs had split up, and the ambassador was now discussing the Afghan situation with a Polish diplomat, while his wife, Ana Maria, was describing the *feria* in Pamplona to an enthralled Indian. Two Australian businessmen wondered if they shouldn't leave the country like their compatriots, especially now that Pakistan had announced missile tests in order to show the Indians that two could play at that game. Their Indian companion simply smiled.

"Vajpayee is away on holiday in Manali. If it were that serious, don't you think he'd stay here in New Delhi?"

The Australians seemed even less convinced.

A fresh glance at the door revealed that Vandana had just arrived, resplendent in a burgundy sari, and she wasn't alone. Henry Caldwell and William Sandmill were with her in Bernatchez's place. He was probably in Canada by now. Sunil Mukherjee brought up the rear. Max would rather have been alone with her, so, disappointed, he headed once again for the garden, where the darkness would afford him better protection. He kept his eyes on Vandana and her escorts, who were now the centre of attention. Don Miguel dropped his conversation with a chubby Argentinean to welcome the new arrivals. Renewed courage — "We won't be cowed by terrorists."

The ambassador took Caldwell by the shoulder and drew him to one side, treating him like an old friend from way back, a confrere at an *escuela ecuestre* in Madrid or Jerez. Sandmill made a beeline for the bar, while Mukherjee was cornered by an Indian journalist, judging by the notebook the man whipped out of his jacket pocket. Max took the opportunity to pounce on Vandana, who was taken aback. "What are you doing here? They know who you are now. The police were tipped off."

It had to be Luc Roberge. He was quicker than expected. Max would have to act swiftly. He dragged Vandana behind a banana tree. He knew his brusqueness was off-putting, but there was no time for politeness and etiquette.

"What is this charade, and who exactly do you think you're fooling?" he said.

Vandana looked up at him. "I don't know what you're talking about."

"David and his inner conflict, feeling torn and clamming up ..."

She frowned. "What ...?"

"Your little trysts at the foot of the Himalayas. Kathmandu."

"There's never been anything between David and me."

"You rushed over to his place the day after the attack, and you knew about the safe under the stairs. It wasn't the first time you'd been there."

"What safe?"

"You were in a real hurry to open it. What were you looking for? Letters, notes, messages? Things to implicate you personally with David, things that would compromise you with the police if they started rifling through the young diplomat's past."

Vandana stared at him in amazement. "You're out of your mind!" She started to leave, but Max blocked the way.

"An affair? A little slip-up, maybe? But it was still going on when you went to Kathmandu. Otherwise, David would have postponed the trip till after Montreal."

Max heard a murmur behind him and turned to see two security agents blend into the crowd. Don Miguel was already hurrying over to them, his hair flying. Max couldn't hear what they said to him, but he could guess: they couldn't have been admitted without his government's permission. They were explaining to him while sweeping the room with their eyes. There was no doubt about what they were looking for. Max. He grabbed Vandana's arm and rushed her out to the garden.

"I want to know what happened between you and David in Kathmandu."

"Nothing happened … nothing at all."

"Look, David's dead, so please stop lying to me, okay? I'm not here to preach at you."

By now, the Indian police were being accompanied by embassy employees, as they jostled their way through the crowd, which was intrigued and entertained by it all. In a few seconds, they'd be here.

"What happened in Kathmandu?" he repeated.

Vandana stared fixedly at him and appeared to hesitate. He'd been right to insist.

"I went by myself," she confessed after a long pause. "David didn't come with me."

"He stayed in Delhi?"

"I don't know, but after the bombing, when Juliette started saying he'd changed after Nepal, I realized he hadn't been with her as I thought."

"Did you tell the police?"

"No. I didn't want Juliette to get involved."

"Another woman?"

She shook her head. "Juliette and David were in love. He'd never do that. Never. Not with me or anyone else."

Max looked at her for a long time. He felt sorry he'd accused her.

"Does the name Tourigny mean anything to you?"

"No, nothing. Who's that?"

Loud voices emerged from the crowd as three policemen joined the others to everyone's delight.

"You haven't a hope of getting out of here," Vandana said, but Max just smiled.

"Don't worry. I'm used to this." And he snaked through the guests at the bottom of the garden and out to the alley by an opening he'd spotted in his previous reconnaissance. It was deserted and dark, and though he wanted to run, he settled into a brisk walk and never looked back. At the corner, he wondered which way to go, but then his attention was caught by the coughing of a rickshaw motor drawn to its potential customer.

"*Aray!* Rickshaw, *sahib*? Rickshaw?"

Max climbed inside and sat down without even dickering about the fare, something the *Lonely Planet* he bought at Heathrow had expressly told him never to do.

No way Max was going back to the Oberoi, of course. The cops were certainly sitting on it. It was by showing his photo to taxi drivers that they had probably traced him to the Spanish ambassador. The rickshaw skirted India Gate and headed for Tilak Marg.

"Do you want to stay at my place?" asked Jayesh over the phone. That could work, but it would compromise the young Indian. He'd thought about hiding out at the inn on Akbar Road, if it still existed, but the police would certainly check there.

"Some place discreet, Jayesh. Better if it's one where Westerners hang out."

After a moment's silence, Jayesh said, "Ask the driver to let you off near the Jama Mosque. Facing it is a small alley leading to the Chawri Bazaar."

Max relayed the address to the driver, who then branched off onto a side road. Suddenly the landscape was different, as Embassy Row and the Ministerial Quarter yielded to a true Indian city, offhand and neglected, a sort of random set of building blocks that, by some miracle, barely held together. Here, unlike the new city, the people were in control of the streets, families sleeping outdoors on *charpai*, a sort of bed they put away in the daytime. Then the avenue narrowed imperceptibly and became a long and winding thread of mud past the shops all barred up for the night. Occasionally they encountered a beggar, one of those who slept in the train station until the police turfed them out to wander the streets in search of shelter. This city was the complete opposite of what one saw in the daytime, astonishingly silent and tranquil, and it would stay that way until the mosques called the faithful to prayer just before dawn: "Never forget, neighbours, that Delhi, Old Delhi is, above all, Muslim!"

Max pictured Bhargava, the "James Bond of Hinduness," dreaming that he could silence these muezzins forever. Send these circumcisees packing to their brothers and accomplices in Pakistan, or anywhere!

There was no missing the red door, Jayesh told him. Behind it was a bright — too bright — illumination, probably neon, and a hand-painted sign announced LIVERPOOL GUEST HOUSE: CLEAN SHEETS. CLEAN SHOWERS. The night watchman was napping on a worn-out mattress behind the reception counter, an older man with ruffled hair and teeth reddened with betel juice. Max signed the tea-stained register but didn't even have to present his passport. The porter showed no surprise that this guest looked utterly unlike his usual customers, whom Max saw early next morning on the sun-flooded terrace. The hotel was a refuge for hippies in wraparound *longyis* and oversized pyjamas — escapees from the West, bigger than life, hairy, and probably fried, smoking *bidis* and nodding incessantly. Max smiled. Jayesh was right. The police couldn't even imagine this place.

18

"Rodger Morency?" wondered Sergeant Demers in amazement. Juliette felt like an idiot. What was she doing at Montreal Police Headquarters? Shouldn't she be holed up at her place, veiled with black lace instead?

"It wasn't his intention to go after your husband. I mean, Morency and Al-Qaeda are not exactly in the same ballpark, are they?"

Still …

He was right, Al-Qaeda and Rodger were worlds apart. Rodger's file was that of a petty delinquent with a monotonous train of police reports that nevertheless became weightier as time went on. He'd woken up one morning as a child who decided he didn't want to be an astronaut or a star hockey player, just a public pain in the ass. His special talent was an alarming ability to get himself into trouble with the justice system, the kind that spared no effort to get nailed by the police: Getting caught at the wheel of a stolen car with a six-months'-expired licence, for instance: *"I was just on my way to get it renewed, Your Honour."* Then an arrest for being found in the basement of an underground parking lot in the company of a minor: *"She showed me her papers. I was sure everything was okay, Judge."* There was also a failed attempt at loan-sharking with Haitian drivers at Lasalle Taxi: *"Honest, I'm not racist, Your Honour."* Little jobs and misdemeanours here and there, none of them worth bothering about.

A very small-time crook with small-time ambitions: corner stores, service stations, metro wickets ... and what about the hospital? Well, sure, he was there to do the rooms, and he admitted it freely: *"Cardiology, now, that's my fetish floor."*

Something didn't sit right in this story for Juliette, but what? The admission was weird coming from someone who always had an excuse for everything, but none for this. He was practically glad to confess for once: *"Sure, I went there to steal."*

"Can we talk to this Rodger Morency?" she asked.

"Between now and his trial in July ..." Demers shaped his fingers to form a bird in flight.

"I thought he was in jail."

"Out on bail, angel that he is."

"But ..."

"His mother came to the rescue, as usual."

Without a word to Béatrice, and especially not to Patterson, Juliette rented a car, crossed the Champlain

Bridge, took the highway through the Montérégie, and had no trouble finding the farm belonging to Morency's mother in Marieville. The father had left the family when Rodger was still young, as she would find out later. For now, she was headed out there to question Rodger, though she had no clue what she would ask him. Mostly she wanted to confirm he was not the mindless idiot that Sergeant Demers depicted: a small-time thug out to rob patients despite the top security.

The other possibility was that Juliette was on the wrong trail, and that was why she'd said nothing to Béatrice or Patterson, though she had mentioned it to Max when he'd phoned the day before. He wasn't convinced either, and Juliette was beginning to doubt her theory. She had to be wrong. A trip to the South Shore would just confirm it.

Born and raised on Chambord Street in the east end, Juliette's only experiences of the countryside were the greenhouse at the Botanical Gardens and pedal-boat rides on Beaver Lake. Outside Montreal lay a hostile world of shady puppy mills, septic ditches, and an anachronistic universe of drunk drivers, incest, and Ski-Doo races. Never mind. A first glance told her Madeleine Morency didn't earn her living from farm produce. The buildings were tumble-down, the fields had gone to seed, and there was a rusted-out truck with no wheels in the yard. In the back, she found the usual bric-a-brac country-dwellers couldn't do without, apparently: mismatched furniture, abandoned tools, an old bike, and two water heaters.

Juliette parked her rental car near a plastic mailbox. Next came a streaking, barking dog trained to eat mailmen. She was confused. Here in this backwater, she felt even more lost than in the alleyways of Old Delhi. How could she let someone know she was here? Yell, maybe, and alert the whole neighbourhood? Suddenly, a woman appeared at the door.

"Brutus, Brutus, here, Brutus!"

Juliette wished she'd prepared them for her visit, and now she was bound to be sent away. The woman — she had to be Madeleine Morency — was already stepping toward the gate. Close up, she looked a lot less hardened than her surroundings. One couldn't tell her age — sixties, maybe — erect and dignified, not the kind to give ground easily. Most fascinating was the long grey hair that fell to her waist. Once blond, she refused to dye it. An aging hippie, maybe?

Without opening the gate, she called across, "What do you want?"

"I'd like to see Rodger." No point beating about the bush. *I guess I should have been cooler*, Juliette thought. *Invented some waterproof pretext, maybe. Well, too late now.*

Madeleine thoroughly examined the visitor's clothes, more curious than aggressive. Perhaps this was the country way. First impressions were everything.

"He's not here."

"Do you know where I can find him?"

Madeleine Morency sighed and opened the gate. Brutus put up some more barking, which she silenced with a wave of her hand. Juliette followed her to the house, mindful of where she stepped. The kitchen was immense and modern, nothing like the outside of the house.

"He promised me he'd get in touch with you," Madeleine said, taking off her shoes.

Juliette wondered if she should do the same, but she hadn't brought anything else.

"No, it's okay, keep them on," Madeleine said, signalling her to sit down at the table. "You prefer coffee, or is it tea, like your partner?"

"Excuse me?"

"Aren't you with the police?"

"No."

Her face hardened at once, and the respect, or rather deference she showed to the authorities was no longer called for.

"What do you want Rodger for?" Madeleine asked aggressively.

"I need to talk to him, ask him some questions." Juliette was getting in over her head, and she knew it.

"What kind of questions?"

Time to think fast. "Oh, questions about his life … you see … I work at the university … in criminology … on what happens to delinquents … that is …"

"You're here to help him?"

Juliette was on the point of saying, "No, I just want to get to know him, that's all," but it sounded desperate, so she said, "Yes." *Now, where to go from here*? She had no idea. "Just putting him back in prison every time won't solve anything."

"Exactly what I've been saying for years," replied Madeleine, "but the police aren't interested. All they care about is filling their quota of arrests each month, period."

Juliette was relieved. "At the university, we think there's another way."

"The cops don't care."

"But I'm not them, Mrs. Morency."

"Rodger never had any luck, sure, but that's no reason to be on his back all the time."

"Mrs. Morency, I'm here to help him, not to put him down."

Rodger's mother watched her without moving, and all of a sudden Juliette felt despicable for making this woman believe she could "fix" her son's criminal tendencies.

"But to do that, I have to get to know him, understand what got him into this in the first place."

Not once did Madeleine Morency shift her gaze from Juliette.

There was more silence.

"So, what'll it be, coffee or tea?"

The life of Rodger, according to his mother, followed the same path as the police reports, but her voice somehow gave it a more personal, intimate hue. According to Demers, Rodger had plunged headlong into crime on purpose, but his mother preferred to talk about his repeated bad luck, one incident leading to another, no matter how hard he tried. There were unscrupulous accomplices, but, according to her, they were opportunists who'd taken advantage of his naïveté and good nature. His long slide to hell had a few bright moments when Rodger could have split from his "negative milieu," but they didn't last. Although his mother kept sending out "positive energy," his lucky star didn't shine bright enough or long enough.

Oh, okay, New Age stuff. Now Juliette twigged to the long grey hair. Madeleine Morency was into pop spirituality, perfumed candles, et cetera, to free her kid from a life of crime, but it wasn't working too well for them, no matter what Rodger promised. He was already too far gone by the looks of it. She wouldn't see him again till the next disaster, probably a call from the police station.

By her third cup of tea, Juliette figured she had enough information. Rodger's path was twisted and tiring. There had been one incident after another, but nothing to connect him to David. He didn't read the papers ("all lies") or watch TV ("more lies"). Above all, Rodger never ever mentioned international politics. The only thing he cared about and his sole subject of conversation was one thing: money. He often got it from his mother.

Just as Juliette was leaving without providing her phone number ("I'm always on the road, but I'll call him"), she saw Rodger's mother blocking her way. Juliette couldn't get out. She had to see Madeleine's photo album.

"Another time, Mrs. Morency."

"I want you to see how much I love him. Please."

There was no refusing Madeleine Morency. Her sanctuary at the back of the house, her "elf garden," as she called it. In the living room and kitchen, she must have been holding back, because here it was a festival for the senses: little angels, clouds, incense sticks, lace, and fine linens. The place was a medieval dump, and it was from here that she sent her positive vibrations to a son who at the same moment was probably emptying the cash drawer of a pizzeria or a car wash.

The album itself seemed to come from the personal collection of some amateur wizard. An oversized, elongated scrapbook held letters his mother had lovingly glued in and news articles relating his criminal career, every petty arrest or incident connected with his shady world, all of it dated and pasted with loving care. It was a painstaking record that spanned from his very earliest days as a delinquent teen to the present.

Juliette thumbed through it with interest, enthralled by this woman's pain at the monument to failure that was her son's life.

"Every letter, every article is glued with my tears."

Once more, Juliette felt bad that she'd lied again. Rodger had done the same so many times in his life. Whatever nonsense her son had been up to, his mother didn't deserve this. Juliette's head was spinning. She should have stopped before her last cup of tea. All of a sudden, she felt like throwing up. Then she passed out.

When she came to, Madeleine was holding out a damp towel: "You're pregnant."

Back in the car, Juliette began to cry long and hard.

19

Temagami Penitentiary was on the edge of a forest, and beyond that, farther north, tundra, glaciers, and the North Pole. In winter, Max O'Brien's cell window provided him with glimpses of deer, caribou, and moose as they ventured into the world of men in search of more food. He felt as though he were in a zoo, a prison invented by some wild-animal lover or by one of the animals, reincarnated as a prison architect. Yeah, why not? Did their ferocity and cruelty condemn them to live out their karma the same as humans ... rebirth in that avatar of destruction, mankind, the worst of all animal species? Had wild animals really driven the gods to this level of desperation?

Max was trying to survive here the best he could: walls around his cell, around the workshop where he made key chains no one would use ... Santa's workshop filled with shiftless young delinquents, a sort of North American gulag where porn films and disco music took the place of forced labour.

Far removed from the city and life itself, Max, at twenty-six, felt like he was dying a slow death. He blamed himself for what had happened, for trusting that green-horn, what's-his-name. The idiot who worked on two contracts at the same time, a no-no under the agreement he'd sworn to, same as the others. Then it happened, the slow decline into the utterly ridiculous. The idiot got caught speeding while under the influence — another rule broken. The cops checked his identity and found he was out on parole, something Max hadn't been told, naturally.

Sitting in the Toronto patrol car on his way to book-ing, the cretin was scared stiff … of what? The speed the cops were driving, their nasty smiles, the leaden darkness that fell around the car? Anyway, instead of shutting his yap and taking the fall, he spilled it all.

"Hey, if you let me off, I'll tell you everything about a job, a really big one — names, details, everything."

The cops probably looked at him sideways with a grin. Deals were usually made further down the line, at least after you'd been charged and knew what kind of time you were looking at; and even then, it was your lawyer who did the dealing, not the joker in the deck. This one couldn't wait.

"You know Max O'Brien?"

Of course they did, but they figured he was in Mexico.

"No way," said the ding-dong. "He's in town, and he's getting something set up on Bay Street."

The two cops were amazed and delighted to hear it, already seeing themselves honoured by the Kiwanis Club of Greater Toronto or cast in bronze facing the CIBC, their reward for saving an unscrupulous banker from the shame and humiliation of his board of governors.

"You accept my offer, and I'll tell you how you can pick him like a daisy."

More like a pimple.

Max and Pascale had just taken shelter at Harbour Square on the 32nd floor of a brand-new building. It felt like a holiday. From the living-room window they could see the ferry shuttling to and from the Toronto Islands, sailboats going by, and the splendid sky of an unforgettable summer. They ate out on the terrace each evening, sometimes chatting about the con that Max and his team were about to pull off. Mostly they talked about what they would do afterward: Hawaii, Guadeloupe, Turkey, or Bermuda? There were long moments of silence. Chit-chat was for jobs, just a tool of the trade, nothing else. Silence was the most precious thing of all. When Max held Pascale in his arms, he couldn't utter a word. Neither of them even tried. They just rolled together like down a precipice, so was this love or vertigo? An endless spiral Max let himself in for, embroiled in a passion he'd never known before.

One last perfect moment to savour, almost as though they suspected what was to come. Max would remember every single detail for the rest of his life: the colour of the sky, the shapes of the clouds, the heat of the sun, but also Pascale's smouldering look as they pulled themselves out of the tangled sheets, and the feel of her soft, trembling skin beneath his fingers. She smiled enigmatically when he asked what she was laughing at, and she said, "I'm not laughing. I'm just happy."

This was normally a word that scared Max, but coming from Pascale, it was the best in the world, the "truest."

"I'm simply happy because you're here and I love you."

He took her face in his hands, and they gazed at each other. Her eyes were brighter than ever, and her face shone with a glow he'd remember always. "I love you, too."

It seemed funny to be saying these words and believing them, knowing that she also believed them. For once, words weren't being used to manipulate someone. He kissed her in a way he never had before. And then they dived back into it.

The next morning, Pascale got up early to go to the gym at the far end of the complex. From her stationary bike, she saw the police storming into the building. Without taking time to change, she ran across Queen's Quay and got on a bus. She looked like an ecology-minded jogger, but also a lazy one who was taking transit to Cabbagetown. That was the location of Max's hideaway and "base camp," a place to ride out the storm. This one was a tornado. The entire gang was arrested, and they all had the fifteen minutes of fame they never wanted on page one of the papers.

When she realized things were going south, Pascale contacted Antoine, who came in from Montreal with Bruce Clayton, a lawyer who was refreshingly down to earth. He advised her to turn herself in. After all, what had she done beside take off when she saw the police coming? She had no record, and for once she wasn't actually part of the plan, so no one could turn on her, and he was right. It was the only smart decision in this whole business that had collapsed with everyone inside, including the pigeon, whose wife left him when he was fingered. The bank put him on ice.

Clayton explained that Max could be tried in Montreal for crimes committed elsewhere and eventually sent away. The Quebec Ministry of Justice only had to make the request to Ontario. Roberge, however, did not come to put his hooks into Max — on the contrary, he wanted him as far away from Montreal as possible, so the trial took place in Toronto, and he was locked up in Temagami. Max was off to the Arctic Circle.

A whole pile of crap, that's what the greenhorn had got Max into — and worse than that, three years at the other end of the world — gee, thanks, Roberge. Max kicked himself for hiring this disaster-prone nitwit. Still, no point in beating yourself up every day.

No sense crying over spilled milk, he told Pascale when she visited him. At first she came by plane, which set her down in North Bay, where she rented a car to drive the rest of the way. After a few months, she settled for the bus: nine hours from Montreal, where she was living near Mimi and Antoine. One day, Max asked her if she had money problems, but she said no — she said she used the long ride to calm herself and do some thinking. He didn't know why, but he felt she was slipping away.

Looking at the forest with her in his arms, he knew he couldn't reach her anymore. She was going through the motions of a ritual she no longer believed in. She had taken up her spiritual quest once more. What was it again? Being reincarnated a hundred times, seated in the lotus position with eyes closed, living in the present, the only time that really exists, and awaiting the *bodhi*, awakening, illumination like Siddhartha. So this cut-rate Buddhism she'd practised before had come back to haunt her, was that it? Antoine swore it hadn't. He put her coolness down to the time and distance that separated them.

Free at last after months that seemed like centuries, Max expected to find her waiting at the exit for him, as agreed. Instead, there was Antoine, with a sad smile and his habitual silence. He'd taken time off from his new job at Dorval Airport — having left Air France — to go get his friend in Temagami. They ate in a restaurant at the edge of the forest, surrounded by heavy machinery. The hamburger was awful. Antoine explained that Pascale had been in France for two months and was out of touch. Antoine hadn't wanted to worry Max. He really thought she'd be home for his release, as she'd promised. "I'm so sorry."

They got back on the road, the taste of rotten meat still in their mouths.

"Please tell me what really happened," pleaded Max.

Antoine recoiled: was it that obvious he was hiding things?

One evening a few weeks before she left, he'd dropped in at her place. There was a man. "No, it isn't what you think. There was nothing between them. I'm sure of it."

Max wasn't.

"But they were both embarrassed. I could tell the guy wanted to be anywhere but there."

Pascale hadn't introduced them, and Antoine never saw him around there again.

"Did you ask her about it? What did she say?"

"To mind my own business."

Antoine was Max's friend, and he persisted. He wanted to know if she was ditching Max, but Pascale paid no attention and just kept telling him to stay out of it. She was old enough to "look after herself."

"Did she go to Europe with the guy?"

Antoine didn't know, but apparently not. She'd left the country alone. "But that doesn't mean anything. She could've met him over there."

As the car emerged from the woods, Max ignored the landscape, brooding, trying to understand. So the son of a bitch had waited till he was locked away to move in and take her thousands of kilometres away. Max had no doubt the guy had handled this elopement, this kidnapping. Even though she had agreed to it, it was still kidnapping. Max blamed himself for not being able to do anything about it. How could he, though? Still, any reaction at all would have been better than not realizing.

Eleven years later, Antoine was on a wild-goose chase through the *ghats* of Varanasi. The silhouette of this stranger, this elusive phantom, had once again undermined his existence. Max felt a shadowy world creeping all around him. He was a pawn in a game with rules unknown, especially to the players. All his life, people had deserted him with no warning: first his mother, then his father. Philippe's death was an abandonment too; Pascale, of course, and now David. All of them had disappeared into a shadow world he couldn't shed light on.

The sound of his cellphone snapped Max out of his reverie.

"The Pakistanis have successfully tested a missile," yelled Jayesh, overexcited. "Of course the Indians couldn't care less!" *They should care*, he thought. "You know what Musharraf said? 'We don't want war, but we're ready for it.'"

The crisis was worsening every day, and government ministries were scrambling. Prime Minister Vajpayee had his top three strong men in an emergency meeting: Lal Krishna Advani, Jaswant Singh, and Arun Jaitley.

"They're even thinking of covering the Taj Mahal with a gigantic camouflage net!"

"The Taj Mahal? Seriously? It's a Muslim monument. Why would Pakistan fool with that?"

"The continent's gone topsy-turvy," Jayesh said with a sigh.

President Musharraf seemed to confirm this by saying his troops would be moved from the Afghan to the Indian border. "In other words, they figure that the Indians are more dangerous than the Taliban!"

"That's got to piss off the Americans," Max replied.

"Sure."

According to the media, Washington was preparing an evacuation plan for its sixty-four thousand citizens in both India and Pakistan.

There would be escalation of paperwork at desks and victims at the front. Twenty dead in Kashmir overnight. Poonch, a town on the Indian side, had been bombarded by Pakistani artillery, leaving seven dead and thirty wounded, and of course the Indians had to counterattack. All along the border, losses were piling up, not to mention the jihadists, who had taken over three Indian police stations, including Doda, north of Jammu. Intervention by Indian forces followed a hostage-taking. Blood and more blood. In Azad Kashmir, Pakistan, schools were closed early for vacation due to the bombardments, or was it so the kids could die in the mountains instead?

Violence reigned through the rest of India, too. Perhaps in tribute to the Nazi SS they admired, Sri Bhargava and a hundred Durgas — heads shaved and tattooed with snakes — had set fire to a store full of Muslims, including some children. The doors were locked, so most could not get out. Later, the Durgas danced in the streets.

But what did all this have to do with David? Well, Max had to go back to the beginning and outline everything he knew or thought he knew. First certainty: David had gone off to a place unknown a few days before he was due to leave for Montreal; like James Bond and Genghis Khan, he had disappeared into thin air. His destination was so secret that no one close to him knew where it was — not Juliette, not his colleagues, least of all his boss. Why such secrecy? Second certainty: the day before the attack, David showed up at Imam Khankashi's place. There was a friendship, or at least a connection going back to his prison days. Khankashi had disappeared, too, or rather, as Jayesh put it, was being hunted by his nemesis Bhargava ...

Why all this sneaking around? Not to mention the safe, which was his third certainty. Someone had opened it without forcing it. Who and why? What about the name *Tourigny* on the airline ticket? What was the connection there, exactly? This was no former employee of the High Commission — Max had verified that. Nor did it have anything to do with the Canadian Co-operation Office in Kathmandu. No mention of a Tourigny on the list of participants at the Montreal conference either. A brick wall. Every clue led to a dead end. Max had spent the night backtracking to pick up the trail afresh. No dice. Each certainty cancelled out the others. It was a set of interlocking traps that yielded nothing. He had to find out where David had gone instead of Kathmandu.

"Any news from Indian Airlines?"

"Nothing," said Jayesh. "No mention of a passenger named David O'Brien for Kathmandu or anywhere else."

"What about the competition ... any quick visits to Pakistan, for instance?"

"No. There have been no India–Pakistan flights since the attack on Parliament."

"Natch."

"I could check Air India."

"No point."

"Trains? Buses?"

"Maybe, but we'd never know unless he travelled first class, which he wouldn't if he didn't want to be traced. He didn't mention the trip to anyone. The only thing left is the Volvo."

"The car was in Delhi the whole time. Juliette and Béatrice used it."

"He could've asked Luiz to drive him somewhere for a few days then bring him back."

"He'd have to take Luiz into his confidence, but not Juliette or Vandana." Jayesh seemed doubtful.

"Depends what he was hiding."

20

Flags and flowers, heavy, downcast faces and dark suits — Juliette didn't know how long she could keep this up: hand extended to receive condolences from people she didn't know and whose sincerity she couldn't gauge. The ritual was just one more "must" for the ants on the diplomatic sandhill, all of them anxious to show the public how big-hearted they were. The funeral home on Laurier was the place for one to "be seen" this week, if one was to convince one's superiors of one's superior character and attachment to one's country's values.

Other majorettes and cheerleaders inhabited this senseless parade. Béatrice, for one, was reliving the death of Philippe. So was Bernatchez, who held Juliette close the moment he got there with his wife, Geneviève, and they stood on either side to keep her from collapsing or committing some gaffe or other, which would be understandable but better-avoided just the same. More crying? No way! *She held herself erect, not shedding a tear, despite her pain.*

After her chaperones had left, Juliette couldn't take it anymore and fled outside. The vibration of her cell-phone distracted her from her anguish while she walked around the block.

"We're on the edge of a hint of a trail," Max said. "David didn't go to Kathmandu with Vandana."

Juliette was lost.

"I haven't got a theory about that yet, but trust me. What about your end?"

Juliette told him about her visit to Madeleine Morency. Maybe the cops were right after all. This Rodger was none too bright. He was capable of landing in a hospital without getting up to speed, not knowing if this was a good time or not for one of his amateur capers. It was tough to imagine murderers, organized perfectionists without a doubt, recruiting such an underachiever to finish off David when he didn't have a prayer. There was silence at the other end.

"Max?"

"I'm thinking about this Rodger Morency character."

"He's a red herring."

"Maybe not. Put yourself in their place. They're led to believe David is at death's door and will never regain consciousness, but really, in secret, he gets gradually better …"

"Yes," said Juliette, "but they still wouldn't have sent that jerk. He'd spill it all, wouldn't he? He'd tell the cops, 'Someone paid me to kill David O'Brien.'"

"Not necessarily. The cops figured it the same as you, so they're expecting an Al-Qaeda hit team, and instead they get Johnny Jellybean. Their mistake was letting their imagination guide the questioning."

"So Morency's smarter than he looks."

"That's one possibility among many. He realizes pretty quickly that the cops don't think he's capable of anything like this, so he plays up the stupidity. He's made for the part, and he's got his bumbling record to back him up: 'So I'm not that dumb, eh? You've seen my file.'"

"A barrel of laughs, but why go through all this to get rid of David? What's the point?"

"Anything else you learned?" asked Max.

"Luc Roberge knows you're in India and what name you're using."

Max was unconcerned. "They can't find me now. I'm safe."

"This guy seems like a tough one."

Tough, maybe. Persistent, for sure. He'd latched on to Max ages ago and had never let go. Pretty ironic just the same, he thought. Except in his early apprentice days, Max had extorted huge sums without any real difficulty, and now came this undertaking, which wouldn't net him a cent, just the satisfaction of unmasking his nephew's killers, and he still had an army of cops on his tail, with this bulldog Roberge as determined as ever.

He was finding the life of a fugitive increasingly unbearable. He thought he was free, but it was just one more mirage. His criminal "career" had bought him the freedom of running farther and farther ... from himself in some ways.

"Roberge blackmailed Patterson," came Juliette's voice from the other side of the world. "He knows things about you."

Forget about it? Tell her to mind her own business? Max's hand passed over his face as if to get his thoughts organized. "Patterson was having financial problems, and I had money to launder, so he laundered it for me."

Max could feel Juliette's disappointment at the other end. She was expecting something a little spicier, worthier of Roberge's delirious imagination, something to do with dark, smoky basements. *Sorry, lady, economic crimes are hardly ever that sexy.*

"But why?"

How could he explain? What should he tell her? Should he open up to her in a way he never had before? Okay, he'd saved Patterson, but only to keep an old promise to Philippe. If Patterson had been ruined, David would have suffered, too.

Juliette understood now why the former diplomat had been so cowed. Luc Roberge could bring him down along with Max.

Despite Max's help, there was still the same uneasiness between the two men. Patterson continued to keep him at arm's length from David, just as Béatrice had done. His activities were still illegal, despite the fact that Patterson had benefitted from them in his darker days. Was Patterson afraid Max would use his "slip" to blacken his reputation with David and Béatrice? Or maybe turn him in to the police, something Max would never do. Out of respect for Patterson? No, not that either. Max cared about David and didn't want to make his world any shakier than it was. David needed someone strong in his corner, like Patterson, instead of a dishrag of a shady uncle.

"Don't go by appearances," he told Juliette, "I'm not doing this for you or even for David. I'm doing it for myself, that's all, to be at peace with myself."

She said nothing.

"I'm not an honest man, Juliette. Everything Béatrice told you about me is true."

Juliette replied, "She says you could've prevented your brother's death."

There was moment's silence. Juliette felt she shouldn't have mentioned it, but she wanted to know. That was all. Béatrice hadn't gone into detail.

"I could've done things differently. I could've got involved, but Philippe asked me not to. I shouldn't have listened to him. One of these days, I'll tell you the whole story." Then he added, "There's a plaque in San Salvador on the house that used to be the embassy."

"Have you been there?"

"Yes. I wanted to see where it happened. I know it's dumb, but I had to be on the spot where he was killed."

"What did you feel?"

"Nothing. I was so sure there'd be something of him left there. Call it what you want: a flame, a spirit, a sign of some kind. I stood in the office, right where he proba-bly fell. I didn't experience a thing, except a great deal of pain, and it wasn't worth crossing the Americas for that. I went to where Pascale died, too, and it was the same. I didn't feel anything but sadness and an incredible sense of waste that just needed death to cap it off."

There was a long silence, and Juliette realized he didn't want to say any more.

After a while, she said, "Hindus say the universe wasn't created out of nothing the way Christians think, but from the ruins of older universes."

Up to this point for Max, Juliette had just been David's widow, his nephew's companion. Now he realized she had a life of her own, her own dreams, secrets, sadness, and beliefs. "You're interested in Hinduism?" he asked her.

"A bit, superficially, anyway."

"Pascale swore by Shiva, Ganesh, and all those other bozos. The apartment smelled of incense all day long, and I had the feeling we were on one long pilgrimage."

Shiva in particular was her favourite Hindu god. One day, facing a statue of Shiva Nataraja, with its four arms, Pascale explained that the lower right hand, with the palm showing, indicated, "Fear nothing. I will protect you. *Abhayamudra*." Max shrugged. He'd never dreamt he'd need the protection of a watchful eye from a benevolent foreign god. *How do you pray to it?* he wondered. *Oh well, no matter.*

"This Pascale," said Juliette, "was she …"

"A crook like me, the best there was."

In his most depressed moments after Pascale left, Max felt like just another pigeon on her trophy shelf.

Imagining her as treacherous, faithless, and nasty like this was the only way to forget her. Yet even slandering her to himself he couldn't get her, or the memory of her body against his own, out of his head. *Eyes that never look away from one another, hers brighter than ever, that sudden glow I will never forget.* Sister Irène's call from the far corner of the globe had confirmed it for him: this was the only woman he'd ever loved or ever would.

21

Goa, 1510, and the Portuguese were on the beach, wading through the water, watched by the natives as if hypnotized. Alfonso de Albuquerque wondered: would this do as a trading outpost? Why not? It would boost Portugal's economic power and eventually compete with the British, who would need a base to the north in Mumbai and one to the east in Kolkata, and the French, who would open another post in Pondicherry in the southeast. It was an ambition that the Portuguese would take quite seriously ... more than just commerce, a colony. The French and English would just wait politely on the dock, not daring to impose themselves, not for the time being, at least. They'd trade discreetly, almost apologetically, but the Portuguese had no such scruples, and from the very beginning, their machine was running at full throttle, not hesitating before the huge task of "civilizing these barbarians" and forcing the Portuguese model on them, as they were soon to do in Africa, Brazil, and Macau. All the French and the British saw in India was a place to make tidy profits for their adventurers in commerce and finance. The Portuguese would be adding soldiers and priests to the mix. Goa was a proper colony, and when the Portuguese finally withdrew, after the Indian Army invaded in 1961, they left curiously empty shells behind on the beach, in the form of Portuguese-sounding names, European-style women's dresses, and, inevitably, Catholicism.

This explained Max's sense of déjà vu as he stepped into the small Roman Catholic cemetery. It was created by the Indians from the former colony who had been exiled to the capital. Its tombstones, cenotaphs, and sepulchres scattered pell-mell over the hill, it could have been a cemetery from Douro or Algarve transplanted to New Delhi.

A woman in black stood before the family crypt. She was the mother of Luiz Rodrigues, the young High Commission clerk who'd been killed along with David. Her white hair was tied back and held in place by her shawl. Her shoulders were stooped, her hands clasped against her stomach like a Madonna abandoned by her Portuguese god. She gripped her rosary with all her might, as Max had seen Sister Irène do after Pascale died. Ten years already. What had happened to the little nun? Probably gone back to France by now to spend her remaining days in a retirement home for missionaries in Toulouse or elsewhere. Her cell would be full of exotic souvenirs, and she'd have trouble getting used to their bland-tasting food. She'd miss the bright and vibrant colours of India.

When the woman in black saw Max and Jayesh, she reacted with exasperation. *Must be two more of those policemen*, she supposed. She hated it when people kept asking the same questions over and over, and now it looked like it was happening again.

"We're not with the police," Max assured her.

She shooed them away. "I've already told them everything I know, now get off my back." She turned to Max. "The Hindus, the Muslims, those degenerate barbarians. Let them kill one another if they want to, but leave us alone."

Max told her he worked for the Canadian Secret Service, and the government was taking the deaths very seriously. He even questioned the honesty of the Indian investigators. "After all, they owe their rank to the BJP, now, don't they? They all eat out of the same hand at the Ministry of Home Affairs. You don't expect them to put themselves out for an embassy clerk, do you, and a Catholic as well?"

That appeared to convince the grieving mother, who must have been thinking exactly the same thing. Her face softened, and a white lock of hair slipped out from under the shawl. As she fixed it, she asked them to follow her. They accompanied her to her home a few streets over, as she insisted on speaking to them only in the presence of her family. It was a modest but tidy house, filled with crucifixes and images of the Virgin, as well as framed photos of Luiz, each with a black ribbon across the corner. The mother of the young man sat beneath the largest frame and began to cry once again into her lace handkerchief. A young girl, timid and silent, with large dark eyes, put her hands on the woman's shoulders. This was her eldest daughter, Teresa — Luiz's sister — the only family she had now. Teresa cast an accusatory glance at Max and Jayesh, as if to blame them for everything.

Max waited for the sobbing to end, then asked, "How long did Luiz work for the High Commission?"

"Since we arrived in Delhi. He wanted so badly to find a job that he visited all the embassies on foot for weeks."

"As a clerk?"

"As anything."

"Did he ever mention David?"

"He loved working for him."

She had dried her tears by now, so her daughter got up and left them alone. That was a good sign. At least it showed she trusted them.

"Did he ever mention any travel plans David might have told him about? Or any other plans at all?"

"He never talked about his job."

"Except that he loved working for David?"

She looked up at Max and said in a strident voice, "My son has nothing to do with any of this."

"Oh no, that wasn't what I meant …"

"But you think it. You have from the start. Luiz wanted to die in his own explosion? According to you, he was some sort of kamikaze, a martyr like those fanatics in Al-Qaeda!"

Teresa was alerted by her mother's rising voice and came back into the room. Max tried to calm things down. "As I told you, the Canadian government wants to clear this whole thing up. I haven't come halfway across the world to find just any culprit. I've come to identify and arrest the people who killed your son, or those who ordered it done."

"Luiz never hurt anyone."

"I'm sure he didn't, ma'am. He was close to David, and they did see each other several times before the attack, am I right? David might have told him he was afraid of something or threats someone might have made."

She shook her head. Luiz hadn't said anything.

"Please concentrate. Perhaps some passing reference, an insignificant comment, something that might mean nothing to you, but …"

"He was a bad driver."

"Excuse me."

"'Mr. David's always distracted.' He said that to Adoor one night when he came here for supper."

"Adoor Sharma, the watchman at the O'Brien house?"

She nodded. "Good friends, they were."

"Distracted over what, did he say?"

"He had lots of worries."

"Did Luiz say that?

"No, Adoor did, that night, and Luiz said, 'He's right, Mama, Mr. David's quite concerned, but the others …'"

"Yes?"

"'They're not there for real.'"

"What did he mean by that, I wonder?"

She shrugged. "I reminded him to keep to his own business, just concentrate on work and avoid gossip, especially with Adoor."

Well, David certainly took his work seriously, but how *seriously?*

"Perhaps it had to do with a trip?"

"He never mentioned a trip to me."

Max looked to Teresa. She shook her head too.

"Is Adoor still recovering?"

"No, he's fine now."

22

*F*ine was hardly the word for it. Adoor Sharma had on a stylish grey *lunghi* and a shirt that was just a bit too small so that it squeezed his waist, slicked-back hair, and his tattooed arm was holding a canvas bag. This was your local thug, Indian-style, the kind who flexes his muscles only around those weaker than himself; now, for instance, as he was harassing some poor girl. She was about sixteen, or less, a pearl, a flower of a girl. Each time she tried to get away, Sharma grabbed hold of her sari.

Yet, despite appearances, there was nothing original about this imbecile. Max and Jayesh had parked on the street and paid a boy a few rupees to watch the car. They were in a part of town even the most daring tourist guides didn't know about. Young girls, children, their faces made up with kohl like adults, but still not able to look older, stood in a row or crouched like beggars in front of Hindu temples. This wasn't a place for charity, though. It wasn't begging bowls or mango leaves they held out to passersby, but their own underfed, emaciated bodies that would probably grow no more.

Max was disgusted. Behind every victim there was a family to support. Selling your body for a few rupees was better than picking through the garbage with the sacred cows.

"They live in the *basti*, the slum over there," shouted another boy they'd recruited for car-watching duty.

Street children? Not exactly, since the whole slum was on the street.

And there was Adoor Sharma, turning away from them.

"Pimp?" guessed Max.

The boy shook his head, no. Mama and Papa were the pimps. Max imagined the *bachas* in the chaos at the end of the day drowsing under filthy sheets while their parents counted out the rupees on the packed earth.

Holding a piece of ripped cotton, the sari of the young prostitute, Sharma moved on to business. A few slaps to show who was boss. She let out a cry of fear to which no one responded, except Max. Sharma never saw it coming. His shirt came apart under the impact, and the blow to his legs floored him. Not such a tough guy now. More like a wet rag. The threat of a fight had stirred the group and their clients, who were all watching, except the young girl, who had fled. Jayesh seized Sharma by the face with one hand and hauled him up. He stood there, trembling and frail.

"We want to talk to you," Jayesh said in Hindi.

Sharma's terrified face looked from Jayesh to Max. This *chootia*, this SOB, was quite a coward. He stammered, "I haven't done anything, I swear I haven't."

"Of course you haven't. You have an excuse. You're still sick, aren't you?" said Max.

All of a sudden, the watchman seemed to grasp what the two were after. "I had a fever!"

"You haven't been to see a doctor, though, have you?"

"You don't go to one when you're sick, just when you're rich!"

"Poor you, with your fever, all alone in a corner."

"I might've been contagious." A sly smile crept over his face as his confidence returned. Sharma had fooled the police, and now he could do it with these two. He straightened. The second time he didn't see it coming either, as Max doubled him over with a heavy blow to the stomach. From his knees, he grimaced and moaned like a dying man. The customers and hookers dispersed as they realized this was only going one way.

Jayesh forced Sharma to stand up again. Max got closer, oh-so-close, and fear returned to Sharma's face.

"They needed someone inside the house to tell them when David came and went, so they paid you off with a whore or some *baksheesh*."

"No, never. I had nothing to do with it!"

"Why don't we ask these girls, say the one you were just beating up? Maybe that one over there? Malaria or no malaria, I'm sure someone saw you around that day."

Sharma's eyes darted around, and Max knew he'd struck a nerve. That night, instead of guarding the house, the fool had come down here to play the tough guy, then got back in the wee hours, just as the boss was leaving for work.

"Okay, so I come down here at night, but nobody ever paid me."

"You tell that to the police?"

"I didn't want trouble. I don't want to have anything to do with all that."

"All that what?"

"You know, the war."

"You think the attack had to do with the Pakistan war?"

"I think nothing. I just hear what people say, that's all."

"Like your friends in the RSS or the Durgas?"

"They're not my friends. I don't know any of them. I don't get into politics."

"Maybe someone promised you a job as watchman at a ministry, or chauffeur, maybe."

"I haven't done anything, honestly."

"Did you meet them at a demonstration? Was that it? Or some looting, perhaps? Say, you do the restaurant, and I'll take the butcher shop. You rape the old ones, and I get the young ones!"

"Not me, I didn't do it!"

"I bet you've got your membership card with you, photo, engraved swastika and all, plus Bhargava's signature."

Jayesh picked up the cloth bag Sharma'd dropped and inside found a wallet with banknotes: American and Nepalese.

"Hey, hey, now you've got me real interested! So you did the safe, too, eh?"

Sharma tried to get away as his fear turned to panic, but Max and Jayesh were too fast for him, and had no problem wrestling him down. Things just picked up where they had left off momentarily. No one was coming to Sharma's defence, and no one was going to ask them to take it somewhere else. Each was in his own world and had nothing to do with anyone else's.

Even panic was not enough to risk telling the whole story. A nod from Max, and Jayesh kicked Sharma in the head. He crumpled to the ground. Overkill? Maybe. No, Sharma was still moving and conscious.

Max bent down. "You know something, and you're going to tell us right now. Got it?"

Blood from Sharma's nose spread fast and dark against his grey shirt. He raised his eyes to them.

"Who did it?" asked Max.

"I don't know. I swear I don't, but Mr. David was scared."

"Scared of who?"

"He never told me anything, but I could see he really was frightened. He was always looking behind him. He was nervous."

"What of?"

"I don't know."

"A trip he was taking?"

Suddenly, Sharma's expression altered — surprise, even astonishment this time. The watchman looked away, but it was too late. Max noticed the shift. The trip — even the cops didn't know about it.

"You know where he went, don't you?"

Sharma hesitated, and the terror showed again on his face. Then resignation. *These two aren't from the government, so I'm okay.*

"One morning, early, when I went over to go on duty, I heard him on the phone to a hotel. He was reserving a room."

"What hotel? Where?"

"In Srinagar, the Hotel Mount View."

Max was perplexed.

"The strongbox. That was you?"

"Yes, I knew the combination. That is … a cousin of mine sells them."

"So you took the money."

"I was certain the police had already searched everywhere, but when I looked inside …"

"When there was no one else around."

"Yes."

"What else was in there besides the tickets?"

"I just took the money."

"No documents, other things, letters?"

"I'm telling you, I just took the money."

23

In prison, Max had received pictures from Philippe, taken when he was on duty in the Moroccan Sahara, pictures of him with local dignitaries appropriately costumed. In one, taken in a *souk*, for example, you could see merchants selling him baubles and grinning from ear to ear. Then, more serious, as befits a "diplomat," he was seated at a mahogany table with officials in European dress, as well as dusty-faced rebels with Kalashnikovs over their shoulders. Philippe's piercing gaze reigned over all — people, situations, insoluble crises — and everywhere he went, he got respect. He inspired people to be on his side and work with him, to feel that serene strength backing them up. His warmth didn't smother or suffocate, but reassured. Max had experienced it as a boy and understood why everyone reacted to his brother the same way.

Philippe had just finished a three-year stint in Rabat and was on his way back to Ottawa to await his next year's posting: Ankara, Turkey. In the meantime, he'd be Mr. Average Suburbanite with his young wife, Béatrice, a translation student who'd wound up at the Canadian Embassy in Tokyo a few years earlier. She was expecting to teach English to the offspring of the "Japanese economic miracle." Then the two had fallen madly in love, and after a lengthy engagement, got married in Rabat. During the long vacation, Philippe had brought his bride to the North Pole to introduce her to Max. She was the very model of an ambitious diplomat's wife: refined, elegant, fiercely intelligent, and ready to sacrifice all for her husband's career. Philippe was beyond doubt a superior being, and so was she, forming an elite duo that, before long, would be unstoppable.

By his side, Béatrice was more like a guide than a shadow. In the thick of things, Philippe didn't have time to stand back and assess every situation with regard to long-term ambitions. Béatrice directed from the wings, and, with exceptional mastery, steered him away from errors of judgment that might hurt his career.

Tokyo and Rabat had been remarkable turns. Of his class, now scattered around the globe, Philippe held the most promise. His finesse, his intelligence, his gift for languages — one year in Tokyo and he was already speaking Japanese — as well as his innate flair for negotiation and human interaction, put him far ahead of the others.

Lost in his "zoo" up in northern Ontario, Max had no idea about Philippe's transformation, or the refinement he'd undergone. Still, nothing had changed between the two brothers. Except Béatrice. The first time he met her, Max saw that the young woman was ill at ease with him. She'd have preferred Philippe to keep his distance, but that wasn't going to happen, so she never accompanied her husband again to Temagami. Philippe often brought Pascale with him on the long drive. These were the happiest moments of Max's incarceration, with Philippe's travel stories and their chats together, all three of them. Everything seemed so easy, simple.

Now, Max found himself reliving the nightmare of Pascale's disappearance, of his return to Montreal in 1980, of the parole conditions that prevented him from packing his bags and going to look for her. He wanted to search every single city and country and house, to walk the streets of the world to find her and bring her home with him and restart their life together. He could forgive her; anyway, it wasn't her fault. It was his for not being there when it mattered. He'd let her down.

"Maybe you should give her the benefit of the doubt," Philippe had said when he was asked for his opinion.

Max hadn't expected this answer. He wanted to send her name and description to every embassy and consulate in Europe. "People have to renew their passports from time to time, don't they?"

But then what? Max knew her. She was probably travelling under an assumed name, and fake IDs were easy to get anywhere.

And, anyway, the benefit of *what* doubt? He knew she was gone and wasn't coming back. Getting her home would take more than his brother's fine and empty sentiments.

"That's what really hurts, her going without saying a word."

Philippe was right about his pain, though. It just got worse and worse. He had no hold over any of this, like a small boy who doesn't get to have a good cry.

"What could you have done, anyway?"

Max had no idea. Maybe things would have turned out exactly the same. At least ...

"She's gone. That we know, and I'm sure she had reasons we can't even guess at. The fact is, she chose to go, and all you can do is rail at the way she did it."

Ever the diplomat. Philippe was discussing this like some inter-tribal conflict in New Guinea: what you do is get each side to consider the other's perspective. The problem with that was they were talking about a ghost. Max was out of arguments and walled himself up in silence. There was nothing Philippe could do to help. Max just had to muddle through on his own.

The next day, instead of reporting to his parole officer, Max crossed the U.S. border at Windsor after an all-night drive, flashing fresh fake papers prepared by Antoine, though Mimi was against it. "You'll dig yourself in deeper, Max. What you need is just the opposite. You need to make yourself look squeaky clean. How can you be any good as a con man with your face plastered over every police bulletin board in the Americas?"

He had a beard now, but it did nothing to hide his suffering, and anyhow, he didn't give any more of a damn for her advice than for his brother's.

Detroit, all lit up, was still a depressing sight. No use hanging around here, so he kept driving till he couldn't keep his eyes open and stopped in some quiet, nameless burg with deserted malls and fast-food places. Still, the motel was full up. Finally, he got a room at the far end of a long row of different-coloured doors and slept a deep, dreamless sleep. He ditched the car in a vacant lot and went south on a Greyhound. His convalescence was definitely over and his new life — his American new life — was underway, but first he had to visit the guru Guvani.

Already Max could pinpoint when it happened, the precise moment when things fell apart between him and Pascale: similar, but not identical to a host of little things he'd not noticed at the time. One day he'd found Pascale searching for information on one guru Guvani, who followed in the footsteps of Bhagwan Shree Rajneesh, a Tantric Buddhist all dressed up in red and who had a hankering for the lifestyle of a maharajah. In the 1980s, he was expelled from the U.S. and fled to Poona in India, where he'd founded his very first ashram in 1974.

Guvani appeared to fall right into step behind his mentor and his competitors, even recruiting the same consciousness-deprived people who'd become jaded toward Western faiths. Guvani even cultivated the same look, minus the red, which he replaced with green, and the used-car-salesman smile. At first, Max had thought Pascale was after the guy's money.

Why abandon Bay Street, Wall Street, and Rodeo Drive for a secluded ashram in Ohio's Hocking Hills? Then again, why not? We all need a fresh start now and then, Max figured. Eastern philosophy was one opportunity. Pascale had other ambitions, though, or rather none at all outside of "transforming" what she called her "life connections." She subscribed to the guru's publications, listened to his meditation cassettes, and even got a small woven rug — probably made by kids at some hole in Rajasthan. She sat on it every Sunday morning and chased away evil thoughts.

At first, Max wasn't concerned, especially since she was as effective as ever. Meditation had given her a clearer grasp of things, and that was a plus in their line of work. He soon lost his illusions about that, though. He realized she was hiding things. Instead of visiting friends in Europe, for instance, she went to Ohio. He found out Guvani had taken a liking to her ("There's nothing to worry about," she said, "He's above sexuality, not like Rajneesh."). That probably accounted for the lecherous smile and the habit of scratching his crotch. *Ah*, thought Max, *the old priest bit*. It worked every time, generation after generation, whatever the religion. It would be just a matter of time before he whipped off his apple-green *dhoti* and frolicked in the fields with his Vestal Virgins.

Then there were the fights and door-slamming, and making up, too. Misdeeds confessed to and half pardoned, swept under the little Rajasthan rug and saved up for the next round. Max had taken Guvani for their next pigeon, and now it turned out he was the pigeon's pigeon. Max was furious. They were after the guy's fortune, but no, he'd taken advantage and stolen what was most precious to him: Pascale, "his" Pascale.

Once in Ohio, Max wanted to see this ashram up close and confront the fraud. At least they spoke the same language, so they'd understand each other perfectly. Instead, he found a modern, up-to-date man, not the sandalled refugee holding court in the luxurious living rooms of bored do-gooder ladies. No, this Guvani was as simple as they come, a diminutive person with too much of a tan for these parts, and his smile was definitely not lecherous. It bore the same fatalism he was to see on many Indian faces later on; millions, in fact. He wasn't rich, either. Max could tell not only from the way he lived, but also as he rifled through his bank accounts and investments. Max had called on a few of his contacts for this. No dice. This guru had nothing, or almost nothing. It was the students who profited from his teaching, not him. Possibly the carpet-seller or the cassette-maker ... who knows?

Brad Wyles — in charge of rooting out victims of esoteric or religious cults — whom Max met in New York, confirmed it. This was Wyles's life-long mission, and he'd like nothing more than to nail Guvani, but the guru was literally above suspicion. He'd gone over the man's early life, as well as his connections in the U.S. and India, with a fine-tooth comb. He'd even sent fake devotees to spy on the ashram and offer him money, cars, yachts, or (more discreetly) investments in tax havens, and they'd been sent packing. He had nothing. He wanted nothing. Even the fanatics clinging to his parka (well, it was winter after all) made him want to get rid of them. Ironically, that just whipped them into more of a frenzy ... Pascale most of all.

Max was like a rabbit in the headlights of this UFO. He was paralyzed, unable to do a thing, least of all use reasoned logic. Pascale would listen to no one, nothing but her own impulses. She was plugged into her own soul with an ardour that literally scared Max. Then one day, the fervour simply disappeared. The prayer rug joined its secular fellows in the back of the closet, preceded by the meditation cassettes. The cure was as sudden as the onset of the disease. Max was just too happy to bother asking why, and their lives picked up where they had left off, in a way. Guvani was gone from their conversations and lovers' quarrels.

In the summer of 1980, when Max got out of prison, Guvani still reigned over the ashram in the Hocking Hills. The master was a little stooped, the smile still resigned, and his modest means the same. His advice was the same as Philippe's. Why go looking for her? Just respect her decision, that's all.

Later, Max did pick up Pascale's trail, when he found out she'd been living in India for years. Perhaps her separation from the guru was just strategic and temporary. Perhaps she'd just wanted to cover her tracks and make things hard for Max, and he'd fallen into the trap. So maybe the man's naïveté, his candour and blindness, had actually been a smokescreen to hide what she was up to after all.

"A swindler like me. The best of the lot."

24

The only way to get past this is to look straight ahead, to project myself into the future, thought Juliette. *From now on, I'm unshakeable; I won't let anything stand in my way. I won't let David disappear, no, never. He entrusted me with his memory, and I won't let him down.* The basilica was packed, obviously. It smelled of rain all the way to the altar. Everyone was wet and uncomfortable. Juliette turned toward the choir and saw Deborah Cournoyer — whom she'd met briefly in Patterson's office — near the organ. One more glance at the body. The Canadian flag was wet, too. Droplets evaporated with the incense. In a trembling voice, Raymond Bernatchez was describing to all a David who was truer than life. Everyone held back tears.

They carried out the coffin, and Juliette fell in behind, accompanied by Béatrice. The younger woman raised her head. Deborah Cournoyer was no longer in the choir, though Juliette spotted her a few moments later getting into the back of a Subaru parked on Saint-Sulpice. Patterson closed her door, and the car rolled toward the Old Port. When Patterson turned around, he saw Juliette. He hesitated. It was as if Juliette had noticed something she wasn't supposed to or been found somewhere she wasn't supposed to be.

Juliette went over to the consultant. "Who was that woman?"

"Excuse me?"

"Deborah Cournoyer, who is she, really?"

Patterson reacted to the question like a slap in the face. He sighed, looking around for a way out, and then sighed again to signal that he didn't want to talk about it. But Juliette stared him down without blinking, and he had no choice.

"She was Philippe's mistress for a number of years. In fact, right up to his death."

"I don't want this business suddenly coming out in public." Now I know what she meant.

The prime minister's favourite caterer had the young wait-staff from the Institut de l'hôtellerie slinking around on cat-feet. There were more flowers, bouquets of them, and a large photo of David, a holiday picture at least, and guests around the buffet table, hesitating between the sauerkraut and the tandoori chicken. Dennis Patterson had done things up grand, as always. Despite her grief, Béatrice was slipping from guest to guest like a bee among flowers: it was just another cocktail party really, a bit tragic of course, but the same rules of etiquette applied, nevertheless. Bernatchez fluttered from one businessman to another with his customary ease. Was this to be a last tribute to David or a chance at privileged access to the high commissioner? To ask the question was to answer it.

Juliette couldn't stop thinking about what Patterson had said a few minutes before and about Deborah Cournoyer's discreet presence at the funeral. Béatrice must have suffered from their relationship. Juliette watched her mingling with the guests and saw her in a new light. She forgave her mother-in-law's insistence, her hurtful comments, her condescending attitude toward people in general, especially to Juliette. Must be a defence mechanism built up over the years. Was David in the know? Surely not. Béatrice could have used this woman to tarnish her deceased husband's reputation, but obviously hadn't. It was to her credit.

Suddenly, Juliette felt she'd had her fill of deconstructing the past, and she took advantage of the general melee to slip discreetly away to the kitchen. The fridge — there had to be some ice. Then her cellphone began to hum. This time it was really crackly on the line.

Max brought her up to date on what he'd found out about David's fear and nervousness from Luiz and Adoor, the watchman; the call from Srinagar in the heart of Kashmir as war threatened between India and Pakistan; David's return to Delhi with his well-kept secret most likely increasing his nervousness and fear. David apprehended what was about to happen: the kidnapping and torture, the explosion under the used Volvo.

"What do you get from that?"

"The attack wasn't a blind, gratuitous, or isolated act. David was not simply in the wrong place at the wrong time, as Patterson and the High Commission people think." David had been selected from among all the diplomats in Delhi for a reason. What that was, Max did not know, but he was going to find out, of that he was sure.

"Kashmir?"

"Maybe."

That Indo-Pakistani wasps' nest, where both terrorist groups operated — Hizb-ul-Mujahideen and Lashkar-e-Taiba. Home of Jaish-e-Mohammed, of Harakat-ul-Ansar, and Al Badr martyrs. "A violence-and-horror competition in its rawest form." Sponsored by Genghis Khan and his jihadis? Sure, why not?

"Maybe the Indian cops were right after all."

"Khankashi plays the moderate, denounces 9/11, and pretends to distance himself from Al-Qaeda, while secretly fanning the flames. David's his buddy, his confidant, so he gives him one more mission … in Kashmir, the lion's den."

Now it was Juliette's turn to be puzzled, as her old theory surfaced again. "So David was charmed by the imam? But that's not like him, not at all." She was wondering more and more how well she really knew her husband.

"From here on, one of two things will happen," said Max. "Either David comes back disillusioned, convinced he's been used for his 'diplomatic neutrality,' and there's a shouting-match in the mosque ('I'm going to turn you in publicly, Khankashi') — but denounce him for what? — no idea, maybe referring to the recent spate of terrorist attacks or his links to ISI. Genghis Khan is walking on hot coals, and David's a troublesome witness, so there's a phone call to one of his nut jobs."

"Or …?"

"Or the Hindu extremists — say, Sri Bhargava, James Bond, for instance. The Hindutva fanatic."

So far extremists on both sides have been banging away at each other while foreigners look on complacently. Maybe David violated this "convention of indifference." Maybe.

"I have to get to Kashmir and retrace his steps," said Max, "see what he saw, pick up his trail in Srinagar at the Hotel Mount View."

Juliette no longer knew what to think.

"Be careful," she said.

The porter at the Liverpool Guest House seemed to be as sleepy in the day as at night. Leaning over a greasy samosa that stained his receipts, he held the room key out to Max without even looking at him. On the terrace, travellers in pyjamas drifted to and fro in slow motion like lily pads floating lazily on a swamp. Not quite the same ones as the day before, but popped out of the same mould. Max was about to slide the key into the lock when he noticed something to his right, or rather someone. An Indian was looking over the message board where the hippies exchanged tips and news or exhibited their poetic talents. Discouraging to read.

Something about this Indian didn't fit. He wasn't an employee. Max was sure of that.

Despite his typically Indian look — shiny pants and belted shirt — he was peering hard as though searching for a *jalebi* recipe or a travelling companion to Annapurna, but what caught Max's eye was the fact that he was *too* normal. That stood out. Something was definitely off.

Instead of going in, Max pretended to have forgotten something in the lobby. The porter had finished his samosa and was perusing the register with the energy of one halfway between life and death. At the bottom of the stairs, however, just in front of the door to the street, was another Indian, definitely not a beggar or a shoeshine boy, but dressed the same as the other and with the same fake debonair attitude. This one had something else going on that Max would have recognized anywhere, anytime … he was a cop, just like the terrace guy. There were probably two more already in his room with guns drawn.

Max was just able to slip past the counter without being seen and dive for the stairway on his left. It led to the roof. Being painfully silent, he climbed the stairs one by one till he faced a door. He pushed it open and was blinded by the sun. After shielding his eyes, he saw five more of them in khaki uniform, and, as he turned to go back down, he found himself face to face with the plainclothes cop from the street. That was it. The only possible way out was to bluff.

"Look, *sahibji*, you're making a serious mistake. It isn't what you think." Then lightning forked through his head and everything went black. Another blow sent him to the floor. The cop he hadn't seen coming gave him a massive blow without even taking a wind-up. Max tasted blood and tried to protect his face with his arm, but it didn't help. It was raining hammer blows non-stop.

Lying on the terrace floor, Max didn't even have the strength to moan. The beating had happened without a word being spoken, almost like a ritual. He was barely conscious. He saw boots approaching, probably a *havaldar*, his footsteps echoing on the tiles as though his head were jammed inside a church bell. He waited for the boot to finish him off, but the voice said, "Okay, the masquerade's finished, O'Brien."

25

Juliette and Vandana fell into each other's arms and then set off for coffee and a chat, the way Juliette had done so often with David. Before leaving for India, they'd lived at the Somerset in the Glebe district, an apartment block swarming with Western members of Parliament when it was in session. The rest of the time, it housed wandering diplomats. A life that was reminiscent of, David liked to say, being "young" again. She was right. He would never get old.

"Mr. Bernatchez asked me to come with him," Vandana explained, "For the conference ..."

She had said too much, and regretted it. But Juliette smiled. "No, no, I understand. You don't need to feel bad because you're standing in for him. Anyhow, you're better off here than there at the moment, aren't you?"

Vandana's face clouded over, and there was a long silence before she said, "The people running my country have gone completely crazy."

They're firing mortars all along the Line of Control, she explained, killing the usual innocent victims: a young woman and five civilians in Garkhal, thirty kilometres from Jammu. At Naugam, in southwestern Srinagar, an Islamist militant was killed by Indian soldiers. It was the same on the Pakistani side — civilians caught in the crossfire, and the media were mostly watching Kazakhstan in the former USSR, especially the city of Almaty, where the regional summit on Asian security was being held. Atal Vajpayee and Perez Musharraf were the stars right now, of course. They alone out of the sixteen heads of state could stop this war.

Talking international politics is her way to keep from crying about David, thought Juliette. Besides, she was glad to see her friend, whom she'd always liked. In Delhi, the young woman had been the first one to visit their home in Maharani Bagh and set Iqbal straight before he stepped too far out of place ("Domestics expect to be treated as such. Otherwise, they think we actually don't respect them."). Juliette had balked at that, coming from a background where equality was the rule, and she was finding it hard to adjust to a country where inequality was the basis of society. Vandana often guided the couple around the *mohallas* and government stores on the weekends. She was able to deflate some of the rug merchants' usual self-assurance, and furniture salesmen used the division key on their calculators more often. David and Juliette had managed to save a lot of money because of her.

Later, at Jawaharlal Nehru University, Juliette had relied on her to correct her Hindi pronunciation. Vandana was the first to tell them about the similarities and common roots between Hindi and French. Both of them were derived from the mythical Indo-European language, which in India had become Sanskrit, thence to the Mediterranean Basin and Greek, Latin, and so on … *Two, seven, nine, ten. Do, saat, nau, das.*

"Few oppose the war. For a peace march in New Delhi," she explained, "four hundred people are nothing. And we're in the homeland of Mahatma Gandhi!"

Major/great + soul (âme) = large soul.

Maha + Atma = Mahatma.

"Meanwhile, embassies lie empty now: Iran, Israel, South Korea …" There was no hiding Vandana's disgust. "The leaders of the BJP really want to sock it to the Pakistanis."

"Why didn't you tell me about Kathmandu?" Juliette asked.

That startled Vandana, though she was expecting it sooner or later. She lowered her eyes. "I don't know. To protect David, I suppose, or rather myself. When I found out he'd lied, I was afraid." Her eyes were moist as she looked up at Juliette. "I shouldn't have done that, I know."

Juliette took her hand for reassurance. No one dear to her heart should feel responsible for David's death. "It wouldn't have changed anything, Vandana, not a thing." Then she said, "I'm pregnant. 'A new universe created out of the ruins of the old,' is how to see it, according to the *Mahabharata.*"

Vandana seemed happy, and she grabbed Juliette's hand and squeezed it. Then, not able to bear it, she turned away. "They've arrested Max O'Brien. Bernatchez told me just after I landed."

Yet again, the world collapsed around Juliette's head.

26

The pain in his face, especially his nose, was excruciating. The cops had really done a number on him. He still had on the same clothes, and his shirt was stained brown with dried blood. Any glimpse of daylight blinded him. Max O'Brien turned his head just a few centimetres, and the effort it required was colossal. He could make out a white wall and a solid door. He thought he was in hospital, but the hammering of boots on the metal floor brought back to him a reality he knew only too well. He was in prison, not a hospital.

An Indian prison.

Here in these cells they piled up foreigners and fed them disgusting slop they had to pay for out of their own pockets. Corrupt guards and bureaucrats — he felt abandoned by all. Soon he'd find out if all those clichés in movies were actually true. He was probably in

Tihar, the same place they'd imprisoned Genghis Khan. At once, he stopped struggling. What was the point? When he woke again a few hours later, it was night. It had to be the next day, and the cell was lit by a naked, yellowish bulb, which made everything seem like a funeral wake. He could hear boots in the corridor once more, but muffled this time. Near the bed was a tray of food that had become a playground for cockroaches, overpopulated like the whole country.

His head still hurt, but the pain had become more diffuse and came in waves like the sea when the tide ran out. At least now he could breathe, and he could smell curry. He retched for a good long time, hoping he could drown all the parasites. He knew he wasn't alone, even before his eyes were fully open. He raised the lids, which, surprisingly, didn't hurt anymore. A familiar silhouette sketched itself against the white of the wall. An unseen guard announced that he was awake, and the silhouette turned round. He made out William Sandmill of the High Commission, not knowing if that was a good thing or bad. What did it matter, anyway? Another man appeared behind him, sweaty and wiping his brow. Sandmill bent over Max, smelling of cologne and wearing a Bulova with a metal bracelet, striped tie, and wrinkled suit. Little splashes of colour and light here and there showed that reality was imposing its presence. Max tried to get up, but his head throbbed. Sandmill put a hand on his shoulder as a signal to stop moving.

He smiled. "Mr. O'Brien. Have they been treating you well, not caused any trouble?"

Treated well? How would he know? He'd been unconscious since ... um ... when, exactly?

"Two days."

Sandmill pointed to another man putting away his handkerchief. "Josh Walkins, RCMP." So this was the Canadian government's token presence kept on the sidelines by the Indian police. "I've got some good news," Sandmill went on, "You're being shipped home. The High Commission's reminded the Ministry of Home Affairs that our two countries have an extradition treaty, so it got fast-tracked."

This was Walkins's cue. "You're lucky, O'Brien. Here in India, counterfeiting and fraud are serious crimes, especially in a country on the verge of war and all that ..."

Max still didn't get it. "So why am I being sent home?"

"Because you belong to us," said a third man from behind the other two, "and you won't be going anywhere after that." Max would have known that voice anywhere, as Sandmill and Walkins stepped aside to let the third party look him over with a triumphant grin. Max closed his eyes and his headache returned, worse than ever. There was something more repulsive than an Indian prison, after all: Luc Roberge.

The detective pointed across the cell to his suitcases. "I picked them up for you at the Hotel Oberoi. You can't say I don't look after you."

The traffic was sheer hell. The road to the airport was jammed with taxis, trucks, government cars, and all sorts of vehicles — destination "some place peaceful." The word was out since morning from every embassy. Washington, London, Berlin, and Auckland had all ordered their diplomats and expats to leave; the same with Ottawa.

"Visa-hunting season is open," declared Sandmill, who was at the wheel. "People will do anything to get out of here."

This explained the choked roads, cars filled with anxious families, kids jammed into backseats, suitcases hastily crammed inside and pushing up against the roof of every car in a fanfare of horns from impatient drivers.

Walkins was sitting in the front, and he swivelled round to address Roberge. "Can't really blame these poor buggers. In Almaty, Vajpayee and Musharraf never even spoke to each other, no matter what Beijing or Moscow say."

"China's kicking itself for helping Pakistan build the bomb in 1998," explained Sandmill, "and now the place is so unstable that no one's in charge, least of all President Musharraf."

"And that's before you add in Kashmir as well."

More dead, tens of dead, hundreds of dead, even thousands or millions if the two countries carried out their nuclear threats.

The day before, Minister Advani adopted a harsher tone. If Pakistan wished to avoid being bombed, it would immediately hand over twenty terrorists they were holding — extremists whom Musharraf and Inter-Services Intelligence were protecting.

Roberge shrugged. He couldn't care less. He finally had Max O'Brien sitting right next to him. So what if the world went up in a mushroom cloud? He had his man and nothing else mattered.

"The Americans can't do a thing," Sandmill shot back. "There's no point in trying to cool the situation down. It won't happen. It never does."

Walkins frowned. "Strategically, they need to get involved because of Afghanistan. The Pakistanis mustn't abandon their western frontier to go fight India on the other side of the country."

"Still, there's no way their mediation can work. On the one hand, India wants Pakistan to stop jihadis from crossing into Kashmir …"

"As if Islamabad could control anything in the country anyway, especially in Azad Kashmir!"

"… and on the other hand, they deny even having any terrorists in their country in the first place."

"So it's a war of wasted words."

"Still doesn't stop the Americans from begging India and Pakistan to settle things without going nuclear."

"I get why the Indians are antsy," Walkins went on. "On the ground, they've got every advantage, but missiles, well …"

"All the Pakistanis have to do is take the offensive. Then …"

Traffic jammed all of a sudden, turning the road into a huge parking lot. Kids from the neighbouring *jhopadpatti* took advantage of the bottleneck to peddle knick-knacks. Max watched them wave their rags, running from one car to another. At least for them the threat of war was a boon, a real business opportunity. He thought about the Pakistani school kids in Kashmir on forced holiday in shelters and refugee camps.

Sandmill turned on the radio. "Maybe the airport's closed."

Roberge suddenly woke up. "Is there another one?"

"For local flights only," Walkins said. But the Indian authorities had assured him there wouldn't be any problems.

"Yeah, but they're swamped, your authorities." Roberge was irritated now.

Back to the pen?

Then, fortunately, traffic started moving again. On to the next slum. The radio talked about Kashmir and exchanges of mortar fire along the Line of Control. The dead were piling up, and already the clinics were flooded with wounded. Max couldn't figure why on earth David had travelled up there for just a few days before Montreal, when the situation was critical even then. Maybe his intuition was right: going to Kashmir and taking part in a conflict that wasn't his went way beyond David's mandate. Maybe that was the reason "they" had got involved.

After the Kashmir junket, was it the Hindus or the Islamists? James Bond or Genghis Khan?

"I've become just like him. I feel just what he felt."

So David was up to something there: some move, some kind of action, probably heroic and/or risky. He was just like Philippe, bound for the same life and the same destiny. His initiatives had been tolerated up to that point, but then he apparently crossed the line for some group or other. What was it? What hornets' nest had David stuck his nose into? Max tried dredging his memory of the papers at the time. He vaguely remembered articles in the *New York Times* and other U.S. dailies, about the tension in Kashmir and renewed conflict between the two countries ... some event. Whatever it was, Max couldn't remember, but one thing was certain: David had chosen that very moment to sneak in. Was there any connection between this secret trip and the upcoming mission in Montreal expressly to reassure Canadian investors? There was no way to tell. There was no one left in the know. He could imagine Roberge's sarcastic reply if he broached the subject. The best he could do was pass his information along to the Indian police, which meant the BJP, who would diligently hide it away or use it for their own purposes.

Close by the airport, traffic was snarled again, but planes were taking off with reassuring frequency. Roberge was in a good mood again. It would soon be time to ditch him, Max figured — in the confusion on the way to the counter in the departure lounge, maybe. But how? Roberge was younger and in better shape, especially given Max's rough time in jail. Max was starving, and his head still seemed about to burst with every movement. Then there was Walkins, too, certainly armed. Sandmill was less of a problem, but he still needed to be dealt with. Three against one was a tall order.

The car pulled into the terminal parking area before he could properly gather his thoughts and work out a plan. The two cops, on the other hand, already had things mapped out. Walkins had arranged for their Air

India baggage check in the VIP room of Terminal 2, out of sight of nosy passengers. A young woman guided them through a crowd of Westerners gathering in front of the counters of their respective airlines. Kids lounged on the floor with their Game Boys, their parents vaguely anxious but relieved to be at the airport. Max recognized some of the diplomats from the party the other night — flashing the middle finger of defiance to the terrorists. They weren't quite so sure of themselves anymore. This was to be a quiet, uneventful slinking away.

At the far end of the waiting room, in a stuffy area stinking of cigarettes, a chubby government official stood waiting for them with a sheaf of papers. Roberge quickly scanned them, while Sandmill and Walkins watched from the sidelines. Walkins kept one eye on the prisoner, and Sandmill couldn't stop looking at his watch, likely waiting for the cops to tell him he could go back and finish packing. Would there even be a plane out the next day, or would he have to barricade himself with the other late-leavers in the High Commission?

The papers were signed, and Roberge tied his tie; one more step completed. He looked at Max. "This is the moment I've waited fourteen years for. You have no idea how happy this makes me."

Max saw the Indian official leave, and past him was the hall where passengers were ready to depart. It was the only way out, and led nowhere.

"You know, I'm gonna miss you," Roberge said. "Your picture's still on the wall behind my desk. Reminded me to keep hunting you. Yessir, that picture ..."

"How about I send you another one? More up to date?"

Roberge burst out laughing, got up, stretched completely, then noticed the mini-bar. He bent down for a look: two cans of Pepsi and plenty of peanuts in case Air India ran out. Roberge sat down facing the prisoner and offered him one of the Pepsis. Max declined.

"Yes, I wish they'd kept you in one of their jails. Ten years times, say, five, the way things are. I'd make sure our union boys sent you a postcard every single day. Whaddya say? A card for a prisoner, now that's depressing, am I right?"

Geez, five hours on the plane listening to this kind of sarcasm, not to mention the stopover in London; Max felt nauseated already. Was this his chance? Nope, Walkins and Sandmill were chatting right by the door. That would be straight-up suicide.

An Air India flight attendant in a sari of the company colours arrived to guide Roberge and Max to the plane. There was good news: the company had upgraded the two of them to first class. Roberge was as excited as a kid in the front row of a puppet show. All the peanuts he wanted and more he could take back to his family.

The waiting room was empty now that everyone was on board, and Max said goodbye to Walkins and Sandmill. What would he do now? Grab the flight attendant as a hostage and drag her into the concourse? That was going too far, even for a Bollywood movie script. Gentlemanly, Max shook hands with the two men. Then came the long corridor, a welcome from the cabin crew, and the smell of disinfectant. The 747 was full, but two places in first class awaited Roberge and his guest, and the cop had the decency not to make a display of his hunting trophy. The people around them paid no attention. Roberge pushed Max over to the window seat.

In a blasé voice, the captain apologized for the delay (probably because of Roberge and his prisoner), then announced still another, a shorter delay. The flight attendant asked them, "Would you like a drink?"

"Mineral water all around," replied Roberge. "I'm on duty, and so's he!"

She got it, of course. She never drank alcohol herself.

This was going to be a long trip, really long. Roberge was positively glowing.

"At least admit you regret all these stupid stunts you pulled," he said a few moments later as he sipped his Bisleri.

"That would change what exactly?"

"Maybe get it off your conscience. Always helps."

"Look, if there's one thing I'm sorry for, it's not doing even more damage. I let you off easy, really. I mean eight million isn't so much." Max had absolutely no intention of feeling sorry for himself or playing the sad little puppy to try to soften up his jailer. In a way, the cop was right to resent him: those millions the Sûreté du Québec union had been forced to take off the books of its investment fund, the incredible promise of huge returns, and the risk-free investment Max and his team had peddled to those suckers. This trap had finally closed on him, just like all the others, but the sound was sharper this time ... and what about their union head who'd wanted to invest even more in it? Eight million, period. Max could just picture the meeting afterward, the anger of the police officers, drained by the naïveté of their broker. All our savings to Max O'Brien!?

"Don't you wonder how I caught you?" inquired Roberge, taking another sip of mineral water.

"Béatrice and Patterson."

"Juliette wasn't so easy. Still, a charming kid, just the same. I bet she doesn't know the part you played in Philippe's death."

"SHUT UP, ROBERGE!"

Passengers whipped around in surprise. Roberge was content just to smile. Max wished he hadn't got carried away.

"Delhi was child's play," Roberge went on, "the night watchman at the Liverpool Guest House is a police informant."

Of course he is.

Max stared out the window. At the edge of the runway there were more slums, people living just feet from the planes and breathing their fumes all day long, never able to talk above the constant roar of 747 engines. Max reclined his seat and closed his eyes so as not to have to listen to Roberge, then willed himself to sleep. Philippe in El Salvador; Philippe the martyr. He finally did sleep. He had no idea how long. Then a voice stirred him.

"Excuse me, sir." The flight attendant, no longer smiling, held out her hand as he opened his eyes. "This way."

Max turned to look at Roberge. He was fast asleep with his bottle of Bisleri spilled all over the tray. The plane was still on the runway, so Max had only dozed a few minutes. He followed the stewardess to the front of the plane. Passengers vaguely glanced at them before returning to their newspapers. The door was still open on the opposite side from the embarking platform. Airport employees were almost through loading food trays on carts with multiple shelves. One of the employees turned toward Max: it was Jayesh. He guided Max down the sloping platform to the catering truck parked next to the plane. The flight attendant followed them. Once inside the truck, Jayesh gave Max some coveralls and an ID badge. The flight attendant also changed clothes as the truck drove to the storage depot. The inside of the truck smelled of industrial *chapati* and stale fried food, but for Max it was the sweetest smell in the world.

"Thanks, Jayesh," he said.

"Don't mention it."

When the door opened at the depot, Max saw the pilot finally get the plane moving at the far end of the runway. Ragged kids were hanging around the tarmac, but they weren't at all interested in the 747. They were completely preoccupied with just surviving for one more day. That was real poverty; kids who didn't enjoy watching a plane take off. Max imagined Roberge's face when he awoke ten thousand metres in the air, alone with nothing but an orgy of peanuts to comfort him.

Jayesh put a hand on Max's shoulder: "Have you heard the news? The Canadiens have re-signed José Théodore!"

27

Hari Singh was the last maharajah of Kashmir. A Hindu at the head of a mostly Muslim state, unable to choose between India and Pakistan, he had taken refuge in Jammu a few months after Partition.

"To make himself useful to the Indians?" asked Max.

"More like to wait and let events determine his political position," explained Jayesh.

Hari Singh hadn't left Srinagar of his own volition. In the fall of 1947, the mountain horsemen of Pakistan had set out for the Kashmiri capital, intent on laying waste to it, and then, while they were at it, annexing the entire region to Pakistan.

"So the dream of Kashmiri independence went up in smoke. An independence no one wanted them to have, for strategic reasons above all."

It was stuck between Islamic Pakistan (a consolation prize from the "international community" after the foundation of the state of Israel that same year) and India, victimized by the caste system and prone to anti-Muslim pogroms, not to mention Tibet to the east, soon to be occupied by Maoist China. There were sentimental factors as well. Kashmir was the entry to Hinduism from the twelfth century B.C. It was also the homeland of Nehru, who, with Gandhi, fathered the modern Indian state.

The approach of the men from the mountains forced the maharajah to request support from New Delhi, which in exchange insisted on the annexation of Kashmir, an offer Hari Singh could not refuse. Indecision is always the worst policy of all. Still, the Indian Army did come to the rescue of Srinagar and succeeded in pushing the invaders back to a few kilometres from the capital. Then stagnation set in, as though the leaders on both sides had studied nothing but the First World War and the Battle of Verdun. This was often the problem with Third World armies, Jayesh said. They were economically too weak to support their military advances.

Then the newly created UN got involved and established a ceasefire line, which is pretty much unchanged to this day. To the southeast lay Jammu and Kashmir under Indian control, and to the northwest, Azad Kashmir, under the Pakistanis, perpetual losers in the wars with India. Now, for the first time, both powers held equal strength due to the nuclear evil that both could deploy.

Buses overflowing with refugees filed past the Maruti, one of many convoys the men had passed on their way out of the capital, *tongas* (horse-drawn carts), as well as other animals whipped on by kids. Such was the ignorance of the poor who thought they could escape nuclear hell by moving a few kilometres farther down the road. Specialists estimated the outcome at 20 million dead. Already, cameramen were in the capital to preserve the mushroom cloud for posterity, as well as the evening news, the first great nuclear boo-boo of the twenty-first century.

Jayesh managed to weave his way between two trucks and get back to the main highway, which was now clear. They spent the night in Chandigarh, then Jalandhar and the Punjab near the crossing into Kashmir at Pathankot, which was swarming with soldiers. Next, they reached Samba, crawling along in the middle of an interminable military convoy. In the opposite direction came Kashmiris headed south in cars smothered in cheap suitcases, and more buses bulging with refugees. This was still an exodus, though different from the better-policed and more "Western" one from Indira Gandhi Airport, despite the numbers. Here, it was a total free-for-all. Only a few kilometres west lay the border of the Pakistani sector where all hell was raging.

Jayesh's car was practically the only civilian vehicle headed back north. Fascinated emigrants shook their heads when they saw Max, just another crazy foreigner with a death wish. Ever since he arrived in Asia, he had the feeling people had been trying to open his eyes and teach him a lesson, but perhaps it was really a distraction or a diversion.

"Why?" he wondered aloud. "What are they hiding?"

Jayesh shrugged. "That attack on David, pretty effective, eh?"

"An organization?"

"Killers are careful people, tenacious too. Nothing gets in their way."

"What are you getting at?"

"Well, we're a long way from our goal, so their attempt to get us off their trail is working pretty good."

"So we're not a threat anymore."

"Not in the least."

"So that's why no one has lifted a hand against us, except Roberge, of course."

Jammu looked like a big resort town after summer holidays were over. It felt abandoned: dusty streets and closed shops with windows boarded up. A capital without its people, mostly Hindus, who were now in flight amid the usual disorder. A ghost town inhabited only by soldiers in combat gear. The "real Kashmir" was still farther north. That was Muslim Kashmir. The wondrous valley. Max would have liked to go on, but they couldn't because of both the curfew and the mountains. Twelve hours of twisting and weaving along the road through steep-cliffed valleys and long, deep ravines. Bad roads invaded by Indian troops sent to support the one hundred thousand already around Srinagar. A few kilometres away from Jammu there would certainly be another roadblock. At best, they'd have to retrace their steps. At worst, they'd be thrown in jail, especially since

Max had no travel papers. The counterfeit IDs Antoine had made were all seized by the cops at the Liverpool Guest House, and even if Jayesh could eventually get him a fake passport, Canadian or other, they'd never get one good enough at Jammu.

They had a another big problem. Max was known to the Indian police now, having escaped extradition, supposing that Luc Roberge had sounded the alarm, and there was every reason to believe he had. Roberge was a proud man, and he'd just been handed a huge humiliation, but he'd still have to get the fugitive tracked down.

The Hotel Sinbad on Canal Road had a pale-skinned manager taller than most Indians. The biggest surprise was his blue eyes and his grey, formerly blond, hair, but despite his European look, the man had an Indian accent. Jayesh told Max that some Indian Kashmiris were descendants of Alexander the Great's troops who decided to settle here instead of returning to their native Greece, a country which, at the time, was tall and blond, not yet mixed with Balkan or Turkish people as it would be in the following centuries. According to legend, the racial purity of these soldiers had lasted to this day. Max realized how this genetic "curiosity" contributed to the Hinduization of the country. Jayesh added that Hinduism had arrived from the north and been imposed on the Dravidians in the south. Thus India was divided in two: the Brahmanic culture to the north, based on purity, and the caste system dominated the Dravidian culture to the south. It was hardly surprising, then, that Untouchables were mainly dark-skinned, and the Brahmins, priests and higher-ups, were lighter.

Their rooms proved spartan but clean, and catered, as advertised, to tourists and travelling officials — so, really, everyone. Line of work? Journalist. What else could you say? A half-dozen of them lingered in the hall, headed, like Max and Jayesh, to Srinagar in the early morning. They were posing as hard-boiled "loose cannons" flying by the seat of their pants at their own expense.

Max fully expected the city still to be marked by the assassination of Abdul Gani Lone, the moderate independence leader, pushed out of the spotlight by the war. Here and there a Durga had scribbled his emblem, a stylized snake emerging from a marigold, on the walls, but nothing else. Horror had given way to terror already.

The noise of Jeeps and military trucks didn't prevent Max from sleeping; he was worn out from all this time on bad roads. At seven in the morning, he was brutally awakened by blows to the door. The reception clerk (didn't this guy ever sleep?) was there with a tray carried by a young Dalit, as though this place were a five-star hotel. There were corn flakes, tea, toast with marmalade, and, once again, *The Times of India* with the headline: WAR IN A MATTER OF HOURS.

The bus was Jayesh's idea. So was the camera. To allow troops to get around easily, intercity transit had been cut back to the minimum, so this vehicle was crowded, and Max found himself as just one more human sardine. There were mostly foreigners, several of whom had stopped over at the Sinbad. Is this the way David had done it? It normally took twelve hours, but today with the military convoys to make way for, it required three or four more.

Udhampur appeared on the far side of the ravine, the last large town before Srinagar. It too was full of soldiers. Then they started out again, bobbing and weaving as always, with hairpin turns and endless waits for convoys to pass. The road was very narrow in places, and reduced to a single lane at best. The ravines contained the carcasses of rusted-out vehicles abandoned after their tumble as much as ten, twenty or thirty years ago. The driver knew what he was doing and took what seemed like senseless risks, overtaking on the edge of ravines, with one hand on the horn and a smile on his face, then whiplash braking behind vehicles loaded with explosives, or accelerating on the long curving declines, as though exempt from the law of gravity.

The first roadblock was at the Banihal Pass, about halfway into their sixteen-hour journey. There was a smattering of police mixed in with the soldiers. Max showed his camera by way of ID: "We're journalists on our way to an appointment in hell." It worked. Then off they were again, fast. The waiting, the dangerous curves. At night, all of a sudden, beyond a moon-shaped mountain, was the famous valley. The heat returned, as well, and there was Srinagar, or so Max guessed, behind the blackout and human presence despite the curfew. Tons of frightened people were hunkered down at home as was their habit these past fifty years.

There was a densely packed crowd at the bus terminal. That was hardly a surprise. People had spent the night there to get the first bus out in the early morning for Jammu. A board on the wall had about fifty ads for hotels and houseboats. Max found the Mount View

Hotel, while Jayesh was haggling over the price of a rickshaw. It was curfew, and the police would be patrolling, but the rickshaw man knew shortcuts and byways, so they relied on him to avoid that sort of problem.

They headed out into the Srinagar night, which a few hours earlier had been like a dark spill of lava submerging houses and businesses. Unlike Pompeii, where all life had stopped instantly, one could see that behind drawn blinds, down dead ends and under the eaves of houses, a world unknown was bustling. The beauties of Srinagar, though, were not to be seen. Every street corner had its sandbag piles, and here and there improvised guard towers had been raised by the Indian Army. Surveillance posts, some of them brand new, others dating from the late eighties, remained from the last really nasty turn in events.

The Mount View Hotel was part of the collective mourning. Its once-luminous sign had been turned off for months. The glimmer of a candle appeared through a parted curtain. There was no other sign of human habitation. The place had its charms, though. It must have been fully booked in the past, but the rear garden where the clients could breakfast or relax — bombardments permitting — had not been kept up.

"Are you phoning from prison?" asked Juliette, when he managed to reach her that evening. Max burst out laughing.

28

The immense register, like those in all hotels long ago, unfortunately held no mention of David. Max's nephew must have had no difficulty using an assumed name. India wasn't in the habit of requesting any ID, passport or other, when one rented a room. Max had already noticed this in Delhi, but the corpulent, stern-faced owner recognized David from the photo Max showed her.

"How many days did he stay?"

"One night I think."

"Was he alone?"

She nodded.

"What did he do? Make any appointments, visit the city, receive any phone calls?"

"Shabir!" she yelled.

The handyman was elderly, frail, barefoot, and dressed in a *salwar.* He seemed better prepared for hunting flies than for painting or woodworking. The owner conferred with him, intoning in a language Max didn't recognize. He later learned it was Kashmiri.

Shabir tilted his head one way, then the other, as though on the point of falling into a trance or passing out, but he was really saying, "I know some things, but only at a price." Jayesh held out a few rupees, and Shabir slipped them into his *salwar* as imperceptibly as a magician. He remembered David, oh yes, because he was the only Westerner in the hotel, in fact the only client who hadn't stayed shut up in his room, especially with the curfew.

"Where exactly did he go?"

This brought a fresh round of nodding and rupee-ing. They'd never find it, he said, without someone who really knew Srinagar the way he did, having lived there all his life. Oh, the horrors he'd seen. More rupees to help him bury the past.

The capital sprang back to life in the daytime, but still a life under military occupation. Armed men looking for possible terrorists patrolled the squares, streets, and markets constantly. David had probably taken this same route and passed the same patrols. He'd no doubt laid out the rupees, too, and that was exactly why he was remembered. The old man walked steadily in front of them, as if he'd done it hundreds of times, as he surely had. He was right — the city was a labyrinth, and, for an hour, they went through narrow streets and narrower ones, even alleys and inner courtyards, as well as false dead ends that actually did lead somewhere, into dark ways apparently designed for throat-cutting, then to a square a little more sunlit than the others, where Shabir pointed to a rundown three-storey building painted sickly green like the rest of the neighbourhood.

"I brought him here," he said with great authority, as though fearful of not being taken seriously, "He went inside here."

How many apartments were there? Quite a few, judging by the number of windows, some of them covered but showing silhouettes. David had given Shabir a generous tip. Jayesh got the message loud and clear, so out came the roll of rupees. After David went in, which apartment did he go to? Why? To do what? Max had to resign himself to the fact that Shabir didn't know. They had no choice but to knock on every door and show everyone the picture of David, risking a few rounds from a Kalashnikov instead. While Shabir waited outside, the two went in. A chubby type, poorly shaven, wearing just an undershirt, who had watched them from his window, emerged at once from a ground-floor apartment.

"Are you here to look at the studio, is that it?"

Then they heard him fumbling for keys as he went back inside. Then he headed upstairs before them without bothering to close his door. He was painfully heavy and slow, and used the handrail not just for direction, but for support. He couldn't get up the stairs otherwise.

"I have to warn you," he said, coughing, "I can't rent it until things are settled, what with this bloody business and all …"

Max pretended to understand, explaining he'd just arrived in Srinagar and was at the hotel for the time being, so he could wait a few days. The fact that a stranger had showed up didn't seem to surprise the caretaker: he probably wasn't the first to visit. Since things had broken down with Pakistan, the city was crawling with foreign reporters.

"And when do you suppose this 'business' will be over?"

The man shrugged. "They've got other things to worry about, and they say I've already had my commission so I'm not short."

"They?"

He, as if noticing him for the first time. "You're not with the papers."

"We just got here from Delhi."

"Well, you'll have to work it out with them, if you want the place right away."

"With who?"

"*The Srinagar Reporter.*"

Max remembered seeing it on billboards when they got into town. It was a daily, like *The Times of India*, but focused on Kashmir. The concierge slid the key into a lock at the end of the third floor in the back, and opened the door. When he turned on the light, the studio was tiny and disorderly. To the right was an unmade bed. To the left were a table, a cupboard, and a sink. The place had the relative luxury of running water despite the outward appearance of the building. At the end, a half-open door revealed a wash basin and toilet.

The caretaker was standing in the middle of it all with arms folded to show he was ready for questions or criticisms. Max showed him David's photo.

"He may have come here to see someone — possibly you?"

The man looked defiantly at both of them. "Police?"

"Do you recognize this guy? His picture was in the papers last week."

"Never seen him here."

Max put the photo away. So, they were going to have to go door to door. They got ready to leave.

"Strange that a newspaper would rent a place like that," Max said before they got to the corridor.

"Owners."

"*The Reporter* owns this building?"

"Yesss. They wanted to pull it down, but they changed their minds. I don't know why. Meanwhile, they rent. That's how Ahmed got the apartment."

"Ahmed?"

"Ahmed Zaheer." He pointed to the furniture and items scattered round the place, "This is all his."

"And where did this Ahmed go?"

"To Canada. To die."

29

The Srinagar Reporter occupied a modern block on the southern edge of town. The windows of the editorial office overlooked the road to Jammu and Delhi a little way off, which symbolized accurately their basic political stance. The daily was "secular and progressive," and, as their highly vocal and visible publicity claimed, an "All-India Publication Promoting Respect & Understanding Among Indians of All Castes & Beliefs." Deepak Vahsnirian, editor-in-chief, was a sort of Indian Walter Cronkite who spoke in a low voice punctuated with sighs of limited dramatic impact, a gentleman, or trying very much to be one. Any minute now, Max expected him to get out a pipe and start stuffing it like a character in some British film from the fifties. Vashnirian prided himself on being a man of conviction, "not an easy thing in this country, even less in this city."

A Hindu himself, he hired a number of Muslims, and not necessarily as sweepers and cleaners, he hastened to add. He, of course, was a member of the Indian National Congress, "India's great party," chased from power by the narrow-minded nationalists of the BJP.

"Still, those of the Congress weren't always up to the standards of their illustrious predecessors, Mahatma Gandhi and Jawaharlal Nehru," Jayesh put in, referring to the state of emergency proclaimed by Indira Gandhi in the 1970s.

Vashnirian's complexion darkened, and Max frowned. This really wasn't the time.

"We aren't here for politics, Mr. Vashnirian. We'd like to talk to you about Ahmed Zaheer."

"How much does he owe you?"

Max and Jayesh exchanged glances as Vashnirian came round his desk to face Max.

"Oh, you're not the first, you know, and you won't be the last, but you'll not get a single rupee from this newspaper, no more than any of the others."

Zaheer had led a dissolute life, he said: baccarat, roulette, *chemin de fer* — he was better known in Macao than he was in Srinagar, debts all over town, not to mention his attitude. He annoyed the staff royally with his spoiled-child act. "Why he even showed up at the office dead drunk, and quite often too."

Vashnirian frowned. "You Westerners imagine them all on hands and knees toward Mecca with a machine-gun slung across their shoulders, as though most Christians are members of the Ku Klux Klan!" He sighed once more his face becoming sad. "Ahmed was the best journalist this paper had. The most formidable ..."

"The kind Indira would have loved to throw in jail."

More poisonous looks from Max to Jayesh, who raised his arms in surrender, "Okay, okay, I'll shut up."

"Ahmed had, I don't know, fifty years of vacation piled up, and he said one morning, 'I'm going to Sri Lanka for a few Adonises, then ...'"

Max looked puzzled, so he explained: "I didn't tell you he was gay? No one knew except for everybody. I mean he wasn't officially out of the closet and not the slightest intention of even opening the door. And Islam, well, that's a closet inside a closet."

"Sri Lanka? I thought he died in Canada."

"Yes, you're right, Niagara Falls."

Now Max was beyond puzzled.

"He changed his travel plans at the last minute, I suppose," said Vashnirian, then. "A stupid accident, really. He fell, and they only found his body at the bottom of the falls next day." Vashnirian paused. "I suppose he should have gone to Sri Lanka after all." He went on to ask them the reason for their interest in Ahmed Zaheer, and Max improvised a story about insurance contracts Zaheer had signed. The editor showed them the journalist's office, now occupied by a serious young intern with large glasses and curly hair. Anything that might have been of interest had been scattered or destroyed, hardly surprising. There was no hope Zaheer would be careless enough to leave anything the least bit compromising lying around, anyway. Next, Vashnirian invited his visitors to eat in a local café ("if it isn't closed for the bloody war!"). He just had to make one telephone call while they waited in the entrance hall.

Niagara Falls, huh?

A Muslim homosexual, barfly, gadfly, and gambler. What kind of nutbar had David got himself in with?

Jayesh was thinking the same thing. "Maybe your nephew was gay."

Max had wondered that, too. Perhaps all this secrecy was just in aid of an ill-fated love-affair. Zaheer would be the inconsolable lover at the foot of the falls. David rushes over to his place to erase all evidence of their liaison. Sure, why not? *Naah.* "David would never do anything like that with me or anyone else," Vandana had said. What if she were wrong?

It was a tempting theory nevertheless, but didn't lead anywhere. David's trip to Srinagar was nearly two weeks after Zaheer's death, so why wait that long before rushing off to "save his reputation"? And who would then be responsible for the bombing? Come to think of it, there was no proof of any kind of link between David and Zaheer at all. The lady at the Mount View and Shabir, her handyman, could have invented anything for a few rupees more. Even if what they said was true, there was no evidence that David went to Zaheer's apartment that night. Possibly any other apartment for any number of reasons.

The more Max thought about it, the more he had the impression his investigation was founded on hypotheses and witnesses who weren't reliable, starting with Adoor Sharma, the amateur pimp. It was all a house of cards that the slightest breeze could bring down in a heap. Niagara

Falls. Adoor Sharma. The strongbox. Max thought and thought, racking his brain, till an intuition, rather an image, took form in his mind. He rifled through his memory — Tourigny and the phone number he'd tried in vain to identify. He thought for a second and looked up. *Why not?*

Max went over to the reception desk and asked the young lady if he could use her phone. She pointed to an empty room a little way off, and he went in, dialled the number for Canada Direct. The young Acadian woman asked if she could help him. He read her the phone number kept in David's safe "… in the Niagara Falls area code, please." One ring, then two, three, and someone answered the phone brusquely. It was a woman's voice, melodious, professional.

"Niagara Parks Police, Joan Tourigny speaking. How can I help you?"

PART THREE

KLEAN KASHMIR

30

Philippe and his son, two shooting stars, David, with his life before him. New Delhi, his first posting, his very own Tokyo, where he was already outshining others, just as his father had done. Max was convinced of it. Sandmill, Caldwell, and Bernatchez himself had already made their beds in Foreign Affairs with the firm intention of pursuing a career free of ups and downs to a comfortable retirement. Max was not being fair, and he knew it. He really didn't know David any better than Langevin, Vandana, or Mukherjee. But still, the young diplomat couldn't help but be exceptional, just as his father had been. He had to be destined for greatness, again like Philippe.

"I've become just like him. I feel just what he felt."

After Rabat, Ankara, and Bangkok, Philippe had become an ambassador himself, slipping in ahead of one of the prime minister's protégés, a shoo-in whose mentor had promised him Thailand while he waited for a Senate seat. However, the minister of foreign affairs had played hardball, and the Asian Tiger was awakening, so a young wolf was required on the scene, not some sleepy bear who'd get eaten alive. The prime minister had agreed, finally. With the protégé gone to Lisbon, Philippe moved into the Silom Road offices. This was a coup in Canadian diplomatic circles. Philippe was one of the youngest ever named to such an important posting. Max understood better than ever the kind of precautions Béatrice was taking. The rocket was on the launch pad and she was not risking a misfire. Philippe was aimed at the upper atmosphere, and flying close to the sun.

David at ten years old. The photos Philippe sent showed him in front of Wat Phra Kaew, temple of the Emerald Buddha. Piloting a motorized pirogue in the middle of the Chao Phraya. A boy with intelligent eyes and an attentive gaze, curious, hands on his mother's shoulders. "Manly." Keeping his promise to Béatrice, Max answered the last messages from his brother, explaining that security considerations forced him to proceed with much more prudence and discretion from now on. So their little ads to one another in the paper became increasingly rare, till they disappeared alto-gether, though Max never stopped looking for them. Béatrice was surely satisfied. The break was complete.

Thus, after Pascale came Philippe.

Would anything have been different if Max had refused Béatrice's demand at the Plaza? What if he had told her to take a hike and mind her own business? She could not possibly understand the bond that united them, or with Gilbert and against Solange. All three huddled together like players in Sunday afternoon football. Max figured it was the best thing to do at the time, but since Philippe's death, he'd come to doubt his decision, and even more so since David's murder. He kept replaying it in his head over and over, shuffling the deck each time, but with the same result.

What was he doing in India, anyway? Was he looking for his nephew's killers, or was that just an excuse for setting his own house in order, or understanding it at least?

Philippe's life took a sudden turn, Max recalled: fresh blood for the Canadian government's electoral machine, which was badly in need of it. He was rumoured to be "ministrable." Meanwhile in Bangkok, Philippe had not yet decided, but he'd been approached and was "interested" in this scenario. Journalists used to grazing on Parliament Hill found themselves interviewing the ambassador down by the *klongs*, holding their noses against the putrid stench of the water … no connection with the Rideau Canal. Bangkok was an open-air sewer.

The leak came from inside the party, of course, or else Philippe himself. He wasn't about to jump into the lions' den without first having an idea of what the opinion-makers thought of his change of career. At worst, it would be viewed as a meaningless "parachute-drop," a make-up operation, additional proof that Ottawa's opportunistic administration was dead on its feet. Well, none of that happened. For once, the media agreed that the future candidate had potential, that plus the fact that the young ambassador had sent a wake-up call, as they say. Philippe's initiatives in Southeast Asia had shown that Canada was no longer the lapdog of the U.S. Now, it could not only bark, but bite, too. This was necessary to the country's independence. It did not go down well with the American ambassador, but won the admiration of the French and Australians, who disliked the increasing encroachment of the U.S. in the region. Vietnam was still fairly fresh in their minds, and the Americans with their two left feet were not welcome there.

Philippe played his cards right, and his performance did not go unnoticed by the head-hunters. Today the minister, tomorrow the prime minister, and why not? Canadian diplomacy had already yielded Lester B. Pearson, and Philippe O'Brien was cut from the same cloth. The red carpet was rolled out from Bangkok to Ottawa, now it was up to him to commit, and to inform his family ... all of it.

The brothers met at La Guardia during Philippe's stop-over on the way to Toronto, their first contact in months.

"So, what does David think of having the future Minister of Foreign Affairs for a father?" Max asked.

Philippe smiled. "You don't approve?"

"Who am I to tell you what to do?"

Philippe looked ill at ease. The decision had been a hard one, of course. Max could imagine them: Philippe and Béatrice, unable to get to sleep at night, discussing it on the barred verandah of their home. David would be napping, unaware that he'd have to change schools in mid-year, yet again. Max had a hard time with ambition: having any, cultivating it, even considering it a quality in someone. In his line of work, it was a fault, a weakness, a failing, the soft spot for another crook like himself to exploit. Philippe's, though, was not your run-of-the-mill ambitiousness.

"I'm tired of representing people I don't respect or trust. I'd like to change things."

From the depths of the backstage, far from the spotlight, Max could see his brother was taking his new role very seriously. He was as good at politics as diplomacy. He was photogenic, but not smug, and he knew how to play credibly to the camera without being boring or pompous. With journalists, he always had just the right word at hand, the perfect quotable phrase for headlines. He wasn't alone in this, of course. There was an army of scribes ready with speeches and jokes, but he never gave the impression he was just reading from a script, holding forth or making people laugh on cue.

By mid-campaign, he was considered a shoo-in, but that didn't stop him from crisscrossing his future riding with constantly renewed energy; Béatrice and David by his side: the holy family, the ideal family, once more.

"I'm here to learn," he used to say, quoting the Russian hockey players who came to scare the daylights out of North American players in the 1970s. Well, everyone lapped that up and laughed. He was a good learner, and quicker than other diplomats. One day, though …

Béatrice was seated across from Max in a New York café, the second encounter without Philippe's knowledge, and she'd come with a definite purpose in mind that she found hard to put into words. Finally, she came out with it. She'd had a visit from Luc Roberge, who had done his little number about how he respected Philippe and believed, like everyone else, that he'd be a great minister. Still, his job wouldn't let him feign ignorance about the younger brother. The crook, the counterfeiter, the invisible man. Here's what he proposed: if Max turned himself in to the police, Roberge would treat the whole thing "confidentially," so as not to compromise Philippe's budding political career. This is what Béatrice had come to New York to discuss with Max in secret one more time, to ask him, beg him, not to blow her husband's dream out of the water.

"Or else?"

"The usual fanfare."

Never had Max hated Roberge so very much, but what could he do but make the sacrifice? Once more. Was it worth it? Who could guarantee Roberge would keep his promise? What was to stop some nosy journalist from rooting around below the surface of a politician beyond reproach? Then again, what choice did Max have? Could he refuse Philippe, and, in a way the country, the career to which he was already sacrificing his own life?

Of course not. Thinking was required, naturally, over a Scotch in the Westbury on Madison, where Max had set up quarters those past six months. So, Abel was venturing into politics, and Cain was planning his exit. The lightweight but effective organization he'd built up would have to be demolished. Even the operation already underway would have to be ditched. The cadre at Consolidated Edison he'd been grooming patiently for months would have to be left twisting in the wind. Then, of course, there would be prison itself. He hadn't been back since the zoo where he'd been when he lost

Pascale, but one sacrifice deserved another, and Max gradually got used to the idea.

Then, all at once, Philippe appeared in Cobble Hill Park in Brooklyn, taking a break from his campaign. Béatrice had goofed and told him about it. He was furious at Roberge's blackmail. She admitted to being the origin of Max's silence in the *International Herald Tribune*. She drove the two brothers apart.

"Why didn't you say anything to me?"

Max sighed. What difference would it make?

Philippe grabbed him by the lapels. He'd never been violent with his brother before, and now this. "Blackmail is the worst cowardice of all."

"I don't care. I'm ready for it."

"Well, I'm not. What more will Roberge want after this? Favours, free passes, special treatment? Today it's you he wants, but tomorrow what? An in-ground pool, a new car, a cottage in the Laurentians, huh?"

Max broke free. Okay, so Philippe was right, but Roberge's threat couldn't be ignored. He moved away, and felt his brother's arm locking with his.

"I'm not getting into politics to put myself at the mercy of the likes of Roberge, get it?"

"That's just crazy."

"Oh no, it isn't. Honesty and guts …"

"Your voters don't care about all that."

"You're wrong. You are so used to dealing with people's weaknesses you've forgotten they have their good points, too."

Already the politician, Philippe was gearing up for a speech, and Max reproached his naïveté, but big brother wasn't having any of it. Did Max really want to prove that people couldn't be trusted? He could've just ignored Philippe's visit and turned himself straight in to Roberge as planned, but he'd never be forgiven, so maybe Philippe was right. What Max took to be candour was perhaps just courage and determination.

Banking on human weakness was his daily bread, his specialty. Philippe, though, was devoting his life to proving the contrary. His entire existence, it seemed, was based on the notion of pardon and redemption.

Take Kavanagh, for instance. He'd saved the man, even if he didn't deserve it; Solange, too, and now Roberge. Philippe was not going to play the game by the cop's manipulative rules and threats, even at the risk of losing his career.

So it was Max in shadows and silence, and his brother in the spotlight, as always. On the dais, Béatrice was silent and retiring. Wonder what she thought of all this? On TV, she was all smiles, elegance, and refinement — no way to guess what she felt — but Max knew she'd never forgive his selfishness: "You had a chance to redeem yourself." What if Philippe was right, and he, not Max or Béatrice, was in touch with the truth about human nature? Max hoped so with all his heart, but didn't believe it for a second.

The news seeped out discreetly, as though the journalist wanted to apologize for being such a party pooper. A short insert in an out-of-town daily hinted that Philippe had an "invisible brother." Maybe it was worth looking into. Was the public aware that Max, the younger one, was a notorious con man, a chronic repeat offender whose comings and goings were as mysterious as his present location? An interview with Detective Sergeant Luc Roberge, economic crimes specialist, gave a few more details. Roberge painted the picture, true, alas, of an unscrupulous fraud artist, and went on to relate his endless pursuit of this international bandit whose misdeeds sapped the very basis of our society.

It was a juicy accusation that made headlines in all the dailies and news bulletins. Suddenly, Max was the one in the spotlight. Old newspaper photos revealed what had happened to some of his victims, who were only too pleased to soil the older brother's reputation along with that of the younger. All of a sudden, "the successful diplomat" wasn't what captured people's attention, and his exploits in Asia seemed boring. Now what they wanted was his explanation, more information, heartfelt accusations, and fratricide. His advisers thought the same way. Philippe would have to disentangle himself from his wayward brother, a stain on the family's reputation, or watch his rise come to a halt. Internal polls were already dipping, and the Opposition wanted his head before he'd even been elected! The lions were already on him before he even entered the arena.

Philippe insisted on continuing to believe in the power of the truth, and he went into lengthy explanations on TV. He opened himself up wide to the public, asking for their loyalty and confidence.

"If you choose someone, trust him, not those around him." But it only made things worse. His frankness was questioned, and he was suspected of covering up even more crimes.

Official corruption and complicity were implied. What if the failure to put a stop to Max was due to his brother's intervention with the Department of Justice, where he surely had contacts? This was the man to whom they were going to entrust major governmental responsibilities? It would surely come to light that the two brothers were partners in crime with a precise, detailed plan that had been in place for years.

Philippe couldn't sleep. The perfect diplomat by day, he gave the impression this mudslinging wasn't affecting him, but alone with Béatrice at night (David was staying with the Pattersons in Repentigny) he spent long hours at his work-table, haggard and wondering. It seemed that, no matter what he said and promised, his political career was in ruins.

At Dorval Airport, Philippe climbed into Max's car, and the two drove away along the highway to the countryside without saying a word for a long time, till they got to the river's edge, and around them nature in the form of an unattractive, untended forest that guaranteed them privacy at least. For a while, they both stared at one another, not saying a word.

"I could do it this afternoon, if you like," Max said. "I'm already in touch with a lawyer, and he'll make sure it attracts the least possible publicity …"

Philippe smiled sadly. Minimum publicity? There was no such thing. No maximum, either. Just publicity, period. The trap was shut around them. There was no escaping now. Too late for that. Max had been right, of course. Philippe was naive, an innocent soul who did not belong in politics.

For the sake of it, Max went on, "They'll jump on me for sure, but you know what they're like. In a week or two, there will be some other bright and shiny object."

"This Roberge, do you think he'll be content to keep his victory under wraps?"

"I'll make sure of conditions."

"That he'll pay lip service to. He'd be crazy to do any different. All that matters is getting his man. The rest he doesn't give a damn about."

Max kicked a pebble into the river.

"Besides, what difference will it make? It's over, anyway."

Philippe went back to the car and got in. Max hesitated, then did likewise and got behind the wheel. Philippe looked straight ahead without a word. He just stared at the current.

"I'm truly sorry," said Max.

Philippe turned to his brother, smiled his resignation once more, then ran his fingers through his hair the way he did as a boy. "It's not your fault. It's mine, my mistake. I don't blame you."

That evening at the Ritz Carlton, he stood behind the mic, surrounded by distraught supporters and announced his retirement from politics. The hall was deathly silent, funereal. This cadaver exhibited himself returning into the earth before the living. He never should have emerged in the first place. In mere weeks, all of his hopes had been swept away. The solitary man who remained on the stage, deprived of the role he'd prepared for since the beginning of his diplomatic career. Philippe refused to answer questions and comments that came from all sides, leaving that to a volunteer. Backstage, Béatrice embraced him tightly, the only person besides Max he could cling to in this senseless storm, and of course Béatrice hated Max and could never forgive him.

Lost among the gabbling flock of journalists drifting away to the exit, Max was a statue, though inside he felt a strange and uncomfortable sensation: the joy of being free, a joy tarnished by his brother's sacrifice. Philippe's decision had deprived Max of the only redemption available by putting his life in the balance as his brother had done. Philippe, as always, had taken on the entire burden, and Max actually felt cheated by his brother's courage and generosity, by a moral strength that refused assistance.

Max spotted him when the hall was almost empty, and the staff were removing the chairs and other equipment. Luc Roberge was observing it all from a discreet corner of the room. He too seemed disappointed, cheated as well by Philippe's sacrifice. In his world, Max supposed, nothing was free, just bought or traded. Philippe, on the other hand, had given without receiving or even wanting anything in return. He'd ruined Roberge's plans, and Max was still free.

He, in turn, looked back and approached the exit. He hesitated to see if other cops were covering the rest , but there was no one. Roberge hadn't realized Max was in town. He never thought his sworn enemy would be here tonight, so Max left the hotel unimpeded and went back to Mimi and Antoine's. In his little room beneath the gable he figured this Roberge had a good lesson coming to him. The next day, his plan was all set: he'd swindle the investment fund of the Québec Police Force. Sabotage was a game two could play.

31

Hearing laughter made him look around. A pair of lovers was kissing; nothing out of the ordinary, especially here, but an Indian couple, probably from Britain, maybe even India. This is how it was these past few days. All of Max's prejudices about the country had been shipwrecked on reality. So, now Indians were coming to Niagara Falls on their honeymoon. Imagine the looks on the faces of the local hotel owners, who'd just barely got used to Japanese tourists.

They were already providing raw fish at breakfast, served at arm's length by disdainful waitresses. Now they had Indians. Max had already spotted these two at Hertz getting used to right-hand driving, then in one of the restaurants on the main street that provided a view of the Falls.

This was Max's third day back from India, after a series of flights from Srinagar to Mumbai, to Frankfurt, to Detroit. He'd crossed into Canada at Windsor on a bus full of Midwestern American retirees on a trip that began with the Falls. Worn out by thirty-six hours of travel, he'd left them at the floral clock and gone into Hertz, then to the downtown Holiday Inn to change names again, and now India caught up with him in the form of newlyweds.

"Sorry, I'm late!"

Max turned to see Joan Tourigny standing next to his table between him and the Indians, hand held out. She was a determined young woman, confident in her charm, with magnificent blue eyes. Max shook her hand as Tourigny slid into the booth opposite him. A breath of perfume invaded the air.

"Is this your first time at the Falls, Sergeant Sasseville?"

"Call me André," Max said. "No, my second time. The first was with my father and brother when I was ten."

Tourigny smiled, put down her cellphone, then turned it off. This was a small tourist town with not much crime, so cops — especially perfumed ones — could permit themselves the luxury when dining with a colleague. Paradise.

"So you're interested in Ahmed Zaheer?" She seemed genuinely amazed.

"Mysterious are the ways of the RCMP," was Max's answer. "A foreigner dying in strange circumstances, you understand."

"Not really, I mean a run-of-the-mill accident. It happens more often than you think. I was talking to a colleague from the Grand Canyon, and you'd be amazed at the number of …"

"Where exactly did it happen?"

Joan Tourigny was taller than Max. She leaned over the rail that kept the reckless from breaking their necks or doing what couldn't be undone out of desperation. Not Zaheer, though. He'd simply lost his footing and fractured his skull fifty metres below. Tourists made the macabre discovery the next morning and called the police. Next to the body were a camera and a laptop in a thousand pieces.

"Suicide maybe?" suggested Max.

She lifted her head. She'd had to yell above the noise of the Falls since they got there, and now, despite a clear sky, a mist of rain was wrecking her hair, but she gave no sign that it bothered her. Obviously, the young woman was used to life in Niagara.

"Depressives don't usually jump with a camera round their necks and a laptop in their hands."

"What if he were pushed?" yelled Max.

That surprised her. "What on earth for? If he had a record or was into organized crime, okay, maybe, but this isn't that."

On the way back to the car, she added, "His computer was finished, but by some miracle, the camera was practically intact. We developed the film — great pictures of Niagara. This guy had talent."

"A photographer, then."

"That's what we thought at first till we got in touch with his paper in India."

Tourigny and her team had found a hotel key on the body, so they went there to search for an address and phone number. What turned up was contact information for the *Srinagar Reporter* as well as drafts of articles on Niagara Falls as the new tourist hot-spot for Indians wanting a real change of scene. "It's the Chinese thing all over again," Tourigny continued, "all those years we thought they were starving and poor, then one day we woke to find they owned half the businesses in town."

Max's serious expression made her think she'd blundered, so she hastened to apologize. "Please understand. They're fine people, and if they want to invest here, well, that's just great!"

When they got back to town, her car slowed behind a dozen tourist buses and ground to a halt.

"Does the name David O'Brien ring any bells?" Max asked.

Tourigny's mind was somewhere else, and she managed to slip between two huge trucks, then got back up to cruising speed.

"Yes?"

"O'Brien, David. He might have called you about Zaheer's death."

"Nope, the only person I talked to was his editor-in-chief."

"Not family or friends, say, who might've come to claim the body?"

"No."

A while later, Max asked, "Do you follow international politics?" — Tourigny registered surprise — "A car explosion in New Delhi last week with a Canadian diplomat in it?"

"Oh yeah, right, I heard about it."

"That was David O'Brien. We found your name and number at his place."

Now it was her turn to go quiet. "You think Ahmed Zaheer was involved?"

"That's what I'm trying to find out."

Jordan Harbour, about twenty-five kilometres from Niagara Falls. A motel was situated on the edge of the highway, the kind of place one picks on the fly with no reservation. There weren't many customers. It probably only filled up at peak season in July and August. There was only one car parked out front. Max figured Zaheer would have chosen isolation over proximity to tourist attractions, but, in fact, the journalist had really made his life complicated. Jordan Harbour was practically an hour's drive from the Falls, and Max remarked on several places with vacancies along the way, all of them just as cut off as this one, so was Zaheer just a solitary soul, or was he in hiding? If so, from whom or what?

His room didn't yield any clues. It was simple, anonymous, and hadn't been occupied since his death, though his personal effects had been removed by the police and shipped to Srinagar, according to the owner. He was perplexed to see Tourigny again and answered Max's questions politely and precisely. Zaheer had not received any visits or made any outside calls.

Nor had he been there long, barely two nights, and then was hardly ever seen.

"Was he driving a car?" asked Max.

"Oh yes."

"Niagara Rent-A-Car," Tourigny filled in. "It was parked not far from the accident, and we returned it to the agency."

"Nothing in it?" Max asked. Tourigny shook her head.

Nothing at all, except Tourigny's name and phone number at David's, no connection between Zaheer and the young diplomat. In fact, everything so far put distance between them, except India itself, of course, but there had to be something. What was it?

That night, after saying goodbye to Tourigny, Max left the Holiday Inn and checked into Zaheer's motel. He asked to have the same room, though he didn't really know what he expected to find. He took a long, hot shower that numbed him, sat on the bed, and dialled the phone.

32

A gay Muslim and compulsive gambler ... in Niagara Falls, thought Juliette. *Found dead at the bottom of the walkway. Was he a journalist following a hot tip? No, just a very straightfoward article on honeymoon vacations, Indian style. For the* Indian Geographic Magazine.

"That would explain the cover story about a wedding in Sri Lanka," Max offered. "He was supposed to be exclusive to *The Srinagar Reporter*, but he was topping up his salary with some freelance stuff for the competition in Mumbai."

Nothing suspicious or unusual in that, thought Juliette. *Zaheer was telling all kinds of stories to his various employers.*

"Unless the idea was to hide something else," wondered Max, "something illegal, but what?"

Juliette was more bothered by the name and number of Joan Tourigny in the vault. How had David got hold of them? Perhaps from the editor-in-chief of *The Reporter*, even though he denied knowing her husband. Weirder still was the fact that once he had them, he didn't get in touch with her. Why was that?

"He might have used an assumed name, of course, but then Tourigny would remember."

"Or she's wrong."

"Not likely," mused Max. "Tourigny's not overworked, more like the opposite. She probably knows all her files by heart. That's her style, organized and everything ..."

"David didn't have time, so he put her info away, maybe to contact her once he got back to Canada."

Max had the receiver in his hand for a while as he stared at the telephone plug over the baseboard and the wire running under the carpet to the phone on the bedside table. The plug intrigued him, though he had no idea why. First was its curious location in the room. The bed was pushed up against the far wall, so normally the plug would be behind one of the bedside tables; then the extension wire wouldn't be needed. Was it bad planning? A lazy technician? Then something else puzzled him: how old it was. The wire came out of a small hole in the wall and had been painted over plenty of times, so this had to be a permanent installation and old-fashioned, something laptop users must have cursed. Say, for instance, Ahmed Zaheer.

So, we had an Indian journalist washing up in an out-of-the-way motel in the heart of America, not at all

surprised by modest accommodations but at least expect-
ing them to be modern enough for a computer connection.
No Internet meant no emails in or out.

"Juliette, I'll call you back."

Max slipped on his jeans and a T-shirt, then exited
the room. It was dark, and the car belonging to the one
customer he'd encountered was gone. Max went into
the office. The owner had left, replaced by a young man
called Steve, according to the card on the desk. He was
long and gangly in a polo shirt that was too big for him.
He got up to tell Max where the ice machine was, but
Max cut him off: where and how could he get online?

"CopyKat in town or some Internet café … you
could go there." Steve fumbled through the display case
for a leaflet, while Max flashed his fake RCMP badge.

The young man looked up, intrigued.

"The client who had my room before me, the Indian
guy found dead at the foot of the Falls," he said. "He
asked about that, too, right?"

"I got nothing to do with this."

"No one's accusing anyone of anything. Besides, it
was an accident."

Steve looked very uncomfortable.

"So did he come for that, yes or no?"

"Well, not for the Internet, but he needed change."

"Change?"

Steve pointed to the phone booth at the far end of
the parking lot.

"What time was this?"

"About four. I had just come on."

"Did he go back? Make other calls?"

"I dunno."

Max went out of the office and across the parking lot to the phone booth. There was just a phone, nothing else, not even a directory. Kids must have ripped it out long ago. So why would Zaheer use this instead of his own cellphone? Maybe it wasn't a satellite phone like Max's. You can't use them in North America, so why not call direct from his room?

Max jotted down the number there and contacted Joan Tourigny at home. "Look, I'm sorry to bother you …"

"No problem, André."

"Ahmed Zaheer made a call from the phone booth in front of the motel. Could you trace the number he called?"

Child's play, Tourigny told him, but they wouldn't have an answer till next morning. They'd just have to wait till then.

In the dining room, Max was just finishing breakfast served by Karen the receptionist, when his cellphone rang, and he heard Tourigny's voice: "Stewart-Cooper International, an engineering firm in Hamilton."

There was no way to tell what was actually said, of course, but Max was more intrigued than ever. Stewart-Cooper?

He thanked Tourigny and hung up. Next, he approached Karen, who was flipping through a magazine in the empty dining-room.

"Can you do me a favour?"

‡

Their computer was used mostly to pay bills and contact the accountant, or to receive and confirm reservations. Judging by the parking lot, that wasn't a particularly heavy job. Karen searched Google for Stewart-Cooper International. A long list of links showed up. Karen clicked on the first one, and soon they saw pictures of a number of factories: steel works, an aluminum smelter, and a hydroelectric plant. SCI had major installations all over the globe, run from the headquarters in Hamilton, where two engineers began operations in 1954. A stylized map showed various sites under construction and others already in use. SCI was active in Asia, notably, India. Max asked Karen to click on that one, and a factory and a hydroelectric dam on the Jhelum River both appeared in a place called Rashidabad.

In the heart of Kashmir.

33

Philippe could have ended up anywhere, even Paris. Along with London and Washington, it was one of those prize postings for older and ambitious diplomats. That's what he'd become overnight. Old. The once-fine bird had lost the majesty of its plumage upon contact with politics. It was a physical and emotional shock he had only just got over when the new minister of foreign affairs offered him Singapore. Back to Asia, where he'd previously shone — a hard-working, calm, and uncomplicated city far away enough for him to wind down his career in relative peace. The new minister was assured the political agenda for Singapore and the Malaysian Peninsula was not all that important, nor was it likely to become so. Soon, this "ghost" would no longer be around to embarrass the prime minister and his government.

Philippe preferred to go to El Salvador, where perhaps he'd reclaim the energy and enthusiasm of his youth, everyone thought. But Philippe's intention was self-sacrifice. He wasn't yet conscious of it, of course, though he did feel an impulse to do something surprising and spectacular.

He was going to be a "disrupter of exploitation" as he liked to say. Max knew enough to bet Philippe was going to outstrip his role and mandate, even if at first he had no idea how.

David didn't follow his parents to El Salvador, but stayed in Montreal to start his studies at Collège Jean-de-Brébeuf. This was the family's first time apart, and for reasons yet unknown to Max, Philippe brought him up to date during a secret meeting in a park in Boston. When Max mentioned the business of the election campaign, Philippe cut him off.

"That's ancient history. What's done is done."

"Why El Salvador?"

Philippe shrugged: he didn't want to talk about it anymore. Why bother getting together just to avoid all the subjects they had in common? Philippe knew what his brother was thinking.

"I want you to look out for David … at arm's length. I don't want him to know."

This came as a surprise to Max. He'd rightly guessed since the election catastrophe that his nephew hated him.

"Please do it for me," Philippe insisted.

Max agreed. He couldn't say no to his brother, could he?

Philippe's face darkened. "If anything happens to me down there, if I don't make it back, promise me you'll always keep an eye on him."

"What do you think could happen to you? Diplomats usually die in their beds, don't they?"

Philippe smiled. "Just promise me."

Max agreed once more. "I'll be there always."

They left the park and walked into town without saying anything. Much later on, Max was to remember this day as especially radiant. Workers from nearby offices were out having their lunch, but paying no attention to the two brothers strolling side by side. Then they crossed Quincy Market, went under the John F. Fitzgerald Expressway, and took Atlantic Avenue near the docks.

For no particular reason, Philippe turned to his brother and held him tight, which Max found surprising. They didn't normally do this kind of thing, especially given the practically illicit meetings they were forced to have. Philippe drew back and looked Max straight in the eye.

"Thanks, Max, for David."

Then he left before his brother had time to answer. A car awaited Philippe not far off. Max could have kicked himself for not noticing it before this. It had followed them discreetly the whole time. Max watched it disappear with a feeling of infinite sadness. The solemnity, the silences, the show of affection, the bizarre thanks, none of it customary, gave him the feeling of having unwillingly taken part in a farewell ceremony.

And it was. Max would never see his brother alive again.

"Jayesh Srinivasan speaking. Mercedes, Lexus, Alfa Romeo … what will it be, sir?

"Very funny, Jayesh, very funny." Max's partner had stayed in the heart of the turbulence in Srinagar. He'd spent the time since Max had left going through the files belonging to Ahmed Zaheer at *The Srinagar Reporter*, looking for a trail or at least a hint of a clue, something that could tie the journalist to the murdered diplomat.

"It's chaos here," he continued. "It's all going to hell: Kashmir, Punjab, the north … and the Line of Control isn't controlled at all."

"What about Rashidabad?"

"Eh?"

Max explained what he'd found out. Any mention of Stewart-Cooper in Zaheer's old files? Jayesh hadn't seen any, but he'd look again.

The Queen Elizabeth Way, then an industrial zone that went on forever, with fields of factories bounded on one side by Lake Ontario and the first suburbs of Hamilton on the other. Chimneys, cranes, a grey haze. Leaving Jordan Harbour minutes earlier, Max was now driving through a lifeless zone straight out of a documentary about the delinquency of heavy industry. The choice of motel seemed to make more sense in light of all this. Zaheer had chosen it not for the isolated location. He could reach the industrial zone, and thus the headquarters of SCI, in mere minutes. What, though, was the connection with the attack on David? Max hadn't the slightest idea, but before leaving the motel, he'd called Juliette in Montreal to tell her what he'd found out, and also to ask her to check the archives.

"Esplanade Avenue, corner of Mount Royal, a branch of the National Library, where they keep the old newspapers, like the last five years' of the *Globe and Mail*. You need to search for Stewart-Cooper and India."

Then he set out.

Terry Hoberman, wearing a dark blue suit with the SCI logo on his lapel, held out his hand to Max, who got up and gave him his business card, freshly made that morning at CopyKat. "Thanks for seeing me so quickly. I don't normally just arrive unannounced in a company's offices like this."

Hoberman cut him off: "You know, I just love your articles, but I had no idea you were in Toronto. Otherwise, I'd have …"

"Oh well, I'm afraid *BusinessWeek* is a circus. Things get decided as you're walking down the hall. On Monday, I hardly know where I'll be on Friday."

Hoberman laughed. "Same here, don't worry!" He led Max to the elevator, and the communications director at SCI was still laughing when they got out a few seconds later. Max realized right away the kind of dipstick he was dealing with and how to handle him. Tanned and probably just back from vacation, in his fifties, thought Max, trying to look younger with a discreet dye job in his curly hair. Hoberman was a bit chubby, the jovial type who could have a laugh even reading a press release. His department had been functioning on auto-pilot for ages. With rising profits, sustained growth, and steady development, Stewart-Cooper International was one of those massive but reliable ocean liners that sloughed off minor turbulence. It was immense, profitable, and worry-free, so hardly known to the media, and this in turn made Hoberman's job a breeze. Max figured he probably spent the day leafing through trade magazines and planning his weekend golf tournament. Actually, no, he enjoyed sailing, hence the deep tan.

Hoberman sat Max in one of the leather armchairs facing his huge desk. On the right-hand wall hung a genuine James Wilson Morrice, not a reproduction. He wasn't often visited by the press. The previous day, Max had downloaded a list of *Business Week* correspondents from the Internet and called them one by one until he reached the voicemail of Tim Harrington: "I'll be away from my office for a couple of days, etc." That way, if Hoberman had doubts and called their editorial offices at Penn Plaza … but SCI's communications director wasn't the suspicious type. Max didn't even need to explain his visit before the man began talking about their international activities in the present context of globalization, the company's results on foreign markets, or even their local hiring policies and respect for national culture.

"There's no reason to exploit them — on the contrary — nor to impose our vision of the world." The company was careful to examine the activities of its suppliers, something that companies of this size often neglected, "to the detriment of the stockholders, I might add."

Bit by bit, Max manoeuvred the conversation around to the hydroelectric plant at Jhelum, which had been built in collaboration with the Indian government. Despite huge obstacles, it was a success, exemplary in every respect.

"Obstacles?"

Hoberman sighed. "Well, the same you'd expect in most developing countries: petty bureaucracy, shortage of qualified manpower, unforeseen delays with subcontractors, and so on." Then he added, "It almost cost Mrs. Griffith her health. When she came through Hamilton …"

"Susan Griffith?" Max had spotted her picture in the annual report he'd consulted in the reception area as he waited for Hoberman.

The latter nodded. "She's definitely earned the respect of my colleagues on the board. Not many of us would want to be in her shoes, certainly not me."

"Yet she succeeded."

"Wonderfully."

"And I guess that's why she's now running the company."

"That and other reasons. You see, Mrs. Griffith …" Here Hoberman frowned, a sign of careful reflection. He seemed to be weighing the pertinence of what he felt like saying. Not for long.

"She's an exceptional person from the humanitarian angle, too. Charity campaigns, international co-operation, development aid — she has a long list of good works. From the moment she got back to Hamilton, she started a foundation to assist Canadian and European couples in the adoption of young Indian orphans, especially those of tribal origin."

Clearly, the communications director was in awe of her. Max imagined him on his knees before her, praising her successes and ignoring the rest, an obsequious expert in bowing and scraping. Probably this Griffith was every bit as competent and up to date as he portrayed her, and she in turn had shunted him into a dead-end job to get him out of the way.

"I guess the threat of war over there complicates things, right?"

Hoberman's tan deepened as his good-naturedness drained away.

"I'm afraid I know nothing about it all," Max went on, "but I suppose managing a generating plant like that in the middle of a country which …"

"Uh, it's closed, as a matter of fact." Responding to Max's curiosity, he added, "Since last month."

"Oh, but I thought …"

"Nothing's changed officially, mind you, and we haven't made it public, because we're hoping to reopen it. If those morons can lay off killing one another, that is." Was he disgusted by this or afraid he'd said too much? He turned a stern eye on Max. Some light seemed to go on in his tanned brain.

"Exactly what is it you want to know, Mr. Harrington? What's your article about?"

Time to take the plunge. "I'm not here as a journalist." Hoberman frowned. "I'm trying to understand what happened to my colleague Ahmed Zaheer from *The Srinagar Reporter*. His body's been found at the foot of Niagara Falls." No reaction from Hoberman. Either the name Ahmed Zaheer meant nothing to him, or he was a good actor. "I'm here for the International Federation of Journalists as their American delegate."

"And how does this involve Stewart-Cooper?"

Max kept it short and sweet. "Well, his laptop was wrecked, but they accomplished miracles in the lab, and *voilà*, they retrieved his agenda and address book. Your name was in there along with your phone number."

Max was fishing, but now Hoberman observed with interest. Had Max hooked something?

"He's dead?" Hoberman was anxious.

"An accident at first glance, but the coroner has doubts, so they asked me to dig a bit deeper."

"Well, why would he want to meet me?"

"I was hoping you could tell me that." Max held out another branch. "Zaheer was from Kashmir originally. In fact, he lived there until just recently. He may have met Mrs. Griffith, perhaps talked to her about the closing down, who knows?"

Hoberman was staring at Max.

"Would it be possible to meet her?" Max inquired.

"Excuse me?"

"Mrs. Griffith. I'd like to talk to her."

Hoberman realized he'd gone too far. "I'm afraid that won't be possible," he said smiling. He was back in control. "But what I can suggest is that when you get to New York you fax me your questions and I'll turn them over to our lawyers. How would that be?"

When Max got back to the car, there was a message from Jayesh. He hadn't wasted any time. "I think I have something. Nothing on SCI and *The Srinagar Reporter*, though — in the files, I mean. Same with *Indian Geographic Magazine*, but at noon, I hung around in the canteen at the *Reporter* to see if I could pick up a lead ..."

"Get to it, Jayesh."

"Yeah, yeah, I am. I met a colleague of Zaheer's who told me he worked on pieces for the commentary magazines, as he called them. Small stuff with low circulation and high pretentions."

"Meaning ...?"

"Whistle-blowing, accusations, muck-raking ..."

Max got the picture. Guys with the gift of the gab seated at a round table, passing around hot files to supply them with whipping boys. "Zaheer showed them one on the mad rush to build dams." Since independence, he explained, Indian leaders had been obsessed with dam-building as a way to control rivers and irrigate drought-stricken land. This had been Jawaharlal Nehru's baby. The results, however, had been so-so. Since the fifties and sixties, entire regions had been emptied of their occupants and flooded. The slums of Mumbai and Kolkata were inhabited by peasants who'd been expropriated with no notice and without receiving compensation or damages. Thus the Indian government had created an army of the homeless, and, with its economic policies, had contributed to the depopulation of the countryside and the impoverishment of its people.

The great dams had quite clearly become the rallying point of the ecological left, and that political chameleon Ahmed Zaheer had helped with his freelance pieces.

"So Zaheer would have denounced Stewart-Cooper."

"No, praised them, more likely."

"Say what?"

"Look, the article says the Jhelum dam was the example to follow. Respect for every norm available, both human and environmental, adequate reimbursement for damage and relocation for the peasants. If the government had respected the rest of the population as much, well …"

Max was even more astounded.

"Wait, wait, that's not all," Jayesh said.

Zaheer's article quoted the engineer in charge of the project and the particular difficulties encountered during construction.

"Do you know the Jhelum? It's a mountain river with falls and whirlpools, ravines and everything, as well as being very hard to reach. Well, that might give you some idea of what it was like to do this."

"Jayesh …"

"Okay, okay, so this engineer starts telling him how they got this project going. There were rocks to get through, trenches to dig right through them using CK-Blast 301 to do it." Now Max was listening, as Jayesh went on, "I thought the same as you, so I phoned our friend Ashok Jaikumar of the Indian police and got their reports on the attack."

"Conclusive?"

"The same kind of explosive. Ammonium nitrate, basically."

So there was a link to SCI after all.

"Can we get hold of this engineer?"

"I'm working on it."

34

Max O'Brien had read and re-read the leaflet a dozen times while casting an occasional glance at the entrance to the sports club. It wasn't overly popular, but attended by the "right kind of people" — one of those luxury gyms where clients went around in high-fashion sweatshirts and designer shoes. After leaving Hoberman, he'd immediately headed for Yorkville in Toronto, where IndiaCare had its offices. An old house had been remodelled to suit its purposes: a Victorian home camouflaged by the huge trees that lined the streets. From where he sat and without leaving his car, Max could see employees walking to and fro behind the windows. It was just as he expected: a modest-sized agency, but with luxurious quarters that inspired confidence and reassured eventual adoptive parents with the air of an impeccable organization, which it was. At first glance, one could tell it was as Hoberman described it, efficient, discreet, and industrious — qualities that had allowed Stewart-Cooper International to make its mark.

Still in his car, Max made a reservation at the Sutton Place Hotel, and then, just before five o'clock, he called IndiaCare pretending to be Hoberman from headquarters. He had to reach Mrs. Griffith, but her cellphone seemed to be off: "Would she be at the foundation by any chance?"

"I'm afraid not," said the young woman. "Have you tried the gym?"

"You think that's where she is?"

"Usually late in the afternoon, she is."

"You wouldn't have the number, would you?"

Max was now hoping that Griffith hadn't altered her appearance too much since the photo he'd seen in the annual report.

He needn't have worried, for around seven-thirty, a grey Mercedes with tinted windows, driven by a chauffeur, drew up near the entrance to the gym, and a few seconds later, a woman of about fifty emerged from the club and headed straight for the car. Susan Griffith was elegant and apparently determined; the kind of person who had no time to lose and was always late for appointments. Had Hoberman talked to her since his visit? Max was betting he hadn't. He'd wait for news from the "journalist" before alerting the boss to his existence. He would be in no hurry to admit his recent indiscretions, either.

The moment she opened the car door, Max approached her. "Mrs. Griffith?"

She turned and was on the defensive, but Max smiled and held up his ID card: "Detective Sergeant André Sasseville of the RCMP."

Griffith looked intrigued. "What's going on?"

"Just two or three questions is all. I'm in charge of the inquiry into the death of ..." Max took a card out of his pocket and pretended to read from it, 'Ahmed Zaheer at Niagara Falls.'" He watched for a reaction to the journalist's name, but there was none.

"What does that have to do with me?"

Max explained what had happened to Zaheer. The reception-desk clerk had heard him call SCI and ask to speak to Griffith. It was a bluff, but Griffith was now watching him with interest.

"I have an eight o'clock meeting at home," she said. "If you like, we can discuss it on the way. Then my chauffeur will take you anywhere you like."

Max got in with her. Bloor Street. Choked with traffic as usual, it served Max well. He'd have more time to question her.

The CEO of Stewart-Cooper knew no one named Ahmed Zaheer, nor any other Indian journalist for that matter.

"What about when you were in Kashmir?"

She was surprised he knew about that period in her life, so he quickly followed up: "I found out on the Web, and I thought he might be someone you knew at the time."

"It's true, I did live in India, Kashmir in particular, but I had no time to hang out with journalists."

"Of course." He added, "I heard about the closing of the central. A real pity."

She registered her disgust for all that, her depression about it, too. It was obvious she cared more about that plant than any other. It would be natural, since it was her baby, her own creation, according to Hoberman. Then she had to be the one to suspend activities and lay off the personnel.

"Maybe that was what Zaheer wanted to talk to you about."

Max saw the chauffeur was turning onto Mount Pleasant Road in Rosedale, with its cushy homes, large patios, and Hollywood pools. Griffith was now more distant and reticent, at least as far as this conversation was concerned. She repeated knowing nothing about this Ahmed Zaheer, whom she'd never met.

"Well, we're here. I'm so sorry I can't help you more."

The Mercedes had pulled up in front of a sumptuous residence that outdid its neighbours. Griffith opened the door, and Max got out to walk around to her side.

"There's just one last question. A Canadian diplomat was recently attacked in New Delhi three weeks ago, and the Indian police think he was in touch with Ahmed Zaheer. His name was David O'Brien."

Griffith had heard about it from the papers.

"I didn't know him, but I'm very sorry."

"When you were in India …"

"Look, Sergeant. All this has nothing to do with me, and now if you'll excuse me."

Sure, thought Max. Besides, he really had no choice. She briskly walked toward the house and "Sergeant Sasseville" was already history. Then he heard the voice of the chauffeur behind him.

"Where do you want to go, sir?"

Max waved him away. "Nowhere, I need to stretch my legs." *And think.*

35

The Indo-Pakistani crisis was headlined in every news outlet. Indian Prime Minister Vajpayee had shown imagination in setting up joint patrols with the Pakistanis to prevent terrorists from infiltrating into Kashmir, an idea that Musharraf found interesting. They were still on a war footing: Portugal advised its citizens to leave the region, and Air France had cancelled all flights to Delhi, though beneath the surface, the ice was beginning to thaw, but only on a very slow drip. Musharraf wanted international observers and the UN along the Line of Control, and Vajpayee refused. Then there was the troubling story of a rice truck loaded with arms being intercepted in Gujarat. The Indians said they came from Pakistan and were bound for Ahmedabad, where Hinduist militants had massacred Muslims two months before.

Juliette was right; sectarian conflict couldn't be disentangled from Indo-Pakistani relations.

"In India, everything's connected to everything else, she had said. "You can't separate one event from another."

As Max drove along the 401 in a rental car, Juliette called.

"The 'Report on Business' section of the *Globe and Mail* for November 2000," she said.

"Yes?"

"An article about Brad Thomassin and his small family from Downsview moving to Rashidabad. Here's an engineer who's never been out of the neighbourhood, and he's worried about spending three years without Harvey's, Walmart, and McDonald's, but fortunately Brad had the advantage of some sessions of familiarization with daily life in Asia given by …"

"Dennis Patterson."

"Hired by SCI so their employees know the difference between a Shiite, a Sunni, a turban, and a Sikh."

Max smiled. Some results at last.

"And that's not all," Juliette added. "I asked Vandana about IndiaCare."

"Susan Griffith's outfit?"

"Who do you suppose she got the idea from? Geneviève, Raymond's wife."

Juliette went on to talk about what Vandana called "the budding friendship" between Susan Griffith and Geneviève Bernatchez as the months went by, their common feeling about the unfortunate orphans in this country, their worthy cause taking shape under the benevolent eye of the high commissioner.

Max remembered seeing a photo of Geneviève with Indian babies in her arms on the desk in Bernatchez's office, but something else about Juliette's news bothered him, the orphans, more specifically the orphan girls. The little girls Sister Irène had been forced to abandon.

Suddenly, two worlds collided.

"You still there, Max?"

"Yeah, yeah."

The picture was beginning to resolve itself, even if the content didn't yet add up.

A dam in the heart of Kashmir; the friendship of the woman responsible for the dam and the high commissioner's wife; an international adoption programme; a journalist, now accidentally killed; and his links to David, though cloudy for the moment.

Three hours later, and Max was in Montreal, in the Labyrinth to be exact. Farther off, at the Mughal Palace stand, the nervous young Indian girl of his first visit had gained experience. No more hesitation and gaffes, and she was heating up the bowls of *dal* and curry dishes with the skill of a Culinary Academy of India graduate, as well as sliding the *papadums* and *naan* bread out of the microwave with the ease of a chef at the Taj Mahal Hotel, all of which tickled the boss as he slicked back his moustache behind the cash. His patience had paid off with a smooth fit.

Max took up his usual post behind the palm tree at the Kon-Tiki, where he'd just spotted Dennis Patterson pushing his and Juliette's trays along the counter. Their plan had worked, Juliette having called Patterson to talk about David and suggesting this place, a public spot Max knew well. It would be easy to ditch Luc Roberge, if he was over the initial shock and back on the trail with his pack. No need to worry, though. Max had got there an hour ahead of time, and everything was normal.

After they paid, Juliette guided Patterson to a booth for four and sat down.

Then a third party appeared: Max himself. The consultant realized, of course, that he'd been lured into a trap. "Aw c'mon now, don't be like that," Max said. "Your food's getting cold."

Patterson was ready for the worst, and it showed, so he got out in front of it. "I'm sorry, Max. I had no choice. He forced me …"

"I'll take care of Roberge some other time. Juliette and I've got better things to do, like finding the guys who killed David."

"I have to understand what happened," Juliette said.

For an instant, Patterson seemed to be sizing up the situation. Then, as though he'd settled on something, he asked Max, "What exactly do you want to know?"

"The connections between David and Stewart-Cooper International."

"SCI?"

Juliette told him what she'd found, and Patterson frowned. "Where was the connection with David? I mean, what are you driving at?"

"Terry Hoberman, their communications guy, talked about trouble on the site: bureaucracy, delays from subcontractors, tangled connections with the Indian authorities."

Patterson sighed.

"Look, don't come on all righteous and indignant with me, okay? If the company hired you, it wasn't about delays. No one thinks it was a bed of roses over there. The employees needed to figure out how to muddle through."

But Patterson was still maintaining radio silence.

"What really happened at Rashidabad?" Max asked.

"Bureaucracy, delays, of course, but mostly threats, acts of intimidation, sabotage.... The Indian Army got called in, but it didn't help, so the company had to hire private security to protect the workers. Rotten atmosphere, and pretty soon unsustainable. The site was shut down for long periods, and the company's schedule went to hell. The budget doubled, then tripled, and the place was costing a fortune. The bosses in Hamilton were threatening to pack up and go build that dam somewhere else. In China, for instance, just over the mountain there had to be plenty of rivers like the Jhelum, and a more amenable population."

"Where'd the violence come from? The jihadists? Hizb-ul-Mujahideen?"

"That's what the authorities first thought, separatist rebels, who were unhappy that the population was putting aside their demands to court international capital and the promises of jobs with SCI, but that wasn't it. It was the Hinduists. The extremists weren't about to let the Muslims — and indirectly Pakistan — benefit from the plant. The dam was built only a few kilometres from the Line of Control. One assault and a surprise attack by the Pakistanis and they'd take control of the central committee and use it for themselves, but instead of caving in, Griffith decided to stand up to the extremists.

She went to see the Hinduists at Jammu and confront them. She tried for three days. The hydroelectric installations wouldn't serve one group more than another, just Indians, period. No exceptions. She was even ready to establish quotas by working with Hindus and Muslims, for instance, verifiable by any and all. She had a commitment from headquarters to correct things as soon as any abuse or omission was pointed out."

The Hinduists had finally ceased hostilities, a real feat.

"So the violence stopped?"

"Right. They even came in on schedule. Griffith could now go back to Hamilton with her head held high."

"No wonder the board made her CEO," Max exclaimed.

Patterson nodded. "Too bad the real war blew it all away, for the time being anyway."

"So what exactly was in this agreement?"

"You'd have to ask Raymond Bernatchez about that."

Patterson explained the startup of the central committee at Rashidabad had been planned behind closed doors in the office of the high commissioner, and Griffith wound up in New Delhi from time to time in order to solve some new problem, take care of some new boo-boo.

So, thought Max, *she went to the high commissioner's place and got to know his wife, and the IndiaCare idea came to fruition? Sure, why not? Griffith had played her cards right: make sure you win over Geneviève Bernatchez, so you get the number one of Canadian diplomacy in India on board.*

Raymond Bernatchez and Susan Griffith became the spearhead of a campaign aimed at various government departments and even Prime Minister Vajpayee, from what Bernatchez told Patterson. The rain was nonstop, so dykes had to be built, and for this they needed the Indian Army.

"Did they get it?" asked Juliette.

"Oh yes. The government is co-owner of the installations."

"And SCI is taking part in the Montreal conference, right?" asked Max after a moment's pause.

"Of course, they're one of the chief sponsors."

"Even though they're temporarily shut down. It's an open secret within the industry, and if they ever gave in to panic, it would be a disaster. Hell, I'd go invest in Thailand or buy from Venezuela."

"Did David ever talk to you about a journalist called Ahmed Zaheer?"

Patterson had never heard the name from David or Bernatchez. He knew nothing about him, so Max brought him up to speed about the research, his "natural" death at the Falls, Joan Tourigny's phone number, the kind of explosive used in Rashidabad and on David, all trails leading to the business in Hamilton, not to mention Zaheer's interest in ecology.

"Hell of a lot more interesting than what the Indian authorities are working on, right?" said Juliette.

"You gotta go to the police with this."

Max just smiled. "Like Josh Walkins, for instance? He's a stand-in over there in Delhi. Luc Roberge, why not?"

"The cops have shown no interest at all in any of this," added Juliette.

"Well, they had no evidence to get their hands on. Now, though …"

"More like trails that Juliette and I have followed the best we can. Now that we've started, you want me to just hand things over so they can sit on them?"

Patterson turned to the young woman. "You're playing one hell of a dangerous game, Juliette."

"She's playing with me, and that makes it a whole lot safer," Max cut in.

Three phone calls when they got back to the car and drove away. The first was from Jayesh in Kashmir.

"Good news. The engineer gave me a run for my money. Nobody at his old Srinagar address, the one I found at the newspaper's offices. *Klean Kashmir*, they called it. After the factory and dam were built, farewell all! He collected his marbles and left the region. Then I discreetly got some info, and I walked all over the neighbourhood. I went to the mosque, the butcher shop, and the café. Finally, I stumbled on an old friend of his …"

"Jayesh …"

"Okay, in the summer of 2001, Najam Sattar went back to his home village to take care of his family. According to this guy, he's still there."

"What's it called?"

"Chakothi in Azad Kashmir."

"Pakistan?"

"I'm doing the best I can."

The second call was from Roberge. "I oughta be furious, I don't mind saying. But now I just feel like laughing about it. The main thing is you're back in town. Oh, so close …"

He too had big news. "The main perpetrator of the attack was arrested this morning and you are virtually the first to know after the RCMP and us, of course. David's wife and mother haven't even been told yet."

Max was caught short on this, and he looked to Juliette, who wasn't privy to the conversation.

"You still there, O'Brien?"

"Huh? Yeah, yeah."

"One of those nutjobs, and a communist to boot."

"I thought that model was obsolete."

"Guess not. In India, they're still current, active, and dangerous."

Max got the idea.

"The Canadians are beginning to see the Indians as foot-dragging, so Chief Inspector Dhaliwal goes back to an old list from the eighties and dusts off a few suspects. Hmmm, let's see, this one's not too bad. Besides, he lives nearby."

Roberge's sigh came across the line. Obviously, he didn't share the sense of humour at the other end.

"The guy confessed he kidnapped the diplomat with two accomplices, and …"

"Things just get better and better. An asterisk next to the name means he couldn't withstand electrodes to the nuts. The perfect suspect."

"Look, O'Brien, this isn't *The Lonely Planet* anymore. This is the end of the road, so you've got a choice. Come in quietly and give yourself up without harming your 'hostage,' and I'll take it into account in my report.

Otherwise, I throw the book at you."

Max hung up the phone and looked at Juliette. "So, now you're my hostage."

"Who turned you in? Patterson?"

"Probably thinking of your safety."

Max spent a long time looking at her.

"What you're doing is illegal, you know. If they arrest me, they'll accuse you of aiding a fugitive."

"I'm big enough to know what I'm getting into. No warnings necessary."

He shook his head. Boy, she had guts, this young woman.

"So, where do we go now?"

He paid no attention to that one. "David sure was lucky finding a girl like you."

Juliette, ill at ease, looked away. "I'm just doing what he'd do for me," she said. "I won't stop asking questions till I know what happened."

Max had on a canvas money-belt filled with American dollars and three passports, all of them maybe "burned" already. He could just see Roberge before the computer juggling aliases and playing with Photoshop to try out different combinations. For the first time since returning from India, Max had the feeling he was an easy target for the police because he was with a woman who wasn't part of "the scene." He absolutely needed a place to rest. He stopped next to a phone booth, opened the car door and let his cellphone slip through the grate into a sewer.

"Have you got a quarter?" he asked Juliette before heading into the booth. His third call was to Mimi.

36

During their one-way conversations, of which there were more and more before Pascale left, she'd tried to make him understand the inevitability of fate, *karma* for the Hindus. Life flowed as a river whose course was fixed forever. There was no point in trying to alter its direction. The current irresistibly brought us back, not into the "right path" as Christians would say, but into the path, for good or ill, that had been set for us since the beginning of time. This fatalism enraged Max, who considered life an obstacle course, a test in the sporting sense, and one for which he had chosen not to obey the rules. But when Philippe died in El Salvador in 1989, he finally understood what Pascale meant. His brother's political mishap had been a futile attempt to change the progress of things. Philippe had returned to his river-bed, which now took him to Central America, and not just anywhere, but specifically to El Salvador, where the menu presented a military clique working for the big landowners, generals who imposed order and terror with machetes and prohibitive taxes. It was a country run by death squads supported by the U.S. Army. Rebel groups hidden in the mountains stood up to them. Assassination and kidnapping were the signs of a perpetual civil war.

A hundred thousand dead in ten years, just one more senseless conflagration on a planet that held to them with demonic persistence.

Max was sure Philippe knew what hell he was getting into and even suspected he chose El Salvador deliberately, maybe because Lebanon, Burma, and other hornets' nests were unavailable. Philippe had determined the location of his sacrifice the way Joan of Arc had resolutely said to her executioners, "Put the fire and stake here, not over there. It's too far!" Karma perhaps, but one he had chosen for himself, as if to prove he didn't care about dying any more than about the latest limo.

Sure, and why not El Salvador?

The sacrifice had been calling to him, and sooner or later, he'd have to face it head-on. The generals just had to wait for the right time to intervene. By seeking to provoke the powers that be, Philippe stood himself in front of the bullseye, but he also drew the sympathy of the people of the capital, terrorized by the violence that corrupted the atmosphere in the country, be they of the right or the left. Lo and behold, here was one, at least, who wasn't barricaded behind bodyguards at every private cocktail party. He dared to drive along the

Panamericana without ten motorcycle cops from the Policia Nacional on his tail.

Béatrice watched this provocation, this ritual of death, with anger she could barely contain. What her husband was doing made no sense. If he wanted to die, okay, but why take his wife down with him? That wasn't his plan, either. He chose one of her return trips to Montreal — there were lots of them — to open the embassy gates to some peasants and rebels fleeing the death squads, and in a single night transform his office into Noah's Ark.

Ottawa was informed, and the minister awakened in the middle of the night. Philippe O'Brien once again. He regretted not having insisted on the Singapore posting instead of giving in on this one, but the wimpy prime minister had wanted to soothe his fallen star, and here was the result.

The view from Ottawa showed Philippe creating his own personal crisis to draw attention to himself. This was Bonaparte on Elba plotting his return to the French throne. No question that when this ambitious headline-grabber came home after saving these poor people, his twisted family history would be all forgotten, but what the minister of foreign affairs saw as a rebirth, a resurrection, a roaring comeback, was in reality nothing but an uplifted middle finger. Okay, so Philippe had manufactured his own distinct flashpoint, but he'd done it to be able to make a spectacular exit. A gesture out of the ordinary, the kind that made its agent "useful," no longer a spectator powerless to act on events, but someone with an impact that made him "essential" to his peers. Since Canadian voters had refused his "total commitment," illiterate peasants — who probably had no idea where Canada even was — would be the beneficiaries of his act of bravery.

Things unravelled very quickly. While the whole world watched, Philippe negotiated for the lives of the peasants with representatives of the generals. He offered his own for theirs, despite orders to the contrary from Ottawa. But who were they to get in the way of his sacrifice? The authorities weren't expecting anything like this insane courage. Then there were the television cameras, and the generals were getting to enjoy their new show. They could of course storm the place and kill everyone, including the ambassador, and put an end to the drama. But these morons enjoyed being instant TV anti-stars, bogeymen scaring good suburbanites all across the West.

Ottawa was in panic mode. What the hell kind of game was this cretin playing? Communications were cut off, naturally. Anyway, Philippe couldn't care less about their advice, and within a week, the media getting bored with their clinking medals and grandiose uniforms, and their own grand play, the generals decided that at last they could act. In a crackling fireworks of shots, soldiers invaded the embassy like drunken festival-goers carrying machine guns. They were expecting the usual panic and desperate acts, but what they got was a deserted building that was way too calm for that. This place smelled like shit. They came across the ambassador writing letters in his office. He barely paused to invite them to take a seat.

Not a trace of the rebels.

What was this? A trap? An ambush?

Philippe suggested they take a look in the basement.

A tunnel dug through the wall led to the sewers of San Salvador, which accounted for the infernal smell that permeated the building.

Later on, one of the escapees told American TV reporters that he'd once worked in the sewers and knew the city's underground world by heart. An important conduit was situated nearby, and for a week, while Philippe faced down the generals under the eye of the camera, the fugitives had punched a hole in the cement and dug through the crumbly earth to the main sewer and freedom. They subsequently found refuge in Guatemala, and the media that had once demolished Philippe's political career were now the ones that, despite themselves, allowed him to save these poor people and become a hero.

For the military, Philippe's victory was intolerable, especially when it was so cool-headed and insulting. He ought to be at their feet begging for pity, but instead he was beaming and seemed to be at his all-time peak. They killed him on the spot at point-blank range.

"If I'd turned myself in to the police when Béatrice asked me to," Max sighed, "Philippe would be alive today."

Juliette was moved listening to this story. A few hours earlier, an elderly woman, Mimi, had greeted them with arched black eyebrows and a strident voice, as well as hot soup. Antoine, her taciturn brother, used his equipment in the basement while listening to *Madama Butterfly*. Mimi didn't seem pleased by Juliette's presence, but she kept her opinions to herself. Max let her use his room and he got settled on the sofa. Juliette wasn't sleepy, and neither was he. She joined him in the living room, and that was when she had asked him exactly what happened to David's father. This time, there was no avoiding the question for Max.

"Did David ever talk about him?" he asked.

"He admired him a lot. He was David's idol," and she added, "David would have liked a Central American posting. He knew they'd never send him though." Then, after a long pause, and realizing that Max was silent now too, she continued, "I'm disappointed he didn't tell me what he was up to. What if he felt guilty about something? Maybe he did feel guilty and didn't dare tell me about it."

"Or perhaps he was trying to protect you. Like Patterson just now."

Everyone wants to protect me, regardless of what I want, she thought to herself. *Maybe David did, too.*

"He didn't want you to get mixed up in anything," Max went on, "like Philippe with Béatrice back then. The people who held a grudge against David knew that somehow or other. That's why you weren't attacked as well."

"Your brother had secrets, too."

Max didn't react.

"Did you know about Deborah Cournoyer?"

Max had never heard the name.

"She was his mistress."

"What're you talking about? What mistress?"

Juliette relayed the conversation she'd overheard in Patterson's office, as well as Cournoyer's discreet presence at David's funeral, and the former diplomat's confidences after she'd left. Max was astounded and couldn't understand why his brother had kept this affair hidden from him, and for such a long time.

"I'm sorry. I shouldn't have said anything."

Two hours later, Max still couldn't get to sleep for thinking about Juliette's revelation. Deborah Cournoyer. Why hadn't Philippe said anything, and why had Béatrice let this go on?

37

Philippe's heroic death had been publicized far and wide, and there had been a stamp and a public square honouring his memory. Newborns had been baptized in his honour, there was a planned biography and TV series. There was even talk of renaming the Foreign Affairs building on Sussex Drive in Ottawa. In other words, the canonization was well under way even before his body was brought home. At the Ottawa airport, Béatrice reminded people of a Canadian Jackie Kennedy marked by pain and sadness, but dignified and forever elegant, with David by her side supported by Patterson, as she received her husband's remains with stoic grace.

Max had watched it on TV in his hotel room in Montreal, scanning the crowd for Luc Roberge, but there was no trace of the cop. Still, he had to be there unless he'd sent some of his men instead. No way he would pass up a chance like this. Max tossed his second empty Scotch bottle onto the floor. He'd been drinking since morning, yet he still felt barely drunk. Perhaps it was the pain, the unbearable feeling that this disaster was his own fault, that he could have prevented it, but hadn't, as usual. Had Philippe left him any choice? No, that was no excuse.

Over the coming years, Max was more and more unobtrusive, though still on top of things. From Chicago or Las Vegas, he kept an eye on David and Béatrice as they started a new life, not missing a beat as they went from one thing to another. Of course, forgetting was impossible, but at least they could give the impression of leaving the past behind. On TV interviews, he heard Béatrice say with conviction that Philippe wasn't dead, that the assassins had destroyed his body, but not his spirit. This spirit from now on would help her to continue. For Max, of course, this was just nonsense, pure fantasy once again. All his brother had left behind were furtive images that faded gradually from everyone's memory, even those closest to him. It had been the same with Pascale's passing away. Both their passionate love and her intolerable betrayal began to dissolve as the years went by. The ugly and the beautiful alike petered out in his memory like a slow, continuous second death that never ended. A second death worse than the first one.

Max opened his eyes. The half closed window-shade of the airplane let the sun's light beam in. He looked at the time. Soon it would be London, then Copenhagen.

‡

For David, the adolescent and then young adult, there was no question of having a career anywhere but in Foreign Affairs. He would pick up where Philippe left off, carry on the fight, even if he had trouble discerning exactly what that was.

Max was siphoning the international account of a real estate investment company in Bermuda when he learned that David had been recruited by the Department. He thought about sending congratulations and saying who-knows-what, maybe that his father would be proud or something along those lines, but he decided to let it drop.

"I've become just like him. I feel just what he felt." Karma from father to son, their fates united in the sacrifice of life? The call of martyrdom like Philippe? The longing to spit fire, give one's life for others, the defence-less ones? Possibly, but David's playing field wasn't as easily mapped out as his father's had been. Drunken soldiers, terrified peasants, a providential sewer. David's world was more complex and even more desperate than Philippe's. One thing was certain, though. David had "done something" as his father had. He couldn't leave things alone, stay quietly behind his desk and entertain passing businessmen. This "heroic initiative," whatever it was, had dragged him to his death.

Copenhagen in the rain, and the British Airways Airbus had been circling the runway for some time now. The city emerged from the clouds from time to time, only to disappear once again in the fog.

The day before, Juliette had asked Max, "Do you believe this story of a communist they've arrested?"

"Did they arrest him? Sure. Do they have anything against him? Possibly. But I'm convinced he has nothing to do with David's death." Max had given a lot of thought to this opportune arrest, which meant the Indian police had stopped focusing on the imam Khankashi. Genghis Khan was off the hook?

On the phone, Jayesh told him that Chief Inspector Dhaliwal had filed a report. Doval Shacteree was certainly no angel, but he was also the perfect sacrificial lamb. Still this about-face was hard to swallow. Prime Minister Vajpayee was passing up a great pretext for accusing Pakistan or Kashmiri separatists of being involved in the killing.

"Things are shifting," Jayesh said. "Here it's *détente* for now, or at least a slight loosening up."

Maybe the Russians or the Chinese had something to do with it, or even the Americans and their rumblings? Who knew? At least there was a breather. The freeze was thawing a bit, and India had taken the first step.

"Then yesterday," added Jayesh, "the Indian Navy pulled out of Pakistani waters in the Gulf of Oman, where it's been for the past month."

"So war is off the table."

"For the moment, and India's ready to name a new ambassador to Islamabad to replace the one they recalled in December."

"They can't let Vajpayee blow this by blaming David's

death on an Islamist terror cell protected by 'The Land of the Pure.'"

"Bingo. So that's why they dug around for this communist guy."

A truce, but a fragile one, tissue-paper thin, and made to the detriment of Hizb-ul-Mujahideen and company. So it's back to the bush for the extremists, including Genghis Khan, and the official war appears to be over, while the underground one is on again.

What was going through David's mind in the days before the attack, when he returned from searching Zaheer's apartment in Srinagar, following the journalist's death in Niagara?

"Well," said Juliette, "the final sprint before the Montreal conference, endless meetings at the High Commission."

"David following in his father's footsteps. He's ready to churn everything up, and that's why he's afraid and mistrusts everybody."

"But why Zaheer's apartment, when he was all praise for the Canadian company?"

"Not a clue."

"Did David already know about Niagara Falls? They'd never even met."

"Can't be. Zaheer's in Canada when his boss thinks he's in Sri Lanka, and David's in Srinagar when everyone thinks he's in Kathmandu, both of them hiding out …"

"They've made contact, but when and where?"

Max had nothing. SCI maybe. The enthusiastic article praising them for their remarkable behaviour. Maybe Zaheer interviewed David at the High Commission's offices.

"So he wanted to meet Zaheer?"

"Maybe via Bernatchez. Probably met him, too."

"One thing's sure, they were not strangers."

"Zaheer revealed what he knew to David. And he was grilled to find out what that was."

"But what was it?"

Max was stumped there, too.

"It's a weird set of coincidences, isn't it?" Juliette continued: "Zaheer's death, the closing down of Rashidabad, David's secret trip to Srinagar, Khankashi's escape the day of the explosion …"

"The threat of war between the two countries?"

"Not to mention Rodger Morency's little waltz around the hospital."

"A dog's breakfast, for sure."

In the airport corridor on the way to the plane stood a small man in a raincoat with an umbrella in one hand and a card reading MR. GREGORY in the other. He seemed nervous as he grabbed Max's suitcase, and, in poor English, explained they were late and had to hurry. Three concourses over, about thirty people were twiddling their thumbs: people of all ages, some jolly older folks and serious young ones. Max apologized for his lateness due to the weather, but received only a grunt without any particular sense of engagement. What a fun bunch.

38

The "dynamic duo," Griffith and Bernatchez, con-cocted the startup of the hydroelectric plant behind closed doors in his office. This had been playing on Juliette's mind ever since Patterson first mentioned it. Before Max left, he and Juliette had agreed that she'd ask the high commissioner about it. He was still going to the Montreal conference, but first she wanted to get her things from Béatrice's place. She knew David's mother would be at her hairdresser on Greene Avenue, and Juliette had chosen this opportunity so she wouldn't be forced to explain things. But Béatrice was waiting for her in the kitchen, with a book in her hand: *The Idiot's Guide to Pregnancy*.

"You look awful," she said by way of greeting. "I've taken the liberty of getting you an appointment with my friend Dr. Ménard at Hôtel-Dieu Hospital."

"I'm fine, really."

"The first months are crucial. When I was pregnant with David …"

Juliette closed her eyes. Béatrice was angry, and she had every right.

"Apparently everyone knows but me."

"I'm sorry. With all that's been happening …" *What's going on with me?* she wondered. *She goes through my things and finds this book. Sure I should have hidden it, but still she had no right to.... And I'm the one who is sorry?*

Béatrice put the book on the table.

"Dennis called and told me you'd met him with Max. You know, if Roberge learns about this …"

"Gee, I thought he already knew."

"Don't take that tone with me. I am just concerned for your welfare."

"Max is going to find whoever killed David."

"Too late, they've already got him. It's in the papers."

Juliette was in no mood to argue, and she went to the guest room to get her things while Béatrice looked on.

"Where are you going?" she asked.

She pushed her way past without answering. Béatrice tried holding her back.

"You're making a serious mistake."

"No, doing nothing would be a mistake." And out she went with Béatrice calling from behind.

"Do you really hate me that much?" She looked horror-stricken.

In the past days, thought Juliette, *this woman's strength has faded away. All that's left is a hollow shell.* Juliette had tears in her eyes for her husband's helpless mother, and collapsed on a chair, while Béatrice drew closer.

"I'm so sorry," Juliette said. "You should have been the first to know, but I was waiting for the right time."

All over again.

"I'm happier for you than you can possibly know."

"I'm doing all this for our child," Juliette cut in. "I want to be able to tell him everything that happened, one day."

Béatrice nodded.

"And Max's part in all this will not be left out."

Béatrice's face darkened.

Outside, Juliette hailed a taxi and then asked him to wait in front of the Sheraton Centre on René Lévesque Boulevard. She entered the familiar atmosphere of the government and industry get-togethers she'd sometimes been to with David. The hall was decorated with saffron colours to charm the Indian families and business representatives recuperating from jet lag. Juliette knew Vandana was in Ottawa at Foreign Affairs today to settle a few things before returning to lend a hand tonight, so High Commissioner Bernatchez would be alone in the presidential suite as organizer of all this. When Juliette got to the floor, however, she stumbled upon Sandmill on the phone to New Delhi. Too late to avoid him. He'd seen her already and wanted a word.

"I feel so sad about David," he said. "I wanted to be at the service, but I was just swamped."

"Thanks, I understand."

He'd arrived a few days earlier and was relieved to say things had calmed down somewhat in India.

"Mr. Bernatchez …"

"Is in his suite."

The high commissioner welcomed Juliette a few moments later and asked her to be seated.

"You know they've caught that fanatic, don't you?"

She nodded. No way she would mention Max's doubts on that score.

"Of course, it won't bring David back," added Bernatchez.

"What was their connection to one another?"

"The Indian police say they'd met a few times at the High Commission. Something about a visa application that was refused. I'm not quite sure. Anyway, he took David as his *bête noire* after that, so he got a few henchmen together …"

"They never found them, did they?"

"They will."

So, here was the official version properly corroborated by the accused.

"Do you really believe these guys kidnapped, tortured, and killed David?"

"Excuse me?"

Juliette outlined what Max had found out about the journalist's "accident" in Niagara Falls, the dam construction on the Jhelum, the use of ammonium nitrate explosives …

"Wait, hold on, are you telling me that David's death is connected to SCI in India?"

"I never believed the official theory about the attack."

"That's not a reason to accuse just anybody."

"Then tell me why," she said. "Why was the power plant built in Kashmir? There are plenty of rivers elsewhere, some other region of India, like around Darjeeling, in North Bengal."

Bernatchez was searching her face with puzzlement. Instead of consoling the young woman, here he was giving her an introductory lesson in Indian economics. He sighed loudly.

"The government wanted to develop hydroelectric power potential in the region using foreign capital, but because of the political situation, no engineering firm wanted to get involved.

"Except SCI."

"Right, the company's used to dealing with this kind of problem. They've handled similar projects in Brazil and Indonesia."

"And Susan Griffith tackled things head-on."

"With a mandate from HQ, obviously, and she came to Delhi with a proposal that convinced the new government."

"The BJP."

"The BJP leadership, the ones with the real power in Delhi, coalition power, in fact. That's what allows them to govern with a majority, support from other parties."

"And these other parties looked favourably upon the Rashidabad hydroelectric station."

"A great chance for the BJP leadership to show they were more than creators of fascist slogans and backward policies."

"And better yet, the Canadian government was agreeable to the project, which looked good to Vajpayee and his bunch of fundamentalists!"

"Look, Juliette, I don't really get why this is ..."

"Concretely?"

"Roads had to be built, peasants mobilized, local leaders reassured."

"Because there was opposition to the the construction?"

"Sure, normal. You upset the lives of thousands of people, you have to expect some of them to be hesitant."

"Upset how?"

"Part of the valley had to be flooded, so villagers had to be evacuated, but you need to realize that the company was very responsible about the orderliness of it and about respecting local culture."

This silenced Juliette, and Bernatchez went on the offensive. "I'm not sure what you're trying to prove, Juliette, but you can be certain SCI's attitude was beyond reproach. Susan Griffith, too."

"Not to mention her selflessness and social awareness, especially regarding the orphans of IndiaCare."

Bernatchez darkened, annoyed at Juliette's sarcasm. "Let's leave Geneviève out of this, okay?"

"Still, it's quite a weird coincidence, don't you think?"

"I can assure you Susan Griffith has nothing to do with David's death. The plant was constructed before he ever got to Delhi. That's all ancient history."

So she'd hit a wall, and she could see Bernatchez wasn't going to offer up anything more. The affair was closed, and it wasn't going to be reopened for the weeping widow.

"David knew about the factory closing a few days before the conference," she forged on, "and you discussed it."

"Sure we did, along with several other things. There were still logistical problems to solve."

"The code of silence, did you talk about that, too?"

"Yes."

"How did he react?"

Bernatchez hesitated as he tried to guess where she was headed with this. "David was conscientious as a diplomat. He understood SCI's problems and the concerns of its board for any publicity this might draw."

"It would hurt a company listed on the stock exchange, right?"

"David wasn't working for the shareholders, if that's what you mean."

Next she asked if he knew about an agreement Griffith had signed with the Hinduists when the dam was to be built.

This caught him off guard. "Who told …"

"Patterson."

Bernatchez shook his head. Again he wondered what connection this could have with the murdered diplomat.

"Was David aware, yes or no?"

"I don't think so."

"What exactly was in it?"

"Hiring quotas, mostly, as well as respect for Brahmins in terms of working conditions."

"Concerning purity?"

"Among others."

"Meaning …?"

"Well, a separate environment, the hiring of Brahmin cooks, vegetarian menus, and the site itself: no contact with lower castes or no-castes, Muslims, strangers in general.

"Is that all?"

"That's already a lot."

Juliette was disappointed. Clearly the Hinduists had settled fairly easily.

Bernatchez drew closer to her. "I know what you're feeling, Juliette. Your husband's death is so unjust and absurd that you need to try and give it some meaning."

"I just want to get at the truth."

"It's right in front of you. You just refuse to see it."

For the first time, doubt began to nag at her. Maybe Bernatchez was right. Her doggedness was starting to look like blind panic, a refusal of the inevitable, rejection of the simple and obvious solution, but still …

"Go get some rest, Juliette. Take a few weeks' vacation far away from here, far from India and all its problems."

The taxi driver was reading the newspaper, the public confession of a pedophile complete with a huge photo covering all of page one. Suddenly, Juliette's mind went back to Madeleine Morency, and she leaned over to the chauffeur: "Can you take me to Marieville in Montérégie?"

39

Thirty-four degrees and unbearably humid at the Islamabad airport — some gawkers seemed to be enjoying the spectacle of humanitarian aid, or at least the "eyewitness account" they had come for and these sweat-soaked Westerners were pretentiously bringing them. Cops, customs officers, porters, and tea vendors looked on smiling at these extra-terrestrials in sand-coloured clothes. One pot-bellied Pakistani with a shiny bald head, and a moustached man in a suit and tie, were trying to gather them all together in a corner between a foreign exchange counter, which was "temporarily" closed, and a snack bar full of travellers waiting to leave on Aero Asia or Bhoja Air. In the parking lot were other faces and more moustaches, but also an ultra-modern coach, or so it looked. Max thought the pot-bellied guy had to be the driver. He was watching his fellow travellers worn out by an eight-hour flight: no Americans but a few Brits, and, most of all, Scandinavians (way too blond) who stopped laughing at their own incomprehensible jokes the moment they got on board the Pakistan International Airlines 747. Max also saw a group of soldiers with AK-47s using a mirror to look under a small Suzuki truck. There could be attacks here, just like anywhere else. The Inter-Services Intelligence agents definitely had to be around somewhere, patrolling the airport day and night. The man with the moustache and suit now shepherding the group to the bus might even be a regional ISI man himself. For now, though, he was just being the energetic tour guide trying to hurry them along. Waving his hand without missing a beat, the guide was examining and counting each and every tourist, probably paid according to the number of humanitarian units he could deliver. He tried to weed out any Indians or other undesirables.

No danger for Max in his Tilley hat, just like nine other volunteers, that was tilted down over his eyes so as to make him unrecognizable. Still, as a further precaution on his way out, to avoid the guide's gaze, he turned to a chubby, good-natured lady who seemed to have latched on to him since Copenhagen. Ingrid had three grown kids in Norrköping, Sweden, who'd advised her against this "expedition," but she'd resisted, and as they got off the bus, Max asked her if she'd ever been to Pakistan before. No, and she was thrilled but nervous about "all that." He wasn't sure if she meant the overall international political situation, the icy reception they were getting in Islamabad, or the impression of being circus animals.

The Swedish lady sat with Max behind the driver. The secret service spy stood at the end of the aisle to welcome these "guests" to his country, still checking out faces the whole time, and assuring each and every one of his complete and entire co-operation.

"Don't hesitate to ask any questions you might have. That's what I'm here for — to answer and make sure you have a realistic picture of Pakistan …" There were no laughs there, so he asked if there were any journalists among them. More silence. Max knew perfectly well that three reporters from a student newspaper in Fredericksberg had made the trip — a photographer had come out to snap them before the trip, but these three daredevils were smart enough not to raise their hands. Fortunately, these dipsticks had been briefed at least.

The bus rolled out, and Pakistan appeared amazingly similar to India. The humanitarians had their noses glued to the glass of their rolling aquarium as Jeeps and other military transport roared past. Under the canvasses, soldiers sat in double rows, weapons between their knees. Their look held a fatalism that, for once, didn't look at all religious. More like animals headed for the slaughter, no longer able to howl or struggle. To Max, war seemed more prevalent here than there. Islamabad was very near the Kashmiri border, while Delhi, to the south, seemed less wrapped up in the northern conflict. That had to be why. If not, then this de-escalation Jayesh was talking about was no more than the pipe dream of foreign correspondents.

Delhi would have won any beauty contests, as well. Not that Islamabad was ugly, but it was a new city in the rectilinear American style, and soulless, though maybe that was an advantage in modern-day Pakistan. On Khayaban-e-Quaid-e-Azam Street, a geography nut in the group pointed out the presidential palace. This was where General Musharraf reigned after overthrowing Nawaz Sharif, successor to Benazir Bhutto, daughter of Ali Bhutto, himself accused of corruption, then dislodged and hanged by Muhammad Zia-ul-Haq in 1979. The latter, probably haunted by his victim, died in a plane accident nine years later. Pakistani politics was a morbid game of musical chairs. The geography whiz explained, under the curious gaze of the guide, that the name *Pakistan* had been invented out of thin air in the 1930s by Choudhry Rahmat Ali, an Islamic student at Cambridge combining the names of the Muslim states in the British East Indies: Punjab. Afghan Province, Kashmir, Sindh, and Balochistan. Missing from this amalgam was the other Kashmir, hence the Pakistani insistence in standing up to the Indians. These "mangy dogs" had gone so far as to attack the very name of their country, but a traveller behind Max disagreed. Pakistan, he said in a British accent, meant "land of the pure" in Urdu, a debate that they didn't have time for.

The Hotel Ambassador-Inn on Khayaban-e-Suhrwardy Street was also surrounded by soldiers. In it, air-conditioning awaited the travellers, the guide told them. Piled in front of the reception desk, the foreigners tendered their passports at arm's length, documents that the thugs of the ISI would enjoy thumbing through tonight while their owners were recovering from jet lag.

Max got away from the crowd and slipped into the coffee shop, where the barista served him a non-alcoholic beer without even asking if he wanted it. His worn jacket had the name AZIZ sewn on it, though the letter *i* was unstitched, leaving a slight outline. He observed the humanitarian gaggle in the lobby as he wiped the counter. Max took a mouthful of beer and asked him if the others were expecting to have any problems getting into Azad Kashmir. "Are they fooling themselves?"

"It's out of bounds to foreigners, especially journalists." Aziz was fairly new to this, sloshing water everywhere, or else it was the local custom when cleaning a counter. "You won't have any trouble though; they'll get you out of here tomorrow as planned." In other words, no hitches, no excuses, no pretexts, no sweaty official apologizing for the delays, no potbellied military officer blaming the Indians for the holdup.

"What about Chakothi?"

"That's the first stop. I don't know if your guy is still there, though."

Max conjured up all those old films he'd seen. The question was always, "How will I know him?" With the invariable answer, "He'll know you."

Aziz had a TV, too, and he loved playing this part, the receding hair, the penetrating stare, the fleshy lips just right for the part where information is given under one's breath. No doubt about it, he'd been born in the right country for this game. It was he who had informed Jayesh that the gaggle had arrived bound for Azad Kashmir, and Max had nothing to do but jump onto a moving train.

Their guide of the inquiring eye was now showing them the way to the elevators.

"You think he's with the secret service?" asked Max.

"No idea. First time I've seen him."

A fresh mouthful of beer.

"So Mercedes is the 'in' thing in Pakistan these days?"

Aziz shrugged. "The war, always war." He couldn't wait for things to stabilize and settle into familiar day-to-day corruption. Till then, there would be hell to pay.

The jostling crowd at the reception desk was thinning, so Max got up, emptied his glass in one gulp and left the barman to his "work." He'd much rather slip out now and make his way into Pakistani Kashmir, but that would attract suspicion. It wouldn't be easy to ditch these clowns, but if, unlike what Aziz said, the Ministry of Information was keeping them confined to the hotel under some pretext or other, Max wasn't going to waste precious time. On the other hand, the presence of this Western contingent would lend him much-needed anonymity.

The room was clean, the plumbing modern, and the view of Shakarparian Park not half bad. A little more imagination and Max could have believed he was on holiday.

Juliette answered on the second ring, as if she'd been expecting this call.

"November 1996. You wanna know where Rodger Morency's community service took him?"

"No idea, Juliette."

"Kipawa Summer Camp in Temiscamingue. A country setting for handicapped kids: there were cabins to be fixed up, a wharf to rebuild, a road through the woods to signpost …"

"Okay, Juliette …"

"Kipawa, one of Mrs. Griffith's good works, along with international adoption."

When Max mentioned Stewart-Cooper, the name rang a bell with Juliette, but where had she seen it before? Then, all of a sudden, when she spotted the taxi driver absorbed in his paper in front of the Sheraton Centre, she remembered Madeleine Morency's absorption in her scrapbook. That's when Kipawa appeared before her in a letter Rodger wrote to his mother: "Look Mama, this is me resting!" The picture was a photo from the camp newsletter showing him helping fellow ex-cons. The accompanying text mentioned Griffith, a member of the board at Stewart-Cooper.

So, at last a link between him and David, but why? How?

In the Pakistani hotel restaurant, Max had time to ponder all this. The meal was so-so, since the chef had agreeably watered down the spices in his *qoftas* and *chapli* kebabs for his Western guests. The conversation, though, was spicier. The geo-geek who had managed to locate the presidential palace that afternoon, and claimed to have had a long chat with the Ministry of Information guy, who said they were leaving for Azad Kashmir tomorrow morning without fail. He seemed proud to announce this to table companions, as though personally responsible for the efficacy of Pakistan's government. So why were they going? To show foreigners the determination of the inhabitants of Azad Kashmir to free their country from Indian domination? Though not to the press, because they'd be tempted to interpret things their own special way and pose embarrassing questions. This was a PR exercise under the guise of a humanitarian expedition.

So, there'd be no journalists, but TV cameras from Islamabad, and publicity would replace truth. It worked very well in the West, so why not in Azad Kashmir?

40

They departed on time the following morning in a Mercedes-Benz Sprinter minibus. Max was relieved the Ministry of Information man had been replaced by another, just as attentive and observant, but at least not travelling in the same vehicle. The official travelled with Ingrid, who waved every time they overtook one another. Starting off at top speed and with horns to blare away trucks and rickshaws, the convoy edged its way forward, pothole by pothole, away from Muzaffarabad. As they distanced themselves from the capital of Azad Kashmir, the road started to deteriorate, soon to become nothing more than a winding mountain trail shared by half the country.

At dusk, they arrived in Chakothi, only five kilometres from the Line of Control and Indian Kashmir. It was cold in the village, as the heat and humidity of the plain gave way to glacial temperatures. The wind blowing in from the mountains was punctuated with machine-gun bursts echoing through the night, never mind the truce trumpeted by the media. It was hard to imagine Najam Sattar leaving Srinagar to come and live here at the gates of war.

The Westerners were billeted in different houses requisitioned by the government, Max wound up with a British representative of the Anglican Church, a modern English vicar, aware of the world's hardships, just the sort once recruited by Her Majesty's Secret Service. This wasn't Christopher's first mission: he'd been a human shield in Iraq during the First Gulf War and considered his holy intervention as some sort of extreme sport. The Bible he read before going to sleep at night was blood-stained.

"My blood, actually," he said with a note of pride.

Max was first up in the morning, and the mountains appeared on every side of the village with a splendour that made him queasy. This was the most beautiful landscape in the world turned into a battlefield.

Max was concerned that the engineer who was to be his contact upon entering the village had not yet arrived. A logistical problem? Maybe a lack of confidence ... or worse. Ingrid joined him, followed by the missionary, complete with blood-stained Bible. They'd slept badly and were all starving. In addition, Ingrid had been bitten by bedbugs all night. By day, Chakothi was depressing. There were soldiers everywhere, just like the day before, walking up and down the muddy street at the centre of the village. Half of the shops were closed for good, and most of the inhabitants hadn't been able to return to their villages since the threat of war in recent weeks. The group was to spend the day and following night in Chakothi, then head off to Kotli and Bhimber, farther south. From there, they would go to Gujarat, then Lahore.

One week on the road, a second week for debriefing, a third week for consciousness-raising, then it was back to Europe. If Najam Sattar still failed to show, Max would have to go home empty-handed.

The aid crowd spent the morning visiting a school financed, of course, by the government in Islamabad. In the afternoon, they listened to an elderly lady thanking the soldiers for protecting them from the Indians, "bloodthirsty beasts." Finally, in the evening, they had to convince a shepherd to interpret a traditional song in Urdu that one of them absolutely had to record. They also visited a bunker that a merchant and his family had built beneath their shop. All these humanitarian visits wore them out, and the evening meal was not enough to satiate their hunger. At precisely nine, the members of the group went their separate ways, and Max found a note in his room: *The small bridge at the village entrance … absolutely have to see this spot before leaving the region. Mountains at midnight illuminated by the moon.*

Of course, Najam Sattar. Max sighed. So, this guy was more of a poet than an engineer.

The guns were quiet now, and the wind as well. It could have been a village in the Alps a century ago, with its oasis for shepherds, no hotels, restaurants, or tourist buses. The moon, full, round, and white, lit up the mountains. Najam Sattar was right, the countryside was even more spectacular at night. Max had no trouble getting to the bridge over the Jhelum, and encountered not a soul on the way. At the height of the long-expected war, the village had been shelled. You could still see marks of it on the houses. *It seems a miracle that the bridge still survived despite the artillery barrages*, thought Max. He leaned on the balustrade and rubbed his hands to keep them warm.

Any minute now, he expected a military patrol to catch him watching the stars, but the village was deserted. Everyone was asleep. Max waited twenty minutes, then half an hour. He thought he'd give it another fifteen minutes before he rejoined the bedbugs. Something unexpected must have come up, or the whole thing was one of Aziz's bad jokes. Then a shadow suddenly appeared on the other side of the bridge, a man smoking. Max ambled over to him. It was a frail, tiny old man from the village he'd seen earlier that day.

"Najam Sattar?" He asked. Surely not. This guy was over eighty years old. With his cigarette-hand, he signalled Max to follow him. He fell in behind the man. They walked quickly and soon found themselves on a path leading deeper and deeper into the woods. Max didn't like the way this was going and hesitated. The old man waited for him on the promontory. Then they walked some more, higher and higher as the trail got bumpy. From time to time, Max stopped for a breather, then to lace his shoe, so he yelled at the old man to wait. When he raised his head, a Kalashnikov was aimed at him and more jihadists in beards and scarves stood waiting to shoot him from the side as well.

"Welcome to Azad Kashmir."

Max's first thought was the 1995 kidnapping of tourists who'd ventured here against all advice from their governments and guides. Their reason? The Indian tourist office had assured them there was nothing to fear up there. They'd been captured by Islamist rebels and held for an exchange involving political prisoners. The government didn't budge, and the body of a decapitated young Norwegian was found weeks later. This perhaps was what Max now had to look forward to. He counted about fifteen of them. Armed to the teeth and with cartridge belts slung over their shoulders, bandolier-style. He also figured on hand grenades, submachine guns, and portable rocket launchers in their backpacks. All that had to weigh a ton and hamper their movements. Max hesitated barely a second and threw over one of the men who was stepping forward, then another onto the hillock behind, instantly throwing himself down a ravine to his right. He was expecting a volley of machine-gun fire, but there was nothing. They must have been under orders. He crossed the stream without looking back and ran a long time, till he was out of breath, finally collapsing behind a boulder. Now what? Where to go? Unbearable pain at the back of his neck squelched all further thought. One lightning flash, then another. He was being beaten mercilessly. When he brought his hands up to his head for protection, the third blow crushed his fingers. His knees hit the ground, and he rolled over onto his side. He could see the muddy boots of the rebels and the rocky path, then, one last time, the rushing waters of the Jhelum between the rocks. Then nothing.

When he came to, Max was in motion, carried by the two heaviest of the group. The old man from the village, his delivery completed, had vanished. Off to his right he heard a growl: they'd noticed he was conscious again. The pair dumped him on the path, and the one who'd hit him, the chief most likely, came over to him.

He ordered Max in very bad English not to cause any more problems. Max got up. In pain, his head was echoing like a gong. Sleeping for a hundred years seemed like the only thing to do, but he was pushed onto the trail, and he asked: "So where are we going?"

"Shut up!"

Then a blow from a rifle butt hit him in the ribs.

The Himalayas were a landscape fit for a calendar, with patches of evergreens clinging to the mountain and letting through occasional glimpses of moonlight. Far off, he heard the sound of a water cascade. Max was trying to get oriented. He had seen Ursa Major from the bridge; now he scanned the sky for the North Star. They were walking east toward India. What the hell did all this mean? They were headed to the mountain on a well-laid-out trail, though narrow, so narrow you couldn't get mules along it. This had to be strictly for human use: smuggling and a night trail for people in a real hurry, the connection between two countries that had hated each other for half a century.

The rebels must have been taking this route several times a month, forging ahead without so much as a glance behind. Which group did it belong to anyway?

Max ran through the names of local organizations in his cracked head, from Hizb-ul-Mujahideen to Lashkar-e-Taiba, and not forgetting Al-Badr and Jaish-e-Mohammed. But why on earth were they headed for Indian Kashmir, when it had to be crawling with soldiers and police? Obviously, they weren't about to kill him just yet, or they'd already have done it. Ransom, maybe? Boy, imagine Luc Roberge's face when he found out two hundred thousand dollars was needed to save his sworn enemy! Now that was a hat Max would love to see him pass around to his colleagues! Two hundred thousand? Sure, why not ... to see his throat cut!

If that were true, they'd be taking him to Pakistan instead, then lock him up nice and tight and call his family. Not so. They were walking into the jaws of the lion, India. Maybe, just maybe, he was getting lucky. There'd be Indian soldiers at the Line of Control, and if he could somehow attract their attention, but then he remembered Jayesh saying that the two Kashmirs had been trading freely forever, in peace or war. India's reinforcement of its positions to counter terrorism — Al-Qaeda, for example, liked to take a turn at the wheel — did nothing to change that. A dotted line on some vague map or other, a pencilled mistake over undetermined territory.

They'd been climbing nonstop in single file. Max sometimes felt a rifle barrel in his back, and that sped him up. The trail was surrounded on every side by mountains, and behind them was the Line of Control, so there had to be a road down below for troop transport, but he couldn't see one.

All of a sudden, the sky lit up: the sun was rising. They'd been walking for eight hours, and Max was wiped. Still there was no question of stopping just yet. Shots could be heard in the distance. Another day was dawning. Then a different sound caught their attention, and it preoccupied the chief of the group for the first time. A gesture from him had the others drag Max onto a different path higher up. Then they disappeared behind a bush as an Indian patrol passed where they had just been with the sound of footsteps and clicking of mess kits. It was now or never, but the chief had his revolver barrel to Max's head.

As soon as they were gone, the band returned to their path and continued walking across the mountain. Once in a while, they lost the trail, and found it again farther off, but it was narrower and narrower each time. Max was worn out and famished, having the feeling they were going round in circles. The sounds of gunfire never let up. He couldn't believe they'd kept up this nonsense for fifty years just to give one another a scare.

The small town of Uri suddenly appeared to the side of the path in full sunlight, and behind the houses was the river Jhelum, though they couldn't see it from where they were. A few kilometres east, in the direction of Srinagar, only steps from the Line of Control, lay Gulmarg, a ski resort that kept working intermittently since the fresh outbreak in the nineties. Now they were in India, so perhaps the rebel base was at Uri, where they were headed.

They had now left the pathway for a narrow dirt road passable to vehicles. Max became hopeful once more. They could see tire tracks in the mud, recent traces. The chief looked left to right and seemed worried again, as though for the first time, things were not going as planned.

From behind a rock, Max saw a parked Jeep, with its motor still running and a flag of the Indian Army on the hood. The soldiers must have got out to pee, have a smoke, or hunt a rabbit. They couldn't be far off and might emerge from the woods at any moment.

Confrontation was imminent, and carnage as well, but there was a chance he could make it out of this, so he made a gesture toward …

Then the gong in his head echoed from a blow once more. A thousand little A-bombs went off in his skull as his eyes fell shut.

41

The wind on his face woke him; a glacial mountain gust that made him shiver from head to toe. The pain was atrocious. The noise, a humming, more like a groaning, from somewhere unknown. He felt burning on his eyelids, which opened only to be blinded by sunlight. He closed them again and tried to roll over on his side, off his sore back. He tried opening his eyes once more and found himself lying on a wooden plank in the hold of a boat. Above him was an opening. That's where the wind and sun were coming from. The groaning came from the motor. With difficulty, he managed to get upright, though his head was spinning. Then there was a shadow over him and words he didn't understand, but he fully expected to be struck again. Instead, someone held out a pan of water. Oh great, first concussion, now gastro-enteritis. What the hell? Why not? He drank greedily, and when he moved away from the vessel, he saw three men leaning over him. They weren't mountain men, but other rebels, bearded like the others and with the same dishevelled turbans.

Beyond them, through the porthole, he was amazed by the landscape: still the same mountains, but the forest had disappeared far off. The boat was on an immense lake swept by the wind. It was a sort of tugboat or fishing boat, but he saw none of the usual equipment. He tried getting up, but his legs wouldn't hold him. He fell down and lost consciousness again. Water on his face this time, and he opened his eyes. Same old jihadists. More water. They really wanted him upright this time. How long had he been out, anyway? An hour, two? No way of telling. The sun was still high, and the boat was in the middle of the lake, far from shore. The motor was off now, and the silence was menacing. They had got where they were going, but where was that? Where they were through injuring him, or was he just being held for a specific purpose, if they bothered to transport him by boat from the forest? The craft was flat-bottomed and covered with a canvas scribbled all over in Arabic lettering. The smell of rotting fish gave him the heaves, but no way was he going to throw up here in front of them. They pushed him firmly, but not violently, onto the tarp, and his face hit the floor. The covering too felt disgusting, and he had the urge to throw up again. That would be the last thing to do. Were those inscriptions a prayer to Allah? This wouldn't be Max's first sacrilege by a long shot, but why make things worse? What was going to happen to him? He wasn't so sure they planned to keep him alive after all. Maybe this covering and this flat-bottomed boat were some sort of ritual, a special death reserved for strangers. He'd be carved up right here and the leftovers tossed into the water.

He had more shivers that had nothing whatsoever to do with the wind. *This is it*, he told himself, *it's all over*. He'd just die out here like a dumb beast in the middle of nowhere. Well, that was also how he'd lived, after all, wasn't it? It was logical: his own personal karma. With a brisk motion, one of the rebels whipped back the tarp beneath his head, and it hit a cold glass surface. The boat-bottom was transparent, like those used to view coral reefs and exotic fish. Now he was really puzzled. Was he the first-ever member of Club Med Kashmir? Clearly, they wanted to show him something, so he swept the bottom with his eyes, trying hard to see through the waters. Okay, there were no fish, no coral reefs, so the tourist season would definitely have to wait. The sun had disappeared behind a cloud and now emerged again. That illuminated the water straight to the bottom. That's when he saw it. First the minaret, then the bit of balcony where the muezzin called the faithful to prayer. Then, farther down, the cupola that was still in good condition. So that was it, a flooded mosque.

"And that's not all there is, Mr. O'Brien. This whole part of the valley was submerged. Twelve villages."

Max turned to see a man with thin grey hair and a well-trimmed beard standing next to him. Tall and Kashmiri-dressed, he wore no weapons, at least none that Max could see. Then, smiling, he said, "I'm forgetting to introduce myself. I am Majid Khankashi, imam of the Kasgari Mosque in Delhi."

Genghis Khan in the flesh.

Max had been expecting a dusty and rumpled Osama bin Laden with a machine gun and munitions belt. Here he was, face to face with practically a dandy. Khankashi helped Max up as the rebels stood guard around them. The imam appeared to be their guest, not their chief or their guide. He signalled one of them and spoke a few words in Urdu. Then a pan of water appeared before Max. He drank greedily like the previous time.

Genghis Khan watched him intently, as if trying to read his thoughts.

"David never mentioned you."

He wasn't the only one, thought Max.

"It's truly terrible what happened to him. A horrendous loss."

"Nothing to do with you then?"

"I had much respect for David, much gratitude, also. Without him, I might still be locked up in Tihar."

"And Ahmed Zaheer?"

The imam smiled sadly. "I've read his articles. Never met him."

Khankashi took Max by the arm to the bridge, while one of the men put the tarp back in place along the bottom. The fresh air did Max good, as the two approached the front railing.

"So we are on the lake created by Stewart-Cooper?" Max asked, though he knew the answer.

"Hindus lived in this valley too, not just Muslims. They were displaced. The lives of thousands were turned upside down.

"The company didn't pay damages?"

"Oh yes, of course, they were relocated, free of cost, nearby in better houses around Rashidabad, and that reduced the influx of migrants to slums of Delhi or Mumbai."

"Thanks to the dam, they lived a little better," ventured Max, "better than the rest of Kashmir, at least. Zaheer emphasized that in his articles."

Majid Khankashi said nothing, silent in thought for a while.

"Oh doubtless," he said with resignation, "but the whole valley lost its soul and its reason for being. Before that, the Himalayas set the pace for people, but now, a hydroelectric complex does that for them." Khankashi turned toward the mountains and the shore.

"The Himalayas are forever, but not SCI. You see, the plant is now closed."

The Indus River that irrigates the eastern part of Kashmir on the other side of Srinagar springs from the Ladakh Heights near the Chinese border, while the Jhelum River has its source in Kashmir, and in the West, the two rivers running parallel on either side of the Line of Control. Once past India, they cross Pakistan from North to South. Somewhere around Mithankot, the Jhelum flows into the Indus along with other waterways from the mountains, a rather undistinguished and anonymous end, but here in Kashmir, the Jhelum still retains all its power for both the greater glory and misfortune of Rashidabad.

"The village clinging to the mountainside, the low and probably dark houses, like the sky at this moment, would be deserted by the tourists, in November, for instance, when the inhabitants are left to their devices after a season of bows and curtsies and forced smiles."

Low, dark houses, like the sky at this moment, were clinging to the mountainside. The village looked abandoned, despite the fact that a few inhabitants came and went. As he crossed the town in Genghis Khan's Jeep, Max had no trouble imagining how dynamic the place had been before the personnel of the complex left. He could picture the bustling main street, the vitality of the shops and small businesses drawn by the centre's employees, and its isolation from the outside world. Of course Srinagar was only a few minutes away by helicopter, and Max had already noticed the landing pad covered by weeds as one entered the village, but who benefited from this other than Susan Griffith and the company bosses?

Now it was all gone, and a cloak of sadness and resignation had descended on Rashidabad. The agitation and dynamism from before the war had only left a bitter taste. These people had been fleeced, and they didn't even know by whom, or how, but they felt themselves victims of a disaster they had no way of measuring. Nor could they explain its origins. The wondrous valley of Kashmir had turned into a nightmare, a bad, greyish, and depressing dream from which no one on either side of the Line of Control could awaken.

Down one street, Max was able to see the gigantic complex out of all proportion to its surroundings, almost as though it wanted to challenge the mountains against which it leaned. Curiously, it didn't seem abandoned, or at least it didn't have that air of broken and discarded toys so prevalent in the other Rashidabad constructions. Max knew nothing about the creation of electricity, but he felt as though it could start up again just like that with the flip of a switch. Maybe the bosses at SCI thought that way, but certainly not the villagers.

The imam Khankashi described the enormous poverty of Kashmir, deprived now of its tourism, replaced with the military and subject to almost daily acts of terror. Whereas in Hyderabad or Bengaluru, a new India was setting aside the Hindu-Muslim conflict, here in the north, the battle raged on, to the great misfortune of the population. At the outset, the issue was a legitimate one: develop the region and invest in infrastructure to remove the motivation and reason for financing extremists, according to New Delhi, by Islamabad. Made desperate by the region's extreme poverty, the people had to be shown by real action that terrorism wouldn't solve anything, but economic development would. Stewart-Cooper also wanted to use southern expertise, which of course pleased the heads of the BJP. Thus the influx of Hinduist technicians, drawn by the promise of work at SCI, would move to Kashmir and help "Hinduize" the region. The Muslims wouldn't be left out either, Khankashi added. The population would provide abundant manpower, and the government also wanted to hire professionals from other regions of India or even overseas: hence the hiring of Najam Sattar.

The retired engineer was waiting for them in the dining room of the New Century, the one and only hotel still open. He was small, round, and nervous, the exact opposite of Khankashi, who was tall, thin, and Britannically calm. Sattar greeted them with a nod. What was he doing here? When he learned a stranger wanted to talk to him about the dam and the death of Zaheer, he'd contacted Khankashi in Srinagar. He did nothing without first consulting the imam.

All through the conversation, he cast glances at Khankashi, and with each new piece of information, the holy man acquiesced with a slight movement of his head, an approval he required at every instant. Sattar spoke of his hiring by Griffith, who'd sought him out in Mumbai though he was already earning a very good living there. Someone had tipped her off that this ex-Kashmiri native was very alert to the misfortunes of his people, so the chance to run the site was particularly attractive to him, as was Griffith's determination.

It was a triumphant return home for Sattar, and what deplorable condition it was in! When his parents had left Srinagar in the seventies, Kashmir was still relatively prosperous, at least by Indian standards. The 1971 war ended in favour of India, and Pakistan had been obliged to cede the eastern portion, now Bangladesh. Both countries emerged extenuated from the war which, despite its cost, had once again failed to solve the Kashmiri problem. Both simply needed to rest and recuperate. At about that time, European charter companies were beginning to discover India and Nepal, and Magic Buses were leaving Paris and Amsterdam filled with hairy hippies loaded with cash, at least by Indian standards, again, and they crossed Turkey, Iran, and Afghanistan to Pakistan, then into India via the Punjab. Numbers of them were enthralled with the beauties of Kashmir before going on to Goa or Kathmandu. Srinagar was a destination of choice, not only for Western millionaires, royal families, or heirs to international fortunes, as always, but ordinary tourists, too, who wanted to make the most of houseboats, mountain hiking, and *shikara* rides on Dal Lake. Imbued with these childhood images, and homesick for Srinagar (as a civil servant in Jammu, his father moved with his family to the other capital every summer), Najam Satar discovered a Kashmir that had fallen prey to chaos. Gone were the tourists, no longer daring to venture north of Amritsar. Gone was the influx of foreign revenue and peaceful evenings at Shalimar Bagh. Welcome back to the skirmishes between Indians and Pakistanis at the Line of Control. Srinagar was a city bled to death, filled instead with soldiers, Hindus for the most part, making their presence only too well known with intimidation, theft, and rape, a breeding ground for violence, and a resistance, and a series of small terrorist groups aiming at the occupying troops but mowing down innocents, the universal victims. Seen from Srinagar, the heart of Kashmir, the most insane project of all: building a hydroelectric plant in the middle of a militarized zone that was ripe for guerrilla action and disputed by the two countries. Nevertheless, it still had a certain chance of success.

Well, at first. With the examples of Bengaluru and Hyderabad to guide them, the government was making serious efforts with this one. Skeptical at first, the population of Rashidabad nevertheless played the game. It was explained that they would be the first to profit from this plant; they'd be hired as construction workers and remembered when it came time to put it into operation. Poorly educated, if at all, and with no technical training, they'd have low-grade jobs like drivers, canteen workers, and security guards. Still, they'd be making more rupees than ever before.

SCI had never concealed the impact all this would have on the area, with the valley flooded, some villages being vacated, and the need to move far away. Ahmed Zaheer, for one, had vaunted the company's approach in *Klean Kashmir*. By then the great upheaval was the subject of much information, advance warnings, and reparations payments. In fact, according to Zaheer's article, some of the valley's inhabitants were disappointed when their rocky little lot wasn't expropriated, unlike that of their neighbours. No surprise there, no popular protest movement, not even a spontaneous demonstration, environmental or otherwise, no "save our riverbanks" like elsewhere in India, like the Narmada Valley in Andhra Pradesh, or China with its Three Gorges Dam.

The government of India contributed, but not just by sending troops. For the first time they were taken care of, without the soldiers coming to ransom their shops and rape their women.

"Sure, the company respected its commitments, and the government, too, up to a point," said Satar, "but one day a bomb exploded on the site, and soon this fine project turned into a nightmare."

"Like the one in David's car?"

"A Hinduist job," said Khankashi.

"I suppose that's what Griffith negotiated: an agreement that allowed hiring quotas, separate work spaces for Brahmins, et cetera," said Max.

"Well, the first agreement did."

"The first?"

"There was a second secret one."

Max was amazed.

"Ten million U.S. paid to the extremists. So, basically, the Hinduists agreed to halt the sabotage, provided she finance their terrorism elsewhere in India."

"With Griffith between a rock and a hard place, her Muslim workers deserted, and the site was about to close, so she had no choice."

"Do you have proof of this agreement?"

"Ahmed Zaheer did. That's what David came to look for in Srinagar after the journalist died," added Khankashi.

It was clear to Max at last. David had carried the baton after Zaheer dropped it, and he'd been killed, too, but who exactly had ordered it?

Genghis Khan smiled sadly once more. "You disappoint me, Mr. O'Brien. You haven't yet asked me with which Hinduist leader Griffith did her negotiating."

Max looked puzzled.

"With Sri Bhargava, the Durgas chief, the 'James Bond of Hinduness.'"

"That's what the engineer had revealed to the journalist Ahmed Zaheer when they met," said Max.

"Not at all. Zaheer's only interest was in ecology," replied Sattar.

"So David …"

"I never talked to him, never even knew him."

Max turned to the imam. "But you did. The Indian cops confirmed that David came to see you the day preceding the attack."

"Simply to tell me that Zaheer had been killed at Niagara Falls, probably by Bhargava's men. He was on the point of doing something that gave meaning to his life: 'I know why Zaheer's dead. I know what they wanted from him.' What is going on, I asked, and he said, 'For the first time in my life, I have the power to change things.' The next day, came the kidnapping, torture, and explosion in the Volvo. Years apart, David and his father had sacrificed their lives the same way. For the same reasons, maybe."

I've become just like him. I feel just what he felt.

"Normally, diplomats don't get involved," Khankashi went on. "They stay within a very precise framework, a well-established code of conduct that remains the same from one country to the next: the national interest before all else, especially the individual. For David, it was the other way around."

For Philippe, too.

42

The Hinduists, all of a sudden, were dazzled by the light of "reason." Susan Griffith clearly explained what they doggedly refused to comprehend, and here we are, good buddies straight off. The violence ceases and the site can start up again. You just had to talk to them like grownups, right?

"Oh, sure, way too easy," Max exclaimed, when he finally got Juliette on the phone from the New Century.

A second agreement. Uh-huh, just a few minor adjustments to cover one's tracks. Meanwhile behind the other curtain, a magic trick, sleight of hand for which Indian Muslims were still paying.

David's meeting with Genghis Khan was "doing something that gives meaning to my life" at the very moment they'd discovered Zaheer's body at Niagara Falls. Griffith and Bhargava, not to mention Bernatchez, naturally. Juliette's thoughts were in complete turmoil, when Max added, "David was convinced Zaheer's death was murder, not an accident, as the cops thought. On his trip to Canada, he wanted to meet the cop in charge of the investigation."

"Joan Tourigny."

"He knew why the journalist had been killed and wanted to continue the fight to the finish. What he found in Zaheer's apartment gave him what he needed."

"Concretely to —"

"Blow the whistle on Griffith and neutralize Bharagava, then stop more massacres from happening. What they couldn't get from the journalist, David had on him."

"A photo, document, what?"

"Who knows, but it has to be why David was kidnapped first and killed later, also why they tortured him … to make him talk."

Juliette was half convinced.

They were both bothered by other things Sattar and Khankashi had said. After Zaheer was dead, they must have searched his apartment thoroughly. Yet they found nothing, obviously because David had "it" on him when he got back from Kashmir, unless he found the proof elsewhere, not in Zaheer's apartment. Till now, Max had taken for granted that David had what he wanted already when he came back from Srinagar. What if he hadn't found it after all, and when he realized Zaheer's apartment had already been searched, he looked elsewhere for whatever it was when he went to Khankashi's.

"Try and remember, Juliette. What happened when he returned home — exactly what happened? Did you offer to go get him at the airport?"

"No, I was teaching. Besides, it was trip he made often, routinely even."

"So he took a taxi, probably frustrated. Did he have one suitcase or two?"

"Just one," she replied, "the same one he left with a few days before. He unpacked it in our room as soon as he got back."

"In front of you?"

"Yes."

"Any gifts, souvenirs, surprises?"

She said, "No, not this time. At first there'd been small things, but after a while ..."

Nothing.

She was trying her best to unravel the last hours in her husband's life, but no dice. She had answers to all Max's questions and doubts. If David did bring something back, it wasn't on him when he arrived.

The Montreal conference was tomorrow, and everyone breathed a sigh of relief. On the political front, *détente* was the order of the day. After generous offers to exterminate one another, India and Pakistan were all kissy-kissy. A day earlier, the demonstrations of love took a new turn. Diplomats were exchanged, airline routes were reactivated, and there were moving joint declarations and accolades. Suddenly, it was a festival of love. The media chronicled the return of foreign expats, looking humbled and guilty, to the indifference of locals. They, of course, never believed any of this silly war talk for a minute. These Westerners, they're so fatalistic.

Juliette spotted Vandana near the buffet at the Sheraton Centre, in a hurry to fill her plate before the stampede. She was perplexed by what Juliette had to tell her.

"The slightest detail is important," Juliette told her.

"Look …"

"Please, I beg you."

"Well, David was tense, more than usual," she said, "irritable, in fact. He had the conference to prepare for, and he got a late start on it, so I had to pick up the slack. Caught between two fires, he said."

"What, exactly?"

"A whole lot of paperwork he asked me not to send until he returned. Then he blamed me …"

Juliette closed her eyes. So that was it. So obvious now. She could kick herself for not thinking of it before. The "preparation," the dozens of document boxes put together by the High Commission.

Vandana looked at her in confusion. Then Juliette briefly explained what she and Max now knew.

"David didn't give you anything?"

Vandana shook her head.

"Some object, a document or some 'insignificant' thing?"

"Why me?"

"That was one of your jobs, wasn't it?"

Vandana shrugged, "Well, I wasn't the only one in the office that did that sort of thing."

"Wait a minute, I've just thought of something. One evening he said, 'Vandana's swamped. She doesn't know whether she's coming or going.'"

"So he would have taken the document with him if it was that important."

"He was afraid the same thing would happen to him as Zaheer, so he wanted to be certain that" — Juliette cut her herself off, then continued — "who was in charge of receiving the documents? I mean the ones sent to Canada after the so-called trip to Kathmandu?"

"Foreign Affairs in Ottawa, like all the others."

As well as to any participant who requested them.

The airport in Burlington, Vermont, was dead calm when Max landed after a detour via Philadelphia. At the Avis desk, there was a weekend promotion. He chose a Pontiac Grand Am and headed to Montreal on Highway 89. After Juliette's call, he could understand David's nervousness on his return from Srinagar, not to mention his disquiet and insomnia. He needed to find a safe place for "it" in case Zaheer's killers came after him, too.

"So he hid it in the papers needed for the conference," Juliette explained, but he still needed a contact, someone in cahoots who would keep it safe till he got there.

A friend.

Patterson.

Juliette remembered they'd spoken several times that evening. Late into the night. She, of course, thought it was about the conference, yet when Max met him the first time, Patterson said he hadn't talked to David for days. Lie number one. So, when he got back from Srinagar, David planned to send the famous document hidden among the file material for the conference. Patterson received it at the same moment David was bombed thousands of kilometres away. That also explained why Pattrson had hired private security for David. He realized what the young diplomat had sent him, and he knew how much it could endanger his life, both of their lives now. So that's why he was so suspicious, especially of Max.

All sorts of questions poured through his head. Why was Patterson laying low? Why not tell the cops and neutralize the threat to himself? There were things Patterson had known from the beginning, much more than he was letting on. All he ever told Max was already known anyway. Max lost himself in theories, when Patterson was safe and dry in reality, watching him flailing around without reaching out to help.

The consultant was only too ready to lay the blame for the attack on Islamist groups and steer Max's search in a particular direction. It had taken Vandana to open his eyes later to the Hinduists, something Patterson should have done from the start. They had their own reasons for getting rid of David. The security agents he hired for David in the hospital were to reassure Juliette, who had not asked for any of it. He knew that the terrorists never invaded hospitals to finish off their victims.

For reasons still unknown to Max, Patterson did not want his mission to succeed. He'd even tried to discourage him and put Roberge on his trail. "He forced me," he said. Maybe, maybe not. So Roberge's blackmail had arrived in the nick of time. But if Patterson was playing a double game, why?

Max went around the Champlain Mall in Brossard keeping an eye out for any cops that might be around. Customers, loiterers, and nothing else. He stopped his car at one of the entrances and looked at the time. Still a few minutes to go before his rendezvous with Juliette. If anything went wrong, Max would go to Patterson's office alone. A Diamond taxi stopped in front of the shopping centre, and Juliette got out. Max glanced around but didn't see any suspicious-looking cars, doggedly aimless pedestrians, or overly nonchalant employees. He waited five minutes, then got out, too. Inside, he paid no attention to the hair salon and video arcade, then went up the central aisle to the drugstore, and there was Juliette again by the candy counter, pretending to choose between two chocolate bars.

"Grab one for me, would you?" he asked.

She threw herself into his arms, and the show of emotion surprised him.

"I was so afraid!"

Max just smiled. "How's the son and heir?"

"Great, but I can't say the same for his mother. Nonstop headaches."

"Join the club!"

Out in the car, she told him that Patterson was waiting for them at his place. She'd talked to the consultant on the phone that morning. He was working from home, so they could drop by anytime. The former diplomat lived in the west part of town on the corner of Saint Marc and Lincoln, a crash-pad he'd had since his divorce in 1993, after some financial woes. His wife had kept the house in Repentigny; he got the debts and souvenirs. Here in the middle of all these boxes, he and Max had made their financial agreement. It was humiliating for Patterson, and he'd rather have done without Max's help, but he had no choice. The bank was after him, and his ex's lawyers, too. His life was one very leaky boat, so one day, like Philippe, he'd placed the usual ad in the daily that Max read every day in the vain hope of renewing contact with David or Béatrice. And then one day, surprise, surprise, Max agreed to Patterson's request, for reasons he'd already explained to Juliette. No way was he going to let David's "surrogate father" go bankrupt and leave David high and dry.

The building was populated by divorcées and bachelors drowning their solitude in workaholism and trying to give some meaning to their lives. They got no answer in the entrance — strange — so Max took advantage of one tenant's leaving to slip into the hallway and up to the twelfth floor, where Patterson lived. He rang, but still got no answer. He had no difficulty picking the lock and entering the apartment. The place was dark — the vertical blinds kept out the daylight. Juliette made to open them, but Max signalled her not to touch anything. Besides, by now, their eyes had adjusted. Max looked around and saw three rooms in relative order, obviously the work of a cleaning woman. Minimal decor: white, cold, impersonal, but functional furniture that Max already knew. A worker ant's retreat, one more workaholic. The bedroom was bland, too. The bathroom showed clean towels hung in an orderly fashion around the bathtub.

But where was Patterson?

Max took another turn around the place, drawn by the table in the kitchenette that was strewn with papers. Max took up a file and glanced at it: a series of letters to a Korean fibre-optic company based in British Columbia and some bills. Also a map of Vancouver, an Air Canada schedule, and hotel names and phone numbers scribbled on a notepad.

"He left in a hurry," ventured Juliette.

"Without his agenda?" replied Max leafing through a notebook with rigid binding.

Now Juliette was rifling through a small desk in the corner on the way into the dining room, looking for some clue, a document, something, anything, while Max explored a cupboard on the other side of the room. The desk drawers weren't locked, but all they held were mostly pens, staplers, and Scotch tape; not much in the way of files. The bottom compartment, though, was a filing cabinet. Juliette pulled out some documents and started leafing through them rapidly. Press releases, a lawyer's bill, the lease. Then Juliette opened another file. Personal letters, some very old and still in their envelopes

Out of one of them slipped a copy of an old passport form with the regulation photos stapled to it. She picked it up and glanced at it casually. Then her face froze, and she felt dizzy. She just stood there, still holding it and unable to move. She turned to Max, who was busy rifling through the cupboard. She didn't know what to do … keep quiet and not say anything? Well, not right now, anyway.

She slipped the form and photos of Pascale into her bag.

Max was on the floor near the couch, poring over a box of archives pulled from under a pile of books. Mostly tax accounts and financial records. That's when he noticed something down there, lying in between the carpet threads. Dirt. Someone had been in the living room after walking on soft, wet earth. Intrigued, he looked farther. No plants. Then he looked at the glass door to the balcony and the vertical blinds, which he pulled aside. Light flooded the place and he saw the cement rail of the balcony, an overturned flower box, and a footprint. He opened the door and went outside. The footprint was pretty large, probably Patterson's. The earth was still moist.

He straightened up and looked around him. On all sides he saw balconies identical to this one. He heard the sound of skateboards. He went to the edge and looked twelve stories down to see kids using the garage roof for practice. The noise echoed all the way up there. He was about to go in when he saw something, and so did the teens at the same moment. Patterson's body was jammed into the garage vent. The kids quit skating to get closer. Then came the police sirens.

43

Max grabbed Juliette by the wrist and dragged her out and down the hallway. Still no one around. They took the stairs at the end of the corridor as more sirens sounded. In a few moments, the place would be crawling with cops, and they had to get out right away. They raced down the steps to the laundry in the basement. They found a fire exit across the room next to a soft-drink machine and exited into the alley. From there they saw a cop car racing down Sherbooke Street with lights flashing and siren blaring at full volume. They ran in the other direction, went in the service door of an Italian restaurant, and came out on Maisonneuve, where they blended in with passersby. More sirens and flashing lights, and they ducked into the Metro.

‡

Juliette saw Max's silhouette reflected in the window while the train rushed on to who-knew-where.

Dennis Patterson, dead.

Plus what she'd found and didn't dare tell him … Pascale.

She bit her lips. Then Max turned to her.

"We didn't finish searching. That means the killers easily found what they wanted. Then pushed Patterson over the edge. Why take the risk of being seen by the neighbours?"

There was no way of knowing.

"Or else they didn't find anything, because Patterson wouldn't let them in and tried to escape via the balcony."

"So he slipped?" asked Juliette.

"They searched the place, but fast and not well. Someone could see the body at any time."

"There's nothing implicating us," said Juliette.

"Except the surveillance cameras," said Max. He closed his eyes. So they'd been seen going in. All anyone had to do was call the cops, so maybe it was a trap?

Something Jayesh said came back to him: *"So we aren't a threat to them anymore."*

"Not at all."

"And that's why no one's been coming after us."

Right, for once, thought Max. They must be near their goal, closing in on the guilty parties in a tightening spiral.

"Suppose David had not risked transferring what he found in Zaheer's apartment via the conference after all? What if he'd taken the 'school-bus route,' the long way around? Maybe Patterson was just too obvious a choice. So, what about someone else, say, Béatrice?"

"She was in Delhi, so she couldn't collect it," answered Juliette.

"Collect it, no, but transport it, maybe."

"Béatrice? A courier? No, she'd never go for that."

"Maybe she didn't even realize it."

David's mother, standing in the living room of her Rockhill apartment, was all the more scared of Max's determination than his mere presence here with Juliette as his "hostage." She gripped her pistol firmly, though, the one she usually kept in her glovebox and was as easy to use as a tube of lipstick.

"The radio says the police are looking for you, so don't waste your time telling me they're on the wrong trail."

Max turned to Juliette, who confirmed that he had nothing to do with Patterson's death.

Béatrice slid her other hand into the pocket of her bathrobe without taking her eyes off Max or cancelling her threat.

"Honestly, what on earth have you been telling her? You are so pathetic, you really are."

A cellphone. With her thumb, she was already dialling a number: Roberge, Juliette guessed. She tried to intervene, but was too late. Max sent the pistol flying onto the glass-topped coffee table and grabbed the phone before she could finish, while Juliette picked up the gun. Now, Béatrice really did look worried.

"Don't you want to find out what happened to David and catch the guys who did it? Is that why you turned me in to Roberge?"

"Stop this circus right now, and quit implicating Juliette in your fantasy. She's got nothing to gain. Nothing at all."

"Except the truth," Max said, staring at her.

"The Canadian government's more concerned about its reputation overseas and its commitments in the region than by the investigation into the murder of a diplomat. The Department is just letting the Indians mess around anyway they like, and will swallow anything, no questions asked."

"And what's your version?"

"David was no random victim!" yelled Juliette. "He was hand-picked."

This bewildered Béatrice.

"Juliette's right. The Indians just play the Islamists and Hinduists off against one another to cloud the issue: the imam Khankashi — so-called defender of the Islamists — as well as Sri Bhargava and his inevitable Durgas, not to mention Doval Shacteree, the radical communist who can't hold up under torture. The official version is just gossip, no more than that."

"David never even went to Kathmandu," said Juliette.

"Srinagar, actually," added Max, "following the trail of a journalist, Ahmed Zaheer, who's just died in Niagara Falls. He'd gone there in secret, because he was interested in a Canadian company, Stewart-Cooper International, who were in charge of a hydroelectric project in Rashidabad, Kashmir."

"A deal with the devil to keep the place running smoothly, a deal David wanted to expose."

"When he got back to Delhi, he confided in Khankashi that he was determined to change things."

Béatrice closed her eyes.

"What the hell was going on those last days before the attack?" Max asked. "I want you to tell me all … in detail, and don't leave out a thing, even if you think it doesn't matter. Do you hear me?"

Béatrice had seen David a few times, but rarely out of Juliette's company. "With all that shopping, I hardly ever …"

"Were you staying in the house?"

"The guest room in the back," Juliette said.

Béatrice had several suitcases, but she packed every one herself.

"Was David anywhere around?"

"No, and they were never out of my sight all the way to the airport. The same thing happened the second time."

"Second time?"

"I was supposed to leave on the tenth, but one evening David asked me to stay with Juliette a few more days." She turned to the young woman. "He thought you looked tired, and he blamed himself for being away so much."

Extend her visit in Delhi? Max looked at Juliette, who shrugged. This was news to her.

"There were problems with this. Air France refused to move the reservation to May 13 with the special rate. David fought with them and lost."

Max got it now. He jumped on the phone and got the number he wanted from 411, then dialled it. There was voicemail and endless transfers, then a young woman's melodious voice: "Air France. Customer Service."

"This is Claude Ferron, Transit Travel. Listen, I have a customer whose refund was refused for a Delhi-to-Montreal flight on ..."

"May 10," Béatrice repeated.

He gave the young woman Béatrice's name and heard her typing on her keyboard.

"What's going on, Max?" Juliette asked, but he ignored her.

"I'm not sure I understand. Everything here seems normal," said the lady.

"Normal?"

"Yes, indeed, Mrs. O'Brien travelled with us."

"What about the thirteenth?"

"Yes. She travelled with us twice."

"You're sure?"

"Yes, absolutely."

He put down the phone, as Béatrice and Juliette stared in fascination, but Max had no time to explain.

"I need your car," he told Béatrice.

On Décarie Boulevard, he started speeding. This was the best way to get noticed, but all sorts of things were rushing through his head. He knew he needed to take care and blend in with the suburbanites, especially right now, but now he'd figured out *what*, he needed to find out *who*. Next to him sat Juliette, who'd been silent since they left Béatrice's place. As they turned onto Côte de Liesse Road, he looked at her.

"That piece of evidence. We always thought it was an object, some document, but it was a person."

"What?"

"Yes, an individual, and this was someone whom David went to fetch from Zaheer's place in Srinagar. He went by train and by bus and brought that person back to Delhi the same way in time to take Béatrice's place on the plane. To Montreal."

Juliette stared at him in stupefaction.

"All he had to do was get Béatrice to delay her departure and pretend Air France had agreed unexpectedly to transfer her trip to the later date. David just bought another ticket, and Béatrice was none the wiser. So, on May tenth, someone travelled in her place."

"And it had to be a woman."

"With a fake passport, which could easily be set up at the High Commission. Say, another tourist had lost her papers, for instance." Max smiled. So David was a bit of a crook himself … all for a good cause.

"So this Madame X is in Montreal," replied Juliette.

"Patterson met her at Dorval Airport, to take her into hiding till David got there."

That's what they phoned each other about when he got back from Srinagar. Then the bombing changed everything, and with David in a coma, all Patterson could do was wait for him to recover and try not to attract attention. Max's, for instance.

"But why insist on hiding her himself? He could have got her police protection."

Max had no answer to that.

"His killers thought, like us, that they were looking for a document or some object. First, they tried to make David talk, but it didn't work. Then they wanted to question Patterson, but he tried to escape and died. They searched his place from top to bottom for nothing."

So, "living proof," a helpless woman who dared not show her face, suspicious and terrified by everyone and everything. Who was she, and where was she? What was it about her that made her so dangerous to those tracking her?

Max parked in the short-term lot at the airport and, before getting out, cast a look around: the usual travellers with wheeled suitcases and today's paper under their arms. The police would certainly be on patrol, especially on the departures floor. Max had no intention of taking flight, though. Exactly the opposite. He took Juliette across the lot to the ground floor, where friends and family gathered to welcome their loved ones home. Without drawing attention to himself, he opened a door marked for authorized personnel only and found himself in a neon-lit corridor. Some men were chatting by a coffee machine. An unwatched TV showed a report on the discovery of Patterson's body behind his building. Interview with Detective Sergeant Bruno Mancini of the Criminal Investigation Branch at the QPF, who was in charge of the inquest. Max was afraid they might mention his name or show his photo, but no, there was nothing. They went down yet another corridor, and Max knew where he was. Same office at the end of the hall.

Totally unperturbed, Antoine turned to him and said, "You want to close the door behind you?"

The crowd was stepping fast and jerky, like an old silent movie at the wrong speed. On the tape, Juliette recognized the arrivals area they'd been in only moments before. Some Indians were waiting for a cousin or a brother-in-law. Mothers and fathers awaited their kids returning from a trip to France or a long voyage to Nepal or Thailand. On the first screen, automatic doors opened and closed to passengers with their baggage carts. A second showed those waiting for them, some with a sign with the passenger's name on it, The third panned over the space between the passengers' exit and the main doors. If Patterson had come to meet David's unknown person, as Max thought, camera two would most likely give them what they wanted.

Max had been looking from one screen to another for half an hour, trying to identify the former diplomat. Antoine, off to one side, leaned into his console, silent as always. Juliette watched, wondering if he knew what she'd found going through Patterson's files.

His sister, Pascale, was alive.

She asked Antoine to pass her the phone book from the shelf, and she leafed through it, looking for an address, when suddenly on the third monitor, appeared a familiar silhouette, and Max ordered Antoine to switch to normal speed. There was Patterson threading through the crowd. He'd traded his jacket for leather and his normal dress shirt for a T-shirt. Then he disappeared and reappeared to face the second camera. He was in the middle of a group of Sikhs gathered at the cordon separating them from the glass doors. Patterson looked at his watch, then at the people around him.

Antoine, never losing sight of the screen, said, "This guy's the one I told you about, the one I saw at her place when you were in prison."

Max whipped around. "What the hell are you talking about?"

"That picture on TV just now, he's older, but it's the same guy."

This was the mysterious stranger who'd taken Pascale to Europe and kept her incommunicado all those years, the one who'd observed her cremation at Varanasi from on high and then fled, the one he and Antoine had tried to find all over the city afterward to no avail.

What was Dennis Patterson doing at Pascale's cremation? What did she have to do with all this, the second anchor point in his two universes after IndiaCare and Sister Irène's abandoned girls?

Max retreated into his own thoughts, nose to the screen. Patterson, incognito, waiting in the crowd, Juliette off to one side, undecided. *Now*, she told herself, *There's no good time, so now might as well be it.*

"Max ..."

But he was worked up about something. On the screen, Patterson had raised his hand, waving to someone. He went around two people standing next to the cordon, and there, approaching, was a passenger who'd just gone through customs. The person was temporarily hidden behind baggage on the cart. Max glanced at the left-hand monitor. No way to see who it was. Then Patterson himself was in the way, but when he grasped the bar to push the cart, he shifted to the right, and there was a young woman, wearing a *salwar*, turning her back to the camera as they both drifted into the centre of the crowd and off screen. They reappeared on the third monitor, albeit later on, and the young woman briefly moved her head till she was facing the camera.

Antoine paused the tape and zoomed in for a close-up. Her face was still blurred and grainy, but they could still make out her features. Her hair was tied back, her eyes deep, serious, and concentrated. She was scarcely twenty, virtually an adolescent, and she obediently followed Patterson. Oddly, her face reminded Max of someone, and he asked Antoine to replay the tape, and again. Now back to the freeze-frame. Max was sure he'd seen her before.

The Mughal Palace.

She was the young waitress at the buffet where Patterson ate on the ground floor of the Labyrinth.

PART FOUR

INDRANI

44

Of course, that was it ... hide her in the middle of the Indian neighbourhood, among her own and in plain sight. What better way to protect her? thought Juliette. Patterson had done it right. She asked Max to slow down, and he checked the rear-view mirror as he took his foot off the gas. She'd made a point of going with him instead of staying quietly behind with Antoine.

After zigzagging through the traffic, Max turned left on Jean Talon, then right to the Al Sunnah Al Nabawiah Mosque. He stopped the car in front of Athena Park. The Labyrinth was just across from them.

"Okay, leave this to me," exclaimed Juliette, just as Max was about to get out.

"Better stay here. It'll be safer."

But Juliette was already crossing the street, so Max fell in behind.

Office workers on a smoke break crowded the front doorway, so the pair wove through them and headed for the cafeteria, which was full to bursting, as usual. Same crowd, same chit-chat. The Mughal Palace was a gold mine. At the far end, Juliette couldn't see the girl among the other employees. Perhaps she had quit, to hide even deeper among the anonymous city's masses. Max pushed aside a few grumbling workers, thrust aside trays, then planted himself next to the glass-encased counter with *rogan josh* and *dum aloo*, but Juliette beat him to it.

"The girl that usually works here, I'd like to talk to her ..."

With his serving spoon raised, the server looked at Max and Juliette in puzzlement, while customers behind them began grousing once again, louder this time. He turned to one of his colleagues and said something in Hindi. A second man approached them, while a third dialled his phone, and behind him a door opened and closed. Through the half-opening, appeared another uniform — the young girl's.

There wasn't a minute to lose, and Max pushed Juliette aside, leaned on the cash register, and jumped over the counter, jostling the server as he did so. Behind Juliette, customers were shouting, as indignation gave way to panic. Max ran for the door, but the telephone guy was in his way, so a solid punch sent him flying into a pile of dishes that cascaded onto him in a deafening racket. Now the entire cafeteria was dead silent, with all eyes on the Indian counter. Max made the most of it to head for the door, this time with Juliette trailing behind. Before it could close behind them, though, she saw two security firm uniforms running after them with walkie-talkies in hand.

The food at the Mughal Palace was prepared at the restaurant a few streets down and delivered every morning. Max and Juliette found themselves in the storage space that was also the loading dock for some other franchises. At the end of the day, it was also where the empty cardboard boxes were piled, along with the leftovers and other detritus from the clients. In other words, they were backstage, and they saw the Indian girl running for the far exit, and behind them, the two security officers. Everything was stacked against Juliette and Max: the girl and the agents knew the place, and soon the police would have it surrounded. The security agents had to be slowed down, no matter what. Juliette got Béatrice's 25-calibre handgun out of her bag — "easier than a tube of lipstick" — and she fired in the general direction of the men, but into the air nevertheless. Clearly, they weren't armed, because they froze on the spot. This was beyond their pay grade, so they left things to the "real" cops.

The alley was deserted, and the young Indian woman had disappeared. The security agents had given up completely. Now there were sirens, but the officers knew their quarry had weapons and would use them. Max and Juliette looked around. They were in the rear alley behind the stores on Jean Talon, with stairs leading to apartments above. The girl could have dodged into almost any place across the way. Max and Juliette had no way of finding her. It was all over.

Just then, Juliette spotted a statue lying horizontal next to the brick wall of what appeared to have once been a store. She knew it to be Shiva Nataraja with its four arms dancing in a circle of fire, and in doing so, the right foot crushed Mulayaka, the demon of ignorance. It was the most common god figure in India, and she'd seen it everywhere, from the Ramnagar Fort palace in Varanasi to the off-duty shop at Indira Gandhi Airport. The local Indian population had converted this store into a temple. Juliette dragged Max along with her. If ever they needed the gods, especially Shiva, it was now. Inside, it was dark and deserted, the old statue in the alley having been replaced by a shiny new one. The wheel of flames was larger and even more spectacular.

For an instant, Juliette felt as though she were back in India, instantly transported thousands of kilometres from Montreal. Somehow, nothing mattered much anymore. She was barely aware of police sirens wailing, their pursuers, the shots she'd fired, and she'd fire again if need be. It had all just faded away.

Max seemed similarly affected by the place and atmosphere. Shiva the dancer god was Pascale's favourite — "Fear nothing. I am here to protect you." A sound caught their attention, a rubbing, a bit like a snake sliding across the ground. In India, thought Juliette, the temples were infested with snakes, symbol of Ananta, who watched over Vishnu in his sleep. Had Montreal Hindus gone so far as to import snakes to decorate their temples? First Max, then Juliette looked behind the statue of Shiva, and the rubbing sound recurred. Max heard a wisp of breath, and, in the dimness, spotted a glimpse of silhouette, then the Mughal Palace uniform and the girl wearing it. She was in the corner, rolled up in a ball with her legs bent tight. What they had heard was the scuffing of her shoes on the temple pavement.

She seemed terror-struck, and now that she'd been caught, she didn't hold her breath anymore. Her breathing was jerky and nervous, as though she couldn't choose between howling in panic or breaking down in tears. Max held out his right hand to her, palm open like Shiva, and softly said, "There's nothing to be afraid of. We're here to protect you."

"*Abhaya mudra*," repeated Juliette in Hindi. At last her university courses were of some use.

The girl seemed somewhat reassured.

"You are friends of David's?" she asked hesitantly in English.

"His uncle," said Max.

"His wife," said Juliette.

The girl closed her eyes a long while, but then the sirens snapped Max and Juliette back to reality.

"Do you know this temple? Is there another way out?"

Wordlessly, the young woman got up and took them to a hidden door to the right of the altar, then a stairway behind a partition, along the wall. In moments, they were on the roof among empty cans of spray paint and used condoms. From here, they could see the neighbouring roofs, as well as the terraces for some of the duplexes, and, below them, the streets being throttled by the fruitless search for Max, Juliette, and Miss X. Fruitless for the moment, at least.

The young woman turned to them. "My name's Indrani."

Max recalled a corpulent man, proudly so, as if girth were a sign of success and prosperity, an obesity he displayed with neither embarrassment nor regret, going so far as to select tight shirts that underscored his belly. He'd come to America thin and svelte, but, like a tree over the years, his trunk had acquired new layers. Now the man who stood before them had hollow cheeks, the light in his face had gone out, and his emaciated limbs floated in clothes that were too ample. Siddharth Srinivasan was a mere shadow of his former self. It seemed to Max that Jayesh's father was a sick man.

"Contrariness, that's his problem," exclaimed his wife wiping her hands on her apron. Deepa went around the stationary bicycle that stood in his way and toward the new arrivals.

Jayesh's parents had passed their prominent facial traits on to their son, though he resembled his mother more. Wearing a sports shirt and slacks like her husband, Max felt she was responsible for Siddharth's new look and lifestyle.

"She's been feeding me grapefruit for six months," he sighed.

Deepa turned to Max. "The same food every day, as if it were all my fault! Who's been stuffing themselves these past thirty years? Who, eh?"

Max just knew somehow they had this same discussion every day, too, with or without an audience.

Deepa and Siddharth exchanged accusing glances punctuated with acerbic remarks until they realized Juliette and Indrani were standing behind Max, slightly off to the side.

"You and Jayesh are in trouble again," remarked Siddharth, noticing the two women.

"Jayesh isn't, at least."

"That would indeed surprise me," replied Deepa turning to Juliette and adding, "it is so terrible what happened to your husband."

Their living room hadn't changed a bit. There was the same extravagant furniture, way too massive for the Birnam Street place, the same abstract-but-kitschy pictures testifying to their fumbling attempts to blend in locally.

Max consoled himself with the thought that the bad taste acquired here reflected more on North America than it did on the Srinivasans. The wall also displayed photos tracing the life path of Siddharth; first black-and-whites showing a slim, young Indian man who sold used Oldsmobile Cutlasses, then moved on to new ones in an immense fluorescent-lit showroom.

The Srinivasans could have moved out of the neighbourhood, like numerous other Indians who had "made it," and set up in some cushy suburb on the South Shore, for instance, but they could never bring themselves to leave the triplex on Birnam Street. They'd made one very big move, and that was enough for them.

Siddharth asked Max, "Do you need a lawyer?"

"Just a safe place for Indrani right now."

"Well, she's got that here, but I'm worried about if she's eating enough." Siddharth turned to Indrani and said something in Hindi. She shook her head.

"Okay," Deepa said, "Jayesh's room, but she'll have to excuse the mess."

"Unless she's partial to the Dark Demon," replied her husband with a mysterious smile.

Dark Demon? Through the partly drawn curtain over the kitchen sink was the apparition of an enormous homestyle Daybreak 34 RV, which half-filled the backyard and was about the size of Red Fort in Delhi.

"That horror! He loves it more than his wife."

The Srinivasans were used to eating in front of the TV. That night, while an exhausted Indrani slept in the next room, they, Max, and Juliette finished their meal watching a news report of the Indo-Canadian conference, which had just begun.

Naturally, the death of Patterson, following so soon after David's, weighed on them, and the organizers, who knew Patterson, praised his courage, honesty, professionalism, and great knowledge of the Asian markets. Next came Detective Sergeant Mancini's press conference on the "mysterious" murder, as well as the flight of Max and the complicity — now no longer in doubt — of Juliette. The "hostage" had surely become an accomplice via a particularly shocking manifestation of the Stockholm Syndrome. Curiously, there was no mention of Indrani in the report. Max recognized three Mughal Palace employees and realized the scale of the police search around the Labyrinth, including his old friend Luc Roberge. Standing next to Mancini, Roberge summed up Max's criminal "career" for the viewers. A notorious fraud, he called him, a crook who was a past master in the art of manipulation and self-transformation, a recidivist who had cut a swath of misfortune and desolation over the years, but a murderer? Here Roberge hesitated. He'd known his share of crooks, and very rarely were they killers. He had his doubts about Max's guilt on this score, although with him anything was possible, so perhaps he had changed.

Siddharth Srinivasan pushed away the *thali*, which contained the remainder of his dried grapefruit. This was really not fit to eat.

45

Indrani came from a small village in Bihar, one of the poorest states of India. Nourished by this misery, of course, were also hate, violence, and intolerance. Hindus and Muslims faced off, just waiting for a chance to exterminate one another. Thus childhood for Indrani and her older sister was unhappy, especially with their mother raped and killed by Muslims. All their father thought about was avenging her death, and he turned into an enraged fanatic. Indrani and her sister saw the RSS militants meeting regularly in their home, each more radical than the next, and talking about it long into the night. Gradually, the girls joined with the adults in their way of thinking, renouncing their Muslim friends and boycotting non-Hindu stores. They followed their father to Uttar Pradesh when he went to try and find a better life. What they found was more like a battlefield.

Ayodhya.

The destruction of the Babri Mosque, then the pogrom, saw thousands of Muslims hunted by Hindu extremists.

"That morning, the RSS fanatics marched just outside our windows," Indrani recalled. "My father was among them, and he was proud to be there. Him and his high-flying zealots were finally going to deal with that sacrilegious mosque. For my sister and me, it was the finest proof of love he could offer us. The greatest homage to my mother as well. When they got there they took apart the mosque stone by stone like an army of ants, and they yelled Hinduist slogans while they were doing it."

One hundred and fifty thousand fundamentalists, including Indrani's father in the front lines, exacting vengeance for his wife. Normally, the police would intervene to stop it, but the BJP-run government of Uttar Pradesh ordered them not to.

The killings began the following night all over India, and once again the authorities refused to intervene. Two thousand dead in three days: Muslims, mostly, including women and children, but finally Delhi did apply some pressure, and the cops of Uttar Pradesh were forced reluctantly to do their work and gradually gain control of the situation.

"When my father got home, he was changed," Indrani continued. "He was even proud more spellbound than before, and that's when I got scared. He'd killed Muslims with his own hands. He was even to be covered in the blood of swine, as he called them. Then he told us the most horrible things, and he smiled as he did it. The old men he stripped to see if they were circumcised, then killed. Women and children were thrown in the river, while onlookers smoked *bidis*. Even worse things than that — women with their breasts cut off, young girls impaled as their parents watched before dying themselves, slowly, though, to make the pleasure last."

Then came the calm, the warrior's rest. The father made plans, which he explained to Indrani and her sister. Indrani was disgusted, but dared not let on. Their father's vengeance grew and grew. He wanted a gang of his own, his personal organization, a sort of shock troop. He'd shown what he was capable of, and that's when he decided to create the Durgas.

"Your father is Sri Bhargava?"

"Yes."

At first, it was a small fringe group like any other, but even the hard-liners of RSS were taken aback. The James Bond of "Hinduness" had one sole objective, if he couldn't pursue Muslims into Pakistan, he could at least exterminate them in India. His determination spiralled upward. Bhargava had an organization with disciples and sympathizers. He was all the more terrifying for being soft-voiced and calm, unlike the henchmen who lay around his house. He was always poised and serene, aloof, like a *sadhu*, or Buddhist monk and, with a contented smile he spoke of pogroms as nirvana, his two adored daughters by his side.

"In 1992, around the time of Ayodhya, the Bharatiya Janata Party wasn't yet the political powerhouse it is today," Indrani explained. The National Congress Party of Gandhi and Nehru had almost always held power in Delhi, an immovable object no one could imagine declining.

At the end of the nineties, the BJP had a chance at power, but some convincing and reassurance had to be carried out. That meant breaking with the most radical Hinduists, such as the Durgas. So the party decided to cut off Bhargava, and this made him furious. Being at the grass roots of the Hinduist movement, Bhargava and the others had supplied the BJP with its most devoted and determined members, whose enthusiasm could sway the silent masses. Now the party was going to form a government, and it pushed aside the militant base of extremists who had devoted their lives to Hindutva.

The Durgas were soon going to need a source of funds or cease their operations. So what was Bhargava's brilliant idea? Using SCI, which was building a dam in Kashmir. That was the source to turn to. With this in mind, Bhargava moved there with his two daughters and others like him. They set up in the region of Baramulla, though separately, thus appearing to be workers from the south eager to leave their furnace of a village for mountainside rupees.

Here, playing the Hinduist card was going to be more delicate than in Uttar Pradesh. In the rest of the country, Muslims were a minority, but in Kashmir, they outnumbered Hindus, except in Jammu, the winter capital. Still, Bhargava was a believer. Indrani feigned belief too, but could no longer tolerate her father and sister's murdering madness. Avenging her mother, sure. But Indrani had the impression it had no end, and was even a pretext for the sheer pleasure of inflicting pain.

In her eyes, the Jhelum site was turning into hell itself, a quicksand sucking in the company bosses. The only goal of her father's band of agitators was not to close the site, she explained, but on the contrary, simply to apply pressure and create an impossible situation, yet one with an exit available to Susan Griffith and the other bigwigs. The bottom line was that Bhargava had set the company up so completely that when things had gone far enough south, he showed up in Griffith's office made a proposal: the famous "second agreement."

"Do you have any proof of this?"

"I am your proof. I heard it all, saw it all … my sister, too."

Very soon, the country caught fire. In, Rajasthan, Madhya Pradesh, or Uttar Pradesh once again, and Bihar and even Bengal, Hindu extremists attacked Muslims with steadily increasing daring and violence. Everywhere but Rashidabad. The severely drained and weakened organization had turned into a solid and well-oiled machine with considerable financial resources — courtesy of SCI. Dozens of *shakhas*, schools teaching Muslim-hate, opened all over the country. Hundreds of militants were housed, fed, and trained at the Canadian company's expense.

In March 2002, after a week of massacres going both ways, Indrani decided to act. She had to bring down this industry of violence with its Hinduist militia and pogroms.

"To my father, I was just a girl with no access to anyone, a young Brahmin brought up in the cocoon of her caste and cut off from the outside world. He never thought I would carry through with my threats to turn him in and put an end to this horrid blackmail he was using against Griffith and her engineering firm."

Indrani left Rashidabad in a panic. She boarded a bus for Srinagar, hoping to melt into the crowd in the summer capital. That's where she found Ahmed Zaheer, the young man she'd met and befriended a few years earlier, and who now, when shuttling to and fro, offered the support of the *Indian Geographic Magazine*, based in Mumbai. Two outsiders: a Muslim homosexual and the young Brahmin daughter of a militant Hinduist, not a pair one would expect to be in touch. Then again, nothing was the same. Nothing made any sense in India anymore. The "blended world" we were now forced to live in was polluting every one of us. Well, Indrani was through with "purity." Cleanliness seemed more and more repugnant, and her contact with the "filth" of Zaheer, and his impurity, gave her the feeling of being back in the real world, not that of the Qur'an or the Upanishads, two bibles, she said, that pitted man against man.

She confided in Zaheer what she knew about the Griffith-Bhargava agreement, and told him she wanted to tell all, but she didn't know how to go about it. Talk to the police? She knew they were crawling with BJP supporters who'd been placed there, and even if there were an investigation, she knew it would get adulterated, covered up, and masked by a hundred other files "more urgent and scandalous." Zaheer hit on the idea of spreading it out in the media, going to the news outlets instead of the police. Indrani had thought of it, too, but that too could be blocked by corruption and influence-peddling that would keep it off the front pages. Specialized papers like *Klean Kashmir* would be interested but less credible. As for the Muslim press, forget it. They had zero impact on government.

She recalled Zaheer smiling at that. He wasn't thinking of the Indian papers, but the Canadian ones. After all, Stewart-Cooper International was a Canadian company, wasn't it? Sure, they were cautious about their activities abroad: protection of the environment, respect for local unions, the company's reputation was intact. Zaheer had even praised them for avoiding ethnic scandal, and now here they were financing Hindu terrorism! He could just imagine what would happen when it came out in the Canadian media.

"Why Hamilton, though?' Why confront Griffith, when all he had to do was descend on *The Globe and Mail* or the *Toronto Star* with the industrial scoop of the year?" asked Max.

Indrani did not know, but when they discovered Zaheer's body, she knew she was in danger. If they could get to him, why not her, as well? They'd been very cautious and not mentioned to anyone the real reason for his trip to Canada. Someone else knew and was determined to act, but who?

"Bhargava?"

"Not directly, my sister."

"Your sister?"

"Vandana."

So that was it. Now it all made sense: Vandana, the model employee!

David, returning from Srinagar, was nervously trying to hide what he knew from his colleague, the older sister still faithful to her father, who suspected something strange in the attitude of the Third Secretary ... Bhargava's reluctant accomplice? Not likely, downright enthusiastic would be truer, in fact every bit as impassioned.

"Now," explained Indrani, "Vandana's making sure the money keeps on flowing from Griffith to the Durgas."

"Because your father's back in charge."

"He held his prey, and he wasn't letting go."

"Then the journalist threatened to shed light on it all."

"But how did Bhargava find out about Zaheer?" asked Juliette, still stunned by the revelation.

The young Indian woman shook her head; she knew nothing. What about leaks, or an outright accusation? The young journalist might have bragged to *The Srinagar Reporter* or the *Indian Geographic Magazine*, even indirectly hinting that he had information that would cause trouble for the Hinduists and shake the Vajpayee government. The BJP had ears in every corner of the country, and a zealous Hinduist might have passed on the message to the leaders, who would surely turn their attention to him.

"Well, Ahmed was certainly chatty," she went on. "He liked to brag and show off his journalistic skills."

"Where does David fit into this?" Juliette asked.

"One day, Vandana told me what he'd done for Genghis Khan in prison, and she was furious."

After her journalist friend died, Indrani mistrusted everyone, not even daring to come out of the apartment opposite Zaheer's, where she was in hiding. Then one night, she heard strangers going into his place.

"Bhargava was looking for you."

"So I called David in New Delhi and told him everything. I begged him to help me."

Max and Juliette could fill in the rest: the young diplomat's secret trip to Srinagar to fetch Indrani; then the Delhi airport with a fake passport for Béatrice Gupta O'Brien; the flight to Montreal via Paris. David had it all set up with Patterson, who met her at Dorval and found her a job at the Mughal Palace; a room he could watch from his office on Jean Talon. He was the invisible hand shielding her, an ace up David's sleeve when he needed it.

The conference would be the perfect platform for David's revelations. Griffith would be there, and so would journalists from all over Canada and India. The floor would be jammed with personalities for his denunciation of the CEO. He knew she owed her job to the "Rashidabad miracle," and she stood to lose it all when the scandal became public. She wasn't his real target, though. He wasn't just out to do damage, to accuse people for the sake of it. He was more concerned about the victims of the inter-communal riots Durgas had unleashed, and he wanted an end to the horrors, the way Philippe had done in El Salvador.

His father had mobilized the media, and so would he. Philippe had set fake negotiations while the peasants fled via the sewers after managing to get the reporters together in front of the embassy without even calling on them. David would use the Indo-Canadian press the same way. *For the first time in my life, I have the power to change things.*

"David wouldn't do anything like that," exclaimed Juliette. "It isn't a diplomat's job to get up there and mete out justice!" She was right, and Indrani smiled.

"That's exactly what David said, but he had a solution for that."

Patterson.

The former diplomat had nothing to lose. David's initiative would push him to the forefront, and at David's request, he was the one who would have made the revelation to the whole world from the podium at the conference. For once, he had the opportunity to reach Philippe's level of heroism: *See, I risked my life, too.*

"David would have stayed in the background on purpose, so as not jeopardize his future in foreign affairs."

"So that explains Patterson's silence to us," Max added.

"After David's death, Patterson's glory might slip through his fingers if he told us or the police."

"Exactly."

I've become just like him. I feel just what he felt.

Better yet, David wanted to leave all the credit to someone else.

46

Floral arrangements decorated the ballroom at the Sheraton Centre, marigolds in particular. The flags of India and Canada were crossed on the walls and behind the bar. There was the usual crowd of businesspeople, predictably drab save the turbans and saris that added the occasional splash of colour; the waiters weaving in and out with non-alcoholic drinks and vegetarian hors d'oeuvres; the familiar drone of trivial chit-chat; the murmur of banalities that run endlessly through such events. In a room several stories higher, Max was dialling his cellphone, letting it ring for a few seconds, worried about having to leave a message, but at last he got an answer: a weak, barely audible "Yes" drowned by the noise in the hall.

"Vandana, I need your help."

He imagined her sidling away from the crowd, looking for a quieter spot. As the noise faded, he realized she was in the corridor.

"Where are you?" she asked.

"Right here in the hotel, I have to get out of the country, and you must help me."

Silence from Vandana. Hesitation. The fish was circling the bait, ready to bite. Would she?

"One hour. Suite 2201."

She was on the hook, and Max could practically hear her wriggling down there. Too late for Vandana now. All it took was a net and a sizzling pan.

Max ended the call and turned to the armchair Luc Roberge had comfortably sunk into, frowning nevertheless. He'd made a point of being out of the way while Max talked to Vandana. His older uniformed sidekick, Morel, cap in hand, was playing practically dead over by the window, like his boss. Bruno Mancini, the man in charge of the Patterson investigation, stood next to Max, who had called him a few hours earlier.

"I know who did Patterson," he'd told him. "I'll help you arrest the killer, but you've got to let me run this thing."

"And why would I do that?" asked Mancini with a slight Italian accent.

"Because you'll also get the killer of David O'Brien."

Mancini was interested but cautious. "Trust a con artist? What do you take me for, O'Brien?"

"In exchange, I surrender to Roberge, so he can finally retire to Florida. That way you're rid of him, too. What's not to like?"

Mancini hesitated, but finally agreed, Roberge, too, and now they had him covered with machine guns for eyes. Roberge spoke first.

"Well, you got guts," he said from the depths of the chair.

"Aw, it's nothing. Only doing my job."

Moments before, Mancini had picked up Max and Indrani from the Loblaw's underground parking near the old Jean Talon train station, and she'd retold her story, convincingly. Indrani was to be put up in another hotel — well guarded — in case Bhargava's men tried anything. But soon the truth would be out and she wouldn't have to be afraid of her father anymore. In the police car, Indrani watched Max with admiration. He wasn't used to doing this as himself, instead of one of his asssumed identities. It felt funny, and he seemed to be the most important person she knew.

Indrani was to be put up in another one — well guarded — in case Bhargava's men tried anything. Soon she wouldn't have to be afraid of her father, and the truth would be out.

Mancini had the présence of mind to move Max through the shipping entrance. When the elevator doors opened on the fourth floor for an employee, Max caught a glimpse of High Commissioner Raymond Bernatchez summing up the commercial links between the two countries, and Max could imagine the enraptured attendees, slightly drunk of course, just drooling to sign a contract. Sooner rather than later, the scandal was going to hit them between the eyes, but for now they were still being jollied along.

Mancini had turned one of the suites into his operational headquarters. This was where Max phoned Vandana. Roberge, of course, wanted to arrest him then and there, while he finally had him, but he couldn't interfere with Mancini's plan to catch Patterson's killer. A simple courtesy under the circumstances. Roberge could hardly refuse him those extra moments of suspense. Still it rankled. This was Mancini's operation.

In turn, Max couldn't resist a smile at Roberge's resignation, like a child impatient to play with his Christmas toys.

"Now," said Mancini, "to pluck the fruit."

A young woman came in with a miniature recorder and mic in her hand. Max unbuttoned his shirt, helped her stick the mic to his chest, and slipped the recorder into his back pocket. Another frustrated smile from Roberge, who promptly turned his back as Mancini helped Max into his jacket. Max was eerily calm. He realized now why he'd felt uneasy in Philippe's office in San Salvador. He couldn't get over his own powerlessness to catch up with the killers and make them pay. This time, he was going to make it work, get David's murderer and in a way fulfill his promise to Philippe. He couldn't care less about prison at this point, and anyway, his sacrifice was a way to give meaning to David's and Philippe's sacrifices as well. Max was the final runner in this relay, and in finding Indrani he was picking up where David left off. David, who had done the same for Philippe. The three of them now reunited in Max's efforts and dedication.

Mancini looked at his watch. It was time to go. He took Max to the door, where Roberge's colleague grabbed his arm.

"I lost thirty-seven thousand dollars because of you," Morel exclaimed. "I was supposed to retire two years ago, so if you're blowing smoke …"

As they got out of the elevator, Mancini looked all around, but there was no one. To the left, at one door, a meal tray with bread basket and empty coffee pot lying on its side. They turned right. Mancini had men on all four corners of the floor and the hotel's main exits. Suite 2201 was on the left. Max glanced at Mancini, who signalled him on before disappearing. Max knocked and Vandana opened the door. She was back to that wary look she had the first time they met at the High Commission.

She was very good at it. No wonder Max had been fooled.

"Let's get something straight right off, Vandana. You'r sister's told me everything."

Her face fell. No more need to lie.

"Where is she?"

"Safe."

"What do you want?"

"A deal. You give me the names of David's murderers, and I'll tell you where Indrani is. Your family history is none of my concern."

She went over to the window, while Max stayed in position by the door, not venturing in. Then she turned to him.

"'You feel let down. I understand," she said.

"Why'd you make it so easy for me?"

"What?"

"You were the one who told me David wasn't in Kathmandu, who told me all about the Durgas and Hindu extremism ... and your father."

She shrugged. "You'd've found out about Kathmandu eventually, and one phone call to the Canadian Co-operation Office would've told you I was hiding something. Same thing for the Durgas. At least this way, I could avoid suspicion and influence your search."

"Because of course you knew David had brought Indrani back from Srinagar, and when you realized that, and also about Patterson being his accomplice, same as Juliette and me ..."

"All he had to do was mind his own business."

"So you could carry on yours unhindered. You were the one who gave your father the idea of holding SCI to ransom."

"One way to get financing, as good as any other."

"Better than others, because you were already in place at the High Commission to shepherd the file through oh-so-discreetly."

"Well, along with yours truly," said William Sandmill.

Max felt the muzzle of a pistol against his neck. He turned slowly, fighting to keep his cool. A heavy guy with no light in his eyes accompanied the first secretary, who was standing slightly back. Then he stepped forward.

"Rodger may have laid it on a bit thick with Zaheer, I agree, but at least Patterson didn't require his attention."

Morency smiled.

"Patterson unfortunately didn't have time to answer our questions, but today it's different."

Sandmill and Vandana, partners in crime, with Sandmill discreetly investing his money in a Portuguese *quinta*, a vineyard he planned to retire to when his tour was over, smiling as he spelled it out. Vandana, of course, was doing it in the name of her father and extremism.

"Your perspicacity amazes me," he went on. "Impressive, in fact. Vandana and I made the mistake of underestimating you at the outset. The first time in Delhi, I didn't think you'd go the distance by a long shot, but when you got away from that plane, well."

"What do you do for an encore? Kill me outright just like that in a hotel full of conference-goers?" said Max.

Sandmill smiled. "Obviously, unless you tell us where Indrani is."

"Self-defence," added Vandana. "You broke into my room and begged me to help you get a fake passport."

"Which she naturally refused to do," said Sandmill, "so you took a shot at her. Hardly surprising on the part of a murderer."

"It's my own fault, Sergeant. I'm just not used to hanging around criminals, you know."

Another smile from Sandmill. "All in all, pretty close to the truth, really, isn't it?"

Max turned to him, playing for time. "The kidnapping, torture, and bomb in the Volvo were all you, of course."

"Bhargava's men. All David had to do was tell us where to find Indrani, and all this could've been avoided."

Utterly false, of course, since David would be an embarrassing witness and had to be eliminated at all cost. Sandmill couldn't possibly risk fouling the deal between Griffith and Bhargava. He had interceded with the businesswoman and convinced her to accept the Durga chief's proposal. In exchange, Bhargava had kicked in two million of the money he got from SCI.

"And where did it come from?"

"Money allocated for the relocalization of the valley residents displaced by the dam, so Griffith was playing a double game. She asked the board for twice what she promised the Indian government. The overpayment went to Bhargava, minus Sandmill's commission, of course. Then Vandana had the idea to blackmail Griffith a second time. Being the new CEO, she could manage that."

"Zaheer would have sunk it all," cut in Max, "so Griffith got rid of the journalist by sending her gorilla, Morency, after him."

Yet another Sandmill smile.

"Ahmed Zaheer was not the guardian angel Indrani imagined," he added. "On his way to Toronto, he figured that, if the CEO of SCI had enough money for Bhargava, she had enough for a journalist and inveterate gambler and playboy. He had expensive pastimes, and all he had to do was deal with Griffith, hence his phone call from the booth across from the motel, so it couldn't be traced. He lied to Indrani. That murder was a Griffith mistake. He could have been bought. David, though, was a crusader, so harder to neutralize." Both, all three counting Bhargava, knew Indrani was behind this trip of his to Canada, and not being able get her whereabouts out of David, they couldn't lay their hands on Indrani.

"We must send her back to India!" screamed Vandana. "My father will get her to be reasonable."

Kill her, more likely, and right here in Montreal.

"Indrani no longer exists officially anymore, does she?"

"Where is my sister?"

It all happened so fast. Max grabbed the lamp at his feet and tilted it at Morency, who lost his balance and took just a fraction of a second too long in reacting, when suddenly Sandmill fired his revolver just as the door opened. Once, twice, then he fell to the floor. Max caught a brief glimpse of Mancini and his men, wearing bulletproof vests. Max was on the ground holding his belly with both hands, surrounded by an immense pool of blood that kept growing. Someone yelled to call an ambulance, and then everything went dark — a black hole, an endless pit he knew he'd never come back from. *Oh well, that's that, I'm on my way to join Philippe and David.*

47

Waxed floors, a corridor-length mirror, almost an ice rink with small, bent-over ladies sliding silently by in pale blue gowns. Their hesitant gait suggested prematurely aged, cloistered nuns. The tranquility didn't deter Juliette, though it did affect her somehow as she stormed out of the taxi, now becoming delicate herself. In this convent, slamming a door or raising one's voice was the worst thing imaginable. They'd asked her to stay in the waiting room, but she rushed down the corridor without a moment's hesitation, asking for directions as she went, and finally found herself in the chapel.

Two solid doors with a crucifix marked the entrance. She opened the right one, and received a whiff of incense full in the face. She noticed three elderly nuns seated randomly, none of them the person she was looking for.

Maybe she should have cooled her heels in the waiting room after all.

"I was expecting you."

She snapped around to see Deborah Cournoyer standing behind her, holding a rosary. She seemed so young surrounded by these elderly ladies. Juliette was about to explain her presence, but Cournoyer led her outside and into the corridor and mirrored tiles again. Words failed her.

"The rule of silence," said Cournoyer. "Silence for the past and the present. We are all there. We all have our secrets." She added, "I knew when Dennis died that sooner or later someone would come to question me, asking questions I never found answers to myself."

Juliette had made the connection with the old passport photos in Patterson's apartment, photos of a younger Pascale, but still strikingly similar.

In an earlier life, Deborah Cournoyer had been Pascale.

In the phone book, Juliette had found the Montreal address of the order that Sister Irène in Varanasi belonged to after Max told her the story of the cremation. Now she was here simply to understand. What was Patterson's part in all this? Why not say anything to Max?

Her room was small but sunny. Pascale hadn't kept much from her time in India, and not necessarily the most exotic things, either. That comb on the wash basin, though, Juliette had seen many like it in the bazaars there, those plastic sandals under the bed — Indians all wore them. Pascale turned to Juliette.

"In a city where death is a flourishing industry, nothing could be easier than faking one's own. A few rupees for a blackened body unrecognizable to anyone. Throw it on the fire and scatter the ashes in the Ganges."

"Why?"

"Because Max was close to finding me. He'd searched all through Europe, chased down every clue. I watched him from afar. Dennis let me know Max wasn't letting it go. Naively, I thought he'd soon give up, but no, never. Quite the opposite, he was consumed by my silence and his failure. Max wanted me home at any cost, no matter what I thought. Eventually I realized he'd never give up, not till the bitter end."

There was no way out but this faked death with the help of Sister Irène, a lie, just another con like so many she'd staged in the past with Max and Antoine. But in Varanasi, it wasn't to fleece bankers and millionaires. It was to fool those close to her, her family and husband. Up on the ghats, she and Patterson hadn't missed a thing, and Antoine had almost spotted them when he glanced up in their direction.

"Being present at one's own funeral," said Pascale, "was the most troubling experience I've ever had to face."

"But why not simply tell Max? He revered his brother, yes, but he also loved you above all else. I'm sure he'd have pardoned your liaison with Philippe."

Pascale, at a loss, raised her eyes to Juliette, gazing at her a long while.

"You don't understand, Juliette, not at all."

Her affair with Philippe was just Patterson's ruse to stop Juliette from asking any more questions. The truth was something far more dramatic still, Pascale explained. Dennis, the diplomat, was about to quit Foreign Affairs to make his own way. Philippe often offered Pascale the comfort of his Chrysler on the road to the "zoo" in Northern Ontario. After three months in the bowels of the pen on the edge of the forest and among the deer, elk, and caribou, Max was far from the drama of everyday life. Blind to the plots going on outside the gates.

"I tried to confess it to him several times, but I never had the courage."

"Confess what?"

Pascale paused.

At the time, Patterson was in the passport office, and Philippe and Béatrice sometimes invited him for a meal at their place. Pascale joined them once in a while. One night Patterson was telling Pascale about his work. Her questions became more and more pointed, with an insistence that took Philippe and Béatrice aback. Then, a few weeks later, Pascale told them she was pregnant.

Soon it would start to show. The child was Max's, but she didn't want to tell him. Why? Because she was tired of this life, of the lies, of the running. She no longer had the strength to keep looking over her shoulder, as Max was still doing, and there was no way she would impose this on their son. She wanted to save him that grief. She wanted a new life for him, something to be proud of. She decided to break with Max, her family, and the outlaw world.

Juliette could guess the rest, and she turned away, but Pascale had opened the floodgates, and there was no stopping her. This child was the solution. Philippe and Béatrice had been trying for years to conceive. They'd been to all the specialists and read all the journals on *in vitro* fertilization, when Pascale offered them a solution. *I'll give you this child to bring up and make into somebody.* At first, Béatrice and Philippe had been reticent, but she'd finally convinced them, and Max would be none the wiser. Pascale would disappear, go to India, and start a new life. She had neither the courage nor the strength to explain it to Max. All that remained of her was little David, who deserved better than a life on the run.

Pascale's revelation left Juliette stupefied: Pascale was not Philippe's mistress, but the first excuse Patterson dredged up; Pascale was the biological mother of a child, kept secret from the runaway father, who couldn't help influencing him nevertheless; Pascale's sudden disappearance, sneaking out on tiptoe. Now Juliette understood a little better Philippe's insistence that Max not pursue the search for Pascale. Philippe, who had kept it all secret, then asked Max to look out for David. Now she also understood Béatrice when, in Patterson's office, she'd said it "should not be brought out into the light of day." Shaken by Philippe's death, Pascale had considered telling all, but Patterson had advised against it for David's sake. She had a choice to make: Max's happiness or David's ... David, who venerated Philippe unreservedly. The revelation would be a bombshell, and destroying what remained of the family was out of the question, so the biological mother had opted for silence.

Pascale burst into tears, not bothering to turn away, as though glad to show her grief. After a while, Juliette took her face in her hands.

"You've got tell him now. You cannot hide it any longer."

48

In the Himalayan fortress of Kashmir lies a cave, and in that cave is a *lingam* of ice, a reproduction of the erect male sex organ, phallic symbol of the god Shiva. A natural phenomenon to which Hindus attribute divine powers. They go there every summer in endless lines of pilgrims, by minibus or on foot from Chandanwari to Amarnath, four thousand metres high. At pilgrimage time, the village would resemble a medieval fair, with itinerant vendors, jesters, and profiteers of all sorts. After the recurrence of the conflict with Pakistan and the aggravation of the Hindu-Muslim conflict, this voyage, the *yatra*, required a military escort. Patrols were scatterd along the route to prevent excesses on either side, since the Hindu convoy had to pass through Muslim villages, and since the pilgrims and their families needed reassurance.

The Amarnath road was one that Sri Bhargava took each year, once accompanied by his two daughters, now alone or with a disciple. On his way back from the sacred grotto this time, having accomplished his *darhsan*, or viewing of the *lingam*, there was a surprise awaiting him: a detachment of Indian police with a warrant for his arrest. They apprehended the religious agitator and took him to Jammu. He was arraigned that day and accused of being the leader of the Durgas by the government pursuant to an investigation led jointly by the Canadian and Indian police, with Josh Walkins in the driver's seat. At the same time, in Hamilton, his colleagues were arresting Susan Griffith after a search of the SCI offices that followed the close interrogation of Vandana Bhargava (her real name) and William Sandmill, now recovering from his injuries. Rodger Morency was on the return route to the pen under the resigned eye of his mother, Madeleine. All four were formally accused of the murders of Ahmed Zaheer, Dennis Patterson, and David O'Brien.

Max was unconscious and so knew nothing of the testimony given by Indrani and the ensuing tidal wave it had caused. She was already back in India by now, where a serious de-escalation seemed to be underway. At the Line of Control, Indian and Pakistani troops were shaking hands, and it appeared to be a radiant summer, not radioactive. In Delhi, Prime Minister Vajpayee agreed to meet President Pervez Musharraf, and the arrest of Bhargava and the dismantling of his terrorist group reinforced what Pakistan called the goodwill of the Vajpayee government. All across India, the CBI was scooping up Durga membership lists and their strategies against Muslims and the more moderate members of the BJP government. Vajpayee proclaimed far and wide his determination to root out terrorism from whatever source, Hinduist or Islamist. A pious wish? Perhaps. In the same breath, Vajpayee promised closer scrutiny of foreign investment projects, even from such "commendable" countries as Canada. Airy promises? Perhaps. At the Montreal conference, SCI executives, shaken by the arrest of their CEO, committed themseves to restarting the Rashidabad hydroelectric station. One thing was certain: young Indrani went home to a country much calmer and more serene than when she had left it. Not paradise, of course, but then who wants a paradise promised by extremists?

Max, on the other hand, was sure he'd gone to heaven. White, white everywhere. No walls, no ceiling, just one huge white, pure mass everywhere, one where he'd have to learn life all over again forever. An angel leaned over him. It was Pascale, older, but beautiful as always. He didn't recall those lines around her eyes or at the edges of her mouth. Any second now, he expected to see Philippe, and then — why not — David, but these two probably still had a lot to tell one another. He'd be seeing them later. For now, it was plenty to feel Pascale's fingers running through his hair.

"Doctor, he's coming round."

The voice. It was Luc Roberge. What the hell was he doing in heaven? They must have brought him up from the underworld specially to piss him off. No, that wasn't it. They were both in hell together. Police and thieves.

Handy-dandy. Then he opened his eyes, and Pascale said, "I'm so sorry. Please forgive me. I'm sorry I hurt you."

"Sorry?"

That was all he got to say before night fell on him again. Deepest night. The voices faded, and silence moved in once more. When he came to again, it really was dark, and he saw Juliette sitting at the bedside table, leafing through a magazine. That was what woke him. He watched her read a long while. Through the open door, he heard a car honk, so he wasn't dead after all.

"I had a dream, a weird one. Pascale was there beside me."

"That was no dream, Max. She's alive."

Max was stunned. He closed his eyes again, but Juliette repeated, "She's alive."

He wasn't ready for this thing she'd just said.

Two days later, sitting on the edge of his bed, despite nurse's orders, Max saw the door open ever so softly, and Pascale appeared and came toward him, just as he'd imagined so many times all these years. The same. Older, of course, but the same. He even recognized her perfume when she sat on the edge of his bed; her scent had crossed the years. She smiled the same sad smile he'd so loved the very first time. She repeated all she'd told Juliette about David and added, "I had no choice. It wasn't against you, but *for* him."

Max stopped her there. All he wanted was to touch her, hold her against him, not ask for a reckoning or an explanation. Just erase the lost time for a moment. He took her in his arms, and for too brief an instant, forgot all the sleepless nights and cries in the wilderness. Pascale was here again. Nothing else mattered.

"You know," she said, "I had the good fortune to see David in Delhi. The high commissioner's wife was setting up a an international adoption agency."

"IndiaCare."

"I went to meet her in her husband's office. Then in the corridor with a pile of paper in his hands, there was 'our' son."

She'd looked at him long and passionately, proud of what he'd become. He'd smiled at her without knowing who she was.

Max followed her gaze to the door, where Béatrice was discreetly standing, never daring to interrupt the lovers' reunion. Now she moved closer and said, "I loved him as my own, Max, and so did Philippe, I promise you that."

Max couldn't hold back the tears, and so he cried rather than get carried away and clutch these two women to force them to give back all those lost years, his lost son, but he hadn't the strength or the courage for it. Deep down, he knew Pascale had been right. She had done what had to be done. He couldn't blame her. Béatrice and Philippe had kept their promise and made a fine and honest man of their son.

Today was the day he got out. There were voices outside in the corridor: Luc Roberge and the man in white, probably the doctor. It was time to respect the agreement with Mancini, and Roberge had come for his due.

Juliette helped him on with his shirt under the watchful eye of a uniform, and no, it wasn't the same one with a beef about his retirement.

"You might want a sweater. It's cold up there. I bet they've still got snow."

So it was back to Temagami with the antler troop. Max could see Roberge's smirk out of the corner of his eye.

"It's going to be a girl," said Juliette. "The doctor told me this morning. David would be thrilled."

Max was.

"You can see her any time you want ... and shower her with presents if you like."

Max softened for a moment. "No, keep her away from prison, same as David."

There was a long silence.

Then she said, "Thank you so much for everything you've done. David would be proud of you."

In the elevator, Roberge ordered Max to be cuffed, and he didn't complain.

His life was entering a new phase again. Nothing that would have enraged him before bothered him now. He'd reached that level of serenity that Hindus and Buddhists often achieved, an inner peace that outsiders sometimes mistook for resignation. Max wasn't resigned at all, sad, maybe, but at peace with himself. He felt as though he'd picked up where "his son" David left off, completing what he'd begun and transcended death, made a difference, like Philippe.

Roberge did things up grand. The police van was parked with its doors open in the spot reserved for ambulances. So this was the end of a long race won by the copper, an exit in style for "Public Enemy Number One." That's when Max saw Pascale with Mimi, Antoine, and Béatrice. Pascale stepped forward and squeezed him in her arms just as he was climbing into the van.

"Take care, Max."

He looked at her long and hard. "Adieu, Pascale."

The doors slammed shut on him, and Roberge got in the front with the driver. A second cop faced Max in the back. Pascale and Béatrice, joined by Juliette, appeared in the window. Finding her, erasing all those years of absence, that was what he'd wanted most. That was his dream, just another phantasm. Pascale was going back to India with Juliette and David's ashes. She'd promised to scatter them there in Kashmir. Max was off to the pen. This time, they were well and truly broken up. Death was all that remained.

Montreal slid past the grill-covered window, and for hours the heat had been unbearable. This was like India just before the monsoon. "David, my son" was all Max could hear in his head, over and over, as though he had to convince himself it was true, not just another bad joke. A son he'd lost twice. Suddenly they were shedding the city like a scab. Here was the country. Where were they headed? From behind the Plexiglas where he sat next to the driver, Roberge glanced over his shoulder, and Max did, too, looking at the guard to his left, but just a second too late. Standing over him, the guard struck him solidly in the face. *Christ, another one whose life savings I swiped*, thought Max. He tried to shield himself with his arms, but the cuffs prevented him. Then more continuous blows, steady, relentless and precise. Max tried to lift his arms, then roll himself up in a ball on the bench, but lost his balance. As he fell to the metal floor, Max realized they had stopped by the roadside. *Okay, this is it*, he thought. *Here on the shoulder, this will be for all the cops I swindled.* Then the slam of a door, and cries of alarm from Roberge, who was ordering the guard to stop. "What are you, nuts? Cut it out!" Then he fell in a heap beside Max, just a quivering mass doubled up in pain. What was happening here? The guard knelt by Roberge and handcuffed him from behind. Then he forced Max's face up to look at it.

"Phew, he's okay," he said after checking it.

Max squinted against the sun, which came in behind him through the open door. A silhouette. The driver was Jayesh in a QPF uniform.

"Sorry about the punch-up, *yaar* …"

Max closed his eyes. Now he could die in peace.

"Come on, we've gotta get out of here. Let's go!"

He felt someone lift him up by the arms, then by the waist, lifting his feet clear off the ground. What next? Siddharth Srinivasan's Daybreak 34, the "Dark Demon," more gaudily decorated than a temple in Tamil Nadu, with pictures of goalie José Théodore along with the god Hanuman. Deepa was bitching at her husband about the samosa he was eating instead of grapefruit. A turquoise *kurta*. "Come on, Jayesh!"

To the music of Kishore Kumar, he had to change out of uniform before they reached the U.S. border. One more passport, yet another, was ready for his friend. Max couldn't even pronounce his own name this time.

"Bennington, New Hampshire," explained Jayesh. "A *khumbamela*, a feast in the honour of Shiva. Every Hindu from the East Coast will be there, just like every year."

Reincarnation, eh? Max had to believe in it now, didn't he? Actually, he'd never done much else.

So, a Hindu on a pilgrimage. Sure, why not?

ACKNOWLEDGEMENTS

Many thanks to the following, who helped me during the writing of this novel: Feroz Mehdi, project head at *Alternatives*, for ensuring that references to India and Indian culture are accurate and adequate, including names and expressions in Hindi; Sergeant François Doré, of the Direction des communications — Sûreté du Québec (Québec Police Force), for describing the work of officers in the Service des enquêtes sur les crimes économiques (Economic Crimes Squad); Dr. Gilles Truffy, for revising the text to ensure the exactitude of medical aspects; Reeta Chowdhari-Tremblay, for supplying precious information on Indian society; Christine Boucher and Francine Landry, for comments and suggestions during the writing and revising stages of this book.

Many thanks to everyone at Libre Expression, especially Johanne Guay, Jean Baril, and the late Monique H.

Messier, who encouraged me and allowed me the benefit of her expertise as an editor.

Thanks also to Nigel Spencer for this translation and to Shannon Whibbs and the team at Dundurn Press.

The author can be reached at mbmysteries@gmail.com.